The
Almost
Wife

JADE BEER

The Almost Wife

bookouture

Published by Bookouture in 2018

An imprint of StoryFire Ltd.

Carmelite House
50 Victoria Embankment
London EC4Y 0DZ

www.bookouture.com

ISBN: 978-1-78681-392-3
eBook ISBN: 978-1-78681-391-6

To my darling girls Laila and Clara, find a good one, like Daddy

I love her and that's the beginning and end of everything

F. Scott Fitzgerald

Chapter One

Jessie Jones

'Is it *really* too much to ask that we just lose these two large oak trees,' sighs Jessie, 'so that my photographer's drones stand *some* chance of capturing the aerial shots I have specifically asked for?'

Striding across the hotel's manicured lawn in a pair of entirely too high heels, sinking as she stomps but refusing to break stride so the hotel's incredulous wedding planner can catch her up, Jessie Jones, highly motivated bride-to-be, is heading straight for the trees in question.

'Look, it's very simple,' she says, flicking a freshly manicured finger to the diary page of her smartphone. 'If we start the work now, it will be finished in plenty of time for my guys to begin planting the additional magnolia and cherry blossom trees I also need. You can't expect me to host a champagne reception on a sun terrace that has no sun because your three-hundred- year-old trees are blocking it all. Hugo really won't appreciate the lack of light.'

'Sorry, Hugo who?' the planner is calling after her as she appears to be struggling to think of a single other thing to say to please the force of nature charging ahead of her. And what can she say? This is clearly a woman not familiar with disappointment.

'Oh for crying out loud! *Hugo Burnand!* Royal wedding photographer to Kate and William and Camilla and Charles before them. Don't you read *Tatler*?'

'Um, not always, but I think I have the latest issue tucked away somewhere in—'

'Then let me enlighten you. Hugo negotiated his way through royal protocol with such dexterity for Charles, that he was the only choice when it came to documenting the wedding day of the new duke and duchess of Cambridge.' Meaning that if he possessed the level of diplomacy, tact and planning skills required to successfully present the nuptials of Kate (the commoner) to William (the future king of England) to the world, then he may – *may* – also be able to help her stage-manage the uniting of two of the most mis-matched families Gloucestershire has surely ever seen.

'OK, got it. Hugo's obviously very accomplished, Ms Jones, I don't doubt that but—'

'He spent three days planning the lighting alone in the throne room at Buckingham Palace for William and Kate's official wedding portraits. Lighting is *everything* to him. So you can see that clearly, *obviously*, these trees need to go.'

She's so pleased her mum isn't here to witness this bratty outburst, she would die of shame and so would her mother. Jessie's being a bully and she knows it. And the worst kind. Talking down to this poor girl, in exactly the way she hates other people doing to her. That paralysing fear of being judged, deemed inferior. Perhaps months of feeling that way have rubbed off on her in the worst possible way too.

'It's just the work you're asking for is going to be incredibly costly Ms Jones and I'm not even sure—'

'It goes without saying that I will cover the cost in full for the work that is needed as well as generously compensating the hotel for any inconvenience it may cause. I understand you may be looking for some additional funding for two new tennis courts? Well, there's your answer,' continues Jessie. 'Let's agree a timescale by end of play today.' Jessie raises both eyebrows and cocks her head expectantly at the poor planner.

'That is wonderfully generous Ms Jones and I can put it to the general manager of course but—'

'Having prized Hugo out of semi-retirement to capture this wedding, I am not prepared to let anything stand in the way of a beautiful collection of images – ones that will be expertly edited by me to show what will at least *look* like a stress-free day. I hope I am making myself clear?' Oh God, she's on a roll now, incapable of controlling herself.

'You are indeed but if I can just point out that…' the planner has all but given up trying to finish a sentence now, her presence seemingly surplus to Jessie's requirements.

'Right, I've got my first dress appointment with Helen across the road at The White Gallery in five minutes, but when I come back we need to discuss where exactly the dessert room is going to be positioned, your thoughts on how we scent the day and what progress you've made with the vicar and that God-awful aisle carpet of his. See you in *exactly* one hour from now.' *It's almost as if every ounce of stress that Jessie is feeling about this wedding is being dumped on to the planner. If Jessie has to worry about all these things, then bugger it, the planner can too. Just for once, she wants someone else to get a sense of what she is dealing with, the expectations she must hit, the sheer number of people she must please.*

Jessie spins her head in the direction of the planner, forcing eye contact, and immediately catches the whiff of terror coming off her. Jessie's eyes slide down her body, noticing the not-quite-crisp-enough white shirt and that the very tips of her patent courts are scuffed and muddied. A question slices silently through the air between them: *is this girl capable of bringing to life everything that Jessie's budget can so easily afford?*

When Jessie discovered another couple had booked the seventeenth-century Willow Manor in the idyllic north Cotswold village of Little Bloombury on the very day she wanted it, she simply paid them off – generously enough to cover the entire cost of their wedding elsewhere. She then booked the property – one of the finest in the whole of the West Country and surrounded by centuries-old cottages and boundless English countryside – exclusively for one week, effectively enabling the in-house wedding planner to hit her revenue target for the entire wedding season in one lump sum. So a bit of co-operation would be appreciated.

It's the look of fear in the planner's eye that does it. That and the fact that Jessie is yet to hear the words, *Absolutely, that won't be a problem.* All her mild faffing ignites the low-level irritation that is Jessie's daily default setting and like a precocious child on the rampage, Jessie unleashes a series of wild arm movements so exaggerated by her frustration, that she is in danger of losing the Carolina Herrera pale blue calf-skin bag that is swinging precariously from one of them.

Time to go in for the kill.

'You *are* up to speed on the dessert room aren't you? Because there is a hell of a lot to consider – and you've seen the guest list so you know we're dealing with three hundred very-hard-to-impress people here.

'How *exactly* are you planning to engineer the display of my ten-tier gravity-defying Peggy Porschen Madame de Pompadour strawberry and champagne buttercream wedding cake? Have you even checked that we have height clearance under the crystal chandeliers – not forgetting of course the fresh floral cake stand which, when all seven thousand of the David Austin Avalanche roses are in place, will stretch to at least four metres high and three metres wide?

'Tell me *please* you have given at least *some* thought to the fifteen-hundred hand-painted mini Maitre Choux eclairs, the Bonpass & Parr bespoke jellies I have commissioned in the shape of the church and the hand-piped biscuits decorated to mimic the lace on my dress? I suggest we need a full mood board of ideas on how exactly this lot is going to be presented.' She stops short of sobbing, *because I would really love to be able to sleep soundly for perhaps just one night in the run up to this wedding, without waking in a pool of stress-related sweat, imagining the moment my future mother-in-law arches an eyebrow at me across the top table, slowly shakes her head and silently confirms that I am indeed not good enough for her son – and stupid me for even trying to fool them all I could be.*

Tantrum over, Jessie is off at pace – leaving hot tears to bubble up in the planner's eyes – her freshly blow-dried blonde hair bouncing in the fittingly crisp spring morning air, huffing loudly and feeling relieved that she had dressed for business today.

She had a feeling it was going to be challenging, so opted for Look No. 32 from the new Carolina Herrera Spring/Summer collection: wide-legged cream crepe trousers sitting high on the waist, worn with the matching silk crepe mix blazer, stylishly edged in black ribbon, cut in neatly at the waist and accessorised with Herrera's rose gold and pearl pendant, the matching bracelet and the *don't dick with me* five-inch laser-cut lace courts. Jessie put this look together precisely as the designer intended, right down to the way the blazer's black silk belt is tightly knotted at the front.

In fact, the only thing *not* from the House of Herrera is Jessie's De Beers platinum and diamond engagement ring, its mere presence somehow giving her the right to say exactly what she wants. Even Ms Herrera herself might have winced at the extravagance of the six-carat, cushion-cut diamond solitaire, in its diamond-encrusted halo setting, with yet more diamonds running around the band. The future heirloom had been individually crafted at a bespoke appointment at the jeweller's Old Bond Street store in London just to ensure no one else in the world would have the same ring.

This is Jessie's time and she is determined to let absolutely nothing get in the way of the perfection she is planning – least of all some slow-on-the-uptake wedding planner who simply has no concept of the scale of what is looming, six short months from now.

September 1st, the day when Jessie Jones will marry 38-year-old Adam Coleridge, the only son of Henry and Camilla Coleridge, two of the wealthiest landowners in the county. And the only man on earth with the power to make Jessie feel so much more than good enough. The kind of man whose life never should have collided with hers, but did. Then when he loved what he saw, how he felt around Jessie with all her raw, unapologetic lust for life, she barely dared to dream it was going to happen. He could have had anything, any woman in the world, but he chose her. And Jessie worships him for that. All her happiest times trace directly back to Adam, like an intricate treasure map, his heart the ultimate reward.

But there is a *lot* of work to do between now and the big day, not least of which is getting her socially challenged family to some level of understanding of the magnitude of the event. The etiquette involved in hosting a collection of people whose personal wealth could solve the entire nation's austerity issue… not to mention the level of grooming that Jessie plans to impose on her relatives.

This is all a very long way from the depressing south London council estate where Jessie grew up – and they all still live. She had battled her way past the bullies at the local school who confused her ambition for snootiness and, from as young as she can remember, she would walk the residential streets of the neighbouring and more salubrious Putney-upon-Thames, choosing the houses she might one day live in – wondering what the hell you had to do for a living to afford to live like *that*. Then she'd return home to see the pile of grubby ten-pound notes appear on the mantelpiece each week in their tiny house – her mother Margaret's housekeeping money – and watch as she struggled to stretch it as far as she could to feed and entertain three children and two worn-out parents. Never once did she see her mother spend anything on herself. There was never enough money, ever. Her father Graham's school caretaker wages never stretched quite far enough.

She knows this was what gave her such an incredible drive to succeed, spurred on by two parents who love their family dearly and were sensible enough to spot Jessie's potential and nurture it, somehow managing to support her through university. She beat 269 other graduates to land that first job as executive assistant to the planning partner at Hunter Bentley property developers. On day two she met Adam Coleridge, the company's marketing director, and three days later they were sipping champagne on their first date. She remembers the thrill of excitement coursing through her as the Friday night crowd pushed them closer together at the bar and, as Adam tried not to touch her too often, she silently willed herself not to fall for him. She knew there might never be a second date and she couldn't handle just a glimpse at what might never be hers. But the heady combination of a fizz-fuelled confidence, Adam making it all so easy, attractive women working hard to get his attention when it was all hers, her head swimming with the exciting chit-chat all around her – clever people with fabulous lives – was fatal. By midnight she was completely undone, totally his if he wanted her. But Adam wasn't making any assumptions. He took her by the hand out to a waiting Mercedes, ready to whisk her home. As he kissed her softly on both cheeks, letting his lips linger tantalisingly close to hers, he opened the car door, but didn't follow her in. On the back seat sat an enormous bouquet of hand-tied flowers. About to explode with happiness, she almost missed the smart black ribbon holding the blooms together with the words *Beautiful Jessie* in gold calligraphy running the length of it. Then the handwritten note simply suggesting '*Dinner tomorrow night?*'

Now Jessie Jones, with her limitless wedding budget, is impatiently pressing the doorbell of The White Gallery, Gloucestershire's most luxurious wedding boutique, just as her mobile phone interrupts her with a sharp buzz that indicates a voicemail message. Jessie stabs the play button and hears the painfully slow and distracted voice of her mum.

'Jessica, it's Mum here... I hope you're having a nice day... Dad and I are doing our weekly shop later and I thought I'd better call you first. You know what he's like when he gets in to the Co-op. We'll be in there forever looking at all the deals. Graham, can you grab a handful of carrier bags from under the stairs? I'm not paying 5p for them all again... Are you still planning to visit this weekend Jessica? What would you like for your tea? Let me know and then I can buy it while I'm out today. Anyway, the reason I am calling is I got a huge package from you this morning delivered by a very nice man. It took me ages to open it, it was so well-wrapped. Anyway, I've looked at all the dresses and it was very kind of you to send them Jessica. I am very grateful and the last thing I want to do is upset you but I think they might all be a bit... oh, what's the word, um... *showy* for me. Your dad thinks I should wear the lilac trouser suit he bought me for our wedding anniversary last year. I'll see if Next have some nice shoes and a handbag the same colour to go with it. Maybe you can help me choose them at the weekend? Love you, see you soon, love you. Let me know about your tea. Bye, bye Jessica.'

'Oh for fuck's sake,' Jessie spits at the phone, just as Helen Whittaker, the calm, unshakeable owner of The White Gallery opens the door to greet her.

Chapter Two

Helen Whittaker

Not one for the snooze button, Helen is up and out of bed moments after the alarm – set forty-five minutes earlier than her usual 7.30 a.m. today – stirs her. Heavy white towelling robe on, she is immediately on autopilot preparing a hearty breakfast of two free-range boiled eggs, thickly buttered white toast (crusts discarded) and half a zesty grapefruit – a meal that will set her up perfectly for the full day of back-to-back bridal appointments that await her downstairs in the boutique. In the four minutes it takes for the eggs to reach her idea of perfection, Helen gets the kettle on and lays out her favourite bone china cup and saucer ready for its morning splash of Earl Grey. Already multitasking, she scans the cream leather-bound appointments diary between sips of hot tea to refresh her memory of exactly who she will be seeing today.

As she runs a finger slowly down the page she sees the names of seven women. Two will be pinned today for their first round of alterations, one has decided on the dress and is coming to select accessories, one is shopping for her bridesmaids' gowns, two are collecting their finished dresses and one – the first of the day at 10 a.m. – will be attending her very first appointment. Helen particularly loves these sessions, charged as they are with such excitement and wonder.

'OK then,' she says aloud to herself. 'Time to get on.'

Fifteen minutes and one piping hot shower later, Helen is covering herself in a comforting layer of Ponds cocoa butter, expertly working the rich cream into her middle-aged and slightly dehydrated elbows and knees then sweeping it along her arms, down her once-toned legs, across her tummy and the stretchmarks she made peace with years ago. Trusty Marks and Spencer's cream lace balcony bra and matching knickers on, Helen turns to the whitewashed armoire where last night she sensibly hung out her clothes for the day, knowing she would want to feel organised.

She takes a seat at the antique dressing table next to her divan with its pretty patchwork bedstead to blow-dry her shoulder length light brown hair. She does this in the same unrushed way she does every morning, into the same style she has worn for decades. She's using the hairdryer's warm blast to tease out layers of soft feminine waves that she gently sweeps away from her face – a face that is framed by an expertly tamed fringe, thanks to the can of Elnett that sits on the table alongside several bottles of Estée Lauder perfume, her daily make-up essentials and a useful box of tissues.

Helen retrieves the yellow-gold stud earrings from the glass trinket box in front of her and smiles warmly as she remembers the expensive bottle of Chablis she and Phillip shared over lunch at their favourite local bistro, celebrating her fiftieth birthday. Her husband had waited until they were both enjoying a velvety crème brûlée from the same plate before slipping the small jewellery box across the table to her with a simple, 'Happy birthday, my darling'.

Today every inch of Helen's appearance radiates togetherness – a woman who would appear to have everything under control. And that's exactly the look she's hoping to convey, because the truth is far less palatable. No one wants to hear that, and she's certainly not ready to share it with the world. Not yet. The understated, easy elegance of a successful businesswoman is all anyone will see today.

Helen steps into her shiny cream patent L.K. Bennett mules, grabs the appointments diary and descends the small uneven staircase from her neat two-bedroom apartment above the The White Gallery. It occupies the lower level of Helen's pretty Cotswold stone cottage, one in a row of four that bend gently around the corner, towards the old mill. The shop stands opposite Willow Manor hotel and the local church, separated only by one single-track road and the shallow stream that runs towards the mill.

The frames of the cottage's tiny glass windows are painted the traditional Cotswold green like every other property in the village and aside from the one small white sign hanging above the door, passers-by would never guess at what treasures are hidden inside. Helen designed the boutique so that stepping through its sixteenth-century solid oak front door is like passing from an ancient world into a bright, white, hopeful future.

She enters the boutique this morning from the back door at the bottom of the stairs to her apartment and gets to work lighting her favourite Jo Malone candles. By the time the boutique opens in just over an hour they will have filled the air with the delicate scent of jasmine. She switches on the glass wall lights, softly illuminating the room's Dior Grey walls, the perfect backdrop shade to a sea of white. On the boutique's large, central glass-topped table, Helen has positioned an ornate crystal vase filled with her favourite wildflowers; the same varieties she carried in her own bridal bouquet thirty-five years ago. The pale pink foxgloves, honey-coloured sweet peas and sky-blue lupins mixed with cow parsley provide the only soft splash of colour today. They sit next to a decorative porcelain plate filled with freshly baked biscuits in the shape of miniature wedding gowns that have been iced a brilliant white.

The only other decorations on the table are three beautifully framed photographs. Helen suppresses the swell of emotion building inside her as she tenderly traces her finger along the frame of the first image, swallowing back her tears. No time for that right now. It's a black and white image of a twenty-one-year-old Helen with Phillip, taken on that roasting hot day in July 1981, just after the two of them had said their wedding vows and run out of the Bristol registry office, overflowing with happiness. Buoyed by the excitement of the day, Helen had stumbled on the hem of her ivory taffeta gown, and just as it looked as though she might tumble down the stone steps in front of their assembled well-wishers, Phillip caught her, at the very moment the photographer took his shot. It remains to this day her favourite image of their wedding.

Both had thrown their heads backwards in a fit of relieved giggles. Phillip saved Helen's blushes that day – as he would many times over – and every time she looks at the picture now she can't help but compare her fortunes favourably to that year's other far more famous bride – Lady Diana Spencer. Helen may have been nearly undone by a tricky hem, but Diana – a year younger than Helen at the time – had to make the three-and-a-half minute walk up the aisle of St Paul's Cathedral in front of a global audience of 750 million eyes, all trained on her. The other two framed images on the table are of Helen and Phillip's own children Betsy and Jack on their graduation days, joyous daily reminders of the very best of family times together. She just wishes she saw them more often.

Helen circulates around the boutique, small cloth duster in hand, ensuring there are no rogue fingerprints and no clutter, then checks the small waste-paper bin in the fitting room for tear-soaked tissues from the previous day's fittings. Betsy has repeatedly suggested her mum get a cleaner to help every morning, concerned that she has more than enough to worry about, but it's a role Helen enjoys. Besides, a lifetime of caring for and cleaning up after a hardworking husband and two children has more than qualified her for the job.

9.15 a.m. – plenty of time for Helen to buff the duster around the boutique's single rose-gold clothes rail that runs the perimeter of the room. It is on this rail that all of Helen's wedding gowns are hung, each on its own softly padded white silk hanger, draped so that every hemline softly kisses the thick cream carpeted floor beneath it. Helen starts to the left of the front door, in her experience the direction most brides turn when they first enter the boutique, and where she has positioned her collection of six modern romantic Jenny Packham gowns.

Helen approaches the rail, running her hand carefully between each gown to check none of the beadwork has caught a neighbouring dress, lifting the skirt of each one upwards carefully in one brisk fluid movement, filling it with air to show it off to its very best advantage. She straightens the embellished beaded cap sleeves of one, smoothes the silk tulle overlay on another, before adjusting the sparkling beaded lace bodice on the next. She decides to move one of Jenny's latest designs, a gown with a show-stopping cascading tiered skirt to the front to create some serious wow factor for everyone entering the boutique today.

This season Helen has bought Jenny's more form-fitting silhouettes – those adorned with wild flower and foliage appliqués, crystal illusion bodices, daring open backs, and plunging necklines. They may not be entirely to her own taste, but when it comes to ultimate contemporary glamour, Helen knows that no one does it better than Jenny – and so do her brides, judging by the stream of orders already placed.

Helen works her way along the rail and on to the five expertly structured Peter Langner gowns including her personal favourite, a ballgown in embossed Shantung silk, with flutter sleeves and embroidered with falling chiffon petals. Next come the legendary bias-cut Pronovias gowns – the ones she knows her more fashionable brides are sure to gravitate towards. Sharply cut racer-backs, a second-skin embroidered lace dress, peek-a-boo sheer chiffon and thigh-high splits are not for every bride, but the ones who love these looks are usually more than happy to pay the higher price tag these gowns demand.

There is just time to complete her circuit of the remaining gowns, before finishing with the eight exquisite designs from Oscar de la Renta, all strapless save for one plunging V-neck A-line gown, which Helen takes the time to adjust on its hanger so it sits perfectly symmetrically. Each dress has been given one incredible defining feature which Helen double-checks now: a back adorned with an oversized bow (straightened); intricate guipure lace (smoothed); a neat peplum skirt (lightly fluffed) and a lace bolero edged with mink and fox fur (lifted higher on its hanger).

Happy with the rail, Helen walks to the back of the boutique and enters the sumptuous fitting room with its floor-to-ceiling ornate gold-framed mirrors on both sides. There is a luxurious chaise, generously upholstered in cream velvet running the length of the room, providing plenty of space for mums and maids to perch and an extravagant crystal chandelier hanging centrally over the space. One small glass table in the corner is where Helen keeps her 'Mary Poppins bag', as she affectionately refers to it. Just like the old fashioned leather doctor's bag carried by its namesake, it opens up like a gaping mouth to reveal dozens of individually boxed and ordered pins, clips, ribbons and elastic – everything she might need to turn a too big or small gown miraculously into the near-perfect size for the bride within it.

The fitting room is where three more super special gowns are today suspended from a floating rail. Knowing that these dresses would take some extra time to present properly, Helen positioned them here last night after closing, giving them longer for any stubborn creases to disappear from the fabric. It's important they look perfect and, analysing them closely again now, Helen is happy that she has done her work well.

9.50 a.m. – Helen returns to the front of the boutique and unlocks the door, ready ten minutes ahead of schedule for her first bride of the day. She uses the time to flick through the file she keeps on every bride she serves – the bible that carefully charts each woman's dress progress from her initial measurements to styles chosen, alternations needed, final refinements and delivery dates. The file never leaves a locked cupboard under the boutique's till – Helen knows she would be lost without it. Opening the concertina box to the section marked *Ms Jessica Jones*, Helen re-scans the fifteen emails that she has printed out and logged there – emails that Jessie has sent Helen in the weeks leading up to this appointment with an increasingly specific and detailed breakdown of exactly what she is looking for. Helen runs through the requirements in her head again. Not one dress, but three. The first, for the rehearsal dinner the night before the wedding, the second for the ceremony itself and the third for the wedding evening party. *I cannot wait for her to see these gowns*, thinks Helen, confident that she will be nothing but overjoyed with what is awaiting her. Helen runs her fingers over the swatches of fabric stapled to the emails that Jessie has sent her along with various video links to designer catwalk shows and the password to a whole Pinterest board full of designs from Jessie's three favourite bridal designers.

For their very first appointment, most brides-to-be come to Helen with a handful of pictures torn from their favourite bridal magazines and, if they are very good, a rough budget – a budget that is nearly always blown once they set foot inside The White Gallery.

None – before Jessie – have flown to New York Bridal Fashion Week to personally view the new collections on the catwalk, before insisting that three favourite sample gowns are pulled off their sales shows and shipped immediately to Helen's small Cotswold boutique.

10.05 a.m. – With no sign of her bride, Helen refers back to the appointments diary to ensure no mistake has been made. One-hour Saturday appointments with Helen at The White Gallery need to be booked weeks in advance and once a sought-after slot is secured no bride *ever* cancels and very rarely are any late without an extremely good reason. Helen pauses for a moment to think about the young woman she is about to meet. Up until now there has been no one Helen couldn't disarm. The disinterested mother-in-law, the jealous bridesmaid who can't afford the dress her childhood friend is trying on and so determines to hate it. The mother-of-the-bride who projects all of her fusty style rules on her confused daughter. Or the bride's father who simply sobs his way through the entire appointment, offering no help at all. Helen has advised, educated, humoured and ultimately won over every one of them. And not one of them has ever guessed at the personal sadness she carries inside her every day, she's made sure of that. Every bride she serves is completely indulged by Helen. She always listens eagerly to their wedding plans, and has never once sold a dress to a girl without being honest about how it looked on her. But Helen knew very well as she was writing the name Jessica Jones under

Saturday 1st March, that she has never experienced a young woman quite like this before – not one.

10.15 a.m. – Helen hears what can only be described as foul-mouthed ranting from outside the boutique and heads to the front door, pulling it open to investigate.

'Oh for crying out fucking loud! *Lilac!* A colour that looks good on *no one*. And Next! Perfect! She could be tripping down the aisle ahead of me in thousands of pounds worth of Max Mara but no, we'll go to Next. Please dear God, let there not be a fascinator sprouting from the top of her head. I can't actually cope with it!'

'Jessica, isn't it? Please, come in,' says Helen, as her outstretched right arm welcomes Jessie under the glorious archway of purple wisteria that frames The White Gallery's entrance.

'What?' barks Jessie, still huffing and puffing in the direction of her phone.

Helen sucks in a lungful of the sweet floral scent, letting it wash away the unpleasantness of the bad language she detests so much and politely steps aside to let Jessie enter.

'Everything is ready for you, Jessica. The dresses were all shipped from America and arrived two days ago. I don't know how you did it but all three made it and they are absolutely exquisite. But should we wait? Is someone else going to be joining you for the appointment Ms Jones – your mother or a girlfriend?'

'God, no. I don't need any help thank you. I hope my emails have made it clear that I already know exactly what I want.'

Being snapped at by a strung-out bride-to-be is nothing new. But even Helen is taken back by Jessie's immediate and undiluted rudeness. Her mind flicks to her own Betsy and how mortified she'd be to see her daughter behave this way. But more than anything it's sympathy she feels for Jessie. *No woman should have to attend her first bridal appointment on her own*, thinks Helen. The idea of Betsy doing that is inconceivable to her.

'OK, well if you're ready, Ms Jones, shall we take a look?'

'That's why I'm here,' Jessie rolls her eyes sarcastically towards the ceiling, forcing Helen to suck in a deep lung-expanding breath. She's not sure she has the strength to deal with this attitude today. She wavers for a moment, wondering whether to confront the rudeness head on, then decides perhaps this total lack of friendliness is what she needs, it'll force her to focus on the job at hand. She needs to get on to the dresses, her comfort zone.

She heads to the back of the boutique and with both arms slowly pulls open the fitting room's heavy silk drapes revealing three of the most breathtaking bridal gowns either woman has ever seen.

'On the left, Ms Jones, is the ivory silk crepe shift dress by Oscar de la Renta. I think the pearl and ostrich feather embroidered hem make it more than smart and certainly special enough for your rehearsal dinner. Obviously, we won't know if the hem length is right until we see you in it but looking at you now, I think we could afford to take it up an inch or two. Just look at the way those feathers are already lifting on the breeze. This, Ms Jones, is a dress you can have fun in.'

Aware that Jessie is saying precisely nothing, Helen continues.

'Then we come to the Carolina Herrera, the gown I believe closed her New York show this season. As I'm sure you already know, Herrera is famous for making wedding dresses that are just as beautiful inside as they are outside and the hand-stitched internal boning work in this chantilly lace bodice is probably the best I have ever seen. It will nip your waist in like nothing else and provide all the support you're going to need to carry an explosion of a skirt this size. So clever of Herrera to have incorporated her signature pocket detail too – just keeping it modern enough, don't you think?'

Still nothing from Jessie, who is standing motionless with a blank expression that is proving very hard for Helen to read. Undeterred, she continues on to the third and final gown in the line-up.

'And *this* is your ultimate party piece. Every inch of this metallic fringed cocktail dress is designed to move with you, Ms Jones. Your body will look like it's dancing even when it's not and the jewelled neck negates the need to add any further accessories. It's the first time designer Naeem Khan has included a cocktail dress as part of his main bridal collection and my goodness, he couldn't have done it any better.'

Helen's chest swells as she takes another moment to appreciate the full glory of what is set before her. She can see in a second the craftsmanship, the endless hours of hand beading, the attention to detail on every inch of lace work. She can see how perfectly tailored each silhouette is, designed very precisely with the female form in mind – not restrictive, but built to glide over a woman's curves so she can walk, dance and entertain her guests totally confident in the knowledge that she looks the very best she ever has.

Helen turns away from the dresses now to confront Jessie face on, desperate to finally elicit a reaction. But Jessie is frozen, one blink away from releasing the tears that have filled her eyes and sending them streaming down her perfectly made-up face. Her mouth is struggling to form the words she wants to say and Helen can see she is trembling ever so slightly from the sheer effort of trying to hold herself together. The bolshie arrogance of ten minutes ago has deserted her completely and the embarrassment of losing her composure in front of Helen is starting to take hold. Perhaps others might have let her suffer for a moment longer, payback for the earlier unkindness, but not Helen.

All her warm, motherly instincts propel her towards Jessie and she pulls her into a deep maternal hug, feeling her uptight and stressed-out little body yield slightly – knowing she'll be dry-cleaning her blouse tomorrow to remove the tearstains that are now forming on her right shoulder. And there they both stand for one whole minute, neither of them saying a word but Helen silently promising she will help to fix this girl, whatever has broken her.

'God, how mortifying,' offers Jessie finally, her cheeks flushed and her armpits starting to prick from the sweaty embarrassment of it all.

'Jessie, if I may call you that now?' asks Helen. 'You are looking at three of the most beautiful wedding gowns I myself have ever seen – the sort of gowns that frankly most girls can only ever dream of wearing. If you didn't shed a tear or two, I'd think there was something wrong with you, darling.

'Let's just look at the dresses for now, see what details you might like to change, talk about timescales and whether you would like to try anything on from the broader collection here. And Jessie, please remember that every single bride-to-be before you has at some point shed tears in my company – *every single one*, without exception. You've just got yours out of the way nice and early.'

There is something in the way that Helen's words make Jessie flush a little more that suggests she might already be unpicking the complex character of Ms Jones – and she can't help but feel satisfied that an appointment that started so negatively has finished with a hint of the progress to come.

Six exhilarating appointments later, Helen is turning The White Gallery sign to closed, activating the over-complicated alarm system she always feels is so unnecessary in this village and climbing the stairs back up to her home, weary but proud of what she's achieved today. As she closes the door that leads into the small but homely lounge with its open fire and small fold-out antique dining table just big enough for two, the familiar feeling of dread begins to build in her again. She kicks off her shoes, wriggles her toes free and heads straight for the small kitchen and the much needed kettle, knowing full well that it's going to take more than a cup of Earl Grey to fight off the impending feeling of loneliness that is creeping up inside her.

Helen's double bedroom is just across from the lounge and from where she is standing in the doorway of the kitchen she can glance through to it. There, hanging on the picture rail is the taffeta wedding dress she wore thirty-five years ago when she married Phillip, the love of her life. Even now – three years, eleven months and six days after she buried him – she still can't bring herself to put it out of sight. Phillip's silk handkerchief from the day is still tucked in to the bodice of the dress. On the evenings when she's really struggling to cope, Helen takes that precious piece of silk to bed with her. But the smell of him has long since faded, unlike the pain she still feels so acutely from losing him.

Chapter Three

Dolly Jackson

FIVE MONTHS TO GO

Another bound-to-be-boring day at work begins as Dolly slides into her desk chair, fifteen minutes late and hoping not to be noticed by Rich, the obnoxious boss of the public relations agency she has barely worked at for the past two years. No chance.

'Nice of you to join us, Dolly,' he bellows self-righteously across the grey open plan office so that every one of her colleagues lifts a head to gawp. 'What was it this time, another dress fitting? Sorry we're getting in the way of all your wedding planning, but in case you've forgotten we've got several crucial pitches this week – and everyone else managed to get in on time.'

'Oh drop dead,' Dolly mumbles under her breath, raising her eyes to the sky and exhaling loudly.

She looks at the patchwork of Post-it notes stuck all over her computer screen – each one covered in random, hurried scrawls, intended to remind her of a hundred urgent jobs she needs to get done before Rich works out quite how far behind she is. *Call Daily Mail news desk, Email Green & Black's chocolate re: missing samples, Chase printers for late delivery, Book meeting room for new client visit* – interspersed with the far more exciting wedding ones that she uses to drag herself out of the work-hating fug several times a day; *Honeymoon: Sri-Lanka or Bali? Confirm menus with Willow Manor,* and *Book facial.* Then, in pride of place at the top of the screen, on the only pink Post-it note and written in shouty capital letters, the challenge that gets her out of bed every morning. *Get wedding featured in* Brides *magazine!*

Dolly slumps a little lower in her chair, praying that Rich – or 'The Dick' as he is unaffectionately known in the office – will just bugger off for now, leaving her to waste another morning achieving very little indeed. Glancing at a half-finished printed presentation that should have been on The Dick's desk a week ago, Dolly lacks all motivation to even turn on the monitor in front of her. She looks at her watch and notes it's a whole nine hours until she'll be turning this thing off again. Joy.

'Ignore that tosser and get stuck in to this,' beams Emma, Dolly's ever upbeat colleague, as she plonks an enormous cheese and ham filled Pret croissant in front of her. 'Come on, one's not going to kill you. I've nailed two this morning already, the hangover demanded it!'

Hilarious as she is, Emma is also one of those unfathomable women who either doesn't realise her belly is escaping over the waistband of her trousers, or doesn't care. Either way, she's the perfect visual deterrent that will stop Dolly eating that Pret doorstop of a breakfast – despite the fact that she can think of nothing more she would rather do. She so envies Emma's lack of concern. If she likes it, she eats it. If Dolly likes it, she generally denies herself it.

'Oh, thanks Emma, that's exactly what I need. I'll wolf this down and then deal with The Dick,' Dolly lies.

'No problem,' chirps Emma. 'Are you coming on Thursday night? A load of us are going to the new bar opening on Mercer street. It's half-price cocktails for the first hour, so obvs we're getting there early. Don't be late or there'll be drinking forfeits!'

'Sounds amaze.' Dolly's second lie of the morning. 'Count me in!' Make that three.

She watches Emma grin, her friendly deed of the day done, turn on her heels and retreat back to her own bland side of the office leaving Dolly to deal with the fresh-from-the-oven pastry smell that is wafting agonisingly up her nostrils. She wants nothing more than to sink her teeth into the croissant's comforting softness – just like every other woman in the office appears to be doing right now – washing it all down with a giant sugar-fuelled caffè latte. The smell is almost intoxicating and a starving Dolly can feel her mouth start to water and her stomach rumble – scream, more like – for something that it might actually enjoy ingesting.

Checking that Emma is already on to cheering up the next victim of Monday blues – and there are plenty to choose from in this dump – Dolly drops the pastry enemy into the bin where it belongs. Deception complete. The bitter green juice she hastily blended in the NutriBullet – an unappetising combination of spinach, kale, celery and ginger – is still churning around her gut, making her feel queasy. She tries not to think about how she forced every mouthful down, eyes clenched, nose blocked to the sour stench, focusing on the fact that it's three of her ten-a-day ticked off before she is even barely awake. But so much for energising her; Dolly feels exhausted from last night's usual Sunday food-prepping routine, making meals for the week ahead so she isn't tempted by the likes of the giant evil Pret pastry now taunting her from the bin. While her fiancé Josh was reclining on the sofa with a slice of pepperoni pizza and a copy of *GQ* – stealing ideas for his next photography shoot no doubt – Dolly dirtied every utensil in their white gloss IKEA kitchen. Five hours cooking, cooling and decanting bland food into individual-portion-sized Tupperware. Then freezing the braised fennel, ginger polenta, cashew celeriac soup, cauliflower couscous, hemp-seed pesto with miso brown rice, quinoa-stuffed courgette and enough nasty juice to keep her going for a month. She could have done it quicker if Josh hadn't demanded her attention every two minutes with shouts of, *Where's the remote? Any chance of another beer? Dolly, grab my phone from the bedroom will you!* So used to having assistants run around after him at work, he often finds it hard to adjust to normal boyfriend behaviour at home. Her best friend Tilly has been telling her to kick him into touch for months, but like most of the other things on her to-do list, she just hasn't got around to it yet.

Now is it any wonder her overworked and underfed body is craving some illegal carbs? What it's actually getting is a small tub of grey sludge that Dolly pulls out of her bag: the almond and chia seed breakfast she also made last night. Another meal to be endured not enjoyed. And that bin will have to move, the bloody pastry aroma isn't giving up. Just as Dolly is trying to work out how she can surreptitiously swap her bin for someone else's, the voice of doom reaches her.

'Get that skinny little butt of yours in here Dolly,' The Dick cackles from the safety of his glass cube. 'I've got a job that has your name written all over it.'

Saved from the breakfast sludge at least, Dolly drags herself out of the chair and across the room in the direction of The Dick's office, noting how everything about her appearance this morning says, *I don't care*. Her honey coloured hair is slicked back into a childish ponytail, while a less than made-up face had to settle for just two products this morning; a Laura Mercier tinted moisturiser and a slick of Tom Ford lip gloss. Dolly's cute Mui Mui skater dress needs to be introduced to an iron and her Kurt Geiger black ankle boots are scuffed and in need of some polish. Dolly knows she is letting herself down. Her wardrobe at home is straining under the weight of gorgeous designer dresses and accessories but they all seem wasted on this place. The more disheartened she becomes with the job, the less effort she makes with her appearance and the worse she feels.

Walking at a snail's pace, she registers the room's cheap, grey carpet tiles, long ago stained by coffee that no one can be bothered to clean off. Some are lifting at the corners, others have been replaced over the years with tiles of a different colour, creating an accidental hopscotch game on the floor. She passes four rows of modular desks with partitions built just above eye level to restrict any unnecessary human interaction, everyone already hard at work in their enforced cells. She also knows without looking that her name is a long way down the list of high performers that The Dick has written on a giant whiteboard on the wall near his office. Designed to terrify rather than inspire, this is his way of publicly outing anyone who is underachieving on the team. Dolly can't help sneaking a look as she moves past it and sees she is second from bottom, just above the new girl who joined last week. The TV ticker tape, another one of The Dick's name and shame devices, is also up and running already this morning. Dolly hates this particularly cruel system, which reveals to the entire office the length of time each individual spends on the phone every day – as opposed to online wedding planning. Lots of time talking bullshit with prospective clients is considered good, anything less than two hours a day means a dreaded visit to The Dick to explain why. The numbers from the previous Friday are still there for all to see. Dolly has managed a grand total of thirteen minutes' phone time.

When Dolly tells people she works in PR she knows they're imme-diately imagining days filled with creative brilliance – sparky people bouncing clever ideas off each other, winning business without even trying. Not the cookie-cutter prison where she spends her days and certainly not the dusty Klix coffee machine she's passing now, noticing the pile of plastic cups that it spewed on to the floor last week that even the cleaner can't be bothered to pick up. Now Dolly is at the other side of the room, the only one lined with windows, she can peer out directly into the neighbouring 1950s high-rise office block. It's the same as all the others on the grim outskirts of Cheltenham before you get to the lovely Georgian buildings the spa town is known for. Behind the same wonky grey venetian blinds, Dolly can see a similarly depressing Monday morning scene is unfolding on this dank and overcast March day. The layout next door is almost identical except, she notices, for the faces of much older women than her who are working there. She's twenty-nine, she consoles herself, still time to escape and as soon as this wedding is out of the way she knows she must. She lets out a long, low groan and turns to face the door of The Dick's office, clocking his latest motivational poster, the one he hangs here every week to *rally the troops*. Last week it read, *You miss 100% of the shots you don't take* but, as it's Monday morning, he has replaced it with this week's offering: *Success is not the result of spontaneous combustion, you must set yourself on fire.* Such a wanker.

'I wish he would,' Dolly mutters to herself, wondering if hitting the fire alarm might be a good substitute… it would at least get her out of the meeting she is about to have. Shuffling into his office without bothering to knock or even raise a false smile, Dolly can see The Dick is wearing his usual white shirt, top three buttons undone, leaving it gaping open so his chest hairs are inappropriately airing themselves in public. The sharp cut of his The Kooples suit might look cool on a man not in his late forties or one that is in better shape than the unshaven mess she is looking at now. Dolly pulls at the back of one of his cheap plastic off-white chairs – ready to sit down and hear her fate…

'Don't get comfortable Dolly, this won't take long,' says The Dick. 'Last week when you were busy swanning around wedding venues or something, this agency picked up the new Couture Cupcake business, who are now selling out of Harvey Nichols and Selfridges in London. As you know, they are the largest maker of bespoke cupcakes across America with the marketing spend to prove it. There isn't a woman alive who doesn't love a cupcake and last week a Kardashian was seen scoffing one so getting them on all the right Instagram feeds should be easy enough – even for you. What I need on my desk by first thing tomorrow morning is tasting notes on the whole lot – that's twenty-six varieties – a name for each and a well thought through strategy of the coverage we can guarantee them. Don't mess this up Dolly, it's the biggest win we've had in a long time.'

Running the next twelve hours on fast forward through her mind, Dolly can see three issues that are going to ensure she will indeed mess this up.

No. 1: She has scheduled a double hit of high intensity interval training after work tonight that will leave very little time later for writing the tasting notes and strategy.

No. 2: She has a dress fitting at 10 a.m. tomorrow morning at The White Gallery, which she is yet to tell The Dick about, having decided at the time she booked it that she'd simply blame bad traffic for her mega lateness on the day.

No. 3: These cupcakes, she remembers from the pitch research she has done, contain 700 calories each. That means

she is walking out of The Dick's office with a box
containing more than 18,000 calories. Never. Gonna.
Happen.

Dolly carries the box back to her desk, dropping it clumsily onto
her keyboard – who cares if they break, she has no intention of tasting
a single one of them. In fact, they are all destined for the giant recycling
bin at the back of the building where no one ever goes because who
cares about something as progressive as recycling around here? Dolly
reaches down to the bin beneath her desk, hesitates for a moment, then
scoops the croissant back up out of it, greedily eating half in three big
hungry bites. Then she picks up the phone, dials her home number
and waits for the answerphone to click in. As it does, she places the
receiver on her desk, where it stays until lunchtime. That ought to get
her daily phone time up a bit. Then it's on to far more important business – she emails The White Gallery to confirm tomorrow morning's
appointment. The Dick will just have to do one!

Chapter Four

Emily Hamilton

Another legendary Sunday lunch – or The Sunday Summit as it is now known in Emily's family home – is about to begin around the Hamilton's dining room table. The best Wedgwood china is out, some freshly baked bread is already sat in its basket in the centre of the mahogany table and two bottles of her mum Gloria's favourite Pinot Grigio are chilled and ready to pour. The unmistakable smell of Pledge polish, mixed with a generous dose of Shake n' Vac, is competing for prominence with the roast chicken aroma that is now filling the entire house.

'*Tell me* you've done the roast parsnips with maple syrup, Mum?' begs Emily, knowing full well she has. Her mum's Sunday roasts make most people's Christmas lunch look a bit lacking in effort.

'Of course, why would you *even* doubt me?' comes the quick response. 'Emily, can you ask Dad to stop printing handouts and gather everyone? I'm about to dish up.'

Emily loves these get-togethers, when everyone from her family and Mark's gather around her parents' enormous dining room table in the comfortable family home on the rural outskirts of Oxford where she grew up. Yes, she is about to tuck into her mum's mountain of roast chicken, goose fat potatoes, Delia's cauliflower cheese plus at least another four vegetables – all swimming in proper lumpy homemade gravy. But it is also their fortnightly wedding planning catch up – something her parents instigated the moment she and Mark announced their engagement – and as usual her dad Bill is printing an actual agenda and positioning a notepad and pencil at everyone's place setting. The retired lawyer in him just loves the need for some extreme administrative organisation. Emily is dressed for the occasion – one of communal gluttony – in a pretty floral cotton wrap dress from Topshop with, crucially, an adjustable belt. She isn't about to let something as annoying as being full get between her and a good dollop of her mum's homemade bread sauce.

'OK people, we have a lot of ground to cover today, so enjoy the spread – thank you, Gloria – and then we'll get cracking,' Bill announces, *completely unnecessarily,* thinks Emily. With only five months to go until she and Mark tie the knot, everyone is well versed in The Sunday Summit routine. Emily and Mark sit in their usual position at one head of the table, her mum and dad are at the other end. Also joining their party today are Mark's just-as-excitable parents John and Barbara, as well as Emily's eighty-three-year-old grandmother Joyce, Mark's younger sister Janet and their next door neighbour Philippa.

'Mark, I've done extra red cabbage and sage and onion stuffing for you this week – I know you love them – plus double pudding. There's Eton mess and apple pie with Cornish custard, double cream, vanilla ice cream or all three if you like. Let's see nine empty plates, shall we, and can someone help Joyce with those sprouts please!' trills Gloria as the noisy clatter of cutlery on china begins and everyone starts reaching over each other to get to their favourite dish first.

'You are a legend Glo, don't I always say that Emily?' says Mark, winking across the table at his future mother-in-law.

'Yes you do and yes she is but you are also setting the bar dangerously high for me, Mum. I'll never be able to match this when Mark and I move in together.'

'Good, frankly, then you'll still have to come here and let me do it for you!'

'How is the house purchase going Mark?' asks Bill, as Emily bristles slightly. It still amazes her how old-school her otherwise lovely dad is. She knows he still sees it as Mark's responsibility to provide for her, despite the fact she's been earning her own – admittedly low – salary as a nursery teacher for the past two years. OK, granted, she is still living at home, but that is about to change. She is a grown woman and she is about to become someone's wife.

'Well, thank you Bill, just got to keep a rocket up those solicitors, you know how lazy they can be. You have to chase them on everything.'

'Mark showed me the pictures on Rightmove, Emily, and I think it looks beautiful, what a gorgeous first home for you both,' adds Barbara. 'And two bedrooms too, which will come in handy when…' Mark's mum can't help herself and everyone sniggers at her usual lack of subtlety.

'Wine, Emily?' offers Gloria, cutting in protectively before her daughter feels the need to respond to Barbara.

'I won't actually Mum, thank you,' realising by declining she might be fuelling Barbara's suspicions that family plans could be imminent. 'I've still got a bit of a headache.'

'Still? Did you take the paracetamol I gave you last night? Occupational hazard I suppose. Well, get some pudding in you later, sugar always helps.'

'Yes, every child in the nursery has the lurgy at the moment, so I'm probably getting *another* cold.'

Emily adores her job running the toddler room at the local nursery and surrounding herself every day with the love and giggles of fifteen boisterous two and three-year-olds. But a job that starts at 8 a.m. and finishes at 6 p.m. and where mobile phones are banned, leaves no time during the day for any sneaky wedding planning. Between that and all the new house admin that needs her attention (despite what her dad thinks), the late nights have been racking up a bit and taking their toll on her less than glowing complexion and her now rather limp looking mousy brown hair. There is a limit to what she can expect Mark to do. He's just as busy trying to win new business for the online travel agency he founded in their last year of university.

An hour later and after Mark has cleared the table and stacked all the dishes into the dishwasher, flirting playfully with Glo as he does, the real business of the day can begin. Emily is immensely grateful for these family meetings when everyone pulls together with one shared goal – to make this wedding as magical as they all imagine it will be. But she also knows her dad's uber efficiency is going to keep her awake again tonight, rolling around in bed like some demented rotisserie chicken, feeling just as hot and bothered from the rising fear about how many decisions she has to make.

'OK, Philippa, would you like to kick us off with a cake update please?' begins Bill. *Here we go.*

'Absolutely. Last time we met, Emily, you didn't seem fully committed to the fondant icing, so I've pulled together some ideas for a few different types of naked cakes – you know, the ones with no icing at all where you can see the filling, which is usually colourful berry fruit. I love this one,' she continues, holding aloft an A4 image to a chorus of approving noises from around the table. 'It's five tiers of vanilla sponge, all sandwiched together with blackberries, strawberries and elderflower-scented buttercream. I'm sure I can do it – if you like it of course?'

Thinking about cake when your belly is chock-full of apple pie isn't ideal or comfortable. And it's cake, isn't it? Sponge, sugar, cream. Is there a bad decision? Maybe that's irrelevant. These people need answers. Eight pairs of eyes look expectantly at Emily now – they want leadership, stuff to action, proper focus, a committed pursing of the lips and nod of the head to demonstrate she's as serious about this as they all are.

Whenever there is a birthday, anniversary, graduation or just about anything that calls for a cake in the village, Philippa is the go-to woman. She ran her own bakery business back in the day and loves nothing more now than playing a star role in creating the most special cake of all – the wedding cake. This is her very gratefully received wedding present to Emily and Mark.

'I had elderflowers on my wedding cake,' pipes up Joyce from her roast potato coma, the words belching out of her, accompanied by what sounds suspiciously like a broken snore.

'That's decided then,' confirms Emily, grabbing the first opportunity to power down the agenda.

'Wonderful,' says Bill. 'Which brings us neatly on to the bunting. Have you had much joy on that yet, Janet?'

Emily is marrying in the same church where Glo and Joyce said their vows and in a bid to make them both feel included she suggested at the last meeting they retain some of the beautiful details that both generations before her incorporated into their days.

In the *make do or mend* mentality of the mid-50s, Joyce chose to forgo flowers and instead decorated the church with pretty lace bunting, patched together from old tablecloths, napkins, cushion covers and whatever else she could get her hands on at the time. Emily asked Janet, the craftiest among them, to see if she could source some of the original lace from a couple of old black and white photographs that she'd been given. If she managed it, Emily wanted to recreate the bunting to hang around the marquee which would host the reception in her parents' beautiful English country back garden.

'It's good news, Emily!' beams Janet. 'Several hours trawling Etsy has finally paid off. I have located a woman in Yorkshire who says if we can email her an image of the lace, which I have already described to her in great detail anyway, she will be able to reproduce it – at surprisingly little cost. We just need to work out how many bunting flags you think you need.'

'Leave that to me,' volunteers Bill. 'I know the precise dimensions of the marquee so I will do the equation later.' He writes the words *bunting maths* on his pad under the heading *Actions*.

'I'm impressed, Janet. I honestly never thought you would manage it,' smiles Emily.

'Well, this is going *great* guns! What's next?' Bill is scanning down the list of everything they must achieve today. 'Oh yes, a garden makeover update from me actually. So, I've cancelled my birthday celebrations next weekend so I can do the final bit of landscaping with Mark before we really start to think about what planting we need then I think we should...'

'No, Dad!' interjects Emily. 'No way. I know how much you enjoy your annual golf weekend with the boys and I don't want you cancelling it on my behalf.'

'Don't be silly darling, I made him cancel it months ago. Don't even speak of it!' chimes in Gloria. 'He can play golf any time. Your only daughter gets married once, this is far more important.'

'Hear, hear!' roars Barbara, fuelled by two large glasses of the Grigio. 'And if you don't mind me jumping ahead on the agenda Bill,' – *he absolutely will*, thinks Emily – 'can we *please* talk about dress shopping now?'

'OK, I know you are all desperate to be in on this but I really need to manage your expectations please,' says Emily. 'I have no desire to be married in a dress so enormous it's visible from the moon – it's just not for me. So please don't be disappointed if I go for something a bit more… *subtle* than you all have in mind.'

'Oh, come on! At least try the whoppers on, will you?' pleads an obviously deflated Barbara. 'Humour us a little, *please*.'

'Let's just get you into a few dresses shall we?' adds Gloria, obviously praying that once the tulle takes over Emily will finally become the Bridezilla they all hope she'll be.

'Urghh, to be continued, but for now I've booked an appointment at The White Gallery in Little Bloombury next Saturday lunchtime. I'll understand if any of you can't make it – obviously you aren't invited Mark – but they haven't got another appointment for weeks so it has to be then. Who would like to come?'

Mark aside, and with the exception of John because *this is way beyond my area of expertise*, everyone around the table raises a hand, including her dad. *Good God, what next*, wonders Emily, *all of them piling into bed with us on the wedding night?*

Another hour passes as Bill rattles through a shortlist of locally recommended florists, the pros and cons of various catering options for a reception to feed seventy, council requirements for guest parking and residential noise restrictions after midnight. His list of actions has grown to fifteen points and, at his polite insistence, everyone gets their diaries out and agrees the date of the next meeting. Nearly three hours after they all first sat down, Joyce has nodded off again and is quietly dribbling out of the left corner of her mouth. She has been moved to the more comfortable Chesterfield in the lounge and Emily's headache has reached epic proportions.

As they finish up, Emily kisses Mark goodbye, thanks everyone for all their amazing efforts and disappears upstairs to the same bedroom she has slept in her entire life for some much-needed quiet time – totally over the wedding talk for one day. Her single bed still plays host to her four favourite childhood teddies including a very tired looking tiny pink one she's had since the day she was born. There is an old Polaroid picture somewhere of it lying next to her in the hospital crib, dwarfing her newborn swaddled body. She knows hanging on to them is a bit ridiculous for a twenty-seven-year-old woman but she couldn't bring herself to bin them or even sentence them to the darkness of her parents' cobweb-filled attic.

Emily collapses on to the bed, happy but tired, looking up at a wall covered in the proud achievements of a conscientious schoolgirl. She returned from a weekend away with Mark recently to find the results of Gloria's under-stairs cupboard tidy were now framed and hanging there – a mix of swimming and gymnastics certificates, a class photo taken before her sixth-form leaver's ball and a framed local newspaper article showing a toothy Emily, aged seven, crossing the finishing line first in a school charity fun run. But Gloria didn't stop there, she has also framed Emily's teacher-training graduation certificate, next to a picture of her and Mark on graduation day, tossing their mortarboards high into a bright blue summer sky and finally her professional diplomas, all four of them, charting Emily's progress through to fully qualified nursery teacher. Emily allows herself a wry smile. She didn't have the heart to tell her mum they looked a bit, well, juvenile, killing any idea of passion that the single bed might not have already extinguished. It's pretty hard to think about devouring your fiancé's half naked body when your goofy seven-year-old self is staring down at you from the bedroom wall. Come to think of it, maybe that *is* her mum's idea? Anyway, what does it matter, she is moving out soon so why risk offending her mum by saying anything?

Emily reaches for the tab of paracetamol tablets still on her bedside table from last night, pushes two more through the silver foil and swallows them whole with a gulp of stale water. Then she picks up her mobile phone and searches through her contacts for the number of Liz, her boss at the nursery. In the two years she has worked there Emily has never called in sick, but judging by the stubbornness of the drill going off in her head, she thinks a warning of a no-show tomorrow might be wise. She feels dreadful. She has a new boy starting in the morning and his nervous mum has already warned Emily that he's going to be teary. She's been doing the job long enough to know this means it's the mum who's going to be teary. She wants to be there to make it as pain-free as possible. Feeling slightly reassured that she has at least scanned his new starter profile and prepared all the things his mum had written that he loves most – some musical instruments, touch-and-feel picture books and some small wooden jigsaw puzzles. Someone else could easily take over if necessary. Emily closes her eyes, just for a second to enjoy the quiet. By 6.30 p.m. she is already fast asleep on top of her bed, still wearing the wrap dress and clutching pink ted.

Chapter Five

Jessie

'What now?' Jessie huffs as her mobile phone starts to ring. She exits The White Gallery, en route back to Willow Manor to sort out that pathetic planner. She glances at the phone, thumb already hovering over the decline button when she realises it's Adam and quickly accepts the call. She could do with hearing his strong confident voice right now.

'Hey, gorgeous, where are you?'

'Hi, honey. I've just finished a dress appointment and I'm on my way back to Willow Manor to run through some details.'

'Cool. I'm just calling to let you know that Lady C has invited us over for an early supper this evening. You know they're bloody itching to get in on the wedding planning, so I said no probs, we'll swing by at six-ish.'

'Tonight!'

'Yeah, we're not doing anything are we?'

'Um…' lacking the presence of mind to invent something, Jessie has no choice but to add: 'lovely idea, I'll come home now and start getting ready.' The dread immediately takes hold, wiping any trace of the smile from hearing Adam's voice clean away.

'Well, you can, gorgeous, but it is only 11 a.m. and we're not due there for another seven hours. It's only supper, no big deal.'

This might be *only supper* to Adam but Jessie knows this *must* go better than her last meeting with Lady C – aka Adam's formidable mother, Camilla Coleridge – and her husband, Henry. They popped in unannounced one Saturday morning to find her slumped on the sofa like some giant hungover slug while Adam was, of course, out for a run. As she struggled to conceal herself under a sheer Heidi Klein silk kaftan, the conversation was awkward and stilted. Henry asked endless questions about what she had planned for the day when the unspeakable truth was making love to their son as often as she could manage. The fifteen minutes they all waited for Adam to return felt like an eternity – the moment he did, his charm melted the atmosphere like warm fingers on an ice pop. But the damage was done, the judgements were made… in Jessie's mind at least.

'Jessie, can you hear me? Jessie?'

'Yep, I'm on my way,' and she disconnects the call before Adam can say another word. No time for chit chat now, not even with him.

Jessie knows she's got off very lightly with Adam's family, until now. There were a couple of large parties around Christmas but as Adam's relatively new girlfriend, she managed to deliberately slip into the background, avoiding anything more than a few quick pleasantries before the hosts were swept away by their more gregarious guests. But supper with his parents in their home, on their private estate, as his fiancée, is a whole new level of exposure.

I need a decent blow dry and then time to think of a gift to arrive with that looks thoughtful but not too try-hard. Then what the hell am I going to wear?

Out of the corner of her panicked eye, Jessie sees the planner approaching, this time with Willow Manor's general manager in tow; safety in numbers.

Have I got time to read the Telegraph *cover to cover? What's going on in the world? What's my view on Brexit, I need to get one, why don't I have one?*

'Not now!' she barks in the planner's general direction, raising a hand like a policewoman directing traffic.

I wonder if any of Adam's Country Life *magazines are still lying about, I need a handle on the concerns of your average minted landowner.*

The planner and manager halt abruptly, musical-statue-like, before Jessie changes her route across the lawn to avoid them altogether, leaving them unsure whether to take up the chase or retreat. Perhaps noticing the ferocious scowl on her face they wisely choose the latter. Picking up her pace, Jessie tears at the clasp on her bag, searching for the car keys.

They're going to ask me what my parents do, what am I going to say? They're going to ask me what I do, what am I going to say? Play tennis a lot, get my hair done and shout at wedding suppliers? This is going to be horrific.

So much of what she'll have to admit tonight won't look good to them, Jessie's sure of it. For a start she doesn't work, having resigned from the property company where she was an executive assistant almost as soon as the ring was on her finger. She resisted Adam's suggestion to quit for weeks, but in the end she couldn't argue around his logic. He wants her around more and feeling that desired was just too persuasive in the end. Her salary was miniscule compared to his wealth and when he played his trump card and offered to put her name on the deeds to the Cheltenham house, she felt secure enough to take the leap. But how will that look to the Coleridges if they ever find out? She managed to meet, ensnare and then live off Adam, all in the space of three short months, that's what they will assume. Then there is the small matter of her unappealing background, and only a catalogue of bare-faced lies is going to conceal *that*.

Adam knows, of course, but that will make it much harder for her to gloss over as she normally would. She can hardly sit there evading questions about her schooling and pretend that her parents' property is not an always-cold council house when a few weeks ago Adam was sat in her mum's lounge unable to remove his coat and watching his frozen breath hang in the air as he politely nibbled on a cheap pork pie. Knowing she could only delay the visit for so long, that day she watched as he made such a fuss of her mum, winning himself so many brownie points that by the time they left he was firmly in the can-do-no-wrong camp. Her eyes remained glued to his sweet face for the entire car journey home afterwards, searching for any sign of exasperation, anything that would confirm the visit was a chore, an act. But there was nothing. Then when their naked bodies became tangled together in bed that night, she knew for sure there was no pretence. He wanted every part of her.

And how could she not adore him for that? But just because he's OK with it, that certainly doesn't mean his parents will be, that's the point. The lead weight hanging in Jessie's belly now feels like a rock destined to sink her.

By the time she jumps in her Mini convertible and, powered by road rage, floors it the fifteen miles back to their home in the exclusive Montpellier district of Cheltenham, her stomach is bloated from the knot of anxiety growing there.

Jessie screeches to a standstill in front of the black wrought iron gates outside their white four-storey, double-fronted property and waits impatiently for the sensor to scan her number plate and automatically open them. Once through, she leaps from the car and takes the stone stairs to their polished black front door two at a time, darting past the perfectly sculpted bay trees that sit either side of the entrance. A gift from Adam's parents for his thirtieth birthday, the property is one of the finest examples of a Regency detached period villa in Cheltenham. Huge rooms with decorative sky-high ceilings, giant sash windows and polished French oak floors are exquisitely designed with a muted palette of soft greys and eau de nil. Everything is in its place, clutter free; as it should be when you have a daily cleaner and no offspring.

One hour later, and most of the contents of Jessie's expansive walk-in wardrobe are piled high in one giant discarded heap in the centre of their emperor-sized bed. Jessie's face is smothered in a La Mer deep nourishing serum and her hair is re-washed, blow-dried and in large Velcro rollers for extra glossy bounce. She is slumped on the floor behind the bed, legs outstretched in front of her, having only managed to decide on her bra and knickers and surrounded by a selection of the day's newspapers. Tears of pure angry frustration are starting to roll down her face just as Adam bounds into the room. All these thousands of pounds worth of couture clothes and fabulous accessories, the best luxury skincare money can buy, every make-up product known to womankind and none of it can help her now.

'Go for this,' he says, calmly pulling a chic navy Nicole Farhi shirt dress from the designer jumble sale. Then he drops to his knees beside her, cupping her cheeks in both his hands, smiling at her sticky, teary face as he starts to gently kiss her tears away. 'Come downstairs, have a cuppa with me and *please* calm down. I've got a few more emails to send and then I'm all yours for the afternoon. Let's do something fun together. Honestly, Jessie, I don't know why you do this to yourself, you have nothing to fear.'

In the half an hour it takes Jessie and Adam to drive to the Coleridges' Cotswold estate in their top-of-the-range Landrover Vogue, neither one of them utters a word. Jessie feels like she is being driven to her fate, Adam doesn't want to risk saying anything in case the tears start again. Instead, he places a supportive hand on her tense right thigh.

As they round the corner, past one of the outlying entrance lodges, and turn between the two stone pillars that mark the opening to Swell Park estate, Jessie gets her first glimpse of the 750 acres of grounds. This might be the countryside but there is nothing accidently wild about it. Every manicured blade of grass looks like it is standing to attention on the orders of the head gardener. They make their way slowly along a concrete road that is flanked by farmland on both sides – pasture for the Coleridges' 1800 ewes to roam. Beyond the first field Jessie can see a river gently curling towards a lake that's dotted with mature trees and a flock of Canadian geese. As they continue on up the road – no one could seriously describe this as a driveway – they pass several stable blocks, barns, cottages and farmhouses inhabited by the fifteen staff that help manage the estate. Jessie looks to her left to see denser tree coverage, where Adam says his father, Henry, likes to host his pheasant and partridge shoots. As they sweep around one final bend and the incline gently increases, Jessie can see the house itself and the couple's four chocolate labradors parading along a front lawn that has been cut in to strict stripes.

As she looks up at the imposing Cotswold stone house now dwarfing their four-by-four it is absolutely mind-blowing to Jessie that anyone could call this home. Adam's face is completely nonchalant.

Lady C herself stands directly in front of the main house, waiting for them – looking immaculate. The woman is dressed in a way that is totally at one with her surroundings and the – let's face it – anything but casual supper they are about to share; the perfect embodiment of low-key luxe. She is head to toe Bamford cashmere, from the luxurious caramel coloured cardigan tied neatly at her hip, to the loose culottes falling just above her quilted monochrome Chanel slippers and the neat pearl studs that catch the fading early evening light each side of her serene face.

As Adam brings the Landrover to a halt, the dogs come to life, galloping towards them with such excitement they are body bumping each other all the way. Lowering both windows, Adam shouts 'Lady C! Can you hold the dogs off please? Jessie's not a fan.'

'God, no! It's OK, you don't have to do that,' Jessie tries to correct him.

But it's too late. Lady C is already rounding up the dogs who are clearly not happy to have been dismissed at the very moment they are about to be reunited with their long lost playmate. Jessie is urgently scanning Lady C's face, searching for any sign of disappointment before she even places a foot on the gravel drive while a man in a smart green Barbour jacket and brown Dubarry boots escorts the dogs towards the back of the main house – where they no doubt have their own luxury quarters.

'Darling!' trills Lady C wrapping both arms around her boy. 'I am so, *so* pleased that you could join us. It really has been too long, Adam. Henry is just putting some papers away in the library, he'll be with us shortly. And hello again Jessica,' she adds a touch more coolly, extending a slim hand that Jessie fears is more formal than friendly. 'I'm thrilled that you could both make it. I can't imagine why Adam hasn't brought you for supper sooner.' She's smiling but her gaze lingers on Jessie, perhaps expecting an explanation that isn't coming.

'Lovely to see you again, Lady Coleridge,' ventures Jessie. 'I'm sorry about the dogs but it's just that—'

'Oh my goodness, you mustn't call me that, it's just Adam's silly nickname for me. You might have told her that I'm not actually titled, Adam. I think Camilla will do just fine.'

'Oh, right,' Jessie shoots Adam a discreet death stare but he's too busy laughing to notice. 'Um, these are for you,' squirms Jessie, handing over the box of Rococo rose and violet chocolates she'd hastily grabbed on her way home earlier.

'How sweet of you, thank you.'

'You look great, Lady C,' Adam continues, oblivious to Jessie's reddening cheeks. 'Have you been riding today?'

'Yes, I did a wonderful hack on Marquis this afternoon while your father was walking the grounds. Do you ride, Jessie?'

Still reeling from the dog disappointment and the wrong name gaff, Jessie has some ground to make up and finds herself saying 'Yes, of course… well, a little', which in fact means 'No, but I'm not going to tell you that.' Bloody Adam, why had he never bothered to explain that Lady C is in fact not a Lady at all?

'Well, let's get in shall we,' she says clapping her hands together. 'Sheila has prepared a divine supper for us all.'

The three of them enter the house through a stone archway, leading into a domed entrance hall lined with all the paraphernalia of country living – muddy wellies, dog leads, wax jackets, an assortment of walking sticks and sturdy umbrellas. Camilla leads them through the entrance and into the main hall, off which Jessie can see at least three principal reception rooms overlooking formal landscaped gardens and the rolling parkland beyond.

'Let's go in to the yellow drawing room, shall we? The view is gorgeous at this time,' says Camilla, as Jessie tries her very best not to look intimidated by her surroundings.

The yellow drawing room is indeed very yellow. Three enormous floor-to-ceiling windows that line one entire wall are swathed in rich sunny velvet curtains, and framed with grand pelmets in a matching fabric. Each has a deep window seat, decorated with an equal number of plumped scatter cushions that have clearly never been disturbed. The opposite wall is covered in extravagantly framed art works, one of which looks like an original sketch and floorplan of the house. Jessie sneaks a closer look and wonders what goes on in a loggia, a scullery or a butler's pantry. There is a huge stone fireplace at one end of the room, with two giant log baskets either side that she could easily stand upright in. Three large sofas form a square shape with the fire and between them is a low-lying ottoman covered in symmetrically stacked rural magazines.

'Adam!' booms Henry, striding into the room in slightly too baggy pillar-box red cords, a smart tweed jacket and a pink and blue checked shirt. It's quite a look. Henry slaps his son on the back with one hand, pulling him into a firm handshake with the other. 'Bloody lovely to have you here. And you Jessica,' he practically shouts before planting a firm kiss on each of her cheeks. Henry smells expensive and clean and for the first time it's obvious to Jessie where Adam gets his confident good looks from.

'Right, drinks. What will you have, Jessica?' asks Henry.

'Oh, um, what are you having?'

'Well, we're celebrating aren't we? Let's have some champagne.'

'I must say, Adam,' says Camilla. 'I am more than a little disappointed that you have chosen not to marry here, on the family estate. It would have meant a great deal to your father and I.'

Jessie's throat tightens. It's bad enough that her mum's love affair with the great British soap opera is inevitably going to be exposed to Henry during the two hours they will be seated next to each other on the top table. It is quite another to imagine her arriving at the Coleridge's, wearing nothing but Next and remarking at how *fancy* everything is.

'Well, Willow Manor is booked now and I know Jessie can't wait to tell you all about it,' offers Adam.

Three pairs of eyes flick in Jessie's direction just as she is upending her champagne flute, draining it in three fizzy gulps; Dutch courage urgently needed, the belch that is now building in her throat definitely not. She can't open her mouth through fear of releasing it, causing a rather awkward silence.

'… Well, a toast then!' shouts Henry. 'Here's to getting to know you and your family SO much better Jessica and, in the meantime, welcome to ours.'

All four of them clink their glasses together, Camilla's eyes unfortunately falling straight to Jessie's empty flute.

'As mother of the groom I am, of course, duty bound to enquire what your own mother will be wearing, Jessica, God forbid that we should clash.' *Unlikely, unless Camilla is also a fan of the Next catalogue.* 'And if she hasn't decided yet then please at least give me an idea of her personal style so that I can make the most appropriate choice.'

Jesus Christ. 'Her personal style… well… I'd say it's, it's quite…' How do you describe the contents of a wardrobe bought entirely in the sales – and not even in the first excited flush of them, oh no, three or four weeks in when the final dregs have been pulled out from the back of the dusty store cupboard, styles that no one ever remembers being in the store in the first place because in all probability they never were. 'Safe! Yes, safe, that's it. That's how I would describe her style. She won't go for anything too bold.'

'Gosh, you've got to give me more than that, Jessica. What would she wear to—'

'Sorry to interrupt, Mrs Coleridge.' It's Mr Dubarry boots again. 'Everything is ready for you in the blue dining room, as requested.'

Supper is mercifully more relaxed than Jessie is expecting. Well, the food is – a delicious spread of poached whole trout with salads and vegetables from the estate's own organic kitchen garden – the interrogation not so much.

'So, Jessie, Adam tells us you're no longer working at the estate agency, is that right?' asks Henry with the same casual openness she's heard a hundred times before from Adam.

Here we go…

'Well, I'm not working at the moment, no. I will be of course but there has just been so much to organise between the London and Cheltenham houses and Adam is working so hard and of course the wedding planning is taking over a bit.' God she feels like a fraud, like she's trying to justify her existence to a boss who thinks she's overpaid and underworked. It's making it impossible to meet Henry's eye, making her feel even more duplicitous.

'You could always help me with my fundraisers if you're bored,' suggests Camilla who has turned to speak to a member of the waiting staff, making it impossible for Jessie to read her expression. Is she suggesting some quality get-to-know-you time together? Or making the point that a day filled with such frivolities must be a pretty empty one, crying out for something more worthwhile to fill it. It can only be the latter.

'Actually, Lady C, Jessie has been doing an amazing job of organising the wedding so far. I've done next to nothing – the poor thing has shouldered it all, haven't you, darling?' Adam's defence, while so welcome, just makes Jessie feel even more inadequate, like she needs explaining – justifying. And God, is that what Adam's thinking too? Is he aware of a judgment being made inside the minds of the people who paid for the house she now lives in?

'Tell us Jessica, what *are* the plans?' Camilla has shifted forward in her seat now, arms folded onto the table, her eyes trained squarely on Jessie.

'As you know we will be holding the wedding for about three hundred guests at Willow Manor. We have the property exclusively for a week so after the wedding there will be a garden party on the Sunday. I'm just not sure about the plans for the rehearsal dinner on the Friday night yet.'

'Well, you must have it here then! At least let us do that, Adam,' demands Camilla.

'No!' the word bellows out of her much louder than Jessie intended.

'Sorry?' shoots back an obviously offended Camilla.

'I… I just couldn't expect you to take that on…' With such glib reasoning, Jessie knows the battle is already lost.

'Nonsense! It would be an absolute delight. You can leave everything to me.' It's the most excited Lady C has looked all evening.

'Thank you Lady C, that's incredibly lovely of you.' Adam seals the deal.

The look on Jessie's agonised face says it all. Game Over. And so is supper. But apparently Camilla is not through with her yet.

'Boys, I'm sure you'd love to enjoy a frame or two of billiards. Why don't you leave Jessica and I to get to know each other a little better?'

More than anything Jessie wants this evening to be over. To be sat back in the Landrover with Adam, pulling away and leaving it all behind them. But she has no choice and besides, Adam is already leaving the room, arm wrapped around Henry's shoulders like he doesn't have a care in the world.

Camilla refills Jessie's wine glass and with a subtle waft of her hand dismisses the one member of staff still hovering in case she is needed. The two women are sat directly opposite each other, giving Jessie nowhere to hide.

"Funny isn't it, they used to say you should never marry out of your age, class or religion,' Camilla begins ominously. 'But so many people ignore that now.' The smile is there again but what is it supposed to mean? Is this an invitation for Jessie to unburden herself? Or polite window dressing around the barely hidden context of *you're not good enough for my son*? Jessie honestly has no idea and she's starting to fidget in her seat from the stress of trying to work Camilla out.

Determined to break the rising tension, Jessie attempts to clear away the last remaining dirty dishes in front of them, anything to avoid Camilla's direct gaze for a moment longer.

'Just leave that,' Camilla is on her feet now and leaving the room. 'I have something for you. Wait there.' When she returns a few moments later she is carrying a small leather-bound book that she slides towards Jessie.

'*The Debrett's Guide to Modern Manners* by John Morgan, a sensational piece of work. Take it and read it Jessica, I think it will help you enormously. I still refer to it from time to time.'

'Thank you, Camilla.' It's all a dejected Jessie can think to say because the insinuation is clear to her. She obviously got more wrong tonight than even she imagined. But while she knows she hasn't exactly been the most riveting company, she hoped it wasn't so bad that she now needs the paperback version of finishing school.

'Etiquette, although hugely derided, exists to give people a set of rules Jessica, to help them fit in.' There is a warmth to Camilla's tone that is totally at odds for Jessie with what she's doing. She doesn't sound spiteful at all but in giving Jessie this book she can surely only mean she is not yet up to the job of marrying a Coleridge.

'We all have a universal desire to be part of a tribe, don't you think, to be accepted Jessica, but there is no point pretending to be something you're not. You've got to have courage to take this on. Having great wealth means everyone will have an opinion of how you conduct yourself, *that* is the price you pay.'

'I see.' Jessie gets it now, Camilla's warning her, telling her she will be watching, ready to pull her up whenever she brings shame on the family, the implication being that she surely will of course. Jessie is only relieved that Adam isn't hearing any of this.

'I personally believe marriage needs two out of three things to survive: love, a sense of humour and money. There is a lot of truth in that, don't you think?'

'I love Adam very much, Camilla, I hope you know that?' The suggestion otherwise has pricked at Jessie and her words sound clipped and defensive. She can feel the heat flood her face but Camilla is the last person she can afford to get annoyed with, not tonight.

'Well then in that we are completely united. I am biased of course but Adam is a wonderful man, one of the very best. His achilles heel is that he's often too trusting. That's what needs to be watched. Just like Henry, he has a natural love of people, always seeing the good before the bad. It is honourable but I worry it might be his downfall.'

The three large glasses of wine Jessie polished off over their light supper are proving a real hindrance now as she tries to decipher any hidden meaning in Camilla's words.

'I will try my best.' It's like flunking an exam. That feeling that you are capable of doing so much better but somehow you didn't. Like there is a mountain of work ahead of you now and you'll be playing catch up forever. Can she play it right? Is it within her? Camilla doesn't seem to think so.

'But Jessica,' there is a light laugh escaping Camilla's perfectly painted lips now. 'Even if you were bitten by seventeen dogs as a baby, never admit you don't like them, no one will ever trust you!' She's reaching out her hand across the table now and tapping the back of Jessie's. 'You have to remember that most of the upper classes are emotionally constipated and unable to communicate with each other – call it the side effects of being sent to boarding school at seven, hardly ever seeing their parents except when they were patted on the head before a governess took them back upstairs to bed. It's no wonder most of them prefer to communicate with animals!'

'Got it!' The dog snub is clearly going to be held against Jessie forever more.

'And one final piece of advice, if I may. Adam's friend Annabel. She's been in love with him for as long as I can remember. Maybe it's her day job, but she's shown more interest in this wedding than anyone else. Tread very carefully there. Tilly is your woman. She's one of Adam's closest and oldest friends and he trusts her implicitly. Stick with her.'

This makes only some sense to Jessie – she's yet to meet this Annabel – but the suddenly serious look on Camilla's face tells her it might not be entirely pleasant when she does.

As Jessie and Adam say their goodbyes later that evening and climb back into the Landrover, Jessie has never felt so self-conscious or shell-shocked at the speed and accuracy of Camilla's dissection of her. She has taken her apart in less than two hours.

'I probably should have mentioned this earlier,' says Adam as they rejoin the main road on their way home, 'but Lady C is actually allergic to chocolate.'

'Of course she is,' sighs Jessie, unable to hide her feelings of despair any longer.

As Jessie's Mini turns past the high-rise council flats on the edge of the Roehampton estate, she moves her Asprey ostrich leather handbag into the front passenger footwell so it is out of sight and turns her engagement ring around so the rock is tucked into her left palm. She drives on down the main shopping street, which looks deserted on this lifeless Sunday morning; only the dregs of last night's revelry remain – broken bottles, dumped takeaway cartons and one randomly discarded trainer. She passes the small playground where she spent such happy days as a child, endless hours hurling herself down the slide, making pretty daisy-chains and sharing childish gossip with school friends. This morning, there is a large scorch mark in the centre of the roundabout where someone has attempted to light a fire and two of the three swings have had their seats ripped off and dumped in the bin. Someone has left a broken pushchair where the seesaw used to be and the black tarmac is cracked and lifting everywhere.

It feels so weird for Jessie, returning to her childhood home now where fond memories of late nights out playing in the dark and the tight family bubble of love she remembers so well mix awkwardly with the feeling of no longer belonging. She feels unsafe, like everyone is watching her, wondering how she took a wrong turn and ended up here. Despite the fact she despises and rejects so much about this ambitionless life, it hurts, far more than she will ever admit, that this place is also rejecting her. She's not one of them any more, can't possibly understand their lives when her own is so far removed. It makes her feel rootless, like she no longer has a claim on it. She lost all those rights the day her bank balance swelled skyward, protecting her from the financial worries that are played out every day behind these cheap PVC windows.

Stepping out of the car, Jessie glances up at the block of flats above her, its tiny balconies crammed with washing that has no chance of drying on this damp morning, towers of kids' plastic toys, barking dogs, a barbecue, a pushbike and in one case, an actual washing machine.

She's parked outside her parent's tiny three-bedroom house, which is identical to every other in the street. Her mum has obviously been twitching at her net curtains waiting for Jessie to arrive because the door flies inwards before she can hit the rusty knocker.

'Jessica!' her mum is throwing her arms around her and pulling her in through the front door. 'Everyone is here and we are all desperate to hear about the wedding plans.'

If that's the case, her siblings are doing a great job of pretending otherwise, as neither of them has risen from the lounge floor where they are busy dunking bourbon biscuits into their mugs of tea.

'I'll put the kettle on and then let's hear all about it, starting with when we're going wedding dress shopping. I wouldn't want to miss that for the world, Jessica!'

As she follows her mum into the narrow galley kitchen, Jessie can feel her heart collapsing in on itself. There is never going to be any shared shopping trip, she's already seen to that. And as she watches her mum fuss over the tea making, asking a thousand excited questions about the wedding, she knows she's failed her again, the guilt of that making her feel she has no right to her mum's unswerving love.

How many times can you let someone down before they start to love you a little less? Does her mum have a limit? Standing in the heart of her family home, Jessie has never felt so lonely. With so much work to do to find her natural place among the Coleridges and the sense of slipping further away from her own flesh and blood, the future doesn't look promising; it suddenly looks very empty.

Chapter Six

Helen

Helen folds out her neat antique dining table and begins to lay it for dinner with two placemats, two sets of cutlery and two water glasses. She tells herself it's force of habit but she knows it's more than that. Nearly four years on from Phillip's death, she still clings to the small everyday rituals, somehow keeping her connected to the husband she will love for a lifetime. His favourite aftershave still sits next to her perfume on the dressing table, his toothbrush leans against hers in the glass in the bathroom. The gentle man who was the centre of her world for so long may be gone, but Helen can't let go of him completely – she doesn't want to. She returns to the kitchen and pours herself a small glass of white wine, noticing again the invitation that is stuck to the fridge door:

Cheese, wine & gossip!
with the residents of Little Bloombury
Saturday March 15th at 7.30pm
The Village Hall
Tickets: £7
RSVP: Jayne on 0749 866 741

❦

For two weeks Helen has been staring at the invitation, knowing she should go, dreading the idea of it more. Now the evening has arrived, what is she going to do? Sit here alone, just like every other night? Add the invitation to the stack of others she has declined because she's too afraid to go it alone, because she still doesn't know who she is without him? Or finally seize the chance to make friends and move on? She looks at the redundant place setting across the table from hers, where she so desperately wishes Phillip was sitting. How much longer can she live in the past trying to keep him present in a life he departed long ago? How long can she keep avoiding her neighbours who must be thinking her the rudest woman on earth?

Helen sits in total silence, contemplating another five hours with no one to talk to, just the TV for company, until it's a reasonable time to go to bed. She misses the loud, chaotic madness that was once the soundtrack of her bustling family life. Someone always shouting after a missing hairbrush, a packed itinerary, trips here, there and everywhere as the family taxi, shopping, cleaning, organising, cooking, repeat, repeat, repeat. Now just silence. She flicks on Radio 2 to fill the room with something other than her loneliness.

'I can't do this, Phillip,' she whispers. 'I just can't do it.'

Helen walks into the bedroom and pulls open the wooden drawer of her dressing table. She lifts out a small piece of weathered-looking paper, a treasured favourite poem of Phillip's by Henry Scott Holland. He had buried it within the pages of her novel, when he knew the end was coming. She hadn't discovered it until weeks after the funeral and when she did the tears poured out of her like they were never going to stop. Helen reads the words again now, as she has countless times before.

Death is nothing at all.
I have only slipped away to the next room.
I am I and you are you.
Whatever we were to each other,
That, we still are.
Call me by my old familiar name.
Speak to me in the easy way
which you always used.
Put no difference into your tone.
Wear no forced air of solemnity or sorrow.
Laugh as we always laughed
at the little jokes we enjoyed together.
Play, smile, think of me. Pray for me.
Let my name be ever the household word
that it always was.
Let it be spoken without effect.
Without the trace of a shadow on it.
Life means all that it ever meant.
It is the same that it ever was.
There is absolute unbroken continuity.
Why should I be out of mind
because I am out of sight?
I am but waiting for you.
For an interval.
Somewhere. Very near.
Just around the corner.
All is well.

❧

Phillip knew his wife well enough to know that this was asking the impossible – asking her to live a happy life without him – but that if he did ask it of her, she would try her very best, one last dutiful role for the devoted wife to play.

Helen sits back at the dining table, one hand holding the passage, the other cradling her forehead. 'Why is it so hard, Phillip? I'm trying, I am. But I don't want to wake up every morning alone, thinking of you before anything else…' She lifts the glass of cold wine to her lips and takes a large soothing mouthful. 'Oh, come on Helen, for goodness sake, you can do this. Just go, you can always leave if it's awful. What's the worst that can happen?' There's precious little conviction in her pep talk but as much as Helen doesn't want to go, neither can she bear another evening staring at but not really watching the TV. Tomorrow is Sunday and the boutique is closed so she can't even pretend that there is preparation to do for the working day ahead.

Before she can over-think it any more Helen picks up the phone and dials Jayne's number. After two brief rings, the line connects.

'Hello, is that Jayne?'

'It is indeed!'

'Hello Jayne, it's Helen from The White Gallery'

'Oh, hi, Helen. Is everything OK?'

'Yes, I was just calling about the cheese and wine evening tonight. I'm sure I'm far too late and you probably don't have space—'

'Yes, we do! How many tickets do you need?'

'… just one please.' Immediate regret.

'OK, I'll hold one on the door for you, see you in about an hour.'

'Thank you, Jayne. See you later.'

As Helen walks along the stone path towards the front door of the village hall, she can hear the muffled sound of warm laughter coming from inside and her stomach tightens. It would be so much easier to just turn around and go home. But home to what, another big, empty evening with no purpose? Her hand hovers over the door handle as she takes a deep breath then pushes the door open. Inside, the room is full of about forty people, mostly her age, clustered in small groups, deep in relaxed conversation. She scans the room quickly, not recognising a single face, hardly surprising given her lack of effort to get to know anyone in the village.

After Phillip's death she sold the family home in Bristol and used the proceeds to buy The White Gallery and the small apartment above it. Everyone thought she was mad at the time – and at this moment she would probably have to agree with them – but she couldn't stay in the family home, it was suffocating, paralysing her progress. So she chose the Cotswolds where she and Phillip had spent so many happy weekends away together. That was as far as her bravery went. Sorting the practicalities of buying a new home and business, while complicated, have given Helen something to focus on. The motivation to build new relationships and friendships has eluded her, until tonight – her first big step.

But now she is rooted to the spot, not quite knowing what to do with herself. Everything is so much easier when you have someone by your side. Her eyes are searching the room, desperate for some flicker of recognition that isn't coming. Oh my God, is she actually going to have to walk up to a group of strangers and introduce herself? No, she can't. She starts to shuffle slowly backwards towards the door, just as a slim woman spots her and makes a beeline.

'Helen, isn't it? I'm Jayne and here's your ticket. Now, if you're on your own, can I introduce you to a few people, and let's get you a drink. Red or white? Follow me.'

'White, thank you, that would be lovely,' says Helen, relief washing over her that Jayne is taking charge.

'Susan and David, can I introduce you to Helen, she owns The White Gallery, opposite Willow Manor.'

'Ahh, hello, Helen, lovely to meet you,' offers Susan, an overly animated woman with flushed cheeks and enough cheese stacked on her plate to feed three people.

'I don't think we've ever met,' adds David. 'Have you been here long?'

'Yes, three years actually,' says Helen. 'I'm afraid I haven't been out and about much.'

'What fun to be surrounded by those wedding dresses all day, I often poke my nose up to the window when you're closed, to have a sneaky look,' says Susan. 'It's a long time since I was a size to fit in to any of them, mind you!'

Jayne returns with a glass of wine, hands it to Helen and promptly disappears again, leaving Helen to it. David is also making his excuses, probably sensing there's about to be a lot of dress chat.

'Tell me, Helen, what on earth does a wedding dress cost these days?' probes Susan. 'I think I paid about two hundred pounds for mine back in the day and David thought *that* was ridiculous. That's men for you, though. Are you married?'

'Most girls I see spend upwards of three thousand pounds on their dress—'

'What! Good grief, are you serious?'

'Yes, a lot has changed since our day.'

'I'd say! Did you say you *are* married?'

'No, not any more.' It's like Helen's brain has momentarily disconnected from her mouth. She can't think of a single other thing to say to qualify the awkwardly short statement.

'Oh, really?' Susan leaves the question hanging in the air, obviously expecting Helen to elaborate but she can't and an uncomfortable silence falls between them.

'Divorced?' Susan isn't giving up.

'No.' Surely now she'll stop?

Susan continues to look directly at Helen, seemingly hell bent on getting to the bottom of Helen's marital status.

Helen decides to steer the conversation back to the safer subject of the boutique, hoping that will satisfy Susan for the time being.

'I do love my job,' Helen offers, feeling responsible for the now stilted conversation they're stuck in. 'It's really about so much more than selling a wedding dress. I'm usually only with my ladies for an hour but in that time I'm their therapist, stylist, agony aunt, marriage guidance counsellor, referee, friend and mother. Whatever they need me to be. And it is wonderful to be needed again.'

'How lovely. Do you run the business on your own?'

Just as Helen is thinking that coming tonight is a huge mistake and the first chance she gets, she will make for the door, a man stands up at one end of the room and starts tapping his glass.

'If I could have your attention please, everyone. Please, everyone, ssshhhhhh. They're going to kill me, but there is a very special couple in the room with us tonight that deserve our attention for a moment. Sylvia and Keith, please join me up here. Not all of you will know this but these two are celebrating their fiftieth wedding anniversary today and look at them, will you – just as in love now as they always were!'

A shocked but clearly chuffed Keith and Sylvia walk hand-in-hand to the front of the crowd to a huge round of applause.

'If there are two people more in love than you pair, then I am yet to meet them,' continues the man. 'Gill, bring out the cake!'

On his orders a tea trolley is wheeled through the crowd, carrying a large white cake with the faces of Keith and Sylvia beaming out from the top of it. Someone pops a champagne cork to shrieks of laughter and cheers from the crowd. Just as Keith plants a huge kiss on his wife's cheek, Helen's face crumples and she is suddenly sobbing uncontrollably and making a dash for the ladies'.

She locks herself in one of the two small cubicles, leans her head back against the cold wall tiles and lets the tears flood down her face, cursing herself for thinking she could do this. She tries to stifle the sound of her sobs as they echo around the room, drowned out anyway by the loud celebrations that are still going on back in the hall. The sadness is suddenly so overwhelming – the realisation that she and Phillip will never celebrate fifty years together, will never have a surprise cake presented to them in front of a room full of well-wishing friends. They'll never do anything else together. He's dead and he's never coming back. She's alone and always will be now.

When she gets home tonight there will be no one to kiss goodnight, no warm lips softly pressed against hers, no hand to reach out to in bed, no one to share a hot cup of tea with and reflect on the day. It is all so unfair. Why her? Why him? She had played totally by the rules. She married a man she loved, who loved her. They had a happy honest marriage with no agenda other than to care for and support each other and raise their children in a bubble of protective love.

There's no way she can walk back through the hall now, her face must be a mess, and as far as she is aware, there is no back exit out of here. *How ridiculous*, she thinks, a grown woman, nearly four years on, and still not able to do something as simple as share a glass of wine with new neighbours and potential friends – friends she knows she needs to make.

She hears the creak of the outer door to the ladies' push open and instinctively lifts her hand to her mouth to muffle the sobs. Her body is shaking internally from the effort of trying to get herself under control.

'Helen, it's Susan, are you OK in there? Helen?'

'I'm fine, Susan. Please go on out, I'll be there in a minute.' The only thing possibly worse than crying in the loos like this is having a total stranger witness the horrible big messiness of it all.

'I'm not going to do that, Helen. Please come out.'

'I just need a minute Susan, please.'

'I'll wait.'

That's it, no choice now but to open the door and face the embarrassment and probably better to do it before anyone else joins them in the loos. Helen unlocks the stiff bolt and slowly pulls the door towards her. Susan is standing right there; there is absolutely no avoiding her.

'I'm sorry Helen, are you OK?' Not waiting for an answer, she wraps an arm around Helen's shoulder and pulls her out of the cubicle, guiding her towards the sink so she can start sorting out the mess that was her make-up. Helen wets a handful of tissue under the cold water tap and starts to blot her mascara away, enjoying the cool feeling under eyes that are sore and puffy now.

'I lost my husband, Phillip, four years ago to lung cancer. This is really the first time I have come to anything on my own. I wish I hadn't now obviously.'

'I'm so sorry, had you been married long?'

'Thirty-five years, although I met him long before, when I was just a child really.'

'Come on,' says Susan, 'let's go back outside and get you a glass of wine and some nice cheese and you can tell me all about him.'

Susan takes Helen's arm and gently steers her out of the ladies' to a small trestle table at the back of the hall, the only one no one else is sitting at.

'How did you meet?' starts Susan once they are sat down together.

'Our families lived in the same street so we'd spend hours playing with all the other local children,' begins Helen, 'doing everything we could to stay out as late as possible. Then I did what most women did in those days I suppose, I married my first serious boyfriend – that was Phillip.' Now that she's talking about him, Helen can feel the tension that was so tightly balled up inside her at the beginning of the evening start to slowly ebb away.

'Everything was simpler then. I compare my life then to my daughter Betsy's today and hers is much harder in many ways. She lives miles away from me in Birmingham with her boyfriend Jacob. She works so hard, all the time, and I worry who is looking after her? Where is her support? Who can she lean on when she needs it? It's much harder for young working women now I think.'

'Yes, baby in one arm, laptop in the other, flying between the office and the nursery they're paying a small fortune for. Both partners earning, but spending it just as quickly. I know, Helen, I have a career-mad daughter too. The things she expects of that poor husband of hers, well, I'd never say this to her obviously but I'm amazed she gets away with it.' Susan is definitely warming to her theme, sending a fountain of blue cheese crumbs across the table as she talks.

'Funny, Phillip and I never discussed how the work was divided, it just happened naturally in the same way it did for my parents. I ran the house, he provided for us, we got on with having a family. Phillip never changed a nappy, or got up in the night to a screaming toddler and he was a total stranger at the school gates but it worked and we were both so happy. I never resented my role, I loved it.'

Why is talking aloud about Phillip so much easier than the solitude of her private memories, the ones she relives night after night? wonders Helen. She might not agree with everything Susan is saying tonight but the female company is very welcome. And the worst has happened now so she may as well try to enjoy herself.

'I used to have my daily routine down pat. I cooked all our meals from scratch – Phillip loved my cottage pie – did all the laundry and cleaned that house from top to bottom at least twice a week. And we never had any credit cards or bank loans. If we couldn't afford it, we didn't have it.'

'Try saying that to someone in their thirties today, they'd think you're mad. If they haven't got the latest iPhone and three foreign holidays booked, then their lives aren't worth living.'

'Every summer we'd pack up the car and head to a caravan park in Cornwall. It was the cheapest holiday ever, but the kids loved it. They spent every day building sandcastles on the beach, whatever the weather, eating sandy sandwiches and begging for ice creams. Then in the evening it would be fish and chips and card games, all huddled around the tiny fold-out dining table that turned into a bed, in the same caravan we always booked – perhaps a trip to the clubhouse if we were feeling flush. I wish I could turn the clock back and do it all again, I really do.' Helen can feel the weight of every one of those memories made real for her, a cruel, contorted mix of the happiness she once felt and the desperate sadness at knowing such treasured moments are long gone now.

'Look at it this way, Helen, you're still young enough to meet someone else.' Susan on the other hand is all cheerful optimism.

'That would be great if I wanted to meet someone else, I suppose, but I don't. That was never the plan, Susan. I wanted to grow old with Phillip, no one else.' The lump is back in Helen's throat.

'I know what it's like to lose someone,' ploughs on Susan. 'I've been divorced so I know *exactly* how you feel. Actually, I must introduce you to Roger. He lost his wife several years ago.'

'*Please* don't do that,' says Helen reaching a restraining arm towards Susan. The thought of having another man's eyes on her, assessing her potential for something she doesn't desire, is making Helen want to bolt for the door. Even the most innocent friendship with a man is beyond her right now. She wouldn't know what to say to him, how to act or manage his expectations and the mere suggestion of it is scrambling her thoughts, reigniting all her panic.

'Oh! There you are, Roger.' Susan is glancing over her shoulder at the table right next to them at a tall, distinguished-looking man in his late fifties who is sat close enough to have overheard their entire conversation.

Before the evening can get any more embarrassing Helen gets to her feet and starts to excuse herself, to escape.

'I'm going to head off, I think, Susan, if you don't mind?' Never more has she wanted to be back in the cosseted safety of her own home, drawing the curtains and shutting out all unwanted intrusions.

'Not before you've met Roger, Helen. Roger, say hello to Helen, she owns The White Gallery in the village.' Already Helen can feel her palms pricking and while she knows it's rude she busies them collecting her things, avoiding Roger's friendly outstretched hand.

'Lovely to meet you, Helen,' Roger is forced to talk to the back of her head. 'If you're heading that way, I'll walk you back, I'm just a little further on from you.'

'That really isn't necessary, thank you, Roger. I'm only two minutes away.' It's hardly the outgoing approach Helen was planning tonight but she needs to cut this off.

'Really, I insist.' Roger is grabbing his coat and attempting to help Helen on with hers. She knows they've reached the point where only real rudeness will deflect him now and she doesn't trust herself to attempt a further decline without the tears bubbling up again. She has no choice but to capitulate, much to Susan's obvious delight.

'It was lovely to meet you, Helen,' Susan adds through an enormous smile. 'I'm just around the corner at Roseberry Cottage if ever you want to, you know, talk.'

'Thank you, I'm sure I will. Goodnight.' Helen is moving towards the door at speed, forcing Roger to jump ahead of her to open it.

The two of them make the short walk back through the village towards The White Gallery, Helen's mind clambering for things to say beyond the obvious trite reflections on the evening, her body rigid under her coat at the thought of him touching her in even the most polite way.

As they approach her front door Roger turns to Helen and smiles. 'It's not easy, is it? People can say some incredibly crass things at times. Well-meaning, of course, but until you've been in our position you just don't know how hard it is.' If he's inviting her intimacy, he's not going to get it. Helen is as clenched and unyielding as the balled fists at her sides.

Roger pauses for a moment, presumably sensing her deep discomfort before adding; 'I think your husband, wherever he is Helen, is probably very proud of you tonight.'

It's a lovely thing to say and exactly what she needs to hear but Helen doesn't want to dwell on the subject with a near total stranger.

'Thank you Roger, that means an awful lot, as I suspect you know.'
She allows herself a fragile smile before reaching for her keys and
heading straight through her front door.

Helen climbs the stairs to her apartment above the boutique feeling
just a little impressed with herself now. She heads straight for the
bedroom, exhausted from the sheer effort tonight has required of her.
She carefully removes all her make-up, brushes her teeth and drops
her clothes into the laundry bin. As she climbs in to bed she gently
kisses the framed photograph of Phillip that sits on her bedside table,
just as she does every night. But there are no more tears this evening
and she is asleep moments later.

Chapter Seven

Dolly

Sweat is sliding down the sides of Dolly's puce face as she fights for air, barely able to remain upright through the force of her own breath escaping her lungs. Her hands are shaking uncontrollably, every drop of lactic acid gone from her body after another painful forty-five min-ute training session.

She arrived home from work at 8 p.m. tonight to the tiny two-bed flat she shares with Josh, shattered from another brain-numbing day trying to make crap products sound exciting. But with no sign of him, she's decided to get her workout done without his usual running commentary on how pathetic her press-ups are. After chucking her pile of work guff onto the floor – the cupcake strategy will just have to wait – she got ready for a double hit of her usual high intensity interval training – the first of five sessions she's scheduled for this week.

The yoga mat is in its usual position in the small space between their breakfast bar and dining table. She's changed into an old pair of trainers, shorts and a sports bra and her laptop is open and logged on to The Body Coach YouTube channel. Despite every inch of her tired body begging to collapse on the sofa, she hits play on another gruelling session, getting her one step closer to her eight and half stone wedding target weight – nice and skinny for her five foot eight inch frame.

The vision of the fat kid she once was is all the motivation she needs tonight, that and a looming wedding day of course. Age twelve and sporting a triple chin that melted into her neck, arms that bulged body-builder-like out of every top she owned, a barrel of a belly that engulfed her waist and wobbled its way through her all-girls school with a life of its own and an arse that was always five seconds behind the rest of her, such was its size. Then came the bullying, the whispered jokes behind her back, the look of disgust on the skinny girls' faces, the friends she never made just because she was bigger; the memory of it all is as fresh in her mind now as it ever was. She can never go back to that, no matter what.

Now for the sodding cupcakes. Having binned the entire box on the way out of the office so there was absolutely no chance of letting a morsel pass her lips, Dolly has the tricky task of naming twenty-six varieties she no longer has in front of her, as well as writing a press strategy to sell the bloody things. Should she text Tilly? Her whipsmart friend would have this nailed in no time. Nope. No point. It's cocktail hour in Tilly's world and she'll be out schmoozing clients. In hindsight, perhaps taking a quick pic of those cupcakes might have been clever. Whatever, Josh is due home any minute and she wants to wrap this up quickly, there are more important things to do, including another email to *Brides* magazine. They *need* to feature this wedding, her future happiness depends on it. Land this coverage, demonstrate her then undeniable styling credentials and boom! A route out of the misery of her own dead-end job would be hers.

She scans through her saved documents on the laptop, thinking there must be something vaguely relevant in there. She runs the cursor down a long list of failed pitch presentations – one for a Greek wine company (undrinkable), a new range of savoury donuts with flavours like chicken liver and blue cheese that no one was ever going to eat, some deluded client who thought reversible tights were the next great thing and then finally, a cupcake brand. Yes!

Dolly remembers this one from about a year ago, they had a decent product but nowhere near enough money to launch the brand effectively, at least that was The Dick's excuse when they failed to win the business. She opens the document and starts to scan its contents. Joy of joys! It's all here. Dolly has seen enough cupcakes in her time to know every company essentially sells the same product, they just give them different names. This is too easy. She starts to copy and paste huge swathes of the old document, lifting the list of names and flavours straight into her new one. The Tuxedo, a rich blend of white and dark chocolate ganache, The Cakey Perry, a light vanilla sponge smothered in pink buttercream and scattered with multi-coloured mini jellies and sweeties, The Florabunda, decorated with an elaborate buttercream piped flower and The Bananarama with its chunks of fresh banana swirled into rich salted caramel, the list goes on. Everything she needs is here, including a long list of press contacts on all the relevant foodie blogs, websites and weekly print titles plus an outline of a half-decent social media campaign that will get these cupcakes all over Instagram. Twenty minutes later and it's job done! There is no point agonising over this because let's face it, this is an American client, they'll want to rewrite the whole lot anyway once six vice presidents of everything have read it.

She fires off an email containing the *new* strategy to The Dick – that will keep him busy while she's at The White Gallery in the morning – then checks her inbox, hopeful there might be something from *Brides* magazine. For God knows how many weeks she has been relentlessly campaigning to the editor's PA, trying to get her wedding featured on the prestigious magazine's glossy pages, convinced it might somehow kick-start a new career in styling, enabling her to give the long-desired two-fingered salute to The Dick. But despite a running total of fifty-six emails, twelve phone calls, one embarrassing and highly ill-judged attempt to actually get in to the *Brides* office and a small fortune spent on tickets to *Brides* reader events in the hopes of actually chatting to Annabel, the ice-cold PA, Dolly has got precisely nowhere. If she made this much effort at work, the agency might finally be profitable.

She makes a mental note to send the PA a box of the cupcakes tomorrow, there are loads knocking around the office, then begins another shamefully sycophantic email to her.

Dear Annabel,

Can I just start by saying I absolutely love your piece in this issue on how powder blue is the new blush – I couldn't agree more! You're such a wonderful writer.

I wanted to update you on my wedding plans in the hope you might suggest it to the Editor for possible inclusion in the magazine – which of course you know I adore. All of my ideas have been taken from *Brides* and I simply couldn't have planned this wedding without your expert help so thank you so much.

We've decided to turn the running order of the day on its head. Josh, my fiancé – who shoots some of your fashion stories – and I will be hosting a large dinner party reception first in the grounds of Willow Manor in the Cotswolds. Starting early evening, the dinner will be served in a glamorous Sperry tent, just like the one in your Real Weddings Special. Guests will enter along a festooned walkway, dotted with globe lanterns before they are seated on large banqueting tables for sharing platters, all organic of course. As bespoke is such a hot trend right now, there will be personalised menus for each guest with their names hand painted on the top. Then we're having a party area with a dance floor and giant mirror balls suspended above it. I've hired the same band you had at your Designer Ball at Goodwood last year! We're having a chic white champagne bar that leads into a chill out snug with giant day beds and reindeer skins to cosy up under.

After reading the last Editor's Letter, I've decided I'm not having any flowers at the wedding at all, just foliage which I agree is so much cooler – probably a mix of giant palms, ferns and smaller succulents and the cake won't be a wedding cake but a towering croquembouche inspired by the one Dolce & Gabbana served at this season's London Fashion Week party.

After dinner, we will walk with our guests through the grounds of Willow Manor and into the nineteenth-century church where we will marry in a romantic candlelit ceremony at midnight. Then, as everyone leaves they get an individual brunch hamper which they are invited to bring back with them the next morning to join us in the tent.

I'm choosing my dress tomorrow morning at The White Gallery. I'm thinking about the 'Niara' by Pronovias. I'm sure you know it, it's the one with the sheer tulle back covered in tattoo lace. It's more skin than fabric to be honest! Shoes have to be Charlotte Olympia mink silk satin with accessories from Jenny Packham's midsummer collection. If you have any questions, please ask as having my wedding featured in *Brides* would be the ultimate compliment and I would be truly honoured to see it there. Do you think you could present my ideas to the Editor soon?

As I think I've already mentioned, the wedding date is August 25th and I hope you won't think this is odd but perhaps the best way for you to experience it is to come? I will put an official invitation in the post to you tomorrow. Look out for it, I had it designed to look like the one you did for the last *Brides* The Show, with hand drawn watercolour calligraphy. And please feel free to bring a plus one too, obviously!

Yours hopefully,

Dolly Jackson

XXX

Inviting anyone else to this wedding is insane, Dolly knows it, the budget is spiralling out of control as it is, but for Annabel she is prepared to make an expensive exception. Dolly hits send on the email just as Josh spills through the door trailing armfuls of camera equipment behind him. He looks bloody hot in a pair of jeans that are skimming his tanned hips and a charcoal t-shirt that is just tight enough across his chest. It's been three years since they first rubbed up against each other on a sweaty night in the Shangri La tent at Glastonbury music festival and one look at him is still all Dolly needs to feel everything tighten inside of her. He's gorgeous, no denying it. Too gorgeous, perhaps. Looking at him now she still can't believe he's hers. They were both drunk the night he proposed, celebrating him landing a lucrative advertising job and she half expected a hasty retraction the next morning when they woke with screaming hang-overs. When that didn't come, she ploughed on with the planning – admittedly without much input from Josh. The ring had come much later, after several weeks of nagging; Dolly remembers that too. Any-way, if their sex life is anything to go by, he is fully committed.

'Grab me a beer will you babes, that was some shoot. Ten hours non-stop. I'm whacked.'

'Who was it for this time?' asks Dolly.

'*GQ*'s Sexiest Women of the year. My God, the bodies, I've never seen anything like it. These women are total perfection, legs that go on and on, not an ounce of fat on them, perfect tits, the absolute best shape of their lives.' Josh pauses briefly, perhaps debating whether to deliver the killer blow before going for it anyway. 'I tell you, Dolly, it's like being addicted to chocolate and surrounded by it all day but told by your dentist you mustn't touch it.'

'Er… right, I suppose I'm the dentist then, am I?'

'Dolly, seriously, no one can compete with these women, they're like a whole different breed. Don't even bother trying, you'll just depress yourself.'

As a wounded silence hangs between them, Dolly considering telling him to bugger off back through the door, he quickly adds; 'But, *obviously* they're not the sort of women you marry. Now, come here.'

Dolly reluctantly moves in closer. Perhaps if she wasn't stuck in the world's shittiest job she might have more time to hone the thigh gap she has been working on for months, un-noticed by Josh, of course. He tightens two arms around her and takes hold of her bum firmly with both hands, pulling her into him. She can feel immediately that he is hard from a day surrounded by all that perfect female flesh. He pushes his tongue into Dolly's mouth making it clear this is no hello kiss and there is plenty more to come.

'Go and put on those black knickers I love, will you.'

Dolly does as she's told, wishing she'd made time for a shower before Josh got home. No chance now, judging by the look on his face, he isn't in the mood to wait for it tonight. In the bedroom, still flushed from her workout, she slips the sheer black knickers on, sucks in her non-existent tummy and examines her rear view in the full-length mirror. Cellulite is a stubborn bitch. Out of the bra, her boobs look pathetic, nothing like the vision of the aforementioned perfect tits she's competing with tonight. She decides on some Prada heels for much needed added sex appeal and totters back into the kitchen, topless. Josh is draining the last of his beer, and pulling his t-shirt over his head, revealing a body that is chiselled, toned and strong. He strides towards her, slipping two fingers straight down under the top of her knickers and pulling her towards him with them there. Before Dolly has chance to catch her breath his whole hand is there, working its way in between her legs, gently teasing them open. 'You're so ready for me, babes, you must have been looking forward to this.'

'Always, Josh,' Dolly pants into his ear, knowing that hearing his own name does it for him every time.

He takes hold of her hips, spinning her around and forwards over the breakfast bar, then grabs her right leg, lifting her thigh up on to the bar too, spreading her open for him. Dolly can feel the cold granite surface beneath her as her boobs are flattened against it. Josh is using his body weight to hold her in position while he unzips his flies and pulls himself out of his jeans, not bothering to remove them. Then he pulls her knickers to one side, pushing himself inside her in one movement, moving her backwards and forwards on the hard surface, appealing for her to *keep it going* just as she imagines he said to the models on set from behind the camera. She's trying to channel Victoria's Secret model fuckability, but she can feel her bum wobbling with every thrust he makes and cringes at the thought of what it must look like.

Josh pulls her down on to the wooden floor and continues until they are both moaning so loudly they can't take any more. They lie there for a minute, neither saying anything, both slightly shocked at the force of what just happened. Josh gets up and helps himself to another beer, leaving Dolly feeling crumpled and slightly vulnerable on the floor. 'Fuck, I needed that,' he pants.

As Dolly gets up and heads for the bathroom she is pretty sure it isn't her still sweaty body that inspired that performance. Josh's day has obviously been an arousing one. As she turns the shower on and steps under the piping hot jets she hears him behind her. My God, he's not after more is he?

'You might want to shave your armpits while you're in there babes, they're a bit, you know, on the hairy side. It's not a good look.'

Dolly wakes the next morning to find Josh has already left for work without saying goodbye. She climbs out of bed, her back sore from the pummelling it took on the kitchen floor last night. *No matter*, she thinks, *it's choose your wedding dress day!* And she has every intention of picking something that is going to blow Josh away.

Chapter Eight

Emily

Last night's sleep, if you can even call it that, was horrible. Fitful, sweaty and punctuated by several startled wake ups, due to the vice-like headache that has now worked its way into one small spot behind Emily's left eye. She has woken again as the first rays of sunlight are peeping through a crack in the bedroom curtains her mum must have drawn after she crashed out. She is still wearing the wrap dress – no way Mum could get that off her without waking her up – but it feels clammy against her hot skin now and as she turns her head to check the time (urgh: 5.53 a.m.) she feels an unpleasant cold wet patch on the pillow and realises the hair on the back of her head is sodden too.

God, she feels tired. She lies there for a moment, wondering what to do at this hour. The room is taking a while to shift into focus, everything is doubled and fuzzy. No point taking any more paracetamol, she has far exceeded the six in twelve hours that the box warns you about. She hasn't got the energy to get up and make a cup of tea, but neither can she lie here any longer in this germy sick bed. She feels gross and wishes someone could open the window and let a cool breeze wash over her, cleansing her of the horrible night sweats, taking the stale smell back out of the window with it.

She pictures the small boy, Daniel, she sent home early from nursery on Friday. How his skin had been roasting hot, cheeks flushed an angry pink, small dry lips fallen open, drained of energy. He'd held his head all morning complaining of a headache, hadn't eaten a thing all day, but still managed to be sick all down her twice before lunchtime. His mother had arrived in a flurry of panic after Emily had called, and whisked him home to the sofa for four-hourly spoonfuls of Calpol, ice cold Ribena and dry toast no doubt – the Holy Trinity for any working mum with a sick child. Obviously Emily is now paying the price for nursing him, inhaling his hot breath straight into her own mouth after she had stripped him down to his tiny Superman underpants and held him in her arms to soothe him. She knew when she finally left the nursery later that evening with her own head banging that this would happen.

The thought of the chilled Ribena makes Emily realise how parched she is. She's desperate for water and starts to imagine it gushing down the back of her throat, washing away the choking dryness that has spread there overnight.

She is going to have to get up or dehydrate away to nothing. As she swings her legs over the side of the bed and pushes herself up on her right elbow, the headache intensifies. It's like someone is forcing a screwdriver through her left eyeball, pushing it deeper and deeper into her head, through cornea, muscle and brain until it will go no further, lodged there as the pain pulsates around it. Poor Daniel, this is truly awful. Emily makes it to the bedroom door and tiptoes across the carpeted landing, arms outstretched either side, steadying herself, towards the family bathroom at the end. Maybe it's the tiredness but the floor is blending into the wall, which is blending into the ceiling and everything is off kilter. Then she is bent over the sink, legs wobbly beneath her, filling her hands with cold water and splashing it over her face, mouth open, gulping it in at the same time. *The relief.* When she stands up and looks in the large mirror she can see that despite the heat she feels boiling through her veins, she is deathly white. Her skin looks pallid, not like her own at all. Like she has been dug up from the grave. Her eyes are tired, the left one noticeably drooping, pupil engorged. Very far from the radiant blushing bride she is soon to be.

Now that she is upright, the feeling of nausea is taking hold, her mouth is suddenly swimming in saliva and she knows she is going to be sick. Wrapped in her favourite fluffy lilac dressing gown, Glo arrives just in time to pull Emily's hair back from her face as she empties the entire contents of her stomach into the pristine white sink, bending and retching until there is nothing left inside her. Glo is squeezing toothpaste on to Emily's brush, handing it to her and lining up a lid full of mouthwash. 'Just a quick rinse, you'll feel much better for it.'

'I haven't got time to be ill this week, Mum, I've got to choose my wedding dress,' is all she can manage before Glo steers her back to her bedroom. She sits Emily in the upholstered armchair next to her dressing table while she strips the bed, remaking it with fresh linen. Emily is even more grateful for the expertly ironed and Comfort-scented pillowcase that is now going on. Glo pulls a pair of shorts and a loose vest top from one of Emily's drawers and helps her out of the smelly wrap dress and into the clean clothes. Thank God for mum.

'You stay in bed, Emily. I'll call Dr Blake and get you an appointment this morning. It's Monday so they'll be busy but I'm sure she'll do it for us. No point having a GP as a close family friend if you can't jump the queue every once in a while, eh? Those germy kids! Have you been using the hand sanitiser I bought you? You must or you'll be ill all year.'

Emily is too exhausted to respond and is starting to close her eyes as her Dad's concerned face appears in the doorway.

'Everything OK, sweetheart?'

Emily smiles weakly, her eyes closing, just catching the sight of her Dad blowing her a kiss before she is asleep again.

Emily sits in the doctor's surgery waiting room, hiding behind a pair of giant sunglasses, trying not to touch anything or anyone. People are coughing, spluttering and sneezing all over the place. A small child is going nuts in the corner because she's been ordered not to rip pages out of the old magazines piled high on the coffee table. Her screams are more than Emily can bear. What she would give for a pair of ear plugs. The child's mother looks worse than Emily and she wonders how she has the energy to restrain her.

Emily is clutching an empty Sainsbury's carrier bag, her mum's idea in case she vomits again. Imagine the telling off she'll get from the prison-warden-like receptionist if she does. The thought of it is making her feel more sick. *This is such a bad idea*, thinks Emily, *I'll be even more ill by the time I leave*. Glo has driven her to the surgery, sad that Emily won't let her stay after having insisted they squeeze her in. Not even this receptionist would dare say no to Glo. Now a hundred wedding thoughts are skipping through Emily's already over-busy mind.

1. Should I make a speech? Will Dad in some way be offended if I do? What would I say? Too much pressure?

2. Canapé menu. Does anyone even *like* duck liver pâté? Wouldn't fish and chips in those cute mini paper cones be better? Trad Dad's not going to like that though is he?

3. Flowers. Dad wants answers on the planting. For God's sake make a decision, Emily. But what's seasonal? What doesn't cost the earth? How many flowers do I even need? What do I want in my bouquet? I don't know any actual flower names beyond rose, daffodil, daisy and tulip and I'm pretty sure three of those aren't appropriate.

4. The dress. No idea. Get one. You've got your first appointment this week and there's a large audience coming with you that need entertaining.

5. Mark wants answers on the honeymoon. Can't he just decide himself? But if I let him are we going to end up on some exhausting mountainous trek through Bhutan?

6. Gift list. Should we? Shouldn't we? Too grabby? Or very useful for guests? I wonder if Mum will write me a list of everything a household needs. She *is* the expert.

7. Bridesmaids' dresses. Decide on the actual bridesmaids first.

After an agonising forty-five minute wait during which Emily is now painfully aware of how much more wedding planning there is to do, the reassuringly friendly face of Sarah Blake appears.

'Emily, come on through.'

The two of them walk down the narrow corridor towards Dr Blake's room, Emily noting the peeling paint on the mismatched doors – the flickering strip lighting doing nothing for the headache – past the bright pink door of the ladies' loos and a giant metal cabinet straining to contain the mountain of dressings, paper kidney dishes and sample pots inside. The air is thick with the smell of disinfectant, doing nothing for the nausea. She takes a seat in the fraying leather chair next to Dr Blake's desk, sorry that she's not feeling more effervescent. Sarah Blake has been their family doctor and a trusted friend to her parents for as long as she can remember.

'Not long now, is it?' begins Dr Blake, trying to make sense of the clutter all over her desk.

'Sorry?' Tiredness is grabbing at every part of Emily, robbing her of the power of conversation.

'The wedding! What is it, five months? I've chosen my hat, you know. Anyway, what can I do for you Emily? You don't look great.' Her focus is shifting now from the swamp of paperwork escaping all over her desk, to Emily's sallow, lifeless face.

'I just need a prescription for some mega painkillers, please, to rid me of this filthy headache.' Emily is slumped low in the chair, legs outstretched, as close to lying down as it's possible to get while sitting.

'How long have you had it?

'This is the fourth day.'

'Non-stop? Has it let up at all?' Sarah is fighting to find a pen among the dog-eared prescription books, medicine journals and an index box that has tipped on to its side, sending a fan of address cards all over the place.

'No.' Keeping her answers so brief isn't exactly deliberate, but Emily lacks all enthusiasm for this conversation. She just needs the damn painkillers.

'And where is the pain?'

'Behind my left eye. It's piercing, like I've been impaled on something.' Her own description is so accurate it's making Emily heave a little.

'OK. You don't normally suffer with headaches, do you?'

Having given up the hunt for a pen, Dr Blake is refreshing her memory of Emily's family medical history on her computer screen, tapping away as Emily speaks.

'Not ones that last four days but I am surrounded by thirty screaming toddlers every day so the occasional banging head is not that unusual. Plus I'm planning a wedding, buying a house and trying to keep two big-day-obsessed parents under control.'

'Any other symptoms? I'm guessing from the sunglasses you're feeling a bit light sensitive?'

'Sunglasses?'

'The ones on your face, Emily.' Dr. Blake's eyebrows join each other briefly in a concerned frown.

'Oh God, sorry, I'd forgotten they were there. Yes, they're not exactly easing the pain but I feel worse with them off.'

'OK, any sickness?'

'Yes, once this morning.' She's trying not to swallow, the burn is still there in the back of her throat from all that retching.

'Temperature?'

'I haven't checked it but yes, I do feel hot. One of the kids at nursery had exactly these symptoms on Friday so I'm sure I've just picked up his bug. Is there something I can take that will wipe this out today?' She starts to shuffle more upright in her chair, sure she'll be handed a prescription soon and be on her way.

'Let's check you out first, shall we?'

Emily likes Dr Blake a lot but this is mildly annoying. She's already wasted the best part of an hour in the waiting room. She just wants to get home, mainline some drugs and crawl in to bed to catch up on all those missed hours of sleep from last night. But no, Dr Blake is taking her temperature (39°C), checking her blood pressure (high, apparently), shining a blinding light in her eyeball (*seriously?*), squeezing hard on the glands either side of her neck and asking a whole load of questions about her extended family's medical history, none of which Emily can recall anyway. Perhaps any other day she would appreciate the thoroughness, not today, not when she's this exhausted.

'Tell me more about the position of the pain, Emily.'

Oh come on...

'I can pinpoint it exactly. It's behind my left eye but stretching deep into my head. That is where is has been for the whole time, getting progressively worse. I'm just super stressed. It's hardly surprising.' A big irritated sigh is filling the space between them.

'That's my concern actually, Emily. What you're describing to me is not a stress headache, that would typically be directly across your forehead. You'd feel as though you were wearing a hat that was too tight. And that's not what you're telling me. The more precise location of the pain coupled with your other symptoms make me think we ought to get you in to Oxford General for a quick MRI scan.'

'What? Bit over the top isn't it? Anyway, I can't, I haven't got time.' She's bolt upright now, body language making the point loud and clear that she has to be somewhere else.

'You're not going in to work today, I presume?'

'Well, no.' Busted.

'OK, well let's do it then. The radiologist is an old colleague of mine and I know she'll fit you in if I ask her to. I'm not going to prescribe you anything until I know more about what we're dealing with, Emily. The scan will give us a nice clear view of all your brain's blood vessels so we'll be able to see if there is any trauma there or a minor blockage.'

'I don't need to start Googling brain tumours, do I?' Emily asks flippantly.

'No, Emily. Your symptoms would have been present for considerably longer if it was that. Look, I'm not overly worried, so you shouldn't be, but let's be sure. There is a real limit to what I can tell from looking at you. If there is a chance to know for sure what's causing the headache, why wouldn't you want to take it? If I call them now, there is a good chance we will get you in today. Go and take a seat in the waiting room again and I'll let you know when I've spoken to them. And book an appointment with your optician so we can rule that out too.'

Back in the waiting room Emily calls her mum from her mobile but it goes straight to voicemail, so she opts for a local taxi firm instead. She can do without the fuss a lift from Glo would involve anyway. Fifteen minutes later and with her appointment confirmed by Dr Blake, she's in the back of the minicab on her way to hospital, when her mobile goes.

'Hi Mum, yes I'm feeling much better actually. I'm just going to pop in to the florist's in town to get a few ideas. Won't be long, home soon.'

That's the great thing about wedding planning, it gives you a thousand reasons and excuses to be somewhere else, even when you're not.

Thrilled she is wearing the biggest, ugliest pants she owns (*buy honeymoon lingerie can join the to-do list*), Emily is undressing in a small room in the hospital's radiology department and changing into a stiff green gown – one with unreachable ties at the back so there is no hope of doing it up. Having been asked to remove anything metal – jewellery, clothes with zips, underwire bra – and place it in the small grey locker along with her valuables, Emily has opted to take everything but the giant pants off. If she has to lie down for an hour, she may as well get comfy. She's heard about these scans before, how the magnetic pull is so strong inside the scanner it's known to send medical equipment flying across the room, sucking in bits of furniture. Now she can see it, Emily is thankful for two things. 1. She is fairly petite, because the tunnel she'll have to lie in is surprisingly narrow and 2. She isn't claustrophobic, because the space between where her head will lie and the top of tunnel is minimal.

The whole thing is so random. She should be wiping Coco Pops off the nursery floor after the kids' breakfast time about now, but instead a studious-looking older woman called Mary is asking her to lie on her back on the scanner bed, while she positions some pads under her knees to make Emily more comfortable. The bed is heavily padded with a groove where her head goes and there are blankets to keep her warm. Mary offers her some headphones that will pipe music into her ears during the scan and a handheld panic button in case she freaks out halfway through. Far from panicking, Emily, is looking forward to the lie down. This, she thinks, is actually the problem with having such a good relationship with your GP. Would Dr Blake have sent someone else, less well known to her, off for this scan today? Is she just being super thorough because she has a personal relationship with the family? Maybe Emily is being harsh but it just all seems so unnecessary. It's a headache – admittedly a bloody painful one – but who goes to hospital for a headache? Is she missing something here? Is there some awful congenital strain in her family medical history that has been kept from her? Was Dr Blake putting in an Oscar-worthy performance as mildly concerned doctor when in fact she thinks Emily is about to expire? No, that just doesn't ring true. It's just fuss… that and probably Dr Blake's fear of what Glo will do to her if she misses anything. Emily feels like one of those time-wasters you read about, squandering precious NHS resources when she should be taking an ibuprofen and getting the hell to bed. This is some palaver to go through just to get some nice strong codeine out of Dr Blake.

As the strains of Nat King Cole's 'Unforgettable' fill Emily's ears, a whoosh of cool air rushes through the tunnel and Emily closes her eyes. Laser-firing sounds come in a series of repeated strengths and volumes all around her head, like machine gun fire but slightly muffled by the music. The cool breeze gives the illusion of fresh air and Emily's thoughts drift to her honeymoon – she and Mark walking hand in hand along a sun-soaked beach, toes sinking in to the warm sand. She pictures coconut-infused sundowners next to a private pool, the air scented with the sweetness of frangipani; days spent lounging on giant sunbeds ordering skewers of fresh fruit; sipping rosé under a striped umbrella while they tuck in to lobster and prawns fresh from the sea. But more than anything, she imagines the two of them chatting and laughing together, making plans for the future. The home they will build, the good times they'll have, the babies they'll love, the solid family they will become. The daydream is so good, she almost doesn't want the scan to end, but one hour later it does and she is back in the changing room, wriggling free of the gown.

'Do you have any plans this afternoon?' asks Mary.

'No, just heading home to do some wedding planning,' says Emily. 'I'm getting married in a few months.'

'Oh,' Mary's face seems to drop ever so slightly before she regains herself. 'Well, good luck, Emily. Keep your mobile on, the results will be through quickly.'

'OK, goodbye.'

As Emily exists the room she glances back over her shoulder to see Mary pick up the phone.

'Yes, it's Mary from Radiology,' she's saying. 'Who is the most senior consultant on today please? I need them to look at something.'

While Emily waits outside for her return taxi on one of those sad memorial benches with its shiny gold plaque dedicated to a 'devoted husband and father', she thinks about Mary's phone call.

The radiologist had surely scanned lots of people that morning, she wasn't necessarily talking about Emily's results. How could she be anyway, they'd only just finished? Besides, the people who do the scans are never the ones to interpret the results, she knows that.

She slumps into the back of the taxi, finally heading for home, noticing a missed call from Mum on her mobile. Oh yes, the florist fib, she'd better get her story straight. The good news is the headache has eased (*see, she just needed some rest!*) and she knows she wants an exotic honeymoon, probably Thailand or Bali, so that decision can be crossed off her list. The morning wasn't an entire waste of time, after all. But the twenty-minute journey back home is taking forever, thanks to the taxi driver finding every red traffic light and road jam he can. Twenty minutes becomes forty minutes until finally she is rounding the corner into the village, just as her mobile phone rings.

'Emily, it's Sarah Blake.'

'Oh hi, Dr Blake. You're not checking up on me, are you? I did go for the scan, in fact I'm just arriving home now.'

'I know you did, Emily.'

Blimey, she sounds like a woman who wants her shift to end.

'Oh, right. Well, it was fine, all good and to be honest I quite enjoyed the me-time. Sorry I was so grumpy earlier.'

'I need you to come back to the surgery, Emily.' Dr Blake's voice is devoid of all jolliness, not her usual cheery self at all.

'What? Have I left something there?

'No, you haven't but I—'

'Oh, my prescription. Would you mind emailing it to the village pharmacy, please? I've spent a bomb on taxis today and no offence, Dr Blake, but I'd rather see my bedroom now if you don't mind!'

'Emily, I am calling because I am looking at your scan results and I need you to come back in the surgery, please. Is there someone you can bring with you? Is Glo around today?'

The smile is immediately wiped from Emily's face. She stops the taxi driver just as they get within sight of the house, redirecting him back to the surgery.

'I'll come now,' she says before the taxi turns, leaving her family home behind them. Emily glances in the driver's wing mirror and catches sight of her Dad pottering in the front garden, getting the flowerbeds ready for the big day.

The moment Emily gives the evil receptionist her name she is told to go straight through to Dr Blake's room. She knocks once and enters to find her doctor poring over what looks like x-ray images of her sliced-open brain.

'You came alone, Emily?'

'Yes, although looking at your face now I am beginning to wish I hadn't.'

Dr Blake looks as though she has been crying. Her eyes are glassy and there is a telltale soggy tissue next to her keyboard. She gets up from her side of the desk and pulls her chair around next to Emily, taking her hand.

Oh shit.

'I'm afraid your scan results are not good, Emily. They show you have a cerebral aneurism behind your left eye. It's very large, just over an inch and imbedded deep in the brain tissue. I have been on the phone to the senior consultant at Oxford General for the past half an hour and while there are lots of further discussions to be had, the initial feeling is that because of its position and size it is probably inoperable.'

Emily's hands move involuntarily to her face, cradling her cheeks as she takes a deep intake of breath. Aneurism. Inoperable. Why is Dr Blake assuming she knows what an aneurism is? She doesn't. 'What does this mean?' she asks as the tears are starting to come.

'I'm not an expert on this Emily and we have to get you referred to a specialist a.s.a.p. but essentially it means you have an inflamed blood vessel that has ballooned inside your brain and is compressing one of your cranial nerves, creating the pressure that has probably been causing your headache. Judging by the size of it, it has been there for some time. What we need to work out now is how we stop it rupturing, how best to treat it. But it's important to remember Emily, you have been living with it fine up until now.'

Can she really be hearing this right? Her first feeling is one of total stupidity. Why hadn't she taken the headache more seriously, been more grateful for the immediate referral? But none of this makes sense.

'How did it get there? Is it really serious? There is something they can do about it, right? Drugs, to shrink it?' The questions are firing out of her more quickly than her brain can keep up. The words sound hollow, echoing, like they're not coming out of Emily's mouth at all.

'Am I going to die, Dr Blake?' She almost feels silly for saying it. How melodramatic is she? How weird is it to hear herself asking that question when an hour ago she was planning her honeymoon.

Silence. Dr Blake is obviously struggling to think of a nice way to say whatever it is she needs to. Emily decides to help her.

'Are you going to be taking your hat back, Sarah?'

'I can't answer that, Emily,' she whispers with the sort of thundering honesty that is not expected.

Then Emily notices the one solitary tear travelling down Dr Blake's face and watches as it lands, exploding on to her lap. In the twenty-seven years Sarah Blake has been her doctor and friend, she has never seen her cry.

Chapter Nine

Jessie

Bridesmaids. Jessie needs bridesmaids. The question is, who? She has already bowed to some major hint-dropping from Camilla and allowed her to invite the offspring of two friends to be flower girls. The Nicki MacFarlane peony-coloured dresses with their smart box-pleated skirts and puff sleeves are already ordered – if it was good enough for K-Middy… Now Jessie needs some grown-up attendants. Or does she? Would it matter if she just skipped that bit? There are no obvious contenders. No old school friends she cares enough about. No former work colleagues she has stayed in touch with, no new friends full stop. She knows she should ask her make-up-dodging younger sister but at five foot four and fourteen stone with hair that always looks like it needs a good wash, Jessie doesn't want that lolloping up the aisle behind her, ruining the elegant aesthetic she is paying well over the odds to create. But Claire *is* her sister. It's only natural that she should be involved in the day and she knows very well Claire will be hurt if she's excluded. *Yes, of course she should ask Claire*, it's the only right thing to do but somehow Jessie just can't convince herself to act on that thought, she's so jumbled between doing the right thing and ensuring every element of the wedding looks perfect.

Perhaps if she didn't have to worry about all this nonsense, she might not be late to her first ever hunt meeting, although looking at this positively, maybe she'll meet someone today who'll fill the bridesmaid-sized hole in her wedding planning.

As Jessie approaches the satnav-invisible field where the hunt is due to start, Camilla Coleridge's words are ringing in her head. *There is no point pretending to be something you are not.* Having given Camilla the impression she is a more accomplished rider than she actually is – a few rushed, last minute lessons covering the very basics like how to get on the thing is clearly not going to cut it today – Jessie now finds herself on the duke of Beaufort's estate (a personal friend of the Coleridges', of course), desperately trying to locate the rest of the hunt who are due to set off in, *shit*, ten minutes. Camilla has kindly (stupidly) lent Jessie one of her *finest horses*, Horace, for the day: now where is Adam? Jessie knows she can't be far off, the four-by-fours are lining the narrow country lanes she has been bombing aimlessly around for the past thirty-five minutes.

Then she spots them, on the other side of an open field. There must be at least two hundred riders, all decked out in, oh God, nothing like what Jessie is wearing. When Adam shouted *dress for the hunt* over his shoulder this morning as he belted out of the house, why the hell didn't she press him on the specifics? When his text arrived an hour later advising her to *ask Lady C about hunt kit, she's expecting your call* she ignored it, not wanting to look clueless again. So Jessie got dressed for riding, not hunting. So, so wrong. And now look at all those dogs, huge dogs, looking hungry for the kill. *Do not admit you don't like dogs.*

She abandons the car and starts to sprint across the muddy field, growing sweatier by the second, earrings jangling, pink lippie smudged across her mouth by the time she reaches the outskirts of the group. Now she's close she can really see what a colossal mistake she has made with her outfit. The hunting die-hards are all wearing what look like dark navy velvet top hats (nothing like her riding hat with its pink and orange silk and jaunty little bobbles dangling from the edge), navy blazer-like coats with buff collars (hers is tweed), fawn breeches (sports luxe black leggings), starched white shirts with ties (the tweed jacket is at least hiding her boob-skimming Abercrombie t-shirt) and knee-length black leather riding boots (Jessie's Hunter wellies are mercifully black, she nearly went for the fun red ones).

'Shit, shit, shit. Oh God, I'm begging you, *please* let this not be happening,' Jessie pleads skywards. It's like the clock has cruelly skidded backwards and she's turning up for a double science exam on the day she should be doing her French oral. She is totally and utterly unprepared for what awaits her.

While still just out of earshot, Jessie starts to rant for all she's worth.

'This bastard wedding, it's taking over my life. How could I not realise what they'd all be wearing? Why the hell didn't I just call Camilla? It's a sodding hunt, I'm on a duke's land. *Of course* it's going to be formal. I am a total arse who deserves to be humiliated. But why does anyone get this dressed up to get covered in mud?'

The atmosphere is one of a formal drinks party, and Jessie's just walked in wearing a nasty nylon tracksuit while everyone else is in cocktail dress. She is dressed for a casual hack, not an exclusive invite-only hunt. *Big bloody difference.* Let's just be grateful Camilla is not here to witness it too. All around her people are greeting each other officially with boisterous good mornings, between swigs of sherry and port from leather-bound hip flasks and nibbles of sticky sausages that are being passed between the riders. Except now they are all looking at her – thinking loud thoughts. Jessie is the unwanted focus of arched stares and shared whispers – from the very same people who in four months' time will be enjoying a five course fine dining menu at her expense – OK, Camilla's expense, but still.

One not-quite-beautiful woman – all perfect skin, big white teeth and an air of superior refinement – locks eyes with Jessie and looks horrified, like someone just wafted a spritz of Britney Spears' latest fragrance under her nose. Jessie knows they've never met before but this woman is so familiar… she knows that face, she's sure of it, but where from? Her panicked brain can't work quickly enough to make it a useful conversation starter.

The woman is sitting astride an impeccably groomed horse with its mane and tail tightly plaited, but on sight of Jessie whirls the mare around, as if in protest. As her horse shifts position, Jessie can see the woman is talking to a confidently breeched and booted Adam, who looks like he's stepped off the pages of a Jilly Cooper novel, a hotter version of Rupert Campbell-Black except that his mouth has dropped open and he's starting to laugh in her direction.

'I take it you never called Lady C, then?' Adam throws an arm protectively around her. 'Come on, we need to sort you out.' Her gaff is rolling off him like the unimportant silliness it is, the cast-iron cloak of confidence he always wears protecting him from even the slightness hint of social embarrassment. But Jessie couldn't possibly feel more the marked woman, her brain burning from the knowledge that she could so easily have saved herself from this if she'd just taken his advice in the first place and made the call. Now she's shone an unwanted spotlight on herself and is praying that somewhere deep down inside, Adam's not feeling the pinch of shame too. Although if he is, he's doing a remarkable job of playing the crowd.

'You are funny, Jessie! You can't wear that hat or the hunt master will send you home. Take it off and I'll get you another. And if you value your ear lobes, I'd lose the earrings too. Just wait here, I'll go and get your horse.'

The temptation to leg it is extreme, but the haughty woman who had been chatting to Adam is edging nearer, her horse taking neat little side steps, totally under the control of those superior shapely thighs.

'You *are* aware you just ran through a freshly sown cornfield, I suppose? You'd better hope the duke didn't see you.'

'Oh, no, sorry. I was just trying not to be late.' Everyone else has seen her, what difference would one more pair of scornful eyes make?

'You must be Jessica,' the woman looks down at her in every way imaginable from the lofty height of her shiny brown saddle, as if Jessie isn't fit even to clean her boots. 'I'm Annabel. I'm sure Adam will have mentioned me.'

No actually, but Camilla has: you're the maniac who has been in love with Adam since forever. Definitely not bridesmaid material.

'Yes, hello.'

'You obviously haven't been on a hunt before.' Her tight, thoroughly pleased with herself smile suggests she is not about to help Jessie navigate her way through it either.

'No, but I'm so looking forward to it. Apparently I have one of Camilla's finest white horses, one of her absolute favourites.'

'It'll be a grey,' corrects Annabel. 'There's no such thing as a white horse.'

'Oh, right. Well, whatever colour it is let's just hope it's not spooked by all these dogs barking.'

'There aren't any dogs here I'm afraid, just hounds, and they're *crying*, not barking.'

At this moment Jessie can think of no greater joy than seeing vile Annabel's horse rear up unexpectedly, sending her over the side like a sack of potatoes into the mud beneath her. Snooty cow. And here comes another – a broad battle-axe of a woman with a mountainous cleavage, thighs like a couple of hams and more than a hint of moustache, who truthfully should not be wearing something as snug as breeches. The hunt for bridesmaids has well and truly stalled.

'Your cap, please,' she motions to Jessie.

'Sorry?'

'Your cap.'

'Er….' She looks at Annabel, searching for an explanation that she's clearly determined to make her wait for, enjoying this little moment of suffering before finally adding:

'She means your payment, Jessie. As you're obviously not a member of the hunt you need to pay a day rate to ride on the duke's land.'

'Oh, I didn't bring any money with me. If you don't mind waiting a moment, I'm sure Adam will have some on him. Look, here he comes now.'

Horace is magnificent with sharp patterns clipped into the hair around his legs and stomach, his mane plaited into tight, neat knots running the length of his neck, each foot covered in a sturdy black bootie. *He's* nailed the dress code. Full peacockery and full marks to Horace. He's spotlessly clean and impeccably well behaved, until he sees Jessie, at which point he starts trying to back away, retreating towards the horse box he just came from, drawing yet more attention Jessie's way. Hacked off that this morning is already not the romantic outing she imagined and furious that Annabel is so obviously enjoying having the upper hand on her, Jessie is keen to remind her that it is she, not Annabel, who is about to marry into this family.

'Oh my goodness, he's so adorable. Perhaps I need to find a role for him at the wedding!' she goads. 'And how lovely of Camilla to put red ribbons in his tail for me.'

'Oh Jessie, the ribbon is there to signify to others that your horse kicks. It's not a good thing. Kicking another horse or rider is bad enough but kicking a hound is the worst thing you can do. I suggest you stay well back in the field because if that happens you're likely to be sent home.'

'Jessie, here's your horse – and I've put some rocket fuel in the stirrup cup if you need it,' says Adam. 'Meet darling Tilly, a dear friend of mine who is going to ride with you.'

'You mean you're not?'

'No, I'm a whippers-in today which means I will be up front with the hunt master, in charge of the hounds. That stout-looking chap over there is the field master, he's in change of the mounted field – that's you, Jessie. Just do whatever he tells you to and you'll be fine. Tilly will look after you .'

And with that Adam is off, Annabel at his side, disappearing across the mist-covered countryside like something out of *Pride and* bloody *Prejudice*, while Jessie is left behind with Tilly, her nanny for the day, and three small children on toy ponies – all of them looking considerably more competent than her.

Jessie barely has time to slide her feet securely into the stirrups before a horn is sounded, long and clear, and they are off, thundering through the great English countryside, Jessie not knowing it yet, but about to give her thighs the workout of their life. Staying on the horse is her one and only objective – that and not killing Camilla's beloved Horace – which means jumping all the fences, hedges and gates en route is out of the question. So she is bringing up the very rear, miles back from Adam and Annabel and having to search out gates, endlessly dismounting and mounting to get through them all – she may as well be at an entirely different event for how included she feels.

They say each time you fall off a horse, you become a better rider, in which case, shortly after setting off Jessie should by rights be the proud owner of a couple of Olympic gold medals. But then it's hard to concentrate when you also have a million wedding thoughts galloping through your head.

I wonder if that vicar has caved yet? He'd better have, because I'm not walking up an orange aisle carpet, end of story.

The air is knocked forcibly out of Jessie countless times today. She's been bucked off, hurled off the back, dumped on her face, landed on, trampled, skewered on trees and somersaulted into ditches as the beast between her thighs does everything other than what she is screaming at it.

I need 'wow' moments everywhere the guests go, different coloured flowers in every space, 3,500 cut white roses dotted along the front lawn, creating the illusion of a field of wildflowers. Every imaginable shade of pink at the reception. Giant fluffy clouds of pink hydrangeas on top of crystal candelabras. A double height flower wall behind the top table, framing every picture of me, the new Mrs Coleridge. Bloody Annabel... where have I seen her before?

If this is Camilla's finest horse, then dear God let Jessie never meet the worst one. Even kind Tilly who has spent the past three hours ineffectually shouting *Hands down, grip the saddle* and *tighten your bloody reigns!* is exasperated by it all, to the total glee of their over-privileged mini companions.

I must get Willow Manor to cordon off the village, no one wants a coach load of Japanese tourists photo-bombing their big day. Campaign to

*the local parish council, get every resident to agree. Offer a hefty donation
to the village hall.*

That Jessie hasn't broken any bones is nothing short of a miracle, but
her now thoroughly pissed-off body is a bruised shade of purple all over.

*I'll need extra rooms for the dress handler, the fine jewellery security
guard and my hair and make-up teams. Confirm numbers for the guests'
welcome bags. Organic goodies from Soho Farmhouse and Daylesford and
a treatment at Willow Manor Spa should do it.*

Any cheerful ignorance Jessie may have felt at the beginning of the
day has been replaced by wild fury and the depressing realisation that
she needs to step away from her addiction to *Vogue* and get on board
with the *Horse & Hounds* scattered all over the house. Magazines, that's
it! She's seen Annabel in a magazine, she's sure of it now.

*The guest's bespoke caricatures! Deadline looming. Must liaise with
illustrator a.s.a.p. – and tell him to take at least ten years off Camilla,
that should please her.*

By the end of the hunt a battered and bruised Jessie has at least
made one crucial decision. Annabel can bugger right off if she thinks
she's getting a good table at the wedding. Then it comes to her. Yes!
The magazine she's been poring over for months – *Brides*. How could
she forget that smug face smarming out at her from those glossy pages?
Annabel's the bloody editor's PA and was plastered all over last month's
issue, writing some bollocks about powder blue being the new blush.
And what's more, Adam has promised her exclusive coverage of their
wedding, apparently earning her major brownie points with the boss.

Well, that's a wedding she'll now be observing from the very back of
the room, perhaps on a table with Jessie's own family. If Annabel enjoys
watching people who are clearly out of their comfort zone squirm their
way through the proceedings, let's see how she copes with that!

❧

'Good grief, what on earth has happened to you?' asks Helen, as Jessie undresses in The White Gallery fitting room, revealing the full extent of the scrapes and bruises lining her bashed-up little body.

Jessie considers lying her way out of this one – car accident (too dramatic, even for her), ski incident (we're out of season, Helen may know that), over-exuberant sex session (poor Helen, no).

'They hate me, Helen.'

There is little point pretending she doesn't care. The defeated dip of her mouth and the sadness swimming around her eyes gives Jessie away anyway.

'Who does?'

'Adam's friends and family, every last one of them and there isn't a thing I can do about it.'

Chapter Ten

Helen

A text from Betsy always brightens Helen's day – unless it's like this one, showing a picture of her boyfriend Jacob's latest attempt to write something that might help to pay the bills one day.

'What d'you think Mum?' It's the question she always dreads being asked because the honest answer is *not a lot*. But how can she tell her that when Betsy herself is trying so hard to be supportive? Exactly the sort of support Helen would want her to be shown if the tables were turned. But they're not and Helen's job is to worry about her daughter, not long-term layabout Jacob, whom the jury is still very much out on.

Helen doesn't have long, Jessie Jones is already undressing in the fitting room and as she's trying to tap out an appropriate response with her too-slow fingers, a second text pings through.

> *And I'm really sorry to ask Mum but do you think you might be able to stretch to another mini loan again this month please? Just until Jacob gets something published – I just know he will, soon.*

Helen has seen for herself how good they are together, like two giddy teenagers, united in their love of life. She's seen how much her daughter laughs – big raucous belly-wobblers – when he's around and how her stories have been peppered with mentions of the man sharing her life – and her bank balance – for four years now. But those laughs aren't paying the mortgage, Betsy's constant overtime at the recruitment agency is. She resolves to have a proper chat with Betsy as soon as she can, but for now a simple *of course I can* is all she has time for before she rejoins Jessie.

And my goodness, what a sight awaits her. Helen is discreetly scanning Jessie's near-naked body. Everything from her neck down looks painful. There is an angry bruise the colour of an over-ripe plum spreading across her left hip, forcing the poor girl to shift her weight awkwardly on to her right leg, then an even bigger one running the length of her lower right arm. Helen notices the palms of Jessie's hands are blistered and stripped of skin but injuries aside, Helen can also see she is just about ready to crack and yes, the tears are coming now, between wails of 'They hate me!' and 'I'll never be good enough!' Jessie's first appointment ended with her face buried in a box of Kleenex, so upset she couldn't even try on the dresses Helen had prepared for her. Now it looks like the second one is starting that way too.

'I seriously doubt they hate you, whatever makes you think that?' Helen has got to get through to this girl somehow.

'I'm not one of them, Helen. I didn't go to boarding school, I don't have a trust fund, my parents don't own land and clearly I did not spend my childhood weekends competing in gymkhanas. This isn't my world, Helen, I just happened to fall in love with a man who lives in it. I'm killing myself to make this wedding perfect in every way for a bunch of people I doubt will ever accept me. The harder I try, the worse it is.'

This is not an unfamiliar story to Helen. Countless brides before this one have stood in her fitting room, unloading their tear ducts with tales of unwelcoming relatives, family politics and jealous friends. Maybe it's something about the anonymity of the setting, the fact these women are passing through on their way to somewhere more exciting. They can unload on Helen knowing that in a few short months she will be gone from their lives, bearing no witness to the secrets told. Her advice will have been dispensed and they will be relegated to the arch lever file under the till. If they send a thank-you card, as so many do, they are remembered each morning when Helen glances up at the notice board in the kitchen where they're all pinned. But otherwise they are gone, along with the confidences they have shared.

Standing here now, looking at Jessie, Helen knows what *is* unusual are the lengths this girl is going to, to win everyone over. She looks like she should be in a doctor's surgery, not a bridal fitting room.

'It shouldn't be like this, Helen. I should be happier than ever, trying on my wedding gowns, surrounded by new friends, laughing, not blubbing all over you for the second time. You must think I'm a lunatic.'

'What I'm actually wondering is if you are simply trying too hard?' ventures Helen. 'Adam loves you. He's asked you to marry him. Isn't that enough?'

'No! Are you *even* married Helen? Do you have any idea how much I am dealing with?'

Now it's Helen's turn to wince. 'I was married for a very long time, thirty-five years, actually.' Her head dips slightly, cutting off any invitation to question her further on the subject.

'Oh, right, well then you must have some idea of the nightmare involved in managing your husband's family?'

'No, I'm afraid I don't.' Jessie's experience is so at odds with Helen's own feelings, it's opening up an emotional void between the two women that Helen is keen to close up. 'Which dress would you like to try on first? Shall we go straight for the Herrera?'

Jessie nods vacantly as Helen lifts the gown from its hanger, whooshing it out so that the light as air tulle skirt spreads beautifully across the carpeted floor in front of them. Helen can feel Jessie staring at her, apparently more interested in what she has to say than the exquisite dress she is about to step in to. But then perhaps a bit of a talking to is exactly what this girl needs.

'Think of this as the opening ceremony, Jessie, to a much more strenuous lifelong event, marriage, one that requires a very different set of skills to planning a wedding.' She's holding Jessie by the hand, steadying her, as she steps into the full skirt. 'Instead of focusing on every little detail, in my experience you have to do the exact opposite. You have to let go.' Helen's wriggling the dress up Jessie's body now, bringing the expertly boned lace embroidered bodice up to sit perfectly at Jessie's waist.

'Let go! Are you actually mad? This wedding is going to set the tone for the rest of our lives together. Everything has to be perfect or it will be imperfect forever.'

There is something so incongruous, thinks Helen, about seeing a beautiful girl, in such an incredible gown, look so unhappy. 'Can I ask if you have spoken to Adam about this, does he feel the same way?' Helen is working her fingers down the run of silk-covered buttons that sit at the back of the gown, the dress fitting more perfectly with every one she does up.

'I don't need to, he's not the one being judged, is he? They all love him. Being loved comes naturally, some of us have to work a little harder.'

'Perhaps that's the point. This shouldn't be hard work, should it?' Helen is placing a flawless powder-blue suede shoe on each of Jessie's feet, giving her the height needed to make this gown drape effortlessly from her slim frame. 'There's nothing wrong with aiming for the perfect wedding. But aiming for the perfect marriage isn't the best idea. All people are flawed and so are all marriages. *All* of them.'

'Look, it's like this. I am the CEO, Helen, I'm in charge of the smooth running of this wedding *and* the marriage – and the growth strategy is getting everyone in Adam's circle to accept me, love me even.' The tears have dried up now and Jessie is miraculously back to her ball-busting best, a hand on each hip, stamping her authority on the conversation.

'If I were you, I'd give myself a demotion.' Helen lifts Jessie's glossy hair, twisting it into a loose bun and pinning it at the back of her head. 'Or at least remember the best bosses sometimes sit back and let people work it out for themselves and have the confidence to know that everything will be fine. Trust me, Jessie, no one is looking at you to have all the answers, least of all Adam, I suspect.'

Silence now as they both admire the vision staring back at them in the mirror. Helen is relieved that finally Jessie is allowing herself the first smile since she arrived.

'Do you have all the Carolina Herrera accessories I requested?' asks Jessie.

'I do – but honestly, I'm not sure you need them.'

'But that's how the designer pulled this look together and I think she knows what she's doing, don't you?'

'Of course she does but the accessories are very expensive and—'

'Do you really think I care about that?' Jessie snaps back.

'Just because something costs a lot of money, it doesn't make it right for this look or, more importantly, right for you. This dress is perfect in its simplicity. When Herrera paired this gown with these accessories she was creating drama for the catwalk, it was a piece of theatre. You don't necessarily need that. Trust your own instincts on what looks good for you, Jessie. Let me show you.'

Helen spends the next fifteen minutes transforming Jessie into the carbon copy of the bridal vision that Herrera created for her last New York show. She adds a billowing silk sash that explodes into a giant bow at the back of the gown, a pair of oversized pearl earrings that extend all the way to Jessie's lightly tanned shoulders, a floor-sweeping lace-trimmed veil fanning out magnificently over the already heavily detailed dress.

'It's an incredible look,' Helen concludes when she is finished. 'Beautiful in fact. But is it wearable, Jessie? Are you comfortable in it?'

Jessie looks baffled. 'I don't know. What do you think?'

'How do you *feel* in it?' Helen is walking around Jessie now, eyes all over the dress, giving Jessie the space and time to form an opinion.

'A bit self-conscious, actually, and I'm worried the earrings are a bit much.'

Helen removes them.

'And does the bow seem a bit over the top?'

'If you're worried about that, let's lose it too.'

As Helen removes the sash, the smile returns to Jessie's face and Helen can see her work is nearly done. She pins the dress where it's needed, raising the hem slightly, tightening the waist a fraction, taking her time to ensure the fit is precisely what it should be for Jessie's body. The two women stand quietly for a moment admiring what Helen has created before Jessie breaks the silence.

'What was your flaw?'

'Sorry?'

'You said all marriages are flawed, how was yours flawed?'

The hairs on the back of Helen's neck lift and the tug in the pit of her stomach returns the second she thinks of Phillip. She lets out a long slow breath, preparing herself for the words she doesn't want to say.

'It was too short. That's what was wrong. We were running out of time the moment we met, we just never knew it.'

'Oh, right.' Jessie's hand instinctively moves towards Helen, understanding the loss she isn't yet being explicit about, but she pulls it back before it makes contact, perhaps fearful it will be rejected after all the crass comments she's made today. 'When did you lose him?'

'Nearly four years ago but it hurts as much today as it ever did.' It's impossible to confess such painful words and maintain the bright and breezy demeanour Helen is aiming for, knowing Jessie's sympathy is only going to make it worse.

'I'm so sorry, Helen. What kind of man was he?' She can see asking Helen to talk about him is going to be hard, but she is genuinely interested. What kind of man would a woman like Helen devote herself to?

Another deep breath, as Helen tries to busy herself putting some of the accessories away – but having delved so deeply into Jessie's life, she senses the weight of expectation, she must allow Jessie to do the same. But how does she sum up a man like her Phillip in a few quick sentences – giving someone enough to satisfy their curiosity so the conversation can move on, but not so much that she plunges herself back in to the abyss of her own grief? Having cheered Jessie up the last thing Helen wants is to drag her back down with her own sadness. Depressing clients is not exactly in the job description.

'He was everything to me, Jessie. He was gentle, kind, honest, devoted to his family.'

'But why him, over any other man?'

Helen places the earrings back in their soft velvet pouch and the two of them take a seat on the chaise, Helen leaning back against the wall, fingertips lightly sweeping under her eyes in an attempt to halt the tears that are perched there.

'He made me feel loved, Jessie. Even towards the end, after so long together, he looked at me in a way he never looked at anyone else, even his own children. It's hard to explain but I was more precious to him than anything. He would have done anything for me, I know that – one of those rare people who lived his life for someone else; my happiness always coming before his own. He kept his promise, to love me until the very last moment.'

'He sounds wonderful.' And despite the years that divide them, Jessie might actually get it. Helen is articulating so beautifully the exact essence of what she hopes for from her own marriage.

'He is. He was.' Helen turns to face Jessie, placing a hand softly on hers, eyes finally giving way to the tears they can no longer hold back.

'I envy you Jessie, you have it all to come.' Helen's forced smile reveals the torture she feels as she recounts what she had and how she must live without it now.

'There is a life full of happiness stretching out ahead of you. I'll never experience that feeling of togetherness again, I know that. But you will for a long time to come. Don't waste it by worrying what everyone thinks of you.'

She looks so broken now. Not the strong, together woman Jessie first met. But so fragile, exposed and vulnerable, like she's baring her very soul to Jessie. But even in this moment, Helen's instinct is to help, warning Jessie not to walk a path that can only end in disappointment and feelings of total inadequacy.

Helen makes an excuse to step back into the shop knowing she needs to collect herself, grabbing a tissue and fixing her face a little in one of the ornate wall mirrors. As she leans closer to the mirror she is surprised to see a figure at the door in its reflection. There's no one booked in for at least another hour and she can see from the outline through the glass that this is a man. Adam, perhaps, here to collect Jessie?

She quickly removes the last traces of smudged mascara, takes a deep breath and opens the door to find probably the last person on earth she wants to see right now. Roger.

'Oh, hi Helen, are you OK?' His face is already full of misplaced concern.

'Um… I'm fine thank you, but with a client at the moment, I'm afraid.' Helen can feel the heat rising in her cheeks and isn't entirely sure why.

'I wasn't sure whether to bother you or not but I was wondering if you might like to go for a drink one night this week?'

'No! I couldn't possibly.'

'Or, um, I could cook you dinner, if you prefer?'

'No, no thank you.'

'OK. I just thought it might be nice if—'

'I really can't, Roger, sorry, I don't know why you thought I would.' Helen's cheeks are flaming now, she knows she's being rude and the atmosphere between them is instantly, horribly tense. Roger is looking at his feet, probably searching for the words that will excuse him from this horror.

'If you change your mind, just let me know.' He's jabbing his hands in and out of his jacket pockets, desperate for something to do with himself, visibly shocked by such a determined rejection.

'I won't.'

As rebuttals go, this one is brutal. And also quite foolish – wasn't company the one thing she craved right now? Someone to call on, to share a joke with, someone to look out for her and punctuate the long lonely evenings with happy conversation that didn't need to carry any significance or hidden agenda?

But the thought of an actual date, with another man? She couldn't. As if physically recoiling from the very idea of it, Helen is backing away from the door now uncomfortably imagining the innate intimacy of the two of them sharing a bottle of wine, the questions he might ask, fingers that might touch each other's across the table, the assumptions people might make. Roger is lingering, needing to be excused. But Helen is struck silent by the thought of another man's hand in the small of her back, as Roger insisted on walking her home again. No. '*I have only slipped away to the next room*'; that's what Phillip had said. Damn Roger for forcing this on her and at work too, her one sanctuary from those awful feelings of Phillip's loss – usually, at least. She is nowhere near ready for this. Surely he must know that. Helen mutters a quick goodbye, noticing the colour of Roger's claret cheeks now match her own, and shuts the door, burying her face in her hands, knowing how badly she just handled the situation. He didn't deserve that.

'Well *that* was awkward!' Jessie has stepped out of the fitting room and observed the whole wretched thing.

For the first time, Helen is genuinely annoyed by her, bordering on angry that she could intrude into a private moment, making light of something so excruciating for her. Has she understood a damn thing Helen has said today? Her face must say it all as a less mocking Jessie quickly adds, 'You *are* entitled to be happy again, Helen, you know.'

'So are you, Jessie, so are you,' is all Helen can manage through gritted teeth knowing she has just pushed away the one man who might just understand how she feels, the private pain she is living with. Knowing also, that the chances of him ever asking – wanting even – to share her company again must surely now be non-existent.

Chapter Eleven

Dolly

Dolly's eyes flick to the torso of the beautiful woman leaving The White Gallery, just as she arrives. The woman's expensive looking skinny jeans are perched stylishly on her hip bones and there is a small flash of tanned flesh where her crisp white t-shirt, one that looks nonchalant but probably costs £300, doesn't quite reach the denim. *Gorgeous*, thinks Dolly, as her heart sinks, now hating the jeans she's wearing. Unfairly gorgeous. Where's Tilly when she needs her ego stroking? She makes a mental note to squeeze in an extra core session later, regretting that she's eaten breakfast this morning. Nothing wrong with the egg white omelette of course but that lovely empty feeling would have been better for her first crack at wedding dress shopping. Who was it who said *nothing tastes as good as thin feels?* They were spot on, whoever it was.

The woman wafts past, engulfing her in a cloud of expensive-smelling perfume, not even registering Dolly's existence. As the two women pass each other Dolly's eyes shift to her tight butt sitting neatly above the, yep, there it is, the thigh gap. Bloody hell. She hates the thought that her own body is about to be compared to *that* in the fitting room.

'Ahh, you must be Dolly. I'm Helen, please come in.' The two women shake hands briefly and Dolly is instantly reassured by her warmth, the confident eye contact and a face that already seems to be inviting friendship.

As Dolly steps into The White Gallery she feels a fresh buzz of excitement surge through her. The past twelve months have all been building up to this moment – when she steps into the kind of dress that will make Josh forget every woman he's ever mentally undressed. And there are plenty. Because what Dolly is looking for is so much more than a white dress with so much more to do than simply make her look good. She needs a gown that will finally extinguish any last remaining thoughts of girlfriends past or models present. The catalyst to the ultimate moment of clarity. Of all the men she could have had – she chose *him*. He's not just going home with her tonight, he's curling up with her *every* night. For once she wants to see that thought engulf him, spread out across his proud face, finally making her feel that she's no longer second best to the unreachable beauty Josh spends all day scrutinising down the phallic lens of his camera.

'Do you have any thoughts on the kind of dress you're looking for?' breaks in Helen, forcing Dolly back in to the room.

'Something really cool, sexy, not traditional.' Dolly is already scanning the rail, eyes drawn to a body-con dress with sheer cutaway panels running down each side, pure Jessica Rabbit; definitely no room for knickers under *there*. 'Something that's going to make me look really hot, like that.' She is pointing at the gown.

God, why couldn't Tilly have joined her this morning? She's feeling her absence terribly now. Of all the days to be taking a bunch of over-smug bloggers on a press trip to some swanky five star spa, why did it have to be today? Until very recently Tilly was the only thing that made the office bearable – largely because she took no shit from The Dick and Dolly loved her for that. Then one day the awful moment Dolly had been dreading came, and Tilly marched into his office and told him to stick it, she was setting up on her own, taking a couple of his favourite clients with her just to really turn the knife. Of course, Dolly was thrilled for Tilly, but overnight she lost her office crutch and she desperately misses their daily updates, tearing The Dick to shreds. Her on-staff personal style, relationship and career therapist was gone. Because, despite their wildly polarised lifestyles, Dolly trusts Tilly's judgement implicitly. One scan of this room and she would know exactly which dress would have Josh dragging her out of the reception to satisfy himself before dessert was even served.

'You're very slim, Dolly, which means there are lots of different looks we can try.' Helen's smiling knowingly. 'I'll pop the gown you love into the fitting room, then let's have a look around and see what else you like.'

It's 10.30 a.m. and Dolly should be at her desk. She knows The Dick will notice her absence, hopefully he's buried in her masterpiece of a cupcake strategy. Chances are a colleague will cover for her for a while (traffic, dentist, crucial client breakfast overrunning, as if) but they won't be able to hold him off for long. She scans the emails on her phone. Nothing from him yet. But there is a message from the entertainment company where she had, after several fruitless weeks of research, found the perfect band for the wedding night. Josh loves them too.

Hi Dolly,
I'm just getting in touch about your provisional booking for
The London Essentials. The deadline to confirm the booking

and pay the 50% deposit has passed and so the booking has
been released. Another couple have now secured the boys but
I'd be happy to pass on any recommendations if you'd like?

Shit! Josh! He promised Dolly he'd taken care of this. She's chased him, confirmed it with him, emailed him relentlessly making sure the bank transfer had gone through; he told her it was all sorted. The entertainment company must be wrong. They will just have to explain the double booking to the other couple. Dolly was first so surely they will honour it? She pings a quick email back, copying Josh in, feeling *almost* sure he won't have messed this up.

Helen returns and the two of them begin to work their way around The White Gallery's breathtaking collection of gowns, Dolly selecting everything that looks spray-on: a red-carpet-worthy tight white fishtail; a clingy satin column; a backless empire line that dips dramatically from the bust around to the base of the spine, all join Jessica Rabbit in the fitting room where Dolly is starting to undress. As she discards her clothes she's revealing over-exercised sinewy arms, a washboard stomach where a six-pack might exist if there was enough flesh on her to create one, topped with a rack of angular ribs that jut out as she bends to remove her jeans. Months of sugar deprivation have earned Dolly a pair of shapeless thighs and the non-existent chest of a thirteen-year-old girl. It's the part of her she hates the most – that and the way the line of her knickers creates the tiniest lip of flesh across her belly. Her boobs used to be the first thing Josh made a grab for but he barely notices them any more – as her bras have got smaller and smaller, so has his interest in that part of her decreased too. Recently he has started to refer to them as her *titties*, like they don't even warrant the full title of tits.

'The thing to remember at this stage is that we are just getting an idea of what shapes look good on you.' Helen is removing the fishtail from its hanger, preparing to help Dolly into it.

'Josh will *love* this dress.' Dolly is beaming. 'It's just like the one Jennifer Lawrence wore on the cover of *Glamour* last month. He shot that image and he didn't shut up about how good she looked for weeks.'

'Well, this one is far too big for you, Dolly, but let me see if I can recreate the silhouette.' Helen pulls the dress in tight across Dolly's narrow back, using giant bulldog clips to hold it in position, her usual pins incapable of gathering so much excess fabric together. When she's finished, the gown is tighter to Dolly's body but has somehow lost all of its intended sex appeal. Having nothing to fill it, the strapless bodice is gaping open across her chest, crying out for some plump womanly boobs to fill it. With no curves to cling to, it's dropping straight to the floor appearing much longer than it should, ruining the shape of the fishtail that should be fanning out beautifully at her feet but is instead pooling shapelessly there. Despite Helen's best efforts, the gown is ruching in all the wrong places, tragically missing the hips and bum that would transform it into the showstopper it wants to be.

Dolly looks at herself in the unforgiving full-length mirror.

'It's awful. *I* look awful.' She's imagining the look of utter disappointment crashing all over Josh's face as he turns over his left shoulder at the altar to see her for the first time.

'The shape isn't right for you, that's all,' Helen consoles her. 'This dress is designed for a girl who is at least a size twelve, you're more like a very small eight.'

Helen slides the dress easily off her, readying the satin column.

Ping! Another email lands in Dolly's inbox as Helen is lifting the next dress up her tiny frame – but Dolly is distracted by the response:

I'm so sorry, Dolly, but we called Josh several times last week, he said he was on a shoot and couldn't chat but promised he would make the payment. When it didn't come, we emailed him again and heard nothing so I'm afraid we had to assume you'd changed your mind.

One fucking thing. That was it. Book. The. Band. I've done all the hard work finding them. Spent hours watching shit YouTube videos of naff wedding performers, hating every single one of them until I found these guys. They played at the Brides *Designer Ball. I've told the* Brides *PA they're booked. How could Josh screw this up for me?*

Now the shimmering satin dress is swamping her, like she's decided to play dress-up in her mother's expensive nightie. It's flapping open at her armpits revealing the pathetic curve of her tiny bud-like breasts and hanging far too low at the neckline, exposing her bony décolletage. It's creepy almost, like a child wearing a woman's wedding dress. She looks scrawny, not sexy, the last thing that's going to ignite Josh on their wedding night.

'I hate it, Helen. Why does everything look so dreadful on me?'

'Can I make a suggestion? I know you love these dresses and I do too, but something so slinky is always going to be tricky on such a petite body. We need to create some curves for you.'

'What? Make me look bigger? That's the last thing I want.' Dolly is going to have to forgive Helen's ignorance on this one. She doesn't know Josh and therefore can't possibly understand the value he places on a woman's physical perfection. Dolly has had enough reminders of that in recent weeks – whenever she came close to cracking and headed in the direction of the fridge, only for Josh to jump in with some put-down about her waddling up the aisle or not being able to do up her dress on the morning. Both scenarios played in loop in her nightmares for weeks.

'No, but we need to create the illusion of curves. It will make the dress look more interesting and will flatter you so much more than these dresses do. Maybe something that's cut on the bias; the curving side seam will give you plenty of va-va-voom. Or maybe a ball gown that cinches in at your naturally small waist then descends into a full, flowing floor-length skirt. It will capitalise on your slenderness but also camouflage your lack of hips. Or we could try a bodice with some detailing to create volume there. The extra fabric up top will help fill out your upper body, as will some of my lightly padded halter neck styles.'

'So much for skinny meaning you can wear what you want! I *need* to look sexy. I think Josh will want to see me in the sort of dress most women *can't* wear. Isn't that what all men want? You tell me, Helen, am I missing something here? What kind of wedding dresses do men love? What do they want to see coming up the aisle towards them?' This sounds so much more desperate than Dolly intends. Urgh, she's become one of those tragic women who dress for men, not themselves. To be honest, she loves the softer, less-structured silhouettes of the pretty tulle overlay dresses, but knows Josh won't. He'll think they're shapeless and boring. Bloody hell. Maybe she should just refix the appointment for when Tilly is free.

'In my experience, most men just want something recognisable on their bride, no mad departure from their everyday style.' Well, that might be as far as most men's vision of their bride goes but Dolly knows Josh won't be that easily pleased. She's lost count of the number of times he's banged on about how a woman should look her absolute best on her wedding day, reaching a level of grooming and style that she's unlikely to ever equal again. And let's not forget how high that bar has been set for him – and therefore for Dolly.

'Also, remember you're going to be in church, Dolly, so you're probably not going to want to feel like you're dressed for a night out with the girls in front of the vicar. Come on, I'll show you. I've dressed a lot of women with your sort of figure and if you trust me, I think I know what will look best.'

Helen briefly steps out of the dressing room to select some more gowns, leaving a deflated Dolly wondering how much she'll need to increase the lingerie budget to compensate for everything she's naturally lacking – and to get somewhere near to meeting Josh's expectations.

When Helen returns she is carrying every dress in the boutique that Dolly would never choose because Josh would never rate it; something that looks like a t-shirt, an enormous puff ball of a skirt and (*seriously?*) something with lace all over it.

'Kate Halfpenny is going to be the designer for you, I think, Dolly. She's known for her bridal separates, which means we can build your look together piece by piece, until we get something that works exactly for your shape.'

'Well, given that everything I've chosen looks crap so far, let's give it a go.' With the clock ticking, Dolly has no choice but to at least try.

She stands still as Helen lifts a skinny slip with thin spaghetti straps over her head. So far, so unimpressive, there's disappointment sagging across Dolly's face.

'That's just our base, we're going to add to it from here. Now, what we need are layers.'

Helen sweeps a silk, full circle skirt around Dolly's body, tying it sharply at her tiny waist, pulling her in beautifully but adding a touch of width across her hips. Then she pulls the slip gently out from under the skirt, just enough to blouse it across Dolly's middle. The skirt doesn't meet at the front so one of Dolly's long, lean legs is exposed from just above the knee, confirming her slenderness, once a six-inch heel is added. The skirt isn't clinging to her like the others, it's more billowing, just waiting to lift on the air as soon as she moves – and the extra metres of luxurious fabric have created the faintest hint of a butt where there isn't one.

'OK, this is more like it.' Dolly is beaming again. 'But what can you do about these?' She points at her schoolgirl cleavage.

'Let's try this.' Helen drapes a light cap-sleeve lace jacket across Dolly's narrow shoulders, adding some wedding-worthy detail and immediately drawing eyes away from her practically concave chest.

'I like it, I really do! You knew those other dresses were going to look dreadful on me, didn't you?' Dolly feels so silly, like she waltzed in here this morning expecting to look supermodel sexy without any of the raw ingredients to pull it off, cringing at the thought of Josh being privy to any of what just happened.

'It's important that you see everything for yourself,' says Helen warmly. 'I can't dictate to you what you should wear, it's your wedding day and ultimately your choice. I am here to advise you, to lend you the benefit of my expertise. I have dressed hundreds of brides, Dolly, so I like to think I know what I'm doing.'

'What about accessories then? Shall we go *enormous*?'

'I don't think so, Dolly. With your frame, if we put something big on your head, you're in danger of looking like a lollipop.'

'I read that Victoria Beckham always carries a massive handbag because it makes her legs look thinner.'

'Good grief, what nonsense. I'm sure she has far more important things to think about than looking thin. How about we try a veil instead?'

'Bit trad isn't it?'

'It's the one single time in your life you'll ever be able to wear one. And since you've asked, I know grooms love them – something about the great reveal he gets to play a part in on the day when he helps to gently lift it from your face.' Dolly tries to stop it but she can't halt the image of Josh demanding a quick powder or lip gloss touch-up the second her veil is raised.

'OK, let's do it!' It's probably not the most feminist thought Dolly's ever had, but she loves the idea of Josh claiming her on their wedding day. Lifting that delicate piece of fabric, loving what he sees and sealing their future with an approving kiss.

Helen takes a fingertip-length veil, dotted with delicate crystal beads and pins it at the back of Dolly's head, then flutters it out so it catches the light, sending mini spotlights of crystal reflections darting around her like paparazzi flashbulbs.

'I feel fabulous! I love it! And more to the point I think he will love it too.'

'You look incredible, Dolly, you really do.'

'Yes! Now, where's my selfie stick?'

The celebrations are interrupted by the loud trill of the boutique's telephone and Helen excuses herself to answer it.

'It's for you, Dolly.' Helen pops her head back into the changing room, catching Dolly pouting seductively towards her iPhone. 'A man, he wouldn't give his name.'

Odd, only Josh knew she was coming here today. Perhaps she hadn't heard her mobile go and he's calling to apologise for screwing up the band booking? Lucky for him she is now in such a giddy mood or he would be for it. Still wearing the full bridal ensemble, Dolly glides out into the boutique, confidence soaring and lifts the receiver to her ear.

'You will not *believe* what I am wearing.' She's all breathless and excited, mind briefly flicking to her wedding night when Josh will be peeling this lot off her.

'Is it a wedding dress by any chance?' The male voice is angry, seething even, barely controlled, ready to explode. Dolly is momentarily sideswiped. This is not Josh.

'Two things, Dolly, if I may intrude upon your precious time for a moment.'

Oh good fucking God, no! The Dick.

'Number one, if you're going to bunk off work like you don't give a toss about your job, then don't leave Post-it notes all over your desk with dates and times and contact numbers clearly revealing where you are.' He's not pausing for breath and clearly not interested in any lame explanation she may have. 'It's bloody insulting to me, and every one of your colleagues who does care. And number two...' His tone is different now, sarcastic and enjoying the moment more, one step ahead of her on something. 'I enjoyed your cupcake tasting notes, I'm just curious as to why, nowhere in your copy or strategy did you *once* mention that they are all sugar-free – the one single thing that marks this product out as different from all their competitors. But you can explain that to me, Dolly, when you get here, because I have cleared my diary for the afternoon so you and I can have a very serious chat in my office. If you've got any plans after work tonight cancel them, you've got some hours to make up.'

The call disconnects and Dolly is left clutching the handset, heart pounding in her ears, mind jumping between the utter joy at the prospect of losing her job and the raw panic of how she will pay for this wedding without it.

All thoughts of the beautiful dress she's wearing have been well and truly pissed all over.

Ping! Another email briefly distracts her from the tears that are inevitably bubbling their way up to the surface. No, this cannot be right. She can see the name right there, in bold black type, unopened. Annabel Coutts, PA to the editor of Condé Nast *Brides*.

Dolly's finger hovers above it, terrified of what one tap is about to reveal.

Chapter Twelve

Emily

Everything is white. The colour of the moment. The colour of happy times. White clouds dotting a promising spring morning sky. A beaming smile. Fresh paperwhites trailing their sweet scent. A dreamy wedding dress.

Not today.

The walls. The floors. His desk. His chair. Even the computer and the keys on his mini wireless keyboard are all clinically white. And the name badge. Dr David Stevens. There are no pens or paper, no personal effects, no brown-stained coffee mugs. Nothing cluttering his desk except one clear plastic file with Emily's name printed in Times New Roman in the top left hand corner, her age following it. Twenty-seven. Far too young to be having this conversation.

'The MRI was a useful procedure, Emily, but I can see from your subsequent CT angiogram, which of course gives us a much clearer view of your blood vessels and their shape and dimensions, that your aneurism is going to be incredibly difficult to operate on.' Dr Stevens is holding direct eye contact, studying Emily, needing to see she is taking this in.

'OK.' Emily looks tiny in the large white padded leather chair across the desk from him. She is using her tiptoes to gently swivel from side to side, like a child unsure of the protocol, desperate to alleviate the uncomfortably sterile environment of the neurosurgeon's office. It's not like she's ever thought about how she might behave or act in a place like this. It isn't the stuff of anyone's idle daydreams.

'There are a number of issues complicating surgery as an option right now. You should think of your aneurism as like a blister on the wall of your blood vessel, but I can also see from your results that there is a second smaller aneurism attached and growing from it. As they grow together, the wall of each is getting thinner and thinner, much like the effect of blowing up a balloon, making them both more fragile and more likely to rupture.'

'And if they do rupture?' Emily's not sure why she even asks the question. She doesn't want to contemplate the answer, let alone have Dr Stevens deliver it to her with all the factual brutality that only a total stranger can.

'There are a great many factors that affect the answer to that, but if you're asking me if it can be fatal, then I'm afraid the answer is yes. Some ruptures can also result in permanent brain damage.'

Dr Stevens has had this conversation many times before, Emily can see that. He doesn't flinch, or stumble over his words. There is not the slightest hesitation or awkwardness as he delivers one crushing fact after another and he maintains eye contact throughout. Emily's mind drifts briefly to the other blows he would be brilliant at delivering: 'You didn't get the job, you're not good enough', 'No, I don't want to marry you' or 'You've missed the last two payments so we are repossessing your house next Thursday'. In the right circumstance, he could be a really useful bloke to have around.

'But there is something we can do to stop them rupturing, right?'
There is no panic in Emily's voice. No tears. She is all business-like
calm. Shouldn't there be an epic meltdown of emotion pouring out of
her about now? It feels as if this conversation is about someone else,
that this can't be relevant to her. The headache has gone, it eased off
weeks ago. Perhaps the aneurism and its friend will do the same, just
shrink back into the mass of her brain tissue, taking every worry with
it, freeing her to focus on the edible favours and floral chair backs that
really should be ticked off her wedding list by now. Perhaps Dr Stevens'
methodical and strictly factual approach is rubbing off on her. She has
a feeling there is no room for emotion in his office. Perhaps patients are
expected to show that later, out in reception with the pretty assistant
behind the desk.

'Your aneurism is growing from the internal carotid artery, that's
the main blood vessel supplying your brain. What concerns me most is
that it also has normal healthy blood vessels attached from it, making it
very difficult for me to block them off during surgery without serious
risk of causing a fatal stroke.'

There is a long pause while Dr Stevens lets that information work
its way into and through Emily's apparently now quite vulnerable
brain. She can see he is in no way inclined to fill the gaping hole in
their conversation.

'Why me? Why is this happening to *me*? Did I do something
to cause this?' Emily is aware this sounds like a bit of a whine –
the toddler stamping her foot and complaining that life's not fair
because she didn't get the packet of sweets or the later bedtime she
wanted – but in the circumstances, she reckons he'll have to let
her have that. Anyway, she's a bride-to-be, she can be as stroppy
as she likes, right?

'The fact is you're incredibly unlucky. You have none of the obvious risk factors – no family history of it, you don't smoke and your blood pressure is reading as normal. You're just one of the thousands who develop aneurisms every year without any known clinical reason why.'

'Where do we go from here? You never said if you can stop them rupturing. ' Emily is still searching for the positive in all of this, but so far Dr Stevens has failed to deliver. Some wonder drug? An experimental procedure they just happen to be looking for willing volunteers to try?

'They could rupture at any time, Emily. I'm afraid there is little I can do to put your mind at rest there. The more pressing point is deciding on your treatment, and on that subject, I'd like a second opinion. If you are happy for me to, I would like to share your results with the Barrow Neurological Institute in Phoenix, Arizona. It's a centre of excellence for the study of aneurisms and they will be able to advise on the specific degree of risk that surgery may bring. We'll be at the mercy of how busy they are but once I hear back from them, we should be able to build a plan for your treatment.'

'And what should I do in the meantime?'

'Go home. Talk to your family. I'm guessing the fact you have come alone today means they don't know yet?'

'No. I didn't want to say anything until I had seen you.'

'You're going to need their support. There will be some tough decisions to make soon.'

'It's just that we are all planning my wedding and—'

'What date is your wedding?'

'August 25th, twelve weeks' time.' Despite the circumstances, Emily still beams when she says these words. Her wedding day. Not that far off now.

'You might want to consider pulling it forward.' Dr Stevens slams her file shut and motions towards the door. 'My office will be in touch again soon.'

Her time is up.

The red dress. Tonight, it had to be the red dress, Mark loves that one. The way it clings to her hips in a way he appreciates more than she does, and drops a fraction too low at the neckline, revealing a hint of lingerie beneath. She is sitting in their favourite Italian trattoria in Oxford, waiting for him to join her for dinner. She's the first to arrive and has secured their usual table by the window so she can watch the throng of office workers on their way home. She's already getting stuck into the warm focaccia bread, dunking it into sweet olive oil and balsamic vinegar, absentmindedly working her way through slice after slice. It's unseasonably warm for an early evening in May and people are lingering, stopping for a beer, spilling out on to the pavement with colleagues, enjoying the moment, starting to warm to the idea that summer is coming.

Table five has been the scene of many great dates with Mark. Some of their very first, when they nervously spoke over each other and worried about food stuck in their teeth. Now they're more likely to finish each other's sentences and swipe food without asking. This is where Mark caught her totally off guard one rain-drenched Saturday lunchtime last winter. He'd asked her to meet for a quick bite to eat but when she arrived the place was empty, bar one single table in the centre of the room. Mark was standing there, holding a single red rose and the Goldsmith's ring box. She'd immediately burst into tears, feeling with every bone in her body that this was meant to be, the absolute natural order of the universe. To marry Mark was her personal destiny, one that had been written in the stars long before she even imagined what her husband might be like – before she even knew she wanted one. Mark was always going to be hers. She was always going to be his.

On a normal evening out she would be twitchy with excitement, thinking ahead to the great bottle of chianti they'll guzzle over the red-and-white checked tablecloth, faces glowing from the flicker of candlelight, the rich homemade puttanesca sauce that could transport anyone to the pastel-coloured coastline of Naples in one mouthful. Mark always managed to spill some on his tie. The heady sweetness of the ice-cold limoncello that would, as always, finish their meal. But tonight the excitement of seeing Mark has an edge. She knows she'll have to tell him. The neurosurgeon has practically ordered it and however upsetting it is, Mark needs to know. He will want to know. She will just do her best to soften it. There are still a lot of ifs. If it doesn't rupture. If the Americans think it is operable. If she just lives with it for the rest of her life.

Emily glances out of the window and can see him coming. Her sweet Mark. He looks so happy. He's smiling. Who does that? Who walks along a busy city street beaming at total strangers as they go? A small boy is bawling in his pushchair, having dropped a cuddly toy. His mum is oblivious, phone glued to her ear, and as Mark approaches he scoops the toy up and hands it back to the boy. He doesn't even break stride, doesn't wait for the thank you that isn't coming anyway, just ruffles the boy's hair and carries on. There is a lightness in his face. Here is a man who thinks all is right with the world. Emily's job tonight is to shatter that thought. Her jaw tightens with the unfairness of it all, all she can think is *why me? Why us?*

As Mark enters the restaurant he is greeted like a long-lost friend by the maître d' – all exuberant handshakes and big man hugs. They chat for a few minutes, Mark winking her way, letting her know he won't be long, and Emily thinks again how his easy ability to get on with everyone is one of the things she loves most about him.

'You look gorgeous as ever.' Mark kisses Emily's hand in mock formality before sliding into the rustic wooden chair opposite her, their knees bumping as they juggle to accommodate each other. 'God, I love this place.'

Emily is suddenly overwhelmed by sadness. It's seeing him up close. Smelling him, feeling his breath on her hand, locking eyes with him, knowing what she knows. She's never kept anything from him before. He's ordering wine, squeezing her hand across the table, telling her again how stunning she looks, and talking at a million miles an hour about honeymoon research. She can feel herself starting to wobble, so tempted to just blurt it out, get it over and done with but…

'And at the risk of sounding completely soft, can I just say that these past few weeks really have been the happiest of my life. I mean it. How did I get so lucky? I look at you now and I can still see that shy university fresher I met when we were eighteen. And here you are, about to become my wife. I mean, you're buying your wedding dress this week, aren't you? His face is all wide-eyed expectation, barely believing that everything they have planned together is finally going to happen. Every feature on his gorgeous face is alive with the thrilling prospect of it.

'Mark—' She's trying to stop him talking but he is in full swing, not suspecting for a second that this is about to be anything but another great meal at Rossellini's. He takes both her hands in his.

'I love you, Emily. I always have. I just hope I can be the husband you want me to be.'

Everything he's saying is instantly sobering, making it impossible for her to open her mouth and say what she needs to say. How *can* she? He's wrong. This isn't about Mark protecting her, it's about her protecting him, from an awful truth he can do nothing about. She has no choice, she has to know. But there is a choice for him. She can choose not to tell him. Not to shatter his world and fill it with worry.

'Listen, you know we've been invited to the Coleridge wedding – Adam and Jessie's – in a few months from now? It's just before we go on honeymoon.'

A nod is all Emily can manage.

'Well, I just want to check you're not going to be disappointed once you see everything they'll be doing? It's a bit of a shame it's so close to ours in a way because I would hate you to feel our day wasn't as exciting or, well, as flash.' He's searching her face now, ready to spot even the smallest sign of disappointment forming there.

'I could never be disappointed. I'm just so happy to be marrying you.' She's having to force the words free from the back of her throat, pausing to take a large glug from her wine glass, needing him to pick up the conversation.

'I'm surprised we got an invite, actually. I know I've organised a lot of trips for Henry and the family but still, it's very generous of them. We should just go and enjoy it for what it is I reckon, a wonderfully over-the-top day of excess!'

It's so sad to hear him getting excited about things that, from where Emily is sitting, really don't matter any more. Who cares how flash the Coleridge wedding is? All she can think about right now is getting married and getting better – preferably without having to unburden herself to Mark or her family.

Because telling him is selfish, she knows that. It can only benefit her; give her someone to share her fears, someone to tell her everything is going to be OK. But he can't tell her that, so why put him – or anyone else – through it?

'I'm going to put on some lipstick then come back and give you a big smacker if you don't mind.' Emily needs to get away from the table before he can see in her face that something is wrong.

'Er… not at all.' Mark smiles, perfectly boyish and charming at the same time.

Emily excuses herself to the ladies', but ducks out the back of the restaurant into a side alley and leans against the wall where the waiters usually take their fag breaks. She takes a deep breath, sucking air down into the very centre of her, releasing it again through her open mouth, letting every ounce of fear and anger free. She doesn't recognise the sound she's making. Pure, undiluted rage is forcing itself up from the very depths of her in a low, strangulated moan. Her fists are against the wall and she's planting painful kicks at it, sending a sharp spike of pain through her right foot and up into her shin. She places her hot face to the brickwork and asks over and over *why, why why*, knowing this secret is hers to keep now.

The headache is back, stronger than ever.

Well, this is cosy. Emily is half naked in The White Gallery fitting room while a cast of thousands including her mum, dad, Mark's mum Barbara, his sister Janet, her granny Joyce and neighbour Phillipa, are sitting in the main boutique waiting for the fashion show to begin. It's the Sunday Summit on a field trip. Her dad is nestled in the middle, note pad in hand because 'we'll need to refer back to my notes later if we can't remember what we liked the best'.

From behind the heavy curtain of the fitting room, where the owner, Helen, is lining up a rail of dresses for her to try, Emily can hear the excited chatter outside. It's all giggles and champagne glasses clinking. Bill has already had to give Glo a stern talking to after she burst into tears the second they all stepped over The White Gallery threshold. Now there's lots of reminiscing about their own wedding days and how their baby girl is all grown up.

First up is a remarkably affordable – for this place anyway – Amanda Wakeley Maya gown. One of the simpler gowns in her ethereal collection, it gathers slightly at the waist before dropping into a fluid chiffon skirt. The only embellishments are two beaded cap sleeves either side of the V neckline and a jewel-encrusted belt that can be removed for brides watching their budget. But as the opener to Emily's personal catwalk show, it's not giving the crowd what they want.

'It looks lovely on you, obviously,' ventures Glo, 'but does it have the "wow" we are looking for?'

'Well, I personally love it Mum, and just so you know, it's a little more affordable than most things back there in the fitting room.' This lot need to be reined in from the beginning or Emily knows the appointment will veer beyond her control.

'Don't be so crass, Emily, this is not about cost. Sorry, Helen. Can we see something a little more… over the top, please?'

'Mum!'

'Oh, come on, Emily, we're only going to do this once.' Glo is not about to be denied her moment of a lifetime.

'Quite right.' Now Barbara is wading in.

'Emily, you don't want to be upstaged by your old dad on the big day, do you? I read in one of your bridal magazines that lots of girls regret not going big enough with the dress. Let's definitely not make that mistake!'

So in the next hour Emily works her way through every conceivable shape of wedding dress to a varying degree of appreciation from the crowd – the strapless ballgown (*divine*) the sheath (*can someone explain to me how that is a wedding dress?*), the fishtail (*too clingy for church*), the column (*your boobs have completely disappeared!*), tea length (*dated*), the high-low hem (*sorry, we don't want a dress that can't make up its mind how long it wants to be*), drop waist (*I'm going to be honest, not flattering at all*), empire line (*maternity wear!*), A-line (*a contender*) – until the crowd are satisfied and Emily is exhausted.

They collectively decide on a Reem Acra strapless ballgown with a hand-beaded bodice and, at her mum's insistence, a giant cathedral-worthy skirt. The price tag is painful but the gown, Emily has to admit, is incredible – a considerably classier version of the kind of thing Cinderella might tip up in on her wedding day. Impressive in its size but light as candyfloss once on (*first dance-worthy, that's for sure.*) She feels good in it – but more because she has given them all their moment. Wedding dress shopping with your only daughter; creating memories more significant than anyone here today could possibly realise.

In the hour is has taken to reach this decision, Emily's audience has polished off two bottles of Tattinger, devoured a plate of biscuits and a round of pretty pink cupcakes, scattering crumbs all over Helen's previously spotless cream carpet. They are now all slightly slumped on Helen's gold and white chairs, decorum having deserted them.

'Excellent progress today.' Emily can hear her Dad congratulating them all on a 'good day's work' as she is finally stepping back into her jeans and t-shirt.

'Well done Emily.' Helen is back in the fitting room, preparing to finalise her measurements for the Reem gown. 'I think you coped pretty well with all that. You're obviously a very close family, which is so lovely to see.'

'Actually, Helen? Don't worry about the measurements.' Emily lowers her voice to a whisper.

'But I need to take them, or the dress won't be perfect for you.'

'I don't want you to order the dress. I'd like the Amanda Wakeley instead and if there is anything you can do on the price that would be even better.'

'But I thought you…' Confusion is spreading across Helen's face and Emily can see she's trying to work out what went wrong. 'The dress is an old shop sample, Emily, and if you want to buy this one, I could let you have it for much less than a new dress would cost. But lots of women have tried it on, you may not feel it's special enough?'

'That's absolutely fine,' Emily cuts her off before she asks any more questions. 'I know they all love the ballgown but—' But what? I'm about to drop dead? There may not be a wedding? I need to future-proof my parents' finances because they might have a funeral to pay for? Maybe she should have told Mark after all. He would know exactly what to do now, how to handle this. Oh God, why can't she just be a normal bride, lapping up the attention, not caring if it's all a bit gratuitous and self-centred. She just wants to spend the afternoon wanging on about crystal tiaras and whether it should be the teardrop pearl earrings or the vintage sapphire ones Joyce wore. The pretence is already painfully draining.

Emily takes a deep breath. 'But I think it actually looks better on me. I don't need the belt either, thank you. And Helen, no one is to know about this, please.'

'Of course but—' Emily watches Helen struggle to work her out, this is obviously a new one on her. She needs to end this conversation before anyone overhears them or she drops her guard.

'Look, I may not need a dress at all, Helen, so please can you just do as I ask?' Emily's voice is full of exasperation, more clipped than she intended and she hates the way she's making Helen's head bow like she's been told off. The only thing worse is the weight of what she knows she now has to do herself, the lie that she will carry with her for however long it takes.

Chapter Thirteen

Jessie

Claire is filling the armchair she's wedged into, picking away at her already chipped Barbie pink nail polish while she works her way through a family-sized bag of Doritos. *Is this breakfast at 11 a.m.?* wonders Jessie. *Or a mid-morning snack?* She can't remember a single occasion when she's seen her younger sister eat a piece of fruit. Or anything that's a direct descendant of nature, free from the trans fats and refined sugars that are pumped into everything Claire calls food. Her job selling burgers to people who value speed over health has done nothing for her understanding of nutrition. Jessie considers for a moment asking her if she even knows what the word means.

She's trying very hard not to let these thoughts show on her face. When was the last time Claire washed her hair? Christ, is that a scrunchie? Where would you even buy one of those today? Is she aware that those leggings are at least three sizes too small?

Is it disgust or pity that Jessie feels? She finds it so hard to separate the two sometimes, especially where her family are concerned.

Should she be helping Claire? Setting her up with someone who could sort this mess out for her. Is she even aware what a state she looks? Wouldn't it be the kindest thing in the world to tell her? No, it would break her, surely. Their lives may have split and taken very different paths but she hasn't completely forgotten the times they spent together as kids, thick as thieves, before all the differences between them became too hard to ignore. Plotting on the landing upstairs, long after their parents thought they were tucked up in bed and the hours playing make-believe in the back garden, Jessie always the teacher, Claire the keen-to-please pupil. There is a delicate heart masked under that terrible lack of style and Jessie has no desire to shatter it – but neither does she want an enormous Claire-sized shadow cast all over her wedding photos. Christ, what would Hugo think?

'Cup of tea, anyone? Biscuits?' Jessie's mum, Margaret, is in the kitchen as usual, tidying up after everyone, sweeping the remains of sugar-coated breakfast cereal into the bin and reloading a large white plate with a mountain of chocolate digestives.

Everyone shouts yes, without looking up from what they're doing, certainly not offering to go and help. Jessie's older brother, Jason, is sitting on the floor, his offensively loud neon board shorts clashing with the bold geometric grey and red patterned carpet. A copy of the *Daily Mirror* is open across his lap, a full page of a lingerie-clad Kelly Brook staring up at him. He's muttering to himself about all the things he'd like to do to her given half the chance, as if a woman like Kelly would even register his existence. Pitifully oblivious to his own shortcomings, Jason lost his job at the local car mechanic's garage after a Kwik Fit opened in the new retail park around the corner. It forced him home for a few weeks to sponge off his retired parents. That was two years ago and as long as Margaret keeps putting food in front of him, washing and ironing his clothes and tidying his room, he's going nowhere. Thirty-eight and still dependant. How tragic. Last time Jessie was home she saw her mum handing him a roll of ten-pound notes, funding another night out with his mates at the local. She'd whispered something about not telling your father, making Jessie wonder how many other handouts he'd so easily taken. No self-respect.

Jessie's dad, Graham, is on the sofa, glued to *Ice Road Truckers* blaring out of a huge widescreen TV that's dwarfing its orange pine stand. He's barely acknowledged Jessie's arrival home, not a man for kisses and hugs. Always supportive but never demonstrative, he is the product of his own cold father, choosing not to squeeze his children like other more obviously affectionate dads might have done. But he shows his feelings in other ways. Of his three children, it is always Jessie he gravitates towards. Not marking her out for more love, but preferring her conversation, her sharper mind, her ambition. Since he's retired from his caretaker job at the local primary school after twenty-five years' unbroken service scrubbing crayon off walls, mopping the stinking toilets and polishing the parquet corridors, Jessie can see he has shrunk – in size and personality. He's eclipsed now by a wife who has more get up and go, and who appointed herself his new headmistress the day he picked up his final pay cheque.

'OK, here we go.' Margaret places a tray filled with mismatched mugs of weak tea and the digestive tower onto the small coffee table, pushing to one side a wicker basket of pot pourri that lost its scent years ago. *Pointless decoration and ornaments – they are everywhere in this house*, thinks Jessie. The ship in a bottle bought on a trip to the Cornwall coast; the row of mass-produced miniature country cottages that Margaret has collected from one of her magazine subscriptions and – most annoying of all – a light-up nativity scene that for some reason was never put away after Christmas one year. There is nothing of any value. No future family heirlooms, just clutter that, bafflingly, her parents feel attached to.

'Come on, then. How are the wedding plans going, Jessica?' Margaret's face is alight with excitement.

'Good! Actually, Mum, I know you wanted to come dress shopping but I'm afraid I've already chosen my three gowns. I just knew what I wanted and got on with it.' Jessie might be dressing this up as a casual information drop but she knows the spike of disappointment her mum will now be feeling. Despite Margaret's very best efforts not to look deflated, she recoils slightly then tries to hide her feelings by handing out the teas as Jessie scrabbles to think of something to say that will make it up to her, some substitute that isn't dress shopping. Her eyes are glued to her mum, watching for a sign she's going to make more of this, then feeling ten times worse when she doesn't. With a quick bat of her hand Margaret decides not to make a fuss, not wanting to cause Jessie the same hurt she is feeling.

'Sorry! Did I hear that right? You need *three* dresses?' Claire is hauling herself forward in the armchair, interest piqued.

'Yes, Claire. One for the rehearsal dinner, one for—'

'The what?' As someone unlikely ever to turn the head of the opposite sex, let alone marry it, Claire is already struggling to grasp very basic wedding concepts.

'It's the dinner for close family and friends the night before the wedding.' Jessie scans the room to see if the assumption she's dreading will be made.

'Cool, another free dinner then. We're all coming, right? Where will it be?'

Of course they would assume it included them. Under normal circumstances the bride's family would absolutely attend. But these aren't normal circumstances, these are not normal people...

'It's at Adam's parents' estate in the country.'

'Finally, we get to meet Mr La-di-da's posho parents then.' If Claire's mocking tone is designed to irritate Jessie, then it's working.

'If you mean Camilla and Henry, then yes, they will be hosting the evening for us.'

'How lovely of them but we must contribute something, mustn't we, Graham? What shall I do, my haddock pâté with some lovely homemade onion chutney? Or that chocolate and caramel traybake I tried last week. Everyone loved that.'

'No, Mum, that really won't be necessary. Camilla will have it all covered.'

'I'm sure she will, but Adam's parents are paying for just about everything else on the day. Anyway, it's bad manners to turn up empty-handed. By the way, your dad and I really want to contribute towards your dress. *Dresses*, I should say.'

God, it is almost laughable. Jessie has kept the full extent of her new wealth relatively secret from her family, which was surprisingly easy, degrees of wealth being an irrelevance in this house. Their understanding of how Adam's family live is so slight that the questioning she expected just never came, they never made it beyond the incredulity that they have someone who cooks for them. So Jessie decided they didn't need to know that the Cheltenham house is valued at £3.5 million, the staff bill every month is in excess of £4,000, or that the contents of her wardrobe is insured for £750,000. Her mum has never had her nails professionally manicured in her life so she won't understand why last week Jessie paid seventy-two pounds for a lipstick (she only registered the cost at all because she was paying in cash, normally she wouldn't even bother to ask) and her family certainly doesn't need to know her three wedding looks are costing well over £50,000. Any contribution from her parents is not only unnecessary – but of no use; but how do you convey that without sounding horribly ungrateful?

Jessie can feel this conversation slipping out of her control.

'I hope you're not expecting me to buy another outfit?' Claire interjects. 'We all know you're loaded but not everyone has your bank balance, Jess. Anyway, I've already bought my dress from River Island, I'll just change the cardi for the different events or something.'

'Really? What's it like?' The edge has returned to Jessie's voice, giving away her nervousness at what outfit Claire has deemed wedding-worthy.

'Why? Worried I'm going to *embarrass* you?' Claire is on to her.

'Of course not.' *Yes, obviously.* 'I'm just interested.'

'It's green, quite floaty, and has a big old sparkly belt around the middle. Mum says it looks good, and it was in the sale, forty quid. Can't argue with that.'

'It's wonderful to see you in something feminine for once, Claire,' adds Margaret supportively.

Jessie hopes her face doesn't look as horrified as she feels. Why would anyone Claire's size think they could do *floaty*? The girl needed structure. The sort that went into the engineering of a very large building – foundations, underpinning, reinforcements, cladding! And she has no middle. Any belt is just going to disappear.

Jessie is panicking now. She'd hoped to take Claire out shopping, to a designer who understands internal boning. No chance now. Think, *think*. Jessie doesn't want to face the obvious way to solve this problem. But how else can she salvage the situation and stop Claire looking like she's eaten three of the other wedding guests? There will be whispers, stares, cruel comments. As much as Jessie despises the way Claire looks, she doesn't wish that sort of mass judgement on her – or how it will reflect on Jessie herself, obviously.

'So your second dress is for the wedding day – what's the third one for?'

'The evening party.'

'Well if you're changing, then so am I. Yes! I can wear my orange dress I bought for Marbella last year!'

Jessie has seen pictures of Claire in that dress, a cheap knock off of a Hervé Léger gown designed for a woman no bigger than a firm size eight. On Claire it's a giant orange, demented space hopper of a dress; an overblown beach ball ready to burst. She just can't let Claire do this. She has to stop it. No choice now, she needs do the unthinkable.

'Actually, Claire, I wanted to ask if you would be my bridesmaid.' Jessie feels sick, like she's committing wedding style suicide but it's the only way she can have at least some control over Claire's clusterfuck approach to dressing herself.

'Really?' Claire is as surprised as Jessie to hear the words.

'Wonderful idea!' Margaret is made up. 'Oh wow, my two beautiful girls together! Claire, you *must* catch the bouquet!'

Sweet fucking Jesus, she's gone all Mrs Bennett. Claire must be nowhere near me when I launch that thing or every man in the place will be bolting for the exit.

'It would mean of course that I'd buy you three different outfits to cover all the events.' Jessie needs Claire to commit to this now and she's sure a few free dresses will clinch it.

'Done!'

One problem solved, another *huge* one created. How to make Claire look good. Jessie's mind is working overtime now, while the rest of them plough on through the digestives. Vivienne Westwood? Always looks amazing on Nigella Lawson. Rouland Mouret? No, brilliant at shaping but too fashionable for Claire. Lanvin and Lela Rose all have beautiful shaped dresses for fuller figures and wasn't it Marina Rinaldi who dressed the plus-size comedian Melissa McCarthy for the Oscars one year when no one else would? Claire is going to need something couture. Bruce Oldfield perhaps? He's known for being brilliant with bodies of all shapes and sizes: chic and tasteful – two words she needs Helen to introduce her sister to whether she likes it or not.

The rest of Saturday afternoon passes much like any other in the Jones household; Mum backwards and forwards to the kettle three hundred times, Dad never moving. The TV is never off; it plays a continuous loop of soaps, game shows and property programmes until the five of them settle down together, cheese and crackers on laps, to watch the evening movie. It's another re-run of Molly Ringwald in *Pretty in Pink*, Jessie's favourite: the girl from the wrong side of the tracks dating the wealthy, popular guy. And he's lovely, charming and genuinely likes her despite the haters who think she's uncool and beneath him. The date is a success until it's time for him to take her home, then she panics because she doesn't want him to see where she lives.

Jessie flinches, the parallels all too obvious. But no one else notices a thing. Claire has moved on to the sofa next to her mum and dad, while Jason still hasn't made it off the floor next to them, forcing Jessie into one of the armchairs set away slightly. As she looks on she can't help but think how wonderful it must be not to care. Not to be aware of the differences in their lives. They're all enjoying the film for what it is, fluffy feel-good Hollywood entertainment. Except Jessie. For her it's a sharp reminder of who she is and the pretence she's got to keep up. She's so grateful the main light has been switched off and it's just the glow from the TV lighting the room because tears have unexpectedly started to pool in her eyes. She knows her family love her – but they love the version of her they think they know. And that's no longer

Jessie. That girl just doesn't exist any more. She can't. She's had to adapt, move on, move up and blend in to a whole new world. As the TV casts a flattering glow across everyone's contented faces, never more has Jessie felt so relaxed and yet so alienated, this sole survivor on the lonely middle ground between the past and the future.

She glances across to the sofa and at her mum whose head is violently jerking as she keeps catching herself falling asleep. She's shattered and it's not even 9 p.m. Jessie looks at her cheap Primark slippers where the soles are detaching and knows she won't buy another pair until these ones literally fall off her feet. The temperature has dropped and her mum is clutching a hot water bottle to her belly, determined not to waste money on the gas fire. The sight fills Jessie with so much sadness, her mum deserves much more – and she could so easily give it to her.

Jessie steps across the room towards her mum, waking her.

'How about I book us into a lovely spa for some proper pampering before the wedding, Mum? Let's get the full works shall we? My treat.'

'That would be wonderful Jessie. Nothing would make me happier than spending the day with you.' She smiles up at Jessie through exhausted eyes.

That was all it took to fill her mum's heart with joy. *I wonder if she'd still love me if she knew what was going on in my head*, Jessie thinks sadly to herself, despising herself once again for assuming that's another problem easily solved by throwing money at it.

Chapter Fourteen

Helen

Helen wakes feeling awful. But it's a different kind of awful today. Not the usual heartbroken loneliness that swamps her from the moment her eyes slide open each morning. This is different. Still there in the pit of her stomach, like a dull heavy weight but more current. There is a freshness to it somehow that she can't immediately place through the fug of her still sleepy brain. Then it clicks. It's shame. Regret. The unshakeable feeling that she has disgraced herself. Let herself down.

Roger.

She can feel warm blood flooding her cheeks as the memory of the way she awkwardly rejected him washes back over her. The courage it took to ask her to dinner may be every bit as strong as her reasons for declining him. She knows that. Didn't Susan say he's lost his wife too? How would she feel if the tables were turned? Helen lies in bed for a few moments longer than usual, staring up at the ceiling, wondering how to make this right again, wishing that Betsy was here to make her feel better. Should she give her daughter a quick call, chat it through with her? She knows Betsy will say all the right things and put it all in perspective. No, she decides against it. She can't trust herself not to cry and that will only make Betsy worry she's not coping on her own.

When Roger interrupted her appointment with Jessie that day, she was caught off guard, not ready to deflect his advances in the same way she did everyone else's questions about her private life. It's suddenly very important to her that Roger knows she's not the rude, cold and ungrateful woman she came across as that day. Surprisingly important.

Helen slumps her legs over the side of the bed and hauls herself upright, releasing a long, low sigh. She washes and dresses in a pretty coral-belted summer dress with a fawn cardigan and pristine white canvas shoes. It's Tuesday and there is no one due at the boutique for a few hours. She can't let the situation fester for a moment longer. She owes Roger an apology and he's going to get it. Only then can she put this whole horrible episode behind her. But first she has to find him. She grabs her keys and heads out of the apartment, into the bright sunlight of the late May morning. Everything is so green, so alive, so fragrant. Perhaps if she didn't have this embarrassing score to settle she might walk down to the stream, feed the ducks and feel pleased to live in such an idyllic part of the world. It's 9 a.m. Too early for the tourist swarm to have started so Helen takes her time, trying to drink in the birdsong, the perfumed smell of jasmine on the air mixed with the unmistakeable whiff of the countryside that suggests the local farmers are already muck raking.

Helen heads for the small village shop, just beyond the mill, tucked away so it is rarely busy, apart from knowledgeable locals and the odd sightseers who have strayed off the main village road and found themselves at the back of some of the prettiest cottages in the area. The store is run by a middle-aged woman called Irene, who couldn't be more *country* if she tried. Write the definition for farmer's wife and she is it. Well upholstered, wearing not a scrap of make-up, a food-stained, scalloped-edged pinny permanently attached to the front of her, wiry grey hair exploding out of her ruddy complexion. A woman who also expresses plenty of opinions, most of them unwelcome. Helen once heard her taking down some naive newbie to the village, who had committed the cardinal sin of not enrolling her children in the local village school. As the mother had handed over the money to pay for her weekly essentials, Irene had let her have it with both barrels, blaming those *loaded Londoners* for destroying village life and pricing hardworking locals out of the property market. It is a wonder that anyone has the nerve to set foot in there. But the point is, Irene's made it her business to know everyone and while Helen would normally avoid her, today she needs her help. If anyone is going to know where Roger lives, it's her.

Helen steps in to the shop and, while Irene is busy serving an elderly couple who are taking an age to decide between the plain or fruit-filled scones, she ducks down one of the aisles to grab some butter, cheese and a fresh unsliced loaf for her lunchtime break. Irene is deep in conversation with the couple and hasn't seen her arrive. A swell of pride rises up in Helen's chest as she realises their conversation has moved on to The White Gallery.

'What a stunning boutique,' the friendly female customer is gushing loudly as she unpacks a mountain of local treats onto the counter. 'I simply couldn't imagine any place I would rather work. In a pretty cottage like that, filled with some of the most beautiful gowns I think I have ever seen.'

'Gorgeous isn't it!' Irene starts to pack the shopping into a brown paper bag. 'Brides come from all over the country to visit that boutique. The owner Helen stocks dresses that you can't buy anywhere else.

They're not cheap mind you, but they are apparently the best, it's just such a shame…'

Helen is crouching low, completely out of sight now, trying to retrieve a packet of chocolate chip cookies, a little treat for when she hits her mid-afternoon slump.

'… such a shame she's one of the most miserable women you'll ever meet.'

What? Helen freezes. She can't have heard that right. She goes to stand up but Irene isn't finished yet.

'Lost her husband a few years ago apparently, never got over it, people say, so goodness knows why she decided to go in to that line of business. I mean, would you want to buy your wedding dress off a joyless old misery guts? Never mixes with anyone from the local community either, contributes nothing. Just keeps herself tucked away, wallowing in her own grief. All very odd if you ask me.'

Hearing someone speak about her in that cruel, unforgiving, not to mention inaccurate way has completely winded Helen. How could Irene? She knows nothing about Helen or what she's going through. Helen's too panicked to move now, terrified she'll draw attention to herself, wondering how she can slip out of the store before she is discovered. How mortifying. But then…

'I mean, you have to ask yourself what a misery she was to be married to in the first place, the poor bugger, whoever he was.'

Something in Irene's unsisterly tone ignites a fury in Helen that she is totally unfamiliar with. She stands bolt upright, dropping all the shopping she has gathered in her arms, sending the packet of biscuits rolling off down the aisle. She spins around and takes four deep strides towards the cash register so that Irene sees her for the first time, sees how pinched her mouth is, how she is holding her breath, ready to explode.

'How dare you!' Helen screams as Irene ducks as if to avoid a swooping wasp. 'What do you know? Please, tell me one thing you know about me or my husband that is a fact!' Helen is shouting now, blind to anything else that may be going on around her, about to make it personal too. 'Something. Anything you haven't just made up as idle gossip to while away the hours in this lousy shop. Please, I'm fascinated to know. What is it?' She spits out the last words, everything beyond her control now. The elderly couple are rooted to the spot, flicking stunned glances between a seething Helen and a visibly shaken Irene, desperate to see what the next move will be. If there were a panic button under that counter, Irene would be reaching for it about now.

'Helen, all I was really saying was that—' Irene's tone is anything but apologetic; so stubborn, refusing to back down.

'I heard exactly what you were saying, Irene, and you disgust me.' The words are flying out of Helen with barely any thought attached to them. 'How sad your life must be, that you have to attack another woman. How spiteful! Is it any wonder that people avoid this shop? Avoid YOU! For your information, Irene, I am on my way to see a man who has asked me out on a date and I am going to say yes. I socialise with people that I want to see and avoid the vile ones that I don't. Now grow up because someone your age *really* should know better.'

OK, so the bit about Roger is a lie but what the hell. *Let's give her something to really gossip about*, thinks Helen. Lecture over, she spins back around towards the door, just in time to see Roger folding his daily newspaper under his arm, freeing his hands to give Helen a comical round of applause. Two other women who must have heard the commotion and come in to enjoy the spectacle are grinning like naughty school children – perhaps Irene's dressing-down has been a long time coming. Helen's not sure if it's because of her enthusiastic

performance or the fact she has publicly confirmed a date with him
but something about the way Roger's eyes have lit up and the sound
of the chuckle that is bubbling up out of him makes Helen burst out
laughing. All four of them spill out on the pavement before Irene
has chance to gather her thoughts, along with the elderly couple
who, far from being shaken by it all, have obviously enjoyed the free
entertainment.

'Right then, I will pick you up at 8 p.m. tonight, Helen,' laughs
Roger. 'And I will remember my manners if you promise not to tell
me off like that!' Then he's gone, disappearing up the road, all swagger
and smiles, while Helen stands there, mouth gaping open, unable to
say another thing.

Back at The White Gallery, Helen is ten minutes away from her next
appointment – and on a somewhat shaky adrenaline come down.
How did that just happen? She set off to apologise to Roger, managed
to have simultaneously the worst and funniest row of her life, didn't
in fact apologise to Roger but now has a date with him that she's not
sure she's even going to attend. She stands in her kitchen for a moment, bent over the work surface, letting the last of the hot, flustered
air escape out of her. But there's no time to dither. She gulps back a
super strong cup of Earl Grey, changes into a fresh dress, somehow
feeling the switch will help cast off the morning's hoo-ha and heads
into the boutique, just as Dolly Jackson rings the front door bell.

Helen recalls the first visit Dolly made some weeks ago. How they
carefully picked their way through dress after dress, Helen tactfully
rejecting the ones that didn't flatter Dolly's tiny frame until they
found the perfect silhouette. Today, Helen will be taking more precise

measurements and pinning the fabric around Dolly's body so that a made-to-measure gown can be created especially for her.

'Hello Dolly, how are you?' Helen is so pleased to see Dolly's happy face, a noticeable improvement on how their previous appointment started – and ended.

'Never better, Helen. *Never* better.' Dolly is beside herself with joy.

"Let me guess, you managed to book that wedding band?'

'Nope. Haven't even looked. Don't have one and don't care. Guess again.'

'Your boss has forgiven you for skipping work to come here?' Helen recalls the look of utter fear she'd seen in Dolly's eyes when she took the call from him on her last visit. So mean of him to hijack her like that.

'Oh sod him! I couldn't care less about that fool.' Dolly is wonderfully jubilant.

'I give up, Dolly. What is it? What can we credit for the fizzy excitement that is radiating out of you today?' Helen is intrigued now.

'My wedding dress and I are about to become very, *very* famous!'

'Really? How?' Helen watches bemused as Dolly casts her eyes skyward, palm pressed to her heart as if addressing her adoring fans.

'I won't tell you how I've done it Helen because to be honest it's all a bit desperado, but *Brides* magazine is coming to the wedding and they have cleared four pages in their next issue – which, by the way, is the biggest selling one of the year – to feature it! Ha! What do you think of *that* then?'

'Wow! That's great news, Dolly!' Helen wraps her arms around Dolly, absorbing and sharing her joy, so pleased for the happy distraction from her own turbulent morning's events. 'What does Josh think of it all?'

Dolly releases Helen from her grip. 'Josh? Oh, I haven't told him. I doubt he'll even realise they're there – although I've had to make a few changes to the plans. *Brides* featured a Sperry tent last issue so I've scrapped that and replaced it with a Tipi village. But they *loved* the sound of the bespoke brunch hampers so I've upgraded those to the more expensive Selfridges ones. They're costing the bloody earth but the editor apparently loves the idea so I'm going big with it and I've ordered an extra giant one for her. Can you believe this is actually happening? I'm sure when they see what a fantastic job I've done styling the day, they are going to want me on board on the team. Don't you think so? There's got to be a chance at least, hasn't there?'

Helen is lifting Dolly's sample gown off its hanger and searching for her tin of pins. 'I have no idea how these things work, Dolly, but the fact they are coming to the wedding has got to be good. Come on, we've got a dress to fit!'

Helen places the silk slip over Dolly's head and watches as it cascades and ripples down her body. Beautiful; as if it was made just for her. She turns Dolly around so she can see the dress from all angles, noticing then that something looks different this time. It's falling almost exactly as it had before except it's pinching a little across her chest. *I must have missed that*, thinks Helen, *before I added the lace cap-sleeve jacket*. Helen's mistakes are so rare that it troubles her greatly when she does make one – usually on the days when dress details are fighting for space in a head still swimming with memories of Phillip. Anyway, the last thing she wants to do is question Dolly's size so she simply makes a note of the adjustments needed and moves on.

Four more brides pass through The White Gallery that afternoon before 6 p.m. when Helen finally turns the pretty lace-edged door sign to closed and turns off the lights. She's shattered but the small, barely noticeable fizz of nervous anticipation in her stomach is powering her on. Helen doesn't want to admit it to herself, won't even allow the thought to fully formulate in her mind, but she is looking forward to going out tonight. She already knows what she's going to wear.

Chapter Fifteen

Dolly

Ten weeks to go

As months go, June is a shitty one. Work is unbearable for Dolly thanks to the choke chain The Dick is keeping on her, continually monitoring her presence in the office of doom. Josh is constantly absent, shooting one perfect woman after another and failing to grasp the fact they've got an aisle to walk in ten weeks. Any intimacy they're sharing amounts to a string of lusty late night sessions, nothing memorable, just getting the job done; retaining some sort of connection. Both are prioritising their personal ambitions beyond the bedroom.

Now Dolly is a ball of knotted tension and nerves about the impending arrival of the *Brides* shoot team at her wedding and as a direct result her budget is careering out of control. She can't help herself. The pressure of knowing the biggest-selling bridal mag is coming to report on every detail of her day means she's added two courses to dinner as well as doubling the choice on the cocktail menu and adding more waiters to serve them. Then, having decided not to serve canapés (£28 a head!) they are now back on. Plus, there's more giant tropical planting and, because she knows it will make an extra shot, a proper tiered wedding cake covered in an explosion of multicoloured graffiti-style icing has been commissioned from a baker who does all the big London film premier parties.

These pictures need to be good. The editor needs to be impressed. Dolly is depending on it.

But for now she is standing in her tiny white bathroom, starkers, and – staring at the pair of dirty boxers Josh left on the floor this morning for her to pick up – wondering what the hell else can go wrong. She steps on to her Fitbit scales and clearly someone has been fucking with them because according to the digital display she has put on six pounds. She quickly runs through her mental checklist. OK, were the scales on zero to start with? She jumps off to check. Yes. Has she had her morning wee – which she knows can add about a pound on a particularly busting morning? Yes, she has. Did she neck a glass of lemon water yet? No. Did she eat late last night? Yes, but it was only a few slices of serrano ham, the only thing left in the fridge that required no cooking. As there's nothing else she can think of, or remove, that's it, she's getting fat. Fatter with every day that passes before the big one. And there is only one fucker to blame for all this. The Dick.

Dolly's mind flicks back to that awful morning when she sprinted into the office, two-and-a-half hours late from her dress appointment, sweat sliding down between her shoulder blades, pooling horribly at the base of her spine where a wet patch fanned out across her pretty peach Self-Portrait blouse. How The Dick had taken great delight in hauling her straight into his office (stopping her just outside and forcing her to read aloud his latest motivational gem: *Everything you've ever wanted is on the other side of fear!*) then gone to town on her so hard that everyone in the room – and probably the adjoining floors – had heard it. Her punishment was simple, but evil. Spend the following month brunching, lunching, and scoffing supper with the agency's most obnoxious clients. Then just to be a total asshole, The Dick had thrown in a list of up-themselves journalists; the ones desperate to escape their own deadline-driven offices and abusive bosses for a three-hour booze-fuelled lunch (especially when she is paying), or to blag cocktails after work that somehow turned in to a 2 a.m. finish and a monster round of buttered toast when Dolly eventually made it home.

Now Dolly is tired. So bloody tired. What she needs is a week on the sofa. What she's facing is another week of corporate entertaining, schmoozing, pretending to like people, looking enthralled by another yawn anecdote, asking questions she has no desire to have answered, brainstorming lame ideas over another plate of rich, butter-soaked food. Then washing it all down with another glass of expensive champagne, and feeling more disinterested with every sip.

The relentless hours and general loathsomeness of the task The Dick has given her means food is the only way to get through it. Sick of pushing stodge around posh plates in wanky restaurants and too exhausted to fight the urge any longer, she has royally broken every rule in her own book. And now she feels disgusting for it; on a self-loathing low. So far removed from her usual controlled grip on everything that passes her lips, she's struggling to see a way back. Too exhausted and time-starved to exercise, she is the walking, talking definition of demotivation. Worse, in the rare daylight moments they have managed to spend together recently, Josh has noticed, saying she'd better increase the sit-ups because she's looking *doughy* around the middle. And now Dolly thinks about it, the dress was a little tight on her last visit to see Helen, wasn't it? Maybe she'll just skip food altogether today – and tomorrow, and redress the balance a little. It wouldn't be the first time. But even as she's thinking it, she knows she won't. What she fancies more than anything else right now is thick white toast, generously cut from an unsliced loaf, made soggy with butter and topped with an obscene amount of crunchy peanut butter.

Dolly flops back on the bed, which is empty of course, Josh having left at the crack of dawn this morning without saying a word, to shoot another story in London. He may as well move there, it would save a fortune on train fares. It's only now that Dolly's eyes fall onto her bedside table, and the blister pack of contraceptive pills that are poking out from under the novel she hasn't picked up for days. Her eyes linger for a moment too long, while her brain tries to catch up with the nagging little doubt nudging its way into her consciousness.

Shit. Her pills. In all the fuss of dresses, The Dick, *Brides*, Josh and this juggernaut of a wedding, has she forgotten to take her pill? She checks the blister pack. No, she hasn't missed one. She's missed *four*. *Shit! How could she be that stupid? Did she miss any last month too? Probably. OK, don't panic.* She's been playing this particular game of roulette for years and got away with it. *Stop being an arse, Dolly; you're not going to be pregnant just because you missed a few pills. The chemicals swim around in your ovaries for months. No one on the pill gets pregnant that easily. Plus, you haven't puked once so you can't be. And any cells that may be thinking of splitting their way to new life will have been drowned in booze. Obliterated before they even got started.*

The logical part of Dolly's brain is completely satisfied that there is nothing to worry about but… there has been *a lot* of sex. Josh's shoot schedule is insane but every time he comes home, he is on her, even some nights when she is already nodding off. And since she's spent most of the past month drunk, it's impossible to pinpoint dates, times or frequency.

She throws on a thick linen robe and heads into the kitchen, really not needing anything else to worry about. She hasn't had a chance to prep any food so tucks into the toast *and* a bowl of Josh's sugary breakfast cereal, the sweetness immediately making her feel better. Then she flicks on BBC breakfast news and slumps on the sofa. It's all so depressing. Hate crimes. Another high-street favourite closing its doors for the last time. Children injured on holiday by faulty fun fair rides. Her mind can't process it all and it begins to wander. *What if she is pregnant?* She imagines it for a moment; the nursery-rhyme version. Milky babies. Soft downy hair. Someone looking up at her with love-filled, devoted, grateful eyes – that bit might be nice. The gorgeous little outfits. The maternity leave! But… Josh as a dad? Parenthood changes some men immeasurably; she knows that from the endless office chat from new mums who return to work with tales of transformed husbands who've happily swapped late nights for chronically early mornings. But Josh?

Dolly's eyes scan the row of plain white, framed photos lining the lounge mantelpiece. Her and Josh skiing; poshed-up at friends' weddings; their first Christmas together; group holidays surrounded by gorgeous friends, all sun-kissed hair, flawless young skin and hysterical grins. Happy memories. A couple with no one to worry about but themselves. Then she thinks about how Josh had declined an invitation to be godparent to a friend's first born last year, telling them he couldn't commit to something with an obvious religious responsibility, while telling *her* the last thing he wanted to do was spend his weekends pretending to be interested in other people's brats. How every time they entered a café or restaurant together he requested a table that was *nowhere near any kids*. At first she put it down to his lack of tolerance for anything that crashed in on the conversation he wanted to have.

Now she's not so sure. If there's an opportunity to avoid kids, he takes it without fail and he's showing no signs of mellowing. On a very surface level it worries Dolly, she's bound to want them one day and then what?

She remembers how the colour had drained from his face, the look of panic and utter fear gripping him after a pregnancy scare last year. How he had physically stepped away from her when she walked into the kitchen, tears rolling down her face, holding the pregnancy test she was about to take. His body language said it all – *your problem*. Then four minutes later, when he knew he was in the clear, he had recalled a conversation with a male friend of theirs shortly after his wife had given birth to their only child. Josh told how the husband had been there for the whole thing *at the business end* and how it was *like watching your favourite pub burn down*. Dolly got the real version from the new mum herself – the relentless pain, hour after hour, the absent anaesthetist, a string of different midwives and changing shift patterns, a once-perfect vagina ripped to bits, literally days spent in agony. Josh howled about that joke for months, telling every man he knew. Repeated it again and again, obviously believing it to be true.

That pregnancy scare. Dolly is pretty sure there were two tests in that packet – and she'd only ever needed one. The other was probably still wedged at the back of her bedside drawer in amongst old pay slips and unopened official-looking brown envelopes. Of course it would be out of date by now. Probably wouldn't work, certainly couldn't be reliable. But… perhaps she should just see if it's there.

It is. The sight of the Clear Blue box with its oddly cheerful pink and blue wording brings back the awful memory of the last time she picked it up. Like someone's just punched her hard in her chest. She can remember the colour of the nail polish she was wearing the day she ripped off the cellophane and scanned the pages of small type advising about when to pee, how many days to wait after your period was due blah blah blah. She hadn't taken it in then and she isn't bothering to read it now. She's remembering how she hated Josh for days after *the scare*, struggling to even look at him until an enormous bunch of red roses arrived at the office. She should have been more grateful but all she could think was *what a predictable cliché*. And what an idiot for landing her with the need for a quick explanation to satisfy all her nosy colleagues. Perhaps if he'd sent her flowers more often it would be less interesting to them all.

OK, let's just confirm that I'm not pregnant this time either, thinks Dolly. *Then I'll write the day off, forget the past month and get focused again on Monday, starting with some serious HIIT sessions.*

Slight problem; she doesn't need a wee. She perches over the loo willing it out of her, imaging that TV ad where the man is surfing the waves in search of the perfect shave... but nothing. She stomps back in to the kitchen, downs three glasses of water and waits. Still nothing coming. A cup of tea. More water. A rank two-day-old smoothie left in the fridge that has separated into an unappetising half water, half sludge mess. Then back to the loo and it's game on: just enough wee to thoroughly wet the fabric tip of the white plastic stick – and most of her fingers.

She watches as the moisture floods the little window with its pink paper backdrop, turning the whole thing a deeper shade. But nothing else, yet. Now what? She leaves the stick on the side of the sink and pads barefoot back in to the lounge, swiping the new issue of *Brides* off the coffee table. It's not long now until Pippa Middleton marries her hedge-fund millionaire and the Ed's letter is devoted to sketches from leading international bridal designers, auditioning for the role of her chief couturier. Dolly looks at the sketches, imagining which would look best encasing that perfectly peachy bottom of hers. There are gorgeous outfit sketches from Jools Oliver for Princess Charlotte and Prince George too. Dolly is thinking about the kind of wedding she might have designed, with Pippa's budget. There is always someone doing it better. Always someone with more contacts, more money, more imagination.

The piss stick! There is a part of Dolly that can't really be arsed to walk back to the bathroom. She knows she's not preggers. But what's the point pissing on the stick if not to know *for sure*? She may as well indulge this game a little longer now she's started. It's her head that makes it through the bathroom door first, not her body. That stays outside. She is on her tiptoes, head tilted sharply upwards, trying to angle herself high enough to sneak a look at it from above. She can see something, something black. What is it? Not lines, which is what she's expecting. What does it mean? She takes one step into the bathroom and lifts her back leg off the floor allowing her to extend much further forward, ballerina-like, arms steadying herself on the door frame. She's above the stick now and can see the result clearly. Just one word blazing back at her.

Pregnant.

Dolly is not proud of her reaction. Not proud of the very first thought that enters her head in the heart-stopping moment just after her eyes bring the word into sharp focus and she stops breathing for a second: *Will* Brides *still want me? Will they want some big pregnant fatty all over the pages of their stylish magazine?* It's irrational and she knows it but it's important, *so* important to her. She puts the loo seat down and perches there, holding the pregnancy test up close right in front of her face. *Clearly this thing is broken.* She's knows it's not. She's thinking, processing it all, trying to plan her way out of it. How many weeks pregnant might she be? *Fuck knows!* How many months would she be on their wedding date? *Too many.* She'll have a belly. Her boobs will be massive. Fat will cling to her. That's what happens to pregnant women, isn't it? Their bodies start to hold on to every calorie they can, readying themselves to sustain and nurture the tiny life forming inside them. She remembers a woman in the office who boldly confessed to everyone one morning she put on two and a half stone with her first baby and three with her second. The youngest is three years old now and still the baby fat won't let go of her. Dolly expected her to be depressed telling this story but no, the nutter is blissfully content because *that's the story my body tells now. That's how I became a mama.*

Sitting in her bathroom alone with her maddening thoughts, Dolly has no clue what she is going to do. But she does know this. She is not walking up that aisle pregnant. Not going to be immortalised forever on the pages of *Brides* with a stretchmark stained beast of a belly sticking out the front of her. No way.

It's some time later when she is back on the sofa, gazing at herself and wondering what might be going on in there, that another thought finally crosses her mind. What the hell will Josh think?

Chapter Sixteen

Emily

'I've decided they mustn't know. You won't change my mind.'

Emily is sitting opposite a stunned Sarah Blake, trying to make her understand that sharing this news with her family is the last thing that needs to happen.

'They are your parents, Emily, they will want to know, they will want to help you through this. I've known your mum for more than twenty-seven years and please believe me when I say that it will hurt her more *not* to know.' Dr Blake is visibly upset. She's lost all of the cool, emotionless doctor façade, *again*. In an almost funny way, she's handling this whole thing worse than Emily is. She's going to blub again, Emily can see it coming. Should she just tell her to pull herself together?

'What do you think that sort of news will do to them, Sarah? It will destroy them. I'm their only child! I can't do it to them. I *won't* do it to them.'

'Well, then at least tell Mark.'

'I can't! There is every chance *he* will tell them. There's nothing anyone can do about this. And it could all be OK, you know. Have you forgotten that? I'm not dead yet!'

'Don't you think this is going to be a huge burden for you to carry, with no one else knowing what you're dealing with?' Sarah's eyes have completely glassed over. She is leaning on her elbows across her desk, pleading with Emily but the battle is already lost.

'Yes, it is and don't think I haven't spent hours silently screaming at my bedroom ceiling, I have. All of this is so bloody unfair. It shouldn't be happening to me, not now, not when I'm about to marry the man I love more than anything in the world…' She has to stop herself now, change tack before the walls come down, releasing every bit of emotion that she's caged up inside herself.

'But I'm not keeping it to myself, am I? *You* know. You're the one person who can actually help me. You can give me medical advice, make appointments, help me decide what to do when the Americans come back with their verdict. That's all helpful.' Emily's voice cracks. 'I don't want to see their sad faces. They are having the time of their lives planning this wedding and I'm not going to take that away from them. In fact, I've decided to bring the wedding date forward. You know, just in case.'

Emily stands to leave and watches Sarah crumple over her desk, shoulders sinking, head dipping, knowing she is defeated. She feels like giving her a hug but doesn't want to prolong this conversation for a moment longer, inviting more appeals to come clean.

'I *will* be all right. I'm strong. I feel OK, for now at least. Please Sarah, respect my wishes on this. I am right, it's for the best.'

As she pulls the door closed behind her, Emily hears Sarah let out a long, breathy sigh, and feels *almost* convinced that as her long-standing doctor and close family friend, Sarah will do as she has been asked.

❧

OK, what to do? Emily needs to pull some masterstrokes to get this wedding where it now needs to be. Her objectives have changed. Get married as quickly – and cheaply – as possible. Very far from your typical bride now. There's no time to wallow in it, that's going to get her nowhere. Drowning in a pool of self-pity won't help anyone. No, she's facing the fact that life might not be building to everyone's pre-planned happy-ever-after ending for her. And so what can she do now to protect them all, to ensure the dark days to come might be tinged with a little lightness for her beautiful family?

Sitting on her bed, she can hear her parents and Mark downstairs, laughing. Emily has just asked Mark to choose everything he wants on the John Lewis wedding gift list. She isn't going to select a thing. When he looked disappointed that she wasn't bothering to join in – in the one job most brides can't wait to get their hands on, spending other peoples' money – she said there was something more pressing that needed her attention upstairs. It's the closest they've come to having a row in months.

'Oh come on, you can't expect me to shoulder the responsibility of choosing *everything*. What if you hate it all?' It was hardly his fault but Mark's whinging made Emily snap back, 'Just do it, will you please? It's not hard!' before she huffed up the stairs, feeling all their surprised eyes boring in to the back of her.

Now she's left her dad and Mark huddled over the laptop together at the dining table and she can hear her dad advising him on the best BBQ, questioning his choice of tongs and insisting he adds two rain covers because *once that thing starts to rust, you've had it*. This is proper husband-to-be and future father-in-law bonding; dad advising, Mark learning from the master, it's making Emily feel more than ever that this is the right thing to do. What if she'd broken the real news this morning? What would be happening now? They'd all be sitting around, weeping over her scan pictures, squeezing her, telling her everything is going to be OK. Well, it might be and it might not be, so it is down to her to help them all, should the worst happen.

Emily picks up a smart, white Smythson notebook from her bedroom bookshelf. It has the words *Tying The Knot* embossed on the front in shiny gold lettering, a gift from Mark when they first got engaged. She thought it was too nice to fill with inky scribbles – and besides, Dad was taking enough notes for everyone, photocopying them and handing them out at every Sunday Summit. Now it has a real purpose. She opens it to the first page and writes: *Wedding #2* then starts to note down the new action plan, point by point. There is something in the cool, methodical manner she is setting this out that is strangely comforting in a practical I've-finished-all-my-homework way. It doesn't feel morbid, it feels useful and sensible – something she can be entirely in control of. There's more of her dad in her than Emily cares to admit. She's already ticked off the dress swap and getting Mark to choose everything he loves on the gift list. Slowing down the house purchase and delaying booking the honeymoon will be harder but she's determined, she'll find a way. She needs to simplify everything. It's not long until several pages of the book are filled with her all-new important to-do list.

Emily taps out a quick email to the vicar. Are there any other available dates he can marry them, preferably soon? The sooner the better. She scans the calendar page on her phone. The wedding date is currently two months off. Too far. There are birthdays, nursery open days at work and business trip dates for Mark to avoid but one Saturday looks clear. It's in two weeks' time. July 14th. Can it be done? There's no expensive bespoke dress to wait for, they are hosting the reception at home, dad is well ahead of the game with the organising.

It's just the catering which Glo would make work somehow and the guest list; could everyone make it? She may have to accept that some confirmed friends will be forced to cancel, but it's a risk worth taking. She hits send on the email.

OK, this is not a bad start, although number four on the plan is controversial. *Make Sally chief bridesmaid.* Emily allows herself a small smile as she realises the one job *not* on dad's agenda and left entirely to her isn't finished yet.

She knows Sally has a huge Mark-shaped hole in her heart – but that's the point. They've all been friends for years, since those early days at university when Emily noticed the way she looked at him. It's not lost on her how a beauty like Sally never committed to a man for more than a few months. She guessed long ago it was because no one matched up to Mark. There had been a night out years ago when Sally had said as much. She'd had one too many glasses of wine and cried on Emily's shoulder about the state of her love life. The conversation should have stopped there but Sally, loosened by the alcohol, had gone on, telling Emily that every time she looked at Mark she could see what she was missing, how much she envied Emily. But there is nothing sinister about Sally, Emily knows that. She just loves everything about Mark, in the same way Emily does, she can hardly blame her for that. His warm nature, his old-school manners, his ability to see the positive in everything (*that might seriously be put to the test soon*) and his boyish, clean-cut good looks. The two of them would look good together. His foppish blonde locks, her sleek golden bob. His broad shoulders, her girly cheerleader bounce. How perfect he looks in a casual white shirt, the easy way she makes a pair of Gap jeans look cool.

She watched Sally once, gazing at Mark, enthralled by him. They were sat in the laughter-filled beer garden of their favourite local pub. It was a scorching July day and the landlord had organised an impromptu BBQ. Hidden behind her sunglasses and slightly set back from the group of friends, Emily quietly observed how Sally hung off every word Mark was saying, not taking her eyes off him for a moment. It was like no one else was there. A blissfully unaware Mark noticed her glass was empty and offered to get her another drink, causing Sally to practically melt on the spot. Emily didn't say a word about it to either of them. What was the point? What would it achieve? A truck load of awkwardness and not much else. Emily knows giving her this role will put her in Mark's path more over the coming weeks. He'll be reminded of quite how lovely she is – and pretty. He might need a soft female shoulder to cry on and Sally would care for him a great deal, Emily is sure of that.

Under normal circumstances, she would arrange to meet Sally, ask her in person, buy her lunch and make her feel special. But today Emily reluctantly settles for a quick phone call.

'Sally! It's Emily, how are you?'

'Hi Emily, I'm great, thanks. Just up to my eyeballs in work but otherwise all good. How are all the plans going?'

'I'm glad you ask because that's why I am calling.'

'OK… you're not about to ask me to supervise the kids table, are you?'

'Far from it! I'm calling to ask you to be my chief bridesmaid. What d'you think?'

A silence that is ever so slightly too long stretches down the line before Sally responds. Emily can imagine the quick internal trauma she's experiencing. Can you be chief maid to one of your oldest friends when you have been in love with her husband-to-be for years? Fortunately yes, you can.

'Wow, Emily, I am completely honoured to be asked and I would of course love to, thank you.'

'Great. I'm so sorry not to ask you in person but everything has been so manic and I just never got around to making a date to see you. And speaking of dates, we're so far ahead with the planning that we're probably going to pull the wedding forward to July 14th. I hope that's OK?'

'Oh, right. Um… yes, I'm free. But that's just two weeks' time, right? Soon! I'll barely have time to organise anything for you. Any reason why you…'

Emily breaks her off.

'Wonderful! I know Mark will also be thrilled to have you more involved in the day.' She pictures the broad grin that she knows will be spreading across Sally's face right now at the mere mention of Mark's name.

'That's so kind of you both, thank you.'

'OK, let's catch up asap then and I'll fill you in on all the details. I've already spotted a great dress of you.'

'Perfect. Thank you, Emily. See you then.'

Another tick. Then another ping, a response from the vicar. The earlier date is free but she needs to confirm it immediately as another couple have asked about it. *Give me ten minutes and I'll be back to you.* Emily bashes out the words, then sits back heavily on her bed for a moment, wondering how on earth she can sell this idea to her parents *and* Mark, who are all downstairs believing they have months to nail all the final arrangements.

It's a good time to tackle it. She is leaving the house in fifteen minutes to see Helen at The White Gallery. One final try-on of the gown and then she'll be walking out the door with it. But first, *this*.

She closes the little white book, replacing it on the bookshelf and starts to walk slowly down the stairs. What should she say? How can she convince them? In fifteen minutes? *Do not cry, do not cry. This has to be casual.* She's slowing down, stalling for time, her mind racing through some options, none of them even vaguely convincing.

As Emily enters the dining room Mark and her dad are just closing the laptop.

'Job done!' bellows Bill. 'And a very good thing I was involved with that, let me tell you. When it comes to barbecuing, I am the expert, as we all know!'

'Thank you Dad, I really appreciate it. But don't tell me anything else, I'd like all the presents to be a surprise when I open them.' What Emily means is, *I don't want to be tempted to change anything.* 'So, good news. I have just asked Sally to be my chief bridesmaid and she has agreed.' Emily's eyes dart to Mark to catch his reaction. And there it is, the warmest of smiles and the words *great choice* escaping his perfect pink lips. 'And I was thinking, we are doing really well with the wedding plans, aren't we?'

'I should say so! I've got a few pointers to run through with you both later but I feel very confident that in the time we have, we are well and truly on target for a beautiful day. Wouldn't you agree Glo?' Bill is typically full of it.

'Absolutely! Why? Is there something you're worried about, Emily?' Nothing gets past Glo.

Mark is looking at her now, immediately concerned that something is troubling her. They're *all* looking at her. *OK, here we go.* She feels light-headed. *Keep it casual, keep it casual.*

'Nope. What I was wondering is, why are we dragging this out? If we're ready, let's get married sooner.' She's trying her best to look nonchalant, like the words have just slipped out without much consideration, with no deeper meaning at all. She picks up an apple from the fruit bowl and takes a large bite out of it, trying to prove this is no big deal.

'Sorry, *what?*' Bill is not understanding the question at all.

Emily ignores him for a moment and directs her attention to Mark. She needs to get him on side, quick.

'What d'you think Mark, shall we?'

'Hang on a second.' He's standing now, stepping towards her, one hand on his hip, the other rubbing his forehead in concern. 'What's going on here? First you're showing no interest in the gift list and now you want to pull the date forward? I'll happily marry you any day of the week, any time of the year, Emily, you know that. But, is there something else I should know about?' All Mark's usual optimism has been suffocated by her suggestion, she should have known this wouldn't be straightforward. If she doesn't nail this now she'll have to stage a huge climb-down just to halt his questions before Mum and Dad start flapping too.

'I love you Mark, I've always loved you. I don't want to wait a second longer than I have to, that's all.' Her voice is timid and loaded with emotion. 'Sorry, I thought you'd be pleased about the idea.' OK, this is more than a little embarrassing – the verbal equivalent of having a dirty big snog in front of your parents especially as she can see Glo going all gooey out the corner of her eye.

'No, it's me who should be sorry, it's a lovely idea. You're lovely.' He can see her discomfort and wants to end it immediately. 'And I'm an idiot. But are we ready? Isn't there a lot more to do? Don't we all want a bit more time to cover everything, not rush it?'

'I don't think so. The invitations haven't gone out yet so that's not a problem and what is there left to organise other than our honeymoon, which we can easily sort? Mum, do you think the catering can be done in time?'

There is an odd, almost knowing look on Glo's face that is slightly unnerving. What is she thinking? *What does she think she knows?* wonders Emily.

'Consider it done! Depending on how much earlier we're talking, we may have to make some slight changes for seasonality – you're not going to get fresh figs in mid-July – but otherwise, I can do it, of course, if it's what you want. My outfit was sorted months ago, so you've got no complaints from me.'

Which just leaves Dad – and he's not about to play ball.

'I'm sorry, has everyone lost control of their senses? The planting! The rose bushes aren't even in the ground yet and I wanted to get all that moss off the front path and re-turf the bit of lawn there. And the church is booked, for crying out loud!'

'Actually Dad, I have checked and there is an earlier date available – in a couple of weeks' time.' It's three against one now, Emily is feeling reasonably confident this will go her way.

'Sorry, but this is ridiculous! I've got an arch-lever file full to bursting with itineraries, spreadsheets, plans and counter-plans all working towards August 25th and now you're telling us we've got two weeks!'

'Bill! A word if I may, please?' Glo has him by the elbow now and is directing him sharply into the kitchen, closing the door behind them but not before Mark and Emily both overhear the start of his scolding.

'Bill! For goodness sake, isn't it obvious? Why does anyone pull a wedding date forward?'

'OK, you know your mum is in there telling your dad you're pregnant, don't you?' Mark has pulled Emily into a bear hug and is trying unsuccessfully to contain his giggles. 'Just to be clear, you're not... are you?'

'No! Of course not. That's just Glo getting ahead of herself as usual. She'll be off to town this afternoon to pick up the Mothercare catalogue, I bet you.'

'Oh God, really? Well, just so you know it would have been wonderful. I would have been delighted if you were pregnant, I mean. Maybe we shouldn't wait too long for that either?' His face is so full of excitement, if she lowered her head a little closer into his chest she could probably hear his heart pounding out his love for her. Emily's face starts to crumple slightly, knowing what he's imagining may never come to be, then she is distracted as a fully chastised Bill and a jubilant Glo step back into the dining room. Bill's eyes immediately fall to Emily's belly before he snaps them away again.

'Sorry if I seemed a little unreasonable then, of course we can make this happen in time for you, honey. Let's get a meeting in with everyone in the next couple of days shall we, and go over everything that still needs to be organised. I love you and we will make it happen for you, I promise, whatever it takes.'

Emily needs to get out of there.

'Thank you so much, everyone. Must dash anyway, I'm off for an appointment with Helen at The White Gallery and I need to confirm the new date with the vicar. I'll see you all later.' Emily belts out of the front door, hot tears starting to fall down her face before she even reaches the front garden gate. She completely misses Sarah Blake sat a little way up the road, slumped low in the driver's seat of her black BMW. She looks exhausted, on the edge even, but that's probably because she's been beating herself up over the meaning of doctor patient confidentiality, wondering whether for the first time in her long successful medical career she is about to break it.

Emily also misses Glo bounding out of the house two minutes later, her face alight with happiness as she is intercepted by a neighbour jogging across the road to join her. The two of them exchange a few quick words then start to walk away together arm in arm, forcing Sarah to restart the engine and drive off in the opposite direction. She's missed her chance and Emily has got her way.

Now the two of them will have to deal with the consequences, whatever they may be.

Chapter Seventeen

Jessie

Jessie is staring at Adam, hoping the words that are falling so easily out of his grinning mouth cannot possibly be right.

'You *can't* have done that, Adam. You haven't had time. And you would have spoken to me first. I *know* you would.' She's saying it through a pinched smile that's more of a terrified grimace. The fear is creeping up inside her, washing up over her chest and running down her arms like a cold shower. It's pure panic and she needs to contain it.

'Not this time, darling! It's all organised. I could hardly fly off to Miami with the boys knowing you haven't organised a hen do for yourself, could I? That wouldn't be fair so I put the best woman on the job. Tilly was only too happy to help.'

'I wasn't going to have one, Adam!' *OMG I can't actually cope with this.*

'I know you weren't. That's the point!' His grin is widening, the look of a man who is sensationally pleased with himself, which is only making Jessie's blood boil faster.

'Who have you and Tilly invited?' *He surely wouldn't have…*

'All the obvious choices: your mum, Lady C, your sister, Annabel—'

Jessie doesn't hear anything after that, only the sound of her heart banging against the wall of her chest, drowning out all his words.

She knows she's been had – and by the one person she cares about most in this world. Adam knows damn well she would never organise a hen do and she's pretty sure he knows exactly why too. This is his way of *nudging* her in the right direction, encouraging her to face down her demons, make new friends, accept – and my God maybe even *enjoy* – bringing their two families together. That was the cheery version taking shape in Adam's head anyway. What is now going on in hers is a very different story, one she can't see a happy ending to. How could it be – when it would involve having Claire and Annabel in the same room together? Her mum and Camilla? The unspoken judgements that would hang over the evening like a big toxic cloud, slowing poisoning them all against each other.

And all that hard work of hers, manufacturing the image she wants people to see, the back story she wants them to hear, is now all unravelling in a quick series of phone calls and covert plotting. Is Adam just choosing to ignore the sweep of embarrassment that crosses her face every time she's forced to admit what her dad did for a living or the name of the area she grew up in to someone who knows what the answer means? They'd seen her family only a couple of weeks ago and not one of them mentioned this hen do. Sworn to secrecy, no doubt. What would Tilly have made of them during her calls to make the arrangements? It's a grim thought.

'When is it, Adam? When is this hen-do *supposed* to be happening?' Her voice is controlled, measured, unlike the volcanic stress erupting inside of her. Maybe there would still be time to get out of this.

'Oh, it's happening! It's at Claridge's, *tonight*. Everyone will meet you there. It's all arranged. I've organised cars for your family to get them there and back, a private room for you all – cocktails, canapés and as much champagne as twenty women can drink in one evening. Then you'll be staying in one of their top suites for the night so you can have a fabulous time without the hassle of getting home. Tilly says everyone is really looking forward to it!'

Well, she's got that wrong. Jessie knows she should be slapping an enormous smile on her face about now but she can't. How could any sane person find the prospect of tonight anything other than utterly hateful? But there's clearly no stopping it so Jessie does the only thing she can, she wraps her arms around Adam, thanks him as profusely as she can manage then huffs up the stairs of their immaculate townhouse to pack – in the sort of strop her sixteen-year-old self would have been proud of.

As she is leaving the house an hour later, on the doomed journey to London, Adam stops her at the door. He places a firm hand on each of her shoulders, rooting her to the spot before he plants one tender kiss on her lips.

'Don't think I don't know this terrifies you, Jessie. I'm not stupid. But people are nicer than you think, you need to realise that. Have fun. Go on, I dare you!'

Jessie's driver pulls up on Mayfair's Brook Street directly outside the front entrance of Claridge's, taking his place in a long line of slick black Mercedes. She's planning to sit there for a moment, gather her thoughts, one last pep talk before she goes over enemy lines. But a doorman in an immaculate top hat and grey tails is pulling open the back passenger door, making eye contact and extending a hand to help her out. She swings two perfectly smooth legs out on to the pavement, christening her new gold sequin Dior heels that both hit the pavement at exactly the same time, followed by the hem of her Carolina Herrera black silk chiffon dress. She glides through the revolving glass doors and into the famous 1920s art deco lobby with its soaring mirrored fireplaces and black and white checkerboard marble floor, pausing briefly to check in before she makes her way up to her suite.

Adam has chosen well. The Diane Von Furstenberg Piano Suite is ordered, calm and elegant – everything Jessie is not feeling right now. More an apartment than a room, the reception area is dominated by a grand piano and full of carefully placed animal prints, oversized Chinese florals and an actual cocktail bar. Everything is dark chocolate and ivory coloured with touches of deep purples and lilacs. Adam has ordered a bottle of Laurent Perrier Rosé, on ice, with one glass next to it and a handwritten note saying 'Be good!'. Jessie pops the cork, pours a glass and promptly drains it before refilling it. Tonight is going to be painful. The fizz might just get it somewhere close to bearable.

7.10 p.m. She should be downstairs now. They will all be there waiting for her but the thought of leaving the suite is agonising. She wants to crawl into that giant bleached oak four poster bed, pull the DvF cashmere blanket up over her head and stay there until the last Lalique glass of champagne has been drunk. But she needs to get down there and assess any damage Claire and her mother may have already caused. She also needs to make friends and this is the perfect opportunity if she can summon the confidence to do it. All of Adam's circle are here tonight, there is no better time to embrace them – and hope they will embrace her back.

She leaves the butler to unpack her case – a perk of booking one of the best suites in the hotel – and takes the lift to the ground level, passing under the original 1920s crystal chandelier, past the gently curving Victorian staircase, getting swept up in the grand theatrical feel of the place. She's heading for the Fumoir bar that Adam has booked exclusively for them tonight.

The calm elegance of this grand dame of a hotel is suddenly shattered by the sight of Claire across the lobby – in the orange dress. As if the vision of her enormous body squeezed into the sartorial sausage skin isn't embarrassing enough, she has accessorised it with an *actual* hot pink feather boa. It's enough to freeze Jessie on the spot. Why Claridge's can't just throw her out is her only thought – hope – really. Jessie notices her sister's manly fist clamped around a champagne coupe, behaving for all the world like she is entirely at home, just another average night at Claridge's. Not in the slightest bit registering that she looks like a kissogram who took a wrong turn and should be in the boozer around the corner being laughed at by a stag do. Her mother, by comparison, is all C&A circa 1983 – wearing a pale mint green trouser suit that's cut all wrong so the legs come up unflatteringly short above the ankles and the well-worn material sags around her bottom.

Camilla is perched at the marble horseshoe bar making witty conversation with a wolfish Italian bartender who is mixing her a cocktail, when he can take his eyes off her long enough to get the job done. Her rich caramel coloured Max Mara trousers are sitting high on her waist, revealing what all that horse riding is doing for her remarkable figure. A soft cream silk blouse, rose gold cuff and Jill Sander leather loafers complete the louche tailoring look, working perfectly in her elegant surroundings.

Jessie can see from the drink in her mother's hand that she's already ordered her usual red wine and lemonade – at least she was spared witnessing that. She can only imagine what the same barman who is now kissing the back of Camilla's hand would make of it. Everything about her mum is awkward and out of place, while the glossy gaggle of expertly put-together young women filling the room is all long, tanned limbs and expensive balayage highlights. They're all chatting over each other about things Margaret knows nothing about – fashion, property, travel and people. In an act of social self-defence, she's backed herself into a corner and now looks like she's waiting for everyone to leave so she can clear the tables. *Probably the best place for her*, thinks Jessie, *until this is all over.*

Everywhere Jessie looks, expensive embellished clutch bags are dangling from delicate wrists, catching the light from the table-top crystal lamps while at ground level, vertiginous spike heels in snake skin, blush suede and metallic studs are competing with each other. By the looks of it, every one of these women – with the two obvious exceptions – have spent the cost of a good meal out on a professional blow dry. Too fabulous or busy to wash their own hair, they've had their shiny locks teased out over crystal earrings, swept back to reveal long slender necks and Tom Ford highlighted décolletages. Not one split end among the lot of them. Fur-trimmed jackets are tossed over velvet aubergine-coloured bucket chairs like their owners don't care if they're there at the end of the night, and it's all fizzy chitchat. A gorgeous waiter is circulating the room with canapés that no one is eating – not even Claire, who seems to prefer the silver finger dish of nuts on the glass-topped table she has bagged for herself.

'Here she comes, our guest of honour!' Tilly has spotted Jessie and is making a beeline. Margaret's face suddenly looks relieved, her daughter finally here to save her. She won't have to spend the rest of the evening shuffling from one foot to the other, staring into her glass, wondering what to do with herself. Jessie can see she is excitedly reaching into her handbag, trying to pull something out before Jessie joins the group…

what *is* that? As Margaret digs deeper into her grey shopper, Jessie starts to make out the words on the foil sash: *Jessie's Chicks on Tour!* Christ, she's gone to the effort of having it personalised so Jessie can stand in one of the most historically beautiful bars in London looking like she should be sucking cheap cocktails through a cock-shaped straw in a nasty chain wine bar. She holds stern eye contact with her mum, not allowing the slightest hint of a smile to pass her lips, shaking her head slowly back and forth until she can see Margaret start to push the cheap tat apologetically back into her bag.

Jessie is swept up into a cloud of expensive perfume and excited hellos.

'Isn't this just hilarious!' squeals Tilly. 'Adam is such a clever bugger, you never suspected a thing, did you?'

'I certainly didn't, no,' Jessie is trying to look relaxed while scanning the room.

'I'm sure you'll recognise everyone,' continues Tilly, flying through the introductions. 'Carine and Pandora were both at school with Adam. Amber works with him, and Anya and Delphine have known him since university. They all did the ski seasons together so if you're after all the dirt, they'll know it! And Annabel you'll remember from the Beaufort hunt. Of course! You two must have talked, she works in the editor's office at *Brides* and they're covering your wedding. Why wouldn't they be!'

'Yes, that's right,' Jessie says through a weak smile. Annabel says precisely nothing, not deeming Jessie worthy of actual words, apparently.

Tilly quickly moves Jessie on around the room and as they leave Annabel she whispers into Jessie's ear, 'You know it's eating her alive that you're marrying Adam, don't you? My advice? Be as nice as you can bring yourself to be. She's as stuck up as they come, can usually be found drowning in a pool of herself. But you've got the one thing she wants that she can't have, Jessie. You've done us all an enormous favour actually, putting her back in her box, temporarily at least!'

Thank God for Tilly. The one person so far who seems even vaguely human to Jessie, the one who has gone out of her way to be helpful. No wonder Adam has so much time for her. She's going to be useful, Jessie needs to keep her close, not least because Camilla has told her to. The fact that she's had to deal with Jessie's family to organise tonight – and is still talking to Jessie – is something of a major surprise.

As for Annabel, on the few occasions they have been in each other's company, Jessie has noticed the way she stares at her, visually picking her apart, unable to work out why Adam could possibly choose Jessie over her. Everything else has come Annabel's way in life, why not him? As Jessie passes behind her now she hears her sneer into the ear of the woman stood next to her, 'Who *is* that?' She's looking directly at Jessie's mum still languishing alone in the corner.

'I don't know but I can feel the static electricity off those polyester trousers from all the way over here!' The two women erupt into a fit of snorty giggles.

Jessie knows she should defend her mum, should turn on the spot and embarrass the two of them. But she's too embarrassed herself and besides, Camilla is waving at her now from the bar. She pretends she hasn't heard the insult and starts to work her way across the room to Camilla, collecting kisses on the way from women she barely knows, one eye trained on her mother who looks deeply uncomfortable.

As she is about to reach Adam's mum, Claire grabs her roughly by the arm.

'I know you've got a lot of people to say hello to, Jess, but Mum is all on her own over there waiting for you.'

'I'm saying hi to Adam's mum first and then I'll be there. Can't you look after her, Claire? *Great* dress by the way.' Jessie can't help herself and the sneer attached to the put-down is vicious.

Claire stands there for a moment, clearly trying to work out what she did to deserve that, fury starting to fill her face.

'Don't be a bitch, Jess,' she snaps. 'I'd say it doesn't suit you but actually we can all see it does.'

'Seriously, Claire, do you really think that outfit is appropriate for tonight?' The exasperation of months of worry, exhausting herself trying to pre-empt and stage manage the moment her family would have to mix with Adam's, is suddenly weighing very heavy on her. 'Look where you are, Claire. Look around you. Do you see anyone else dressed like a barmaid?'

'You total cow! We're all here for you, you know. Because it's your special time apparently. And that's how you treat me?' The actual insult surely isn't what hurts, Claire's collected a few in her time. It's Jessie's superior attitude that will be killing her.

'Have you got anything else you can put on, Claire. *Anything* less trashy?' Jessie is well over the line now, no way back but Claire is not about to be bullied into submission.

'You don't fool me, Jess. I can see how hard you're working to impress all these people you barely know. How you've changed the way you look, the way you sound – you're so desperate to fit in, aren't you? But you're not one of them, Jess. It doesn't matter how rich you are, you never will be. You do know that, don't you? That none of them would give you a second look if you weren't marrying Adam.'

'Fuck you, Claire!'

'What on earth is going on here?' Margaret is at their side now, trying to stop the two of them ruining the night.

'Apparently, I look awful and need to change,' spits Claire.

'Says who?' Margaret's face is full of hurt and confusion.

'Says me! Look at her, Mum, it's bloody embarrassing.' Despite her best efforts to contain her rage, the volume of Jessie's complaints is climbing too high and heads are starting to turn their way.

'Let's just leave it, shall we, girls? We're all here to have a good time and I don't want a little spat ruining everything. Come on.' Margaret has a hand placed on each daughter's shoulder, trying to take the sting out of their anger.

'She needs to change!' Having gone this far, Jessie can't relent now, not until she gets the result she needs.

'*Leave it*, Jessica.' Margaret's legendary patience is starting to wear.

'Why should I? Look at the state of her.' Even as the words are spilling out of her, Jessie knows she will regret them later.

Something switches in Margaret's face. Any sympathy she may be feeling for Jessica is evaporating swiftly. She is not about to stand by and watch her daughters attack each other.

'Jessica, you cannot control everything around you, I'm afraid. You can't dictate what people wear. How would you feel if this was Adam telling *you* what to put on?'

'Well he doesn't need to, does he, because unlike Claire I have some taste and… and I'm not the size of a small family car!'

'No, you're not but you *are* a stuck up bitch who thinks she's better than everyone else. And I'd rather be a little heavy than—'

'Are you kidding me?'

'That's enough!' Margaret's raised voice has caused the women next to them to stop chatting and openly stare. 'I'm not going to stand here and listen to you both like this. I've been waiting in that corner for nearly forty minutes, Jessica, for you to come and say hello to me. Hoping you would introduce me to Adam's mum and some of your other friends. And you haven't. So, I'm guessing I'm embarrassing you too and if that's the case, I think I would rather just leave.' The last three words are pushed out through tears as Margaret bows her head and makes for the exit.

'Find another fucking bridesmaid, Jess. Perhaps one of the skinny bitches who are looking at you right now, wondering who this total low life is that's been forced on them.'

Jess watches the two of them leave, Claire's arse coming dangerously close to knocking over a table of drinks on its way out.

She glances over at Camilla, who has watched the whole sorry situation unfold and is now trying to pretend she hasn't. She spins back round to enjoy her barman, the whole thing apparently entirely beneath her.

Desperate for someone to blame but herself and noticing the look of pure joy spreading out across Annabel's polished face as her eyes dance between Jessie and Camilla, Jessie heads straight for her.

'I know Adam has told you that *Brides* can cover our wedding in the next issue Annabel…' She's close now, invading Annabel's personal space, causing her to pull back slightly.

'Er, yes. We agreed it months ago, the pages are all planned. *Adam* is very happy with them.' Even now she can't contain the vile smirk.

'Well, I'm afraid I'm not,' snaps back Jessie. 'I don't want our wedding featured, so I'm afraid you'll need to find a replacement.' The sense of superiority is catching and a sarcastic sneer is pitched all over Jessie's face, just as Annabel's is caving in on itself.

Killer blow delivered, Jessie snatches a drink from a nearby table, downs it in one and heads for the bar already wondering how she will explain to Adam how his beautifully planned evening for her has unravelled so quickly.

Chapter Eighteen

Helen

'I am but waiting for you. For an interval. Somewhere. Very near. Just around the corner.'

Helen has re-read those lines a hundred times this evening. Phillip hadn't chosen to leave her. And when he knew the end was close, he made it clear to her through these words that he would never leave her. So what was she doing now, pulling all her best dresses out of the wardrobe and trying to make herself look attractive for *another man*?

The words that have provided so much comfort to Helen for so long are now holding her back. Was this Phillip's way of saying he didn't want her to find happiness in someone else's arms – because he is still with her? But how can that be? Certainly in the visits she makes to her memories every day and the stabbing daily reminders of his gestures and mannerisms. But now, standing alone in her bedroom, her wedding dress still looming large in the background, Helen is questioning his motives. What *was* he expecting of her?

As she pushes dress after dress along the metal rail in her closet with all the speed and focus of a determined sales shopper, discounting every one as she goes, Helen is transported back to that awful Sunday afternoon. When she sat next to him on the bed for hours, too afraid to leave even for a moment, in case he slipped away. The day was bright but she was forced to close the curtains as the sun streamed in and made Phillip squint and twist his head uncomfortably. Helen smoothed his forehead, gently sweeping his hair off his face with her fingertips, softly kissing his cheek and the back of his hand, knowing it might be the last time she would feel his warm skin beneath her lips. A whole lifetime of love flowing out of her and into him.

She read the newspaper to him – avoiding the six pages on the death of his favourite singer Whitney Houston – and updated him on neighbourly news. Then she folded the paper neatly, placed it on the floor and held his hand until it went cold in hers, a final loving act for his wife and dedicated nurse. She hugged him afterwards, taking one of his arms and placing it across her. It didn't feel like a strange thing to do at the time. It felt like an intimate moment together, just the two of them before phone calls were made and the room filled with the coroner and Phillip's GP. Before she forced open the bedroom windows in a panic, unable to bear the presence of death that was engulfing her.

And now here she is, a tear-stained mess and Roger is arriving in half an hour. She isn't dressed. She isn't mentally ready for her first date. She's cursing herself for not just arranging to meet him somewhere, then at least she would have the option of not turning up. As it is, he's going to arrive on her doorstep, all triumphant, and she's going to have to stand there in her bra and knickers, shouting at him through the letterbox to go away.

OK, let's just at least decide what to wear, the rest will hopefully follow, one way or another, thinks Helen. She thought she had the perfect outfit – a beautiful deep-rose-coloured dress with a simple seam detail and a smart asymmetric collar. But now she's remembering how she wore that dress to a close friend's birthday party with Phillip and how the two of them had laughed all night as he'd spun her around the dance floor to an endless stream of Duran Duran – the pair of them thinking they looked so much cooler than they did. She's also rejecting Phillip's favourite dress – a slightly seventies number with its graphic floral print and subtle splits at the hem – the dress of a thousand different dates with Phillip. She can see them now, on a spontaneous weekend to the Cornish coast, sat on the beach until the sun stretched its deep pink arms across the sky and Phillip had wrapped his around Helen.

Everything she owns is heavy with the memory of him, but eventually she settles on a comfortable deep-blue velvet dress with button-sleeves and a high neck. It's elegant, not suggestive. Tailored but not tight. Simple rather than smart.

What would Phillip think if he could see her now? Would he be pleased for her, she wonders? *Jealous? Heartbroken?* On the advice of dear friends, Helen had briefly put herself out there after Phillip's death, before she sold the family home in Bristol and bought the business in the Cotswolds. But on the few times she did venture out, those friends looked just as uncomfortable as she felt with the empty chair next to her, no one to naturally fill it. She was no longer one half of a whole and no one knew what to do about that – least of all her. So, she diligently worked her way through all the stages of grief from denial to anger and depression.

On someone else's well-meaning advice she finished every day for months writing down 'three things I did well today', even if all that amounted to was 'I washed my hair' or 'I made a sandwich' just to help her find some comfort in the mundane and the routine. Helen read every article she could find on how to make herself *emotionally available* – capable of trusting again – to decide whether she was suffering from *analysis paralysis* and too busy fearing another loss to truly move on. She has passed through that mix of sorrow and anger at all the loose ends Phillip left behind. Their loose ends, frayed and exposed, had once found completion in each other. Without him, Helen's had nowhere to go.

But Helen's clever; she's done the homework, passed the theory test. Now it's time for the real thing and she knows it. If she's honest with herself about tonight, it comes down to one simple truth. She's scared. Scared Roger will think she's dull, the conversation will dry up or she'll get emotional. Because *Good Housekeeping* can teach you many things but not how to be a great date when you're terrified inside.

The doorbell sounds, sending Helen's stomach lurching upwards as a hundred butterflies collide with each other. *Once you allow your heart to be cracked open again, you never know what's going to happen,* she thinks, as her hand settles on the door handle, and right now she would trade anything to be free of the loneliness.

When she opens the door, Roger is there in a smart business suit and tie, beaming from ear to ear and holding a single red rose. Helen cringes at the formality of it all, seeing immediately how seriously he's taking this date. She is hoping for a casual supper in the pub, something that would at least look like no big deal, but judging by the way Roger is kissing the back of her hand and telling her she looks beautiful, it's going to be anything but.

'I've booked a fantastic table at Sotheby's, only the best for you Helen.' Roger winks at her, face full of expectation, waiting for Helen to look impressed. But she knows the restaurant, has heard clients moaning about how stuffy it is, how slow the service is. The sort of place that charges the earth for a plate of fish and chips because it's been deconstructed to look nothing like fish and chips. *Such an ill-planned choice for a first date*, thinks Helen, committing them both to hours of conversation in a dining room of white tablecloths, silver cloches and where no one can talk above a whisper. Helen can't let it happen.

'Actually, Roger, I'm sorry to rewrite your plans already but would you mind if we stayed more local this evening? I have a full day of appointments at the boutique to plan tomorrow and something a little more low-key might be better. I'd be very happy at the pub across the road.'

'Oh. Really? It might be a bit rowdy at the weekend, Helen, I wouldn't want you to feel—'

'Honestly, I would prefer it, thank you. If you don't mind?'

'OK. It will be considerably kinder on my wallet anyway!' As soon as the words are out of his mouth, Roger's face gives away his awkwardness and regret. He might have been thinking it but it's a crass start to the date and one that isn't lost on Helen. She hates the assumption that he's paying, somehow making her feel beholden to him before they've even looked at a menu. She would have been impressed by a subtle offer to pay, later in the evening when a glass or two of red wine had warmed them up a bit, but Roger has declared his intentions too early.

The pub is exactly what Helen has in mind, the sort of place you hope to find on a weekend away in the country – all cosy sink-into sofas, low ceilings, flagstone flooring, shelves lined with help-yourself books and most importantly an easy relaxed vibe – thanks to a smattering of weekenders thrilled to have closed their laptops and now getting stuck in to the local ale. But Roger's still trying to demonstrate he knows how a gentleman should behave. He's opening every door he can find for Helen, making a big show of standing back so she can pass through first.

'Right, let's get you sat down and I'll go to the bar. A white wine, yes?'

'I'll have a gin and tonic please, Roger,' replies Helen, very much feeling the need for something stronger.

With Roger at the bar, his back to her now, she can't help herself thinking how different he is to Phillip. He seems older, physically and emotionally. The suit is swamping him a little and he's shorter, less broad than Philip. She knows it's a very ungenerous thought, but while everyone else at the bar is comfortable in jeans and quilted country jackets, Roger looks like he's just finished a corporate conference.

'There you go!' Roger places a glass of white wine in front of Helen. She pauses for a moment, about to point out his error but decides against it, keen to keep the evening as fuss-free as possible.

'So, that was some dressing-down you gave Irene earlier!'

In all the panic of the date, Helen has completely forgotten about the incident at the local shop. It's a reminder of how Roger landed this date in the first place. And also that she still owes him an apology.

'I was actually coming to find you this morning, Roger, to apologise for how rude I was the day you dropped into the boutique unexpectedly.'

'Think nothing of it.' He's flicking a hand dismissively in front of her, signalling the conversation can – and should   move on, probably not wanting to relive the awkwardness or lose the sense of control he feels he has tonight.

'I hope you can forgive me. I just wasn't thinking straight and you caught me off guard. I am sorry though, the last thing I wanted to do was make you feel uncomfortable.'

'I had a feeling you'd change your mind about joining me for dinner so think no more of it.' Roger's not joining the dots, not registering that

Helen was never coming to accept a date, just to apologise. 'Business certainly looked to be booming anyway. How do you manage it all on your own?'

'Because I have no choice, I suppose. It's only me, so I have to make it work. But I like it that way, to be honest. I enjoy running a business, it's given me a whole new challenge since losing my husband. I went from being a housewife to a boutique owner very quickly, but I'm proud to say it's working. I love negotiating with the designers and spending time with all those bright young women every day.'

'Who advises you? Do you have someone very clever helping with the business plan?'

Helen knows Roger is well meaning – he's making conversation, showing an interest – but the question is so inherently sexist, she is struggling to form a response that won't sound confrontational.

'As I say, it's all me.' She takes a large mouthful of wine, allowing it to slide down her throat, washing away some of the irritation she's feeling.

'Well, I've cut a few business deals in my time so if ever you want to run anything past me, feel free. Mind you, I'm not sure how much help I'll be on the subject matter – the frivolities of fashion are much more a woman's territory, I'm sure!'

It's at this point that Helen begins to switch off from what is coming out of Roger's mouth. They need to order and she's looking at a younger couple at the table next to them, perhaps having a weekend away without the kids. They've chosen to sit next to each other at the table, rather than opposite, practically stuck to each other's side. Helen leans over and asks what they're eating, it looks so delicious. Soon, the three of them are chatting away, Helen advising on a couple of other places to visit while they're in the area. Roger isn't joining in and if

Helen isn't mistaken he's a little put out because he wants –expects even – her undivided attention.

He spends the rest of their date trying to assist her with everything: getting up, sitting down, ordering and to physically shield her when the pub gets busy and people are jostling the back of her chair, spilling beer on the floor. It's all too much for Helen. She's used to coping now, looking after herself, she's not some precious but incapable toddler that needs protecting. Roger playing the part of the Milk Tray Man *all because the lady loves being looked after* is turning her stomach a little. She finds herself doing things that are out of character just to try to shock him out of his preconceptions. When he grandly excuses himself to go to the gents', she goes to the bar to buy another round of drinks, even though neither of them has finished what's on the table. It's her way of demonstrating that just because he's buying dinner, he doesn't get to dictate the running order of the evening. If she wants to buy a drink, she will, no outdated code of conduct he still lives by is going to stop her. She pauses at the bar a little longer than she needs to, sharing a joke with the barman, dusting off some mildly flirtatious skills she's forgotten she has – just long enough for Roger to return and see she's a capable woman. Not *his* woman.

Maybe it's the wine or the company she's in that's bringing out the devil-may-care streak buried deep within her, but knowing there is never going to be anything romantic between her and Roger loosens Helen up wonderfully. She finds her sense of humour, starts to feel like an attractive, engaging woman with something more to offer the world than a gorgeous wedding dress.

By the time the date is reaching its natural conclusion – Roger telling Helen loudly across the table, 'I won't hear of you paying a penny, goodness me, I couldn't live with myself!' – Helen is feeling fully patronised. Perhaps Betsy's financial independence can only be a good thing after all? If this is the trade-off for being financially tied to a man today, then she wouldn't wish it on anyone.

Helen knows Roger will insist on walking her home and fine, she'll let him, it's the last time he'll be doing it. In a final act of misplaced chivalry (at least that's what he'd call it), Roger deliberately places her on the inside of him so she isn't the one closest to the road. It's a Cotswolds village, the chances of an HGV steaming through unseen at 10.30 p.m. and dragging her under its giant wheels at the last moment are remote, but that's not why Roger is making the unnecessary fuss.

Helen doesn't care, she's learned an important lesson this evening. Perhaps it was a little mean to practice on Roger and in one sense she should be thanking him for getting her out. But she can see now that all her worrying about tonight was a waste of her energy. She did it! And she didn't just get through the evening, batting off the assumptive behaviour of a man who doesn't know her at all, she took control, she turned it around and she made it fun for herself, despite him. Tonight was easier than she imagined and she can't help but smile about that as she gives Roger the briefest kiss on his cheek, thanks him for dinner and sends him on his way. So what if his mouth is hanging open slightly, about to ask for an invitation in for a nightcap presumably? Helen is already turning the key in the lock and her back on Roger's crestfallen face, surprisingly happy tonight to be going home alone.

Chapter Nineteen

Dolly

Dolly is staring at her baby. The start of it anyway. Turns out it's bigger than she thought. The GP guessed twelve weeks, the sonographer confirmed it. And now Dolly and Tilly are curled up on her sofa together looking at the scan picture to prove it. There's a new significant date in Dolly's life stamped down the side: her EDD or Estimated Date of Delivery is December 30th – *if* she chooses to keep it that way.

'Tilly, *what* am I going to do?' Dolly can feel the weight of her sleep-starved face dragging her features downwards into a sad, defeated frown. Her eyes are puffy and sore from hours of muffled sobbing into the pillow, praying Josh wouldn't hear because she hasn't yet found the courage to say those two simple words – *I'm pregnant* – words that have been so easy to share with Tilly this morning.

'Well, what we're *not* going to do is panic.' Dolly so badly wants to absorb Tilly's confidence, let it flush through her body and straighten out everything that's got so twisted and confused these past few weeks. 'You're not the only woman to have ever found herself in this position, right?'

'I suppose not.' She can see Tilly isn't going to let her wallow in it for a second, which is a shame because a morning blubbing all over her is exactly what she feels like doing.

'So, Josh doesn't know?'

'No.'

'And why is that?' God she's methodical, picking this problem apart like some client's PR disaster that needs strategising. Is she going to start plugging Dolly's answers into a PowerPoint presentation?

'Why d'you think?' Once again Dolly is irritated at having to admit to Josh's shortcomings. It's not like she's shattering any misconception of him being future husband of the year material but still, it's embarrassing and can only reflect badly on her – she's the sap who lets him get away with behaving the way he does. 'He's not going to be bloody pleased, is he? Look what happened last time – and I was just *nearly* pregnant then.'

'And what, you *are* pleased? Is that the problem here, you want this baby and you don't think he will?'

Two minutes after striding through Dolly's front door with an armful of M&S mini rocky roads and chocolate cornflake cakes and Tilly has shot straight to the heart of the problem. Because all those hours spent staring at the bedroom ceiling night after night have been put to good use, trying to work this problem through in her own mind. The idea of holding this baby – *their baby* – in her arms is a happy one. She's indulged the fantasy for long enough on those lonely nights – pictured the Moses basket draped in soft white linen, the nursery shelves lined with cute lop-eared bunnies and balls of fluff that pass for baby sheep. Walls strung with fairy lights, and a porcelain owl-shaped nightlight that throws stars and moons on to the ceiling as a gentle lullaby teases the baby off to sleep. A mini wardrobe filled with rompers and playsuits in white cashmere, organic cotton sleep pods, swaddling blankets and tiny newborn onesies with detachable mittens. More than that, she's daydreamed about her and Josh having something solid, defining, a real achievement they can love together, something credible that will mean something. But Dolly can't kid herself that Josh is part of this fantasy. She suspects he wants to keep their lives exactly as they are – indefinitely. And how long can she be satisfied with that? There's no suits-all solution to this one – not even a compromise to be cobbled together. The baby's either coming – or it's not. There is a future for her and Josh, or there's not.

'Dolly? Is that what you want?' Tilly snaps her back into the room.

'I think I do want this baby, yes.' It might be whispered but *there, she said it.* The first time the words have passed Dolly's lips and it feels so confessional, revelatory and a bit silly actually. Like that day Josh slid the solitaire engagement ring down her finger and she heard herself saying the word *fiancé* out loud, like they were just playing at something so much bigger, more grown up than they are – trying to make the mental leap between what she just said and what it actually means. But that gap feels huge to Dolly right now, maybe too huge. Christ, it's one thing saying she wants the baby, another actually having it. Is she really going to let her belly swell and fill with this new little human being? Does she even have the first clue what being a mum really involves – the sacrifices she'll have to make, the total life adjustment, putting someone else's needs before anything she may want – maybe she's already had a fair bit of practice at that? There are no answers to any of this in the well-thumbed Marie-Chantal and Bonpoint catalogues hidden under her bedside table.

'The fact is, the baby *is* already here,' Dolly's holding the scan picture up so she and Tilly can see the tiny nub of the baby's nose and delicate little fingers that are waving out at them. Looking at this grainy image she can't deny the black and white creature, only five centimetres long, about the size of a plump lime. The fragile little life that's come along to totally upturn hers. She's seen on screen how it can already open and close its mouth, curl its toes, and clench its eye muscles. She has listened to the rapid heartbeat, now undeniably knitted to hers and felt the wave of relief wash over her entire body as she lay there in the hospital maternity unit, belly exposed and covered in cold jelly, hearing how the baby is growing well.

'He or she is already here and I'm not sure I'm capable of...' Dolly lets her words trail off.

There is a pause while both of them accept what she's saying, Tilly sucking in a lungful of air and turning now to face Dolly on the sofa.

'I did.' Her eyes are unexpectedly full of emotion.

'What d'you mean?'

'I had an abortion. About three years ago.' Tilly's tone is matter-of-fact, but not even she can hide the pain that is suddenly resurfacing on her face.

'But... I had no idea, you never said anything.' Fear and confusion are being elbowed to one side now as a sense of neglectful guilt is grabbing Dolly. Tilly is one of her closest friends and she didn't even know. She's no better than Josh. How could she possibly have missed this?

She imagines herself then, wrapped in a green hospital gown, wincing through the induced stomach cramps, legs forced apart by stirrups while the cold, hard metal of the doctor's surgical forceps breaks through her, flushing her free of motherhood with the same procedure he might perform a dozen times that day. Could she really look the other way while the *products of conception* left the room in a bowl, feeling no pain, forcing herself not to think about whether the tiny life that was still beating twelve minutes ago felt anything either. Dolly has done her research, she knows exactly what Josh might ask of her – what she might be forced to consider, in the weeks to come.

'Are you OK Dolly, you've gone very pale?' So typical of Tilly to only be thinking of her, even while she's sharing what must have been such an anguished time for her. 'Listen, I panicked. I was walking back out of the clinic before I even realised what I'd done. It was one stupid night with a client that never should have happened, totally reckless, and I just felt I had to deal with it quickly. I didn't think it through at all and I really don't want you to make that same mistake.'

'I'm so sorry I wasn't there to support you.' Dolly can't hold her own tears back any longer and reaches out to Tilly, clinging to her like she wishes she had done three years ago when it might have made a difference.

'Listen,' Tilly pulls the two of them apart and regains her focus, taking both of Dolly's hands in hers. 'The procedure was quick enough. It was all very early on and I'm fine, honestly. I know I did the right thing for me at that time. But I want you to know that I've thought about what I did every single day since; it's never going to leave me.'

'Oh, Tilly.' Dolly can't bear that she's gone through this alone when she was busy doing... what? Obsessing about her sit-up count that week?

'I'm not saying don't have an abortion, Dolly, the situation you're in is so different to mine, and only you can decide. But I just want you to know that it will stay with you. It's not something you can package up afterwards and stick in a file marked *done*, it's not a tick on the to-do list. You know, my life feels like one long bloody business meeting sometimes. The thrill of landing a new client is paper thin compared to what you now have a chance to experience. And isn't there always the possibility that you're wrong about Josh? It's a while since that scare, he really might not be as horrified as you think.'

Listening to Tilly talk is exactly what Dolly needs today. It's helping her get everything into perspective, thoughts are starting to shift, take their place and form a natural order in her mind.

'Tilly, I'm not sure your situation really *is* that different to mine,' Dolly's getting on top of this now, finding her voice, allowing her opinions to be heard.

'You didn't have any support; you would have had that baby alone, right? That feels pretty similar to what could happen to me. But my problem is so much bigger than this baby, isn't it? I naively thought marrying Josh would elevate us somehow, make our relationship more worthwhile. But he's still the same man, he's just going to be wearing a smart suit for the day, that's all.' It's like every doubt that Dolly has ever pushed to the back of her mind about Josh is finally breaking free, there are so many they won't be contained any longer. 'Sometimes we go days without him asking me anything about *me*, how I am, how I'm feeling, if everything is OK. We talk a lot but somehow it's always about him, his work, his plans, how he wants things to be.'

'Well, I can't say I didn't notice, but how has it got so bad?' Tilly's honesty is refreshingly helpful and, by turning the spotlight on Dolly, is forcing her to be truthful with herself too.

'I've gone along with it because his life is so much more exciting than mine, so we just talked about his more. But there shouldn't be a *his* life and a *my* life should there? It should be *ours*. That's been lost on both of us. The gap between us is so wide now.' Dolly's head dips downwards, knowing she's not painting a picture of two ideal parents here. 'Maybe he's just too selfish to be a good dad. Maybe I'm too selfish too. And if that's true, why am I even considering having this baby?

It's wrong, I know it is. God, I found myself asking his permission last night to put my feet up on the sofa next to him, how warped is that? We're miles apart from each other. We don't even touch each other any more, Tilly. Not in that innocent, naturally close way that most couples do, you know?'

'Yep. I know.' The dip at the corners of Tilly's mouth suggests Dolly's not the only one missing the warm blanket of relaxed intimacy.

'He used to make me feel incredible. Now I just feel like he doesn't know me, not really. What I don't know is whether he would even want to fix us. Will he want to postpone the wedding, take some time to get close again, have this baby and come together like a proper family? Will he actually want to do all of that – or is it going to be too much like hard work?' She's putting the questions to Tilly like she expects her to have the answers. Dolly is beyond tears now; this is mentally a better place to be. All the uncertainly and pretence is falling away and she can see she needs to confront Josh with everything she knows to be true.

'Why don't you just see how he reacts to the news of the baby? You're going to have to tell him, so maybe that's a good place to start? And whatever you decide, I am here for you. Whatever it takes Dolly, you won't be on your own.' Tilly's smile tells her she means every word of it.

'Thank you. And yes, you're right. He'll be home tonight. I'm going to do it then.' Dolly just prays the confidence that Tilly has filled her with can last that long, and not get eaten up by the sadness of how this conversation could go. There will be no presenting him with a blueberry in a gift box, because that's how big their baby is right now, like some women get to do. Or a plate with the words *you're going to be a daddy* inscribed on it for the big reveal at the end of his dinner.

No photo frame with *I Heart My Daddy* across the top and the words *picture coming soon* where their beautiful newborn is destined to go.

Tilly starts to gather her things together, sneaking one last cornflake cake before she's off.

'Actually, before you go, there is one other thing.' Dolly hesitates now, knowing this next issue isn't going to get the same sympathetic hearing.

'Yep?'

'There's not going to be any *Brides* shoot now is there?' Dolly tips forward, elbows on her knees, her face buried in her hands, slightly ashamed to even be raising the subject. And Tilly is having none of it.

'Forget it. It's gone, you've got enough to worry about without all the stress of a load of stylists crawling all over your big day – assuming that's *even* going to happen now. Just send the email, pull out, and give yourself one fewer headache. It's not important.'

It might not be to Tilly, but Dolly is dying inside. Endless months of selling herself to ice-cold Annabel in the editor's office and now she is going to send the unimaginable email telling her they can't cover the wedding. All she can see is The Dick's self-satisfied face, the one she'll now be looking at for a while longer at least, all promise of that future styling career well and truly snatched away. While the realisations about Josh and his failings have been gradual – creeping up on her over weeks and months, allowing her to silently rationalise her way through it all – losing *Brides* is a fresh blow. It hurts. Maybe it even hurts more. But she'd sooner die than be featured all pot-bellied pregnant and anyway Tilly is right, there might not be a wedding after tonight's chat with Josh. She needs to send the sodding email.

'Just bloody do it now before you change your mind,' Tilly is handing Dolly her iPhone. 'And I'll catch up with you later.'

Five minutes later Dolly hits send, hearing the *whoosh* that tells her those devastating words are flying through the ether, soon to land on Annabel's iPhone, no retracting them now.

All she can do is focus on what little positive there is. If she does a good enough job styling the nursery, is it too insane to make a pitch to *Vogue Baby*? In the meantime there have already been some cracking upsides to the current state of play. Knowing her little secret has joyously ramped up her *fuck-you* attitude to critical levels at work. Just imagine if she gets to drop this shit bomb on The Dick. She'll be untouchable. She could milk this pregnancy for all it's worth. You name it, she'll be having it, starting with midwife appointments inconveniently scheduled in the middle of the working day. *Obviously.* The sort of morning sickness that requires regular trips to the office canteen to regulate blood sugar levels, giving herself permission to eat anything and *everything*. Gone already are the late nights and relentless client suck-ups, thanks to a doctor's note conveniently explaining she needs rest without saying why. So, Dolly is looking at a strictly 9 a.m. to 5 p.m. office existence with even less work populating those hours than ever before. Have some of *that,* The Dick!

Less excitingly, the final pair of jeans she can still fit into are cutting painfully into her belly now and she heads to the bedroom to change. She's sucking herself in so she can force the zip down, then holding her breath while she unpops the top button. As her flesh is gratefully unleashed she's reminded of how quickly the pounds are coming for her. Will those gorgeously angular hip bones return? Or the satisfyingly deep curve at her now thickened waist? Will she ever again be able to slide her legs easily into the kind of jeans most women would struggle to get an arm into – once the water retention and bloating kick in?

Dolly spends the rest of the day researching nursery designs on Pinterest, tagging everything that she thinks *Vogue Baby* might want to see in a forthcoming issue, before Josh finally swaggers into the kitchen early evening, pushing a hand through his lightly ruffled hair, looking, it has to be said, pretty bloody special. A quick shower and into a sky blue shirt and his favourite faded denim jeans has worked wonders after a sweaty day in the studio. *He's so beautiful*, thinks Dolly, as she places the slab of steak she's cooked for them in front of him, her own stomach somersaulting at the sight of the blood swimming around it.

'So listen, I'm getting quite close to this client, Dolly, and I think there could be a lot more work coming my way – most of it likely to be in New York.' Josh is hacking into the meat now, spearing it onto his fork, not noticing he's causing Dolly to heave. 'It will mean I'm in Manhattan more but for what they're paying, I think we can suck it up.'

'Oh, right. When do they need you again?' Dolly is already feeling uneasy about where this is going. She'll need Josh. More than he knows yet.

'There will be a couple of smaller jobs over the next few months which will put me out there for a week or so each time, then the big one will come in December when they're re-shooting their global ad campaign. I'll be gone for most of the month, travelling to a few different locations across the States.' In his excitement, he's speaking quickly, Dolly can see the barely cooked steak tumbling around his mouth and is struggling to suppress the nausea.

'But, the good news is, none of this is going to impact on the wedding date. It just means you'll be doing most of the last minute organising – but let's face it, you're much better than me at that anyway. You don't mind do you, babes?'

Dolly can see he's buzzing about the opportunity – who wouldn't be? – but that's because he doesn't know yet, they can't be on different continents when she's giving birth, any man would understand that. There will be other jobs. Josh is good at what he does, he has good contacts, people won't *not* hire him again because he turns down one commission.

'Dolly? Are you even listening to me? I know it's a lot to take in, but they are already hassling me for an answer. I had a text on the way home from the creative director asking if I'm in. What d'you think?'

'I think you'd better look at this!' Dolly slides the scan picture across the table towards Josh and fixes her eyes on him. As the nerves take over she's motionless, barely breathing, waiting for the flash of realisation to slap itself across his face.

Silence.

It occurs to Dolly that this is probably the first pregnancy scan picture he's ever seen, he might not know what he's looking at. She sits patiently, giving him all the time he needs to work it out.

Then, finally, 'Whose baby is this? Not Tilly's?'

Jesus Christ.

'No Josh! It's ours. I'm pregnant!'

'What!' His fork clatters loudly to the floor where it stays. His mouth has fallen open and his head is shaking disbelievingly from side to side, as if trying to erase her words, telling her this can't be right. Dolly's hands slide protectively under the table to her belly, something deep within her already feeling the emotional pull towards her baby, not him, shielding it from the insults she fears are about to come.

'But it can't be… you're on the pill. You take it every day, don't you? I thought we were safe? Shit, have you been forgetting them again?'

As the smile starts to fade from Dolly's face, the corners of Josh's mouth dip into a frown and his eyes burn with blame – it's momentary and he knows Dolly can see it. He doesn't recover himself quite quickly enough and now a prickly silence is spreading between them as they both realise how the other one feels. Dolly goes to push her chair back with her legs, choosing the flight option, but he grabs her arm before she makes it to her feet.

'Shit! Wow! Are you sure?' He's scrambling for words, caught in that brain-freezing no-man's-land between what he *should* say and what he *wants* to say.

'There's the evidence right in front of you, Josh but if you need any more, I'd take a look at my belly.' Dolly's angry now. *Fucking typical. Most men in this position would celebrate now, panic later, out of sight where it wouldn't matter. Not Josh, the selfish prick.* Dolly shakes her arm free from him.

'I've given it a lot of thought, Josh, and I really think we should postpone the wedding, have the baby and then plan a more low-key wedding afterwards. There's going to be so much to pay for, a nursery to plan, we might have to scale back on the wedding. But we need to decide quickly because I'm already twelve weeks and due on 30th December.' Dolly is trying to keep the emotion out of her voice. She wants to sound practical, factual, show him one of them is thinking this through clearly but that's not easy when he's staring at her like these are the words of a raving mad woman.

'But I'll be in New York then!' His hands have fallen open on the table, palms facing upwards as if he's spelling out what should be glaringly obvious to her, mocking her ignorance even.

'Josh! No, you won't. Are you seriously suggesting you'll be on a shoot when I'm pushing this baby – *your baby* out? Has it occurred to you that I might need a bit of fucking support? I can't do this on my own!' Dolly didn't want to get hysterical but the fear, panic and anger are all combining in to what she knows must be an ugly rant face.

'Bloody hell, Dolly, you can't just dump this shit on me and expect me to have all the answers.' Josh pushes the unfinished meal away from him and gulps back some water, buying some brief thinking time.

But it's clear there isn't going to be any celebration tonight. No frantic fantasising about what the future might hold. They aren't going to curl up on the sofa while he rubs her belly and they Google cool baby names. She makes a final plea for his support.

'I'm scared, Josh.' She's reaching a hand across the table to him, then suffering the indignity of seeing it lie there, ignored. She's too embarrassed even to withdraw it so starts to fiddle with the coasters stacked there.

'Yeah, well maybe I am too. We were going to have a fucking great big wedding party with all our mates, then enjoy life for a while. Now we're going to be tied to a baby before we're even married. Have you thought about what that will do to us? A life full of shitty nappies, sleepless nights, babysitters and fucked finances.' His arms are swiping across the tense air between them, like a conductor building to a heart-stopping crescendo, as he spits out his long list of objections. 'I didn't think either of us wanted that.'

'I thought you'd be pleased!' She's not even sure why she says it, not when in her heart she knew how improbable an outcome that was. Bloody hormones had got her hopes up, made her believe she might have the sort of happy ending other women get to enjoy.

'Why? We came close to this disaster before. I thought we were both relieved when that turned out to be a false alarm. What part of you thought less than twelve months on the same thing would suddenly be really fucking good news? It's not!' The palms are fists now and Dolly can see he's spitting across the table as he barks at her, too angry and wrong-footed to control the speed of his own mouth.

'Right.' Dolly slumps back in her chair in an attempt to diffuse the confrontation. She doesn't have the energy for this and there's very little point prolonging the showdown.

'I wanted to marry you, Dolly, have fun with you. Throw stupid dinner parties that lasted all night, spend a ludicrous amount on Italian wine and French cheese just because we could. If you have this baby, we'll be doing it all with one eye on the baby monitor waiting for it to start screaming so we can argue about whose turn it is to go and lie on the nursery floor until it stops. And the other eye on the clock because we'll have to be in bed by ten anyway, too sodding exhausted to do anything else.' He's leaning forward in his seat towards her so she can see his conviction shining in his eyes, the *you-know-I'm-right* arch of his eyebrows, that confirms he thinks he's winning this argument.

'Well, I think that's probably where I'm heading now. You can find somewhere else to sleep tonight.' It's not lost on Dolly that Josh is now talking about his desire to marry her in the past tense. To think; a few hours ago she and Tilly were busy giving him the benefit of the doubt, now she's feeling the full force of his reaction and it is entirely, depressingly, predictable.

'Thanks for your support, Josh. I'll have to make sacrifices too, you know.' She's up now, keen to make a getaway, not wanting to look at that angry face for a second longer. 'Do you have any idea how long it's taken me to get *Brides* magazine interested in our wedding, to agree to come and shoot it so that I might finally escape that shitty job of mine?' The attempted guilt trip is futile, she knows it, but she needs to hit him with something, this can't all be her fault.

'Why didn't you just remind me to put a word in? I could have sorted that for you.'

'But you didn't, did you – when it would have been so fucking easy for you?' Dolly leaves the room before they can hurt each other any more, at a loss as to how this could have all gone so badly tonight.

It's not until much later when she's held her own belly through a good two hours of angry tears, that she tiptoes back into the lounge. Josh is sprawled across the sofa asleep, one arm dangling towards the floor, his phone dropped on to the carpet. She bends to pick it up and can see the last text message he received. It's from the creative director that was hassling him for an answer on New York. It simply says *I'm so glad you're in.*

Chapter Twenty

Emily

This is not the stuff of the movies. And most definitely not what your average bride signs up for. Emily is standing in The White Gallery fitting room wearing the Maya gown, a wedding dress that no one wants her to wear. Not her family, not Helen, not her. A wedding dress that she might *never* wear. If ever there was a moment to hold herself together, this is it. If she cracks now, shows even the slightest chink in her armour and lets Helen in on what's really going on, she will be undone. If the tears come now, they'll never stop. Her plan will implode and all her plotting will be for nothing.

Funny, thinks Emily, as Helen adjusts the embellished shoulder straps of the otherwise very simple gown, *the number of women over the past three months who said how defining this moment would be.* The all-encompassing epiphany when a bride-to-be stands staring at her soon-to-be married self, cloaked in white and realises with total clarity that she is gazing at *The One*. It's usually the veil that does it, apparently. That one unmistakably bridal accessory that transforms a woman from mildly embarrassed pretender to the real *I Do* deal. The problem is, Emily is not feeling it. Her mind is full of the dress that got away. The

Reem gown that everyone chose for her – and how that dress was going to be central to the happiest day of her life. The nerves she would feel stepping in to it on their wedding morning. The heart-thumping walk up the aisle in it, gripping her dad's arm just as tightly as he would be gripping hers. Countless photographs taken wearing it, that would tell the story of their very special day for years – generations hopefully – to come. Mark teasing it off her later that night. Then packing it away in layers of crisp white tissue paper until their first anniversary when she might get it out, sending year-old confetti cascading to the floor, and twirl around the bedroom in it – just for giggles. Then the day she would show it to her own daughter for the first time, maybe even trust her to try it on. See it swamp her little princess as Emily watches, her thoughts thrust forward to when she'll be mother of the bride. *Would she cry?* Yes, she'll be bursting with love and pride, just like Glo will be. Hopefully.

There's nothing wrong with the Maya dress, plenty of girls would kill to marry in it, Emily knows that. It's just that it's not making her heart sing. It's making it feel heavy with the responsibility of what she feels she must do. And judging by the solemn look on Helen's face, she's not feeling it either.

'You know, Emily, if you really want the Reem dress – or any other dress for that matter – and cost is the issue, I'm sure I can come to some arrangement for you.'

'That's so lovely of you, Helen, but no, no thank you.' Such unexpected kindness from Helen is pushing Emily to her absolute limit. Just like a well-meaning colleague asking if you're OK, when you're really not, sending all your pent-up sorrow spilling out in a big unplanned cry. Emily can only hold her emotions in check for so long. This is much harder than she thought it would be. She needs to get these final dress tweaks done and get out of here. Out into the sobering fresh air and back to her to-do list. There is plenty still to be done.

'OK, let me pin the hem for you and then I think we'll be done.' Helen is on her knees working her way around the bottom of the gown, lifting it as she goes and pinning it in place so it is the perfect length for Emily. 'It will take about five days for the alterations and then it's all yours. I'll call you when its ready and then you can pop back to collect it. How does that sound?'

'Perfect, Helen, thank you.'

Fifteen minutes later they're finished. Emily is back in her jeans, buttoning up her delicate silk H&M shirt and fielding text messages from Glo asking about menu changes when everything starts to go dark around the edges until there is only blackness.

I die at 11.05 p.m.

The moment the overwhelming feeling of peace drowns me, like I have come to a point of no return, like there is no need to breathe any more but also weirdly no cause for alarm. I feel so serene.

I know what's happening to me. I've read about it. An account in one of the Sunday supplements months ago about a man who drowned but was then revived, recounted in exquisite detail how beautiful the experience is. How at the moment when utter panic should have been mauling him, as his lungs filled with water and a slow suffocation meant there was no air left to breathe, there was not one shred of fear in him, just a willing acceptance, no desire to fight it as he floated off into the warm cushioning water. And it's the same for me, in my safe place, my childhood bedroom. And I am so pleased I'm here after the embarrassing fainting episode with Helen, not in some hospital bed, surrounded by the stench of other people's illness. Face-planting on to Helen's perfect cream carpet was just the beginning of the end for me. Now I'm comforted by the fact my parents are just the other side of my bedroom door. The trouble is they will never know how easy it was for me. Their imaginations will build a far more gruesome death that I'll never be able to disprove. The pain of that thought is far worse than the act of dying and the only thing I'm fighting against.

Mark and Mum both check on me in the night, before 'the time of death' when I'm going but not quite gone. When Mark comes in he pulls the duvet up a little higher under my chin and kisses my forehead. *My God, how is he going to cope when he realises?* He'll blame himself; spend a lifetime thinking he did the wrong thing and that in the precious few moments when his actions might have made a difference, he advises the weakest over-the-counter painkiller and an early night. I pray in my final moments on this earth that Sarah gets to him soon and takes that weight away from him.

Then Glo arrives on her way to bed and stands staring at me for ages. I lie there, seeing her perfectly clearly. I would give anything to know what she is thinking. I can't ask her – no words will come, I am already too far under, death's grip already too tight on me and my vocal chords. She's smiling and then I remember. She's spent the day planning what sort of granny she will be. If my heart hadn't yet stopped, it was surely breaking now. I try to lift my arms to hold her but they're useless to me, like the moment the anaesthetist's needle takes effect. So I watch instead as she comes closer, her face almost touching mine. More than anything in the world I want to feel her warmth one last time. My life to end as it started, connected to her. And then it happens. One final loved-filled kiss goodnight, so powerful that I hope for a moment it might even bring me back. And unlike the duvet, I can feel it. Not the touch of her lips but the full effect of that kiss – a mother's kiss.

I can feel all the years of nurturing and caring, the unconditional love and devoted support flow from her right in to me, travelling back through my body at high speed, filling my lungs and making my heart swell. Her love inflates me with so much happiness, like a giant helium balloon, I think I might just lift off the bed and float up to heaven right there and then. I wonder for a moment if on some other plane – some intuitive, subconscious dimension in her own brain – she knows what's happening and that's why she's here, to perform the last act of love that will make me feel better. My beautiful mum. I see for the first time how strong she really is. Which is a relief. Her world is about to be smashed into a million shattered pieces that may never be put back together. I'll miss you Mum, I'll miss you Mum… I can't make myself heard.

As she stands to leave the room something catches her eye in the darkness and she picks it up. I can just make out the wording on the front. *Tying The Knot*. Yes, Mum! Yes! Open the book, read it, know how much I love you, how much I desperately wanted to protect you from this! I'm screaming the words at the top of my voice as if in one of those nightmarish dreams when something awful is about to happen but the warning sound just won't escape out of you. She holds it in her hand for a moment longer, running her finger along the spine of its closed pages, then places it back on the shelf without opening it. She's gone and I am left to my fading thoughts.

It's 6.30 a.m. now so I've got a bit of a handle on how this works. I can see my body, I just can't move it. The duvet is on me but it feels like it's floating above me. I can't physically feel anything but my emotions feel heightened and intense like I can sense the settled, unknowing breath as it floats in and out of my sleeping father just down the hallway. It's resonating deep within me on a much more profound level than merely hearing or feeling it. My only agony comes from knowing his calm contentedness can't possibly last.

Lying here now I must admit it, Sarah Blake was right all along. If I'd listened to her the day she begged me to come clean, everyone would have known I wasn't being *that* bride, getting all overwhelmed by the dress and fainting. Maybe I might have known it too. But it was so fleeting. Seconds, that's all it was, before I was back in the room and everything was back to normal. Trouble was, Helen was so convincingly dismissive. 'Oh, I never had you down as a fainter, Emily! Don't worry,' she said, 'it happens, it happens a lot.' In between the cup of sweet tea she forced on me, the fuss about calling Mark to pick me up and the general feeling of being a colossal idiot, the moment passed. I felt fine – not even the hint of a headache.

I always imaged if the rupture came it would be big, explosive, without doubt. That I would be snuffed out in a split second. But that's not how it happens. You can faint, regain yourself, seem fine, but all the while the damage is being done, inside your head where no one can see it or know it, not even you. Or at least that's how it happened to me.

Turns out I was in death's shadow all day. I called Mark, but only because Helen insisted and stood there watching me do it. He pulled the seat belt around me in the back of the taxi before putting his own on and then we set off home, him asking lots of questions: Had I eaten lunch? *No.* Are there bugs going around nursery again? *Yes, always.* Am I sleeping properly? *Obviously not.* I batted back answers easily enough, no big deal. Then I buried myself into the wonderfully warm place between his chest and his shoulder while his hand cradled my face. As blood started to swamp my brain, I pushed my ear closer to him and listened to his heartbeat one last time. The comforting, rhythmic beat sounding so strong while all the time mine was fading. I know now, it was the last time I would feel his strong arms holding me, protecting me. He had no idea I was already gone – well, as good as. Already in that ethereal place between life and death where the chances of being saved are seriously slim. You just don't imagine it will start to happen on the back seat of a cab do you? Surrounded by that stale smell and sitting on the crumbs of the last passenger's cheap supermarket sandwich.

I still felt fine when Mark got me home. I walked from the car – noticing Dad had already made a start on de-mossing the path, bless him. Mercifully he and Glo were both out – imagine the fuss otherwise – that's when Mark gave me the paracetamol, tucked me up in bed and told me to stop stressing about whatever I was stressing about. If only I'd been braver and checked in with Sarah Blake I might have been carted off to hospital. There might have been emergency surgery. The pressure the blood was causing in my skull might have been relieved. I might have stood a chance. I might never have had that stroke. Now I have to ask myself, during my last hours of brain function, did my one great attempted act of kindness cause my death? If I'm being kind to myself the answer is, probably. If I'm being honest, almost certainly.

Now the fact I am lingering is the scariest bit. Do other people linger? Is my beloved and long-departed Aunt Marigold going to appear on the end of the bed in a minute to talk me through the protocol of being dead? Is this normal? No way of knowing. The only logical reason I can think of is so I can witness the goodbyes, but how cruel is that? I'm not particularly religious but I'm also sure whoever is making the decision to keep me here wouldn't willingly inflict that torture on me. But being here feels right, intended, like something else is coming that I need to confront. Otherwise there would just be truly nothing, surely? I don't want to think about what that thing might be. It's too big and requires more brain power than I can possibly muster right now.

Then my thoughts are blown apart and sent smashing into my bedroom walls. Glo is awake and she's coming to check on me.

Chapter Twenty-One

Jessie

'If we're going in, we're doing it my way, OK? And the only time I want to hear from you is when it's time to pay.' Claire is eyeballing Jessie at very close range, ready to pounce at the slightest hint that she might renege on their deal. The two of them are sitting in Jessie's Landover outside The White Gallery with five minutes to spare before their appointment time. And Claire is keen to recap on the terms of the tightly negotiated agreement. 'I am choosing whatever I want to wear and you won't be interfering or arguing about it. Are we clear?'

'I said you could choose the dress and I mean it, but all I ask is that you listen to Helen. She knows what she's talking about and she can make you look… better.' Jessie is choosing her words very carefully indeed. The fallout after the hen do was monumental. Claire has only agreed to resume her bridesmaid duties after Jessie delivered an unreserved and grovelling apology in person and in front of the whole family, performing her biggest climb-down since she was overheard lying to a school friend about what her dad did for a living.

'It's just, I think Mum and Dad are pretty unimpressed with you right now and they have asked me to let them know how today goes.'

Claire's got her and her proud smirk says she knows it. 'I mean, you can't have missed the fact that Dad made himself scarce after your little speech? It doesn't normally take him two hours to go and buy the newspaper, does it? And is it me or did he pretty much ignore you for the afternoon when he eventually did come back? I'm not sure what was worse actually, that or Mum just sitting there in total silence, not knowing what to say or think of you and how you treated us that night.'

'OK, I get it, let's not relive the whole thing please. I have apologised. And trust me, their reaction was not lost on me.' The *apology* was supposed to be the easy way out – blame the stress of wedding planning then move the hell on. Now looking at the smile on Claire's face, Jessie is wondering if this will be easy at all. Did she miss a golden opportunity to come clean, lay bare a few insecurities and appeal to her family for some help and understanding? Instead of pitting herself against her own mother and sister in the battle for her father's support and sympathy – one throw-down she knows she is never going to win.

But there is a faint flicker of pleasure too at what she held back. How could she stand there in front of them all and pretend she was wrong about Claire in the orange dress? There are climb-downs and then there's entering the land of total make-believe. Besides, Claire's not that stupid and has had a frustratingly hot radar for Jessie's bullshit since they were kids. Probably best not to appear *completely* insincere. But she can't deny it hurts a great deal that her own parents don't want to be around her or talk to her right now. The two people on this earth biologically programmed to forgive practically anything she could throw at them, and yet they are ever so slightly rejecting her. Too proud and too lovely to just come out and say it, they're making their point by not returning her phone calls and easing themselves even further into the background of this wedding. Jessie should be pleased, but despite all her bluster and big mouthing, she's not. She's ashamed. *Why do her family always bring out the absolute worst in her*, she wonders, as she sits here now, knowing one more clash with Claire will be the end of her.

Her sister is still prattling on about *the way it's going to be when we get in there*, so puffed up and full of herself, revelling in having the upper hand. There is nothing as effective as a nice bit of family fall-out to flatten all the excitement of a forthcoming wedding. Jessie can still feel the heaviness in her chest, the regret weighing her down. The questions resurfacing to make her wince over and over. *Why did I do it? Why couldn't I have just let it go? What was the worst that could have happened? A few unkind sniggers? A whispered put-down or two? If Claire was game enough to turn up in that dress, I should have let her deal with it herself.* Jessie is well aware of how stupid she's been. That if she had just kept her mouth shut that night then any unkindness would have been attributed to Adam's friends, not her. And now she's torn between wondering how she could have treated her mum and Claire so badly, so publically, and the uncomfortable thought that Adam must never know what happened. As far as he's aware, it was the roaring success he planned it to be. Lovely Tilly is on side to maintain that particular lie. She just needs to pray that no one else squeals to him about what went down. Add to that angst the sense of dread at the impending shopping trip she and Claire are about to share and Jessie's nerves are not in a good place.

So, there may be a deal between them but that doesn't mean Jessie is about to relinquish all control. She has taken the liberty of furnishing Helen with a few of the facts about Claire ahead of time. Namely, her lack of any sense of style and her almost impressive ability to make anything look cheap, regardless of its actual cost. She has also explained to Helen that she would like to see her in something understated and elegant for the rehearsal dinner, wedding day and wedding party. Whatever it takes to pull this off, Jessie is happy to pay.

And Helen is not about to disappoint. As the two women step into the immaculate boutique – Jessie working hard not to focus on her sister's dirty opened-toed sandals – Jessie can see she has already prepared a rail of bang-on-brief dresses. Nothing sheer, nothing spray-on, no revealing cutaway fabrics, no garish colours, just a beautiful rail of chic floor-length gowns in a subtle palette of soft metallics and chalky pastels. She has also included a few discreet cover-ups in cosy fake fur, embellished lace and layered tulle. This is going to be OK. Jessie might even relax. Helen is on the case and if anyone can handle Claire, it's her.

'Good afternoon, ladies. You must be Claire?' Helen motions to the two of them to take a seat while she moves the rail into the fitting room.

'Yes, nice to meet you Helen. I can't *wait* to start trying on!'

'Well, let's get cracking then, shall we? I already know a lot about the wedding obviously, so I have chosen things that are very much in keeping with what Jessie will be wearing and the colour palette of the day. Why don't you take a look, see what you like and I'll help you into anything you'd like to try on.'

'Got it!' Claire stomps over to the rail and begins to rummage through the dresses just like you might on a competitive Saturday afternoon bargain hunting in TK Maxx.

Jessie watches, determined not to say a word. There are at least eight dresses on this rail that she would be very happy to see Claire wear and a few that, while they wouldn't be her first choice, are still a vast improvement on anything Claire might choose herself. But Claire is already at the end of the rail, having failed to pause over a single gown.

'Mmm, they're all very nice, Helen, but I had something else in mind.'

Claire is grinning from ear to ear, knowing she is about to send Jessie over the edge.

'Share your thoughts, Claire, please?' prompts Helen. 'There are lots more bridesmaids' gowns here that you can try. Is there a particular style or cut you wanted to try? A shape you feel more comfortable in that I haven't included?'

'I want to wear white.'

'What!' Jessie is immediately on her feet. 'Are you *actually* kidding?'

'No, I'm not. I don't like pinks and lemons and all these girly colours. White looks good on me, especially with a spray tan, so that's what I want.'

A stunned silence falls between the three women, Helen's eyes flitting backwards and forwards between the two sisters while Jessie stands rigid, furious tears beginning to irritate the back of her eyelids. *Does the actual moron not even know she shouldn't be wearing white, or is this another one of her giant wind-ups?* The fury pumping through Jessie is making it impossible to work out. It's going to have to be Helen who speaks up. If Jessie opens her mouth now the torrent of abuse that will pour out of her will be brutal. Mercifully, Helen sees that.

'I'm sure you know, Claire, that traditionally white is a colour worn only by the bride – a way of marking her out as special on her wedding day. You don't want to spend the entire day being mistaken for the bride, do you?' Helen's voice is light and breezy, like she is offering the sort of kindly advice that is sure to be taken.

It's not.

'Oh don't worry, Jessie is happy for me to wear whatever I like, aren't you Jessie?'

'I didn't say wear a bloody wedding dress, Claire!' Jessie's forced composure is rapidly unravelling.

Claire takes a slow, controlled inhalation of breath, looks Jessie directly in the eye and with all the composure of a serial killer, delivers the fatal blow. 'I forgot to ask by the way, what did Adam say about the hen-do?'

In the wonderful fictional world inside Jessie's mind, her hard, bony fist is connecting with Claire's jaw, catching her completely by surprise as she punches the pleasure right off her face.

'Helen, please let Claire try on whatever she likes, anything she feels comfortable in.' *You know what, sod her. If she wants to look like an idiot, who am I to stand in her way, crack on luv, enjoy. And when everyone laughs at you, you can deal with it.*

Jessie sits back, unbelts her cashmere YSL jacket, drops her quilted Chanel bag to the floor and unleashes a breathy sigh that could blow out a candle. Then she spends the following hour watching Claire try on every conceivable shape and style of dress in the place – each one looking more ludicrous than the last. Helen is trying her absolute best to steer her towards the less obviously bridal styles – plainer gowns, without trains – but of course, Claire is having none of it. What she is having is way more fun than Jessie ever did choosing her own gowns. It's her princess moment. She's twirling from one side of the room to the other, gathering up great armfuls of tulle then dropping them dramatically as she shifts her weight from foot to foot. She's pretending to hold a bouquet of flowers in front of her, walking slowly up an imaginary aisle and at one point even asks Helen to stick a veil on her head *just for fun*.

Why is she doing this, wonders Jessie. Is this wedding day by proxy? It's tragic, truly tragic but the longer this bizarre scene is played out in front of Jessie, the less angry she feels. It's almost quite liberating watching Claire spin around that fitting room without a care in the world. A girl, as far as Jessie can tell, with so little going for her and yet... far happier than Jessie feels right now. She truly believes she looks beautiful. There is no self-doubt. So whatever warped sense of adult make-believe is going on in that head of hers, Jessie's letting her indulge her frothy fantasies, whatever it takes not to be the bad guy for once. And extraordinary as it seems, her sister is coming to her wedding wearing a wedding dress. A new all-time low has been reached.

'Why don't you pop over to Willow Manor and order us some lunch while I settle up with Helen, Claire? I won't be long.' Jessie's voice is heavy with resignation, all the soon-to-be-married joy sucked right out of her.

'Great idea! Thanks, Helen. I'll see you over there.' Claire gathers up her things, swings her bag over her shoulder and heads for the door. Just as she reaches it, she tosses a glance back over her shoulder, her face now cold with distain.

'You know what, Jess; the blue off-the-shoulder dress will do fine for your wedding day and you can pick whatever else you like for me. I don't care what. Because unlike you, I'm not obsessed with what people think of me and how I look. But I hope you enjoyed our little shopping trip anyway. You certainly deserved it.' And with that she is out the door, off to celebrate her little victory, leaving Jessie to scrape her mouth up off the floor.

'Um... can I ask what just happened?' Helen is looking at Jessie for some sort of explanation. 'I'm afraid I'm a little confused. Are you taking the dresses or... not?'

But Jessie is in what can only be described as the brace position. Still sitting, she's cradling her head with both hands and has allowed it to drop, defeated, between her knees. All the frustration, anger and humiliation are causing her whole body to shake as she lets out a pantomime-loud wail. Helen takes a seat next to her, folding an arm around her shoulders and easing her back upright with a gentle, 'Come on, Jessie.'

'I'm so sorry, Helen, I don't even know where to begin with all that.' Her face is flushed bright pink, a vivid stress rash starting to stain her throat and neck.

'You don't need to explain anything to me if you don't want to,' offers Helen. 'I can see clearly enough what you're dealing with. Some advice? You can't control your family, Jessie. People are who they are and the more you try to push them into a corner, to make them conform to your way of thinking, the less likely they are to bend to your idea of perfection. Someone wanted to teach you a lesson today – one I'm guessing could have been avoided?'

'I don't know how things got so ugly. I love my family, I really do. Even Claire. She's my sister, how could I not? But they get everything wrong. *Everything.* If Claire had just one ounce of ambition in her she might see that I can help her. Make her look better, feel happier with herself.'

'From what I can see, she is happy, Jessie. But it's not *your* version of happy, it's hers. Didn't you see her face in those dresses? She was in another world for a moment, totally swept up in the magic of it all. OK, she has some ulterior motives, but I've been doing this job for a long time and that was no playacting for your benefit or mine. She doesn't see herself the way you see her, I'm afraid, and so she doesn't share your view that there is a need to change or work to be done.' Helen has pulled her chair closer to Jessie now, looking like she's going nowhere until this is resolved and Jessie feels better.

'It's not just Claire, though, it's my whole family. I've got a mum and dad I love dearly but they just don't get it. My mum wants to turn up for dinner at Adam's parents' estate with a traybake she's made with Tesco economy ingredients, for crying out loud. Adam's family has a chef! But my mum can't see that because she'll be too busy telling Camilla how clever she is because if you shop well you can make it for 50p a slice. While Dad will be boring the arse off Henry with unwanted advice on the best way to get his car road-worthy for winter.' It's like Jessie has taken an honesty pill, a truth serum – call it what you like, it's all pouring out. And while there is nothing terribly elegant about it, at least she's airing it finally in all its undignified glory.

'Let them.' Helen is smiling as if this is a lot less of a problem than Jessie thinks. 'Adam is marrying you. Does it really matter?'

'Yes! I want them to think I am someone worth marrying. I don't want to be the second class citizen, the girl who got lucky to bag him. I want to be Adam's equal.'

'But you are, Jessie, or Adam wouldn't have proposed. You are luckier than you think. Look at everything you have. A man who loves you, wants to be your husband, have babies with you, grow old with you. And a family that love you too. Parents who are proud and a sister who is still prepared to stand by you, despite whatever has happened between you both. You are rich in so many ways, Jessie. Do you honestly think Adam's parents are impressed by everyone they meet? They've sat through boring dinner parties just like the rest of us, been astounded at someone's lack of intellect and probably felt inferior themselves at some point. They're human. We all are! That stuff happens to us all. It's not important.'

Jessie looks like she's had the wind knocked out of her. 'You're right, Helen. I know you are.'

'Unless you are planning to entirely rewrite history, Jessie, this is you. This is what they get and if they don't love you already, they will come to. Apart from anything else, it's in their interests to. Has it ever even crossed your mind that they might be nervous about what you make of *them*?'

'Never.'

'Don't alienate your own family, Jessie. One day you will look around and they'll be gone. Then when it's far too late, you'll see all this nonsense for what it is. Irrelevant.'

Chapter Twenty-Two

Helen

'Hi Emily, it's Helen again. I hope all is well and you're feeling a little better. I just wanted to remind you that your dress is ready. As I mentioned in my email, I know you need it as soon as possible so I rushed it through for you. Please feel free to come and collect it as soon as you can. Any problems, just give me a call on the usual number. Have a lovely day. Bye.'

Helen hangs up. It's the third message she's left for Emily. And nothing. It's completely baffling; especially considering the tearing rush Emily was in to get her hands on the dress in the first place. But then what was it she said that day? *I may not need a dress at all.* All very odd. Helen has a strict policy never to get involved in the family politics that often surface behind the fitting room curtains, unless she's invited to, but this situation is different, intriguing in a way the more obvious jealous sister, overbearing mother or dominant best friend dynamics are not. Still, nothing she can do about it until Emily decides to get in touch so she resigns herself to simply waiting it out.

She zips Emily's dress up into its protective silk carrier and places it towards the back of the boutique, next to the others waiting to be collected or ready for the final seal of approval. She has a few minutes to spare until Dolly Jackson is due in so rips open the note that has arrived in the post from Betsy this morning – she recognised the handwriting immediately. It's a thank-you card for the last cash transfer she made to Betsy's account. As she reads her daughter's grateful words, Helen wonders if they can only be the precursor to the broken heart she will one day soon need to fix. The card is signed from Betsy alone but the loans have never been for her. Jacob has never thanked her for the money she sends. Perhaps he's too proud? Perhaps he doesn't know? But Helen knows the loans might not be necessary at all if he was earning *something* and surely that is a fault line no relationship can sustain for long?

She lifts the carrier marked for Dolly off the rail and takes it through to the fitting room, ensuring all her pins and clips are ready for her next appointment, just as the doorbell trills.

'Come in, come in, Dolly! I've got everything ready.' Helen has been looking forward to this appointment. It's Dolly's final fitting before she takes the dress away for its starring role on the pages of *Brides* magazine. Dolly was nothing short of ecstatic when she told Helen the news and, while Helen would never say as much, she is also thrilled, predicting a steady stream of new brides through the door once the coverage appears. That dress, on that body, coming alive with all the passion and go-getting energy that only Dolly could bring is going to ensure Helen remembers this girl for a very long time to come.

But Dolly looks very different today. For a start she's dressed rather low key, to put it politely. Helen's used to Dolly swishing into the boutique in something fabulous – a far-too-short skater skirt or a pair of heels that force her right up on to her tiptoes – but today it's a pair of leggings, Converse trainers and an oversized t-shirt that not only looks like it could do with a wash but which is also rather snug around curves that were definitely not there before. Helen can see immediately that they will be re-pinning the dress again today. Dolly's loveably goofy smile has also disappeared, replaced by a large pair of dark eye bags that would look more at home on someone straight off a night shift. And now that she is in under the soft lighting Helen can also see Dolly's skin has lost all its youthful glow. It's blotchy, dotted with an irritable rash of small red spots and the colour of a corpse. Lifeless eyes are sitting under a bird's nest of unbrushed hair.

'Put the pins away, Helen. We're not going to need them.' Dolly's bottom lip is already starting to tremble.

'Oh dear. What's wrong, Dolly? You really don't look very happy.' What on earth is going on today? First Emily goes AWOL, now the world's happiest bride looks like someone sat on her wedding cake.

'I wanted to come and tell you in person,' mumbles Dolly. 'The wedding is off.'

'Oh, I see. Are you OK?' It's less a question and more of an offer to unload. Whatever has squashed Dolly's spirit so it now has all the life of three-day-old wedding flowers, needs unpicking, Helen can see that.

'Not really. It's all gone a bit horribly wrong I'm afraid. Look at the state of me.'

Helen watches as Dolly makes no effort to hold back the tears now, allowing herself to completely unravel, like it was her sole purpose for coming here today. Helen knows Dolly could have cancelled the dress with one swift phone call, email even – but she didn't. It's not Helen's wedding dress expertise that's needed today, it's her unbiased motherly support and a friendly shoulder to cry on. And Helen is only too ready to tap straight back into all that knowledge, all those skills that kept her own family knitted together so well for so long.

Needing no further invitation, Helen gathers Dolly up into a bosomy hug, squeezing her tightly, engulfing her in a comforting cloud of Jo Malone lily of the valley scent. Helen clasps a hand on the back of Dolly's head as she succumbs totally to the kindness, resting her cheek on Helen's shoulder where the sobs start to hiccup out of her. Helen can almost feel the sadness and upset shaking around inside the sorrowful, dishevelled mess that is now flattening her perfectly hair-sprayed do. As she steadies Dolly, Helen can also feel more flesh on her bones, a totally different girl to the almost skeletal one she first met.

And then it all falls into place.

'I'm pregnant, Helen.' Three words that bring everything clattering into perspective, they squeak out of Dolly through childish sniffs, an appeal to make everything better, make all this just go away. The reaction exploding inside Helen couldn't be more different. From a generation who embraced motherhood as their own, taking ownership of every need a baby ever had, Helen is instantly transported back decades when every waking hour of her day was spent happily devoted to raising cheerful children. She pictures herself with a three-week-old Betsy, the two of them falling asleep on the sofa in each other's arms, needing each other in equal measure, more content than she ever thought possible.

'Wow! Well, that's wonderful news, isn't it? Why are you so upset?' Helen pulls her upwards by the shoulders so the two women are nose to nose; Helen all smiles and raised eyebrows, Dolly attempting to wipe tear-sodden hair out of her eyes.

'Josh doesn't want the baby.' Dolly's eyes shift downwards, hiding what looks tragically like shame.

'Ahh.' Helen has sorted out some problems in her time: deceitful bridesmaids, fiercely protective mothers, but this one is not about to be resolved with a couple of shortbread fingers and a fresh brew of Earl Grey – although she'll probably fetch them anyway.

'Oh, Dolly, why ever not?' Helen feels the heaviness in her own voice, laden with disappointment.

'He's not ready for it he says, too much going on with work and he just wants to be married, have fun without the apparently massive burden of starting a family so soon. It's all my fault, I've messed everything up.'

'Well, that's certainly not true. It takes two people to get you pregnant, Dolly. But how do *you* feel about it?' Helen is sitting Dolly down now on the chaise, the scene of so many tears and dramas over the years, and wonders for not the first time this week where all the good men have gone. The sort that would put Dolly's happiness well above his own. Helen places a box of pretty floral tissues between the two of them – another invitation to let it all out – and allows Dolly to completely unburden herself. To hell with the ticking clock on their one hour appointment time.

'It was the very last thing on my mind. I was so geared up for this wedding, so focused on whether the venue was cool enough or the drinks budget big enough and whether the bloody editor of *Brides* thinks my shoes are stylish enough, I just didn't see it coming.' Dolly is up, down, reaching in her bag for nothing in particular, then dropping it again, twitching away like a mad woman. 'Perhaps if I didn't have the world's biggest asshole for a boss this wouldn't have happened. I wouldn't have been trying so hard to get out of there. I might have remembered to take the damn pills.'

'OK, slow down and sit down, let's think about this rationally. Number one, I don't think we can blame your boss for this one Dolly. He may be many things but he didn't get you pregnant.' As Dolly let's out a disgusted snort at the mere suggestion this might ever be possible, Helen's enthusiasm for problem-solving kicks in. Perhaps it's because Betsy is so far away these days and she's rarely asked to swoop in and pick up the pieces, but she can see a real opportunity to help, to save Dolly from the despair that is swamping her.

'The real question is how do you feel about the fact that there is a baby inside of you? How does that make you *feel*?' Helen can't help it, she's making this emotional.

Dolly says nothing for a moment while a fresh waterfall of tears builds behind her wet eyelashes. 'So, so happy.' The hint of a smile is back. 'But then Josh made me doubt everything, endlessly running through his list of reasons why having this baby is a bad idea: cost, it's career limiting, social suicide. We've spent weeks trying to be grown-up about it, talk it through. But it's never long before the shouting, swearing and door-slamming starts. Or he just stomps out of the flat to the pub again.'

'Oh, dear.' Helen can see how Dolly's own hopes for the future are so at odds with the reaction she's getting at home.

'The things he said have really made me question whether I want to be one of *those* women.' She slumps down on to one of the ornate gold chairs usually occupied by a bride's family and friends during fittings and Helen dutifully takes up the seat beside her.

'You know, blocking the pavement with my enormous thousand-pound pram, handing out dirty looks to anyone who swears or smokes within a three-metre radius of my tiny precious one? One of those eyes-to-the-skies types who shoulders her way into Starbucks every day, full of self-importance because *I have a baby you know*, feeding a serious caffeine addiction, over using the word *lovely* about 400 times a day and buying clothes for myself on the basis of how easy they are to wipe clean.'

'It doesn't have to be anything like that! You'll still be *you*!' Helen is smirking now, she can't help herself, not that Dolly's noticed, she's on a roll tearing down every new mum who might be struggling to make it to bedtime each day without bloodshed.

'Will I spend all my time wondering what that awful smell is following me around before realising it's the baby's dinner from three nights ago still crusted on my shoulder? You know, they all pretend to the world they're deliriously happy, thrilled that Finn has eaten all his sugar-snap peas. But you never see pictures of them on Facebook bawling into their pillow at 3 a.m. when the tiny terrorist won't sleep do you? He may not have put it to me very kindly but maybe Josh has a point. Maybe we're not ready. Maybe *I'm* not ready.'

That another woman could have such a different take on mother-hood to Helen's own experience is taking her breath away. Where do such staunch views come from, she wonders? And when did mothers become such a target of loathing and misunderstanding from other women? It's almost laughable in its naivety. Helen shifts position in her seat, getting comfortable, ready to hit Dolly with a serious trip to the frontline of motherhood.

'I understand your fear, I really do, but you are entirely missing the point. You will be living in a different universe to the pre-baby you. I remember those newborn days with my two like they were yesterday. Up feeding thirteen times a night, my head and heart a cocktail of love and fear all shaken up for days on end with no proper sleep. I didn't leave the house for ten days after my first was born.' Helen's gaze has shifted off somewhere near the ceiling where it looks like her past is playing out in beautiful technicolour.

'Oh Christ!' there is nothing beautiful about this for Dolly it seems.

'Yes, I prayed to him a few times. The truth is, if you're not waking them, changing them or feeding them, you're entertaining them, soothing them, educating them – or worrying about whether you are doing any of these things right. But once the fear starts to ebb away, it's manageable and you can do this!' Helen is so animated now, right back there reliving those treasured middle-of-the-night moments spent working out what her own little darlings needed from her.

'You're hardly selling this to me! And what about my body, Helen? It's going to look disgusting forever isn't it? I mean, look at me now and I've got months to go yet!' Dolly is stretching the giant t-shirt tight across her middle, to accentuate the flabbiness already settling in for the long haul.

'I'm not going to lie to you. Yes, your body will change beyond all recognition. It will just keep growing and growing until you can't bend over.'

Dolly's face has dropped even lower than it was when she arrived and she lets out a long low sigh like she's just been told that *Brides* magazine has gone bust. But Helen is undeterred.

'What you have there is nothing compared to what's coming. You'll get so big there will be no room to breathe. To eat even. Your body will stretch so far you'll wonder if it will ever bounce back. You'll be your heaviest, flabbiest and saggiest.'

'I'm not sure I want to hear any more of this.'

'Stay with me Dolly because this is important. When your body does these incredible things, you're not meant to look like Barbie, are you?' Helen has shifted her position so she is facing Dolly now, making sure she is hearing all of this. 'When you are holding your baby, drenched in happy hormones, trust me, you will feel nothing but proud of what your body has just done for you. This is not about who can be up and in the park with the pram the quickest. But when you do eventually get tired of elasticated waist bands, that's the time to do something about it.'

'*If* I'm holding my baby…'

Helen feels the sadness of what Dolly is saying thump through her. Her hands drop into her lap, her shoulders sink but she's not quite defeated yet. She knows she shouldn't but her next words are out before she can package them up into something less definitive.

'Don't do it, Dolly. Have this baby. Learn what an incredible gift you have been given. If I hadn't had my children to help me through my very darkest times I'm not sure I…' She trails off, not wanting to make this conversation about her. Dolly is about to make the biggest decision of her life and Helen is going to do everything she can to ensure it's the right one.

'I'm frightened, Helen.' Dolly is on her feet now, it looks like she's heard enough. Helen needs to end this on a high, give her hope.

'I know you are. Who wouldn't be? But that's OK, I was too. I was much younger than you, Dolly. And maternity care was nothing like it is today back then. I remember thinking in the labour ward when they put the tightly bound bundle in my arms that what I had just done was seen as so normal, expected, nothing exceptional. No one was shouting about it from the rooftops, handing me a medal for what I'd achieved. And they should have been.' It's Helen's turn to look a little deflated now.

'No one is going to throw you a parade for having the courage to go it alone but you are on the precipice of something extraordinary – and I would say don't deny yourself the chance to experience it.'

As she bends to pick up her bag, a sadness creeps back across Dolly's face like a shadow snuffing out any lightness in its path. 'I've got no one to go to antenatal classes with.'

'What?' Helen is talking about the rigours of childbirth and all Dolly is interested in is the networking opportunity?

'You know, the classes where they teach you all about pregnancy and labour. They're full of happy young couples learning massage techniques. How to write a birth plan together. What needs to go in your hospital bag. I've looked into it and most of the classes are for couples because, naturally, everyone expects the man to give a toss. My family live miles away and most of my friends are likely to flake out at the important moment. I can hardly ask them to get up at 3 a.m. and drive across town when my waters break. I don't have anyone to do that with me.' She's walking towards the door now, mind apparently made up. Helen needs to say *something*.

'Yes, you do. You have me. I will be there for you, Dolly. I will see you through this if you'd like me to. Because I'll do everything I possibly can to support you so that you can have this baby – if that's what you decide, of course.' Helen's chest is swollen with purpose and pride, if she was that sort of woman there would be an air punch or a high five happening about now. Because while she barely knows this girl, she does know what two days of labour feels like, the sort of agony that will take you to the very threshold of your capability and hold you there for hours and hours while you rise and fall in and out of your own private world of pain. She can't bear to think of her, or any woman, going through that alone.

'Thank you, Helen, truly, that is an amazing thing for you to offer, it really is but keeping this baby may mean losing Josh and I need to be one hundred per cent sure I can do that.' Dolly's fingers are turning the door handle now. 'It's an impossible choice, and one I never imagined I would have to make. Perhaps there is the slimmest chance he will come around to the idea, but I doubt it. Unless he has a complete change of heart then it's Josh or the baby. But I won't give up hope just yet, not without one last try.'

Perhaps it's the memory of the disappointing date with Roger – which reminds her, she really must decline his last two texts asking for another one – or the realisation that she has been coping alone herself for so long now, but Helen doesn't feel like making any allowances for a man like Josh. One who helps create a problem and then lacks the courage to deal with it.

'I think it's a very cold man who can look into the eyes of his newborn baby and not want to protect and nurture it in any way he can,' Helen adds. 'It's a decision only you can make. But please don't think you're alone, Dolly. I'm here and I'm ready.'

As she watches Dolly walk slowly back down the path, head bowed, missing all that the garden has to offer at this time of year, the magnitude of what just happened hits her. There is a moment of hesitation and self-doubt while Helen questions if she's up to the job, then she is distracted by the pillar-box red light flashing on her phone, telling her there's a new voicemail. It's the first time she's noticed it. How long might it have been there? It must be Emily, she thinks. She hits the button and hears the strained sound of an unfamiliar man's voice. He's struggling to string a sentence together, can't even force out his own name through what sound like muffled tears before he gives up and ends the call. *How disturbing*, thinks Helen, clearly a wrong number. She hits delete.

Chapter Twenty-Three

Dolly

'This doesn't have to be a big deal, Dolly,' Josh is shouting at her in between mouthfuls of toast and hot coffee. 'I'm not saying no to a baby, just no to a baby right now. That's a pretty good compromise, isn't it?'

'Yes! Unless you happen to be the one with the baby in your belly!' Dolly's words are screaming back through the air, powered by the frustration of weeks of trying to chisel her way through Josh's wall of stubbornness. 'Are we really going to try to solve this in the eight minutes before we both have to leave for work?'

'No we're fucking not because I'm sick of going over old ground, it's getting us nowhere.' The door slams so loudly behind him that it sends a framed message that she bought him for Valentine's Day last year crashing to the floor. *I want all my lasts to be with you.* Just as well she'll have to bin it now, thinks Dolly, every morning she looks at it is a horrible reminder of how much their relationship has nose-dived since he'd sat in bed that morning opening it, before apologising for *not quite getting you anything yet.*

And now she's going to be late for work again, not that she particularly cares. She needs somewhere – someone – to vent all this anger at and the office at least offers the perfect candidate.

❣

What is about to happen has been a painfully long time coming. But that is only going to make it all the more sweet. Dolly is standing outside The Dick's office, hand edging towards the door handle while she glances sideways at his latest trumped-up career advice. Last week's poster was a corker: '*If you're offered a seat on the rocket ship, don't ask what seat! Just get on.*' As if anything that exciting could ever happen in this graveyard for broken careers and unlikely ambitions. This week The Dick has opted for something simpler, more *prosaic* by his standards, '*Don't feel sorry for yourself, only assholes do that.*' Dolly wonders briefly what HR might make of that if they cared enough to get out on the floor and see how the troops are coping.

As for The Dick, could the man be any more crass, any less impressive? thinks Dolly as she brushes the pain au chocolat crumbs off the front of her dress, smearing chocolate down it as she does. Then without bothering to knock, she throws his door open, making The Dick jump guiltily. She watches as he quickly closes the *Mail Online*, but not before she sees the picture of some minor celeb bending all over a beach in Barbados.

'What is it, Dolly, I am very busy!'

'Richard! Everything OK? You look a bit sorry for yourself today,' Dolly is fired up, ready to let him have it.

'Be very careful, Dolly, I have three new business pitches in my inbox that need assigning. All three of them could very easily make it to your desk.'

'I'm so pleased you raise the subject of pitches actually, Richard.' Dolly is striding backwards and forwards in front of his desk, sergeant major-like. 'I know you were keen for me to be in the pitch presentation to McVities this afternoon—'

'No, you *are* in the pitch presentation this afternoon.' The Dick's chair is swivelling in her direction now, his arms folded across his pigeon chest. She has his full attention and can see the irritation locking itself across his face – a face that is starting to flush unattractively like it does when he's had one too many Proseccos at lunchtime.

'Well, no, sadly I'm not. The bad news is I've got another personal appointment this afternoon that I'm afraid I really can't miss – you'll recall the doctor's note I gave you recently?'

'Dolly, I need you in that pitch this afternoon. Whatever this appointment is, you need to refix it. It can't be that bloody important. And can I remind you that a doctor's note is not something that should be used as an excuse to bugger off for another bout of wedding planning.'

Dolly winces slightly at the mention of her wedding then regains herself quickly, determined not to give him the satisfaction of glimpsing a moment of weakness.

'It is *very* important actually. I've made HR aware of it and of course they are being nothing but supportive, please feel free to have a chat to them if you need to. I'll be leaving the office at 2 p.m. and won't be back until tomorrow. You'll need to find another sucker to take my place – someone else to stand in front of a room full of people looking for great marketing ideas that they're not clever enough to come up with themselves. I can highly recommend Rachel, she's brilliant at bullshit and for reasons none of us can work out, is desperate to impress you.' Dolly knows antagonising The Dick like this is high risk. While being a single mum is still an option, she needs this job and its pathetic salary more than ever. But she's feeling so emboldened. It's false confidence and bound to be short-lived but while the assertiveness is pulsing through her, she can't help herself, she's going for him.

'If I could just add one thing, please, Dolly, before you go back to your desk to shuffle paper for the rest of the morning. A quick glance at your employment contract will remind you that it is important to dress professionally at all times in a manner befitting the job you largely pretend to do.' He's about to hit her where it hurts, she can feel it coming. 'Well perhaps a quick trip to the ladies' might be in order because if I'm not very much mistaken, that looks like the remains of breakfast stuck to the front of your dress... and there is a hole in the back of your tights.'

The smug bastard, he's hardly one to talk about sartorial standards. I can't be the only one who's spotted the yellowing circles under the armpits of today's once-white shirt.

'Perhaps you should consider retiring that dress altogether, it looks like it's straining at the seams a little. Off you go.' He waves a hand dismissively and Dolly has no choice but to slump back to her desk – via the kitchen where she makes a giant mug of tea with two sugars and helps herself to a handful of chocolate digestives. If someone is stupid enough to leave them lying around that's not her problem, is it?

By the time she fires up her computer the little digital display in the top right hand corner reads 10.15 a.m. She logs straight on to the BabyCentre, the site where she roughly calculated her due date before her first scan confirmed it. As she enters her password a message blazes up on the screen in front of her: *Your Baby at 18 Weeks!* In between biscuit dunking and sending a shower of soggy crumbs that will never get cleaned away into the cracks between the letters on her keyboard, Dolly scrolls downwards. Within five minutes, she's sucked right in, absorbing every detail about what's going on inside her right now.

The progress being made by something – *someone* – so little, so innocuous, so theoretical until now, is astounding. There's some gross stuff about how the top of her uterus is now reaching her belly button that she quickly skirts over. And then, whoa! This baby is already about fourteen centimetres long, it's swallowing, has the beginnings of its first hair-do and it's starting to hear and feel. Before she realises it, Dolly is skipping on ahead to the more advanced weeks where there will be eyebrows, eyelids, tiny little tooth buds.

She is only vaguely aware of the office goings-on around her. People reluctantly making phone calls, filing determinedly into The Dick's office and then out again like they've had the wind knocked out of them but mostly killing time with chat about *Bake Off* and *Strictly*. Someone comes to her desk at one point and asks for a client's contact details so they can return a series of increasingly irate phone calls that she hasn't found time to respond to yet. But she's in her own world, flitting between the incredible story being told on her screen and sad flashbacks of what's going on at home.

But this has been a productive morning, as far as Dolly is concerned. She now knows where all the local nearly new baby sales are in her area, what she can expect to spend every month on formula if she chooses not to breastfeed and the extortionate cost of nappies, bearing in mind that a newborn can get through fifteen a day.

As Dolly sits there, surrounded by the drum of dull office life, she's wondering if there is a future for her, Josh and the baby? A way back through all the rage, to the man who loved her so much, once. Can she see it? She's going to work that out on her way to her antenatal appointment. It's time to go.

❧

The maternity waiting room at the Central Cotswold Hospital is really not the best advert for motherhood. It's full of worn-out, heavily pregnant women, grappling with bored toddlers sick of waiting their turn and now pulling wallpaper off the walls, breaking the pathetic selection of toys on offer or bellowing for food at the top of their tiny lungs. The body language of each of them gives away the length of time everyone's appointments are clearly over-running. Swollen bodies are slumped low in chairs, legs have flopped absent-mindedly wide open, one woman is reclined so low she is resting the back of her head on the chair, teetering on sleep – although God knows how with the noise level in here. Exhaustion, that'll be it. As Dolly checks in at reception a clearly stressed midwife who doesn't have time to make eye contact tells her they are over-running by two hours.

'What! Why didn't you just call me to tell me that? I've left the office early to get here.' OK, she doesn't actually give a toss about that but still, she could be sitting in a comfortable coffee shop instead of in what looks, feels and sounds like the seventh circle of hell.

'Take a look around you. Does it look like we have time to manage everyone's personal schedules? Take a seat and you'll be called when it's your turn.' The entire conversation happens through the top of the midwife's head as she hasn't taken her eyes off her keyboard to visually acknowledge Dolly.

Christ, is this what I will become? wonders Dolly as she takes a seat. Part of this pack of women for whom life is one enormous hassle, dictated by the useless scheduling system of the antenatal clinic or the demands of their aggressive toddlers or needy newborns. She's looking around the room – at the posters on the wall warning of still-birth, at the selection of changing bags, contents strewn across the floor leaving an untidy trail of nappy sacks, pots of indistinguishable creams, wipes,

wipes and more wipes and spare baby clothes – everyone having long since given up trying to contain their own belongings. She watches one woman whose belly is so enormous Dolly is questioning how it stays suspended out from her. Her boobs have been pushed sideways by it so that they are hanging udder-like either side of what probably used to be her ribcage. It's a very different picture of motherhood to the one so beautifully painted on Dolly's computer screen earlier today.

Finally Dolly's name is called and she is led in to a small soulless room. It's dimly lit and contains not much more than a hospital bed, what looks like some scanning equipment, a monitor and a small desk and chair.

'Pop up on the bed for me.' The midwife is so young Dolly is tempted to ask where the real one is. 'Dolly Jackson, isn't it? And you're eighteen weeks?'

'I think so.' Dolly is suddenly hit with a wave of nerves about what they are going to discuss and what she is about to see.

'OK, we're a bit early for your next scan but we'll take a look anyway and see where we are with everything.'

'Yes, this baby isn't exactly planned I'm afraid.' God, why is she blurting this at her – and why is there so much shame attached to that one simple statement?

'You're not the only one, don't worry!' Although apparently it doesn't bother the midwife. 'Lie back and we'll check the heartbeat first, then I'll take all of your baby's measurements.' She's dolloping the cold jelly on Dolly now, taking little care to avoid her clothes.

Having let the weeks slip by, and with the number of unsuccessful attempts to convince Josh about their future sharply rising, Dolly is suddenly overcome with the fear that she really can not do this alone. Even just coming for the scan solo feels wrong. What if she's about to hear bad news? There is no one here to hold her hand, wipe her tears away and tell her everything will be OK because if nothing else, they've got each other. Oh God, oh God, maybe it's not too late to consider the alternative?

'I might need to ask you some questions about the... process, I mean my... er... my *options* from here, if I can, please.' Dolly is struggling. How do you broach this subject with a woman who has rigged her whole career around the fact that she loves babies, or so Dolly must assume. A woman who spends all day, every day bringing new ones into the world, not the opposite.

'Of course, everyone starts to get twitchy about pain relief options at this stage, it's perfectly understandable. We're going to be pushed for time today but I can give you plenty of leaflets that spell out the choices.'

Before Dolly can have another stab at making herself understood, there it is, the fast, fluttering heartbeat of new life filling the room. Dolly catches her own breath, silencing herself completely so she can concentrate on the sound coming from somewhere deep within her. She closes her eyes and lies there, perfectly still in the near darkness and thinks about the baby, Josh, the wedding, the decisions looming large in her mind. The horrible, big, messy situation that she must unpick – and soon.

'Oh, that's unusual.' The midwife says it almost under her breath, as she leans in closer to the monitor, keen to get a better look at whatever it is she thinks she's seen.

'What? What is it? Have you seen something bad?' Dolly's belly is tightening around her as the dread of what's coming next takes hold. *Is this decision about to be taken out of her hands*, she wonders? *Is there something terrible happening in there that means this baby won't make it after all?* In the almost heart-stopping moment when the midwife is forming an appropriate response, all Dolly can think is how bloody relieved Josh will be.

'No, nothing, it's OK. I shouldn't have said that. It's absolutely nothing to worry about, honestly.'

'But you *did* say it and now I *am* worried and you really need to tell me. *Please.*' Dolly is pushing herself up on her elbows, trying to see the monitor herself.

'I'd rather not – but I promise you all is fine.' She looks like she's dropped some real blunder, one that could bring an untimely end to her short career.

'Please, tell me. Whatever it is, I really would rather know. It won't go any further than this room.'

It's obvious Dolly is not about to jump off the bed like nothing was ever said and the only thing the midwife can do is reluctantly capitulate.

'OK. At eighteen weeks it's normally too early to see this but I am pretty sure I can tell the sex of the baby. Perhaps you're a little further along than we thought.'

'On my god!' If hearing the heartbeat made this pregnancy real, then finding out the gender would almost be like holding the baby in her arms. 'Tell me!'

'Are you sure you want to know? I can't be one hundred per cent positive so you will have to bear that in mind.'

'I want to know.' There is not a hint of doubt or hesitation in Dolly's mind.

'It's a girl. I'm pretty sure, Dolly, you are going to have a beautiful baby daughter!'

The tears are immediate. Soft silent ones at first that slide down the side of Dolly's face undetected before she erupts into proper big heaving sobs that require nearly half a box of the midwife's tissues. And as quickly as that, the decision is made. Dolly is going to be a mum.

'That's wonderful,' is all she can manage. 'Just wonderful.'

Chapter Twenty-Four

Emily

I wish I could put a warning sign on the bedroom door. *Do not enter, unexpectedly dead daughter inside.* Or *Go out for the day! Do something fun! But whatever you do, don't come in here.* Something, *anything* that would prepare my poor mum for what she is about to discover.

I hear her get up, pad across the landing, pausing briefly at my bedroom door, her ear pressed to the woodwork probably, *ironically*, listening for signs of life from within. Then she carries on downstairs to make me a cup of tea. The fourteen minutes it takes her are agonising. While she's cheerfully dropping a teabag into my favourite naff Easter mug, I'm lying here counting down the seconds, drowning in the horrible inevitability of what is coming. The tea that will go cold, the biscuits (two of my favourite custard creams, annoyingly) that will be returned to the old Fortnums tin in the kitchen cupboard. I listen to her coming back up the stairs, everything rattling on the wooden Laura Ashley tray I bought her years ago for Mothers' Day with the matching teacups and saucers that she usually likes to keep for best. She's humming to herself, enjoying being the first up and busy with the little act of love she is doing for me. Enjoying just being Mum – *my* Mum.

The door handle turns. *God, I wish I could make this stop.* A crack of light breaks through and I see a flash of her lilac dressing gown before the shattering noise of the tray hitting the floor cancels everything else out. I can't help it but I think about the carpet and what a mess that lot is going to make. Then I'm snapped out of hoping she's got enough Shake n' Vac to sort it by her chilling scream. She's going to wake the neighbours. My father's name is screeching through the air, so high pitched and agonised I wonder if every dog in the village can hear it.

She sees immediately that I'm gone and I wonder how? Are my eyes open, starring lifelessly up at the ceiling? Is there a streak of blood coming from my nose? My ear? My eyeball? Do I smell bad? Am I deathly white? I don't know.

There's a clattering noise from outside the room, the sound of Dad getting out of bed at speed and then his slightly panicked face appears panting in the doorway. Bless him, he's probably expecting a large spider. He's frozen now, eyes flitting from me to Glo and back again for what feels like an eternity. The penny is about to drop – and when it does his face morphs slowly. He was mildly irritated at the early wake-up but now his features are a map of hurt and disbelief – until he looks at Mum, *really* looks at her and sees in her face what she is seeing all over mine. There are shouts of *Do something!* and *What's wrong with her!* and *Call a bloody ambulance!* No one mentions the D-word. Then Dad swoops quick and low, still fit as a flea, catching Mum just before she collapses over me on the bed.

Everything is on fast-forward, like those TV shows when high-speed traffic is pictured by a single streak of bright red light. It's all happening so quickly, blurred at the edges, hectic, stressed and full of confusion.

Dad snatches my mobile from the bedside table and dials 999, panting down the phone for an ambulance. If I could smile I would because he was always banging on about how I should put a security pin on that phone so no one else could use it. For once Dad, I win! He's struggling to make himself heard over Mum's wailing and pleading to *help her Bill! Quickly!* Her cries are so loud I can feel them deep within my ear, like she's in there drumming out the beat of her pain. While Dad is trying his best to sound calm and in control, she's holding my hand, squeezing it tightly, praying for a reaction she's not going to get. Then she's pulling me up and trying to shake the life back in to me. Oh God, this is getting desperate now. *Make her stop Dad, make her stop!*

The second he disconnects the call Mum is screaming at him again to call Sarah Blake because *she'll know what to do.* Then the same man who always keeps a stack of change in a dedicated tray in the car so he never gets caught short at a parking meter is searching for my pulse, a breath, the faintest pump of a heart beat. When there is none, he's closing my eyelids with the soft pads of his fingertips, sending my lovely mum to her knees again.

The room fills with people and quicker than I expect, it comes. One of the paramedics steps back from my bed, hangs his head and blinks so slowly I wonder if his eyes are ever going to open again. A mark of defeat. When they do open he almost doesn't have to say a word but confirmation is needed and he knows it. *I'm so sorry, we're too late. I'm afraid your daughter has been dead for several hours.*

I don't know how many times he's had to deliver this blow but he does it so sensitively, I half expect my mum to thank him for his kindness. But instead she lets a moment pass. She's summoning all her raw strength, I can feel it powering up from the pit of her stomach, building, ready to shout him down.

'No she's not! Don't be so bloody stupid! She's normal, healthy. So… *stop wasting time!*'

'She's gone, luv. She's cold. There is nothing more anyone can do now.' The whispered, reasoned voice of my dad takes the sting out of her panic and I think about how even in the most awful moment imaginable, they are so good together. Solid. Unbreakable.

Sarah Blake arrives bringing some much-needed facts about headaches, scans, the neurologist's opinion, the verdict that never made it in time from the Americans and how she tried so desperately to persuade me to tell them.

'Does Mark know?' The words whisper out of Mum.

'No. Emily was adamant no one must know. She just wanted to get married and spare you all the heartache. I'm so, so sorry Glo, Bill. I wanted to tell you, I really did. I hope one day you can forgive me for that?'

If there is forgiveness to be handed out, it's not going to happen today, not now.

'Can I ask you please to go and collect Mark? He needs to be here and I don't want to leave Glo. His details are in the book next to the phone, under Jacobs.' Well done, Dad. I feel bad for all the times he irritated me with his organisational obsessions – lawns that had to be religiously mown, the central heating timer always changed with the seasons. But that orderly calm is getting him – and everyone else – through this now.

'Of course, I'll do it now,' I can feel the relief radiating off Sarah, now that she has a chance to be useful.

Sarah and the paramedics leave the room while Mum and Dad kneel on the floor by the side of my bed, in amongst the cracked china, spilt tea and broken biscuits. They cradle each other and sob so sadly in each other's arms I just want to vaporise. No one should have to watch their parents' hearts break in front of them like that. I pray long and hard that wherever I'm going next, this memory won't be travelling with me.

Time hangs frozen like that for I don't know how long before Dad says he needs to speak to the paramedics. Now it is just me and Mum and I feel warm again, so safe with her. She starts to brush my hair, taking her time to gently tease out every last knot. She's holding it firmly between the brush and my scalp in case she unexpectedly hits a tangle and I want to tell her, don't worry Mum, do your worst, nothing can hurt me now. She washes my face with a warm wet flannel, removing every last trace of yesterday's make-up (God, I'm so slovenly) tears streaming down her own face as she does it. I wonder if it's possible to run out of tears while she dabs a little lip balm across my dehydrated lips.

She talks to me, tells me that she's cooking my favourite Jamie Oliver garlicky chicken for dinner tonight, she got all the ingredients in yesterday while she was in town, even the expensive heritage tomatoes I love. She met Mark's mum for lunch too and they made plans to surprise us both with a joint photo album of our lives so far – up until our wedding day. Weirdly, I like hearing this, the plan is working and these two wonderful women are becoming good friends.

All the while she's telling me this, she's changing my clothes, heaving me out of my seriously unstylish pjs and into a pretty floral summer dress, the one I wore to our engagement party last year. I remember when I came down the stairs in it that day and she got all emotional. She tried to hide it but I saw Dad hand her a tissue and tell her to stop being so silly. To me she's always her best when she's silly.

As she leans over me, I can smell her citrusy Penhaligon's perfume and I'm transported back through a million happy memories – her pulling a birthday party dress over my seven-year-old head; being pushed on the swings, face crimson with the giggles, cuddles on the sofa hoping she wouldn't notice it's past bedtime, days ill off school with grapes and dry crackers in bed.

By the time Mark arrives, she's even painted my fingernails a light baby pink. That last bit is odd but I get it, I really do. She's only thinking of me. She always did care more about my appearance than I did. Maybe she also knows it's probably the last time Mark will see me and she wants me to look lovely for him.

Dad is back in the room and I'm shouting at him *Look after her Dad, don't let her spark go out.* Maybe those words will hang in the air somewhere and creep into his ear sometime soon when he is sleeping. I hope so.

'Glo, Mark's here. Please can we let him have a moment alone with Emily?' Sarah's obviously broken the news, because I can hear Mark through the brick wall out on the landing making a valiant effort to compose himself. But his breath is ragged and uneven and I can feel the nervous vibrations through the floorboards as he shifts from one foot to another.

Mum doesn't hear a word at first. She's lying on the bed with me, side by side, our fingers interlocked together. She doesn't want to leave me and I don't want her to either. I want to roll over to face her and take in a huge lungful of her comforting smell. What if this is the last time I see her? I might not be here when she comes back. I have no idea how long I'm going to occupy this observation deck between life and death.

Seeing Mark is going to kill me all over again. Mum takes another minute, saying nothing before she slowly gets off the bed and leaves the room. She pauses briefly on her way out and swipes my white *Tie The Knot* Smythson notebook off the shelf. I knew it! She's drawn to it somehow, she knows there's something in there she needs to read, I'm convinced of it. She doesn't look at Mark, she can't, preferring the comfort of Dad's chest instead.

The door closes behind them and it's just me and Mark now. He stands, several paces from the bed, hands clasped to his face, eyes bloodshot and full of sorrow, looking but not believing what he's seeing. He's shaking. My big, strong nearly-husband is shaking all over and there isn't a thing I can do about it. Seeing him is a brutal reminder that this wedding is off. All that planning, decision-making, all those hours spent weighing up the gold foil versus the letterpress stationery and now none of it will come to be. I will never be Mrs Jacobs. My engagement ring is never going to be joined by the simple white gold wedding band we chose together. The thought makes me feel so hollow, so pointless. Why didn't someone just tell me, when I was six years old and role-playing my way to the kind of life I thought I might like, *Get a move on, because twenty-one years from now it'll be gone before you even take delivery of the John Lewis thirty-two piece crockery set.* Mark's burying his face under my hair now into the softness of my neck and I can sense his tears on my cold skin. 'I'm so, so sorry,' he's saying it over and over again and every time I hear that word it's sending a painful stab of guilt right through me. I did this to him.

The living me sometimes wasted time in idle moments, usually hormonal ones, wondering how I might react on hearing life-changing bad news. You know, the really grim stuff – your husband's gone under the wheels of the number twenty-three bus on his way to work. Your mum's blood test results didn't just show a touch of anaemia after all. But what Mark does next really surprises me. Less than two hours after my cold, hardening body is discovered what does he do? He unpeels himself from me, muttering about needing to cancel my wedding dress and calls Helen on his mobile. At least he tries to. The call connects to her answerphone and he tries to choke out his own name but can't. He makes several attempts before the tears take over and he has to hang up. He looks like he's sulking now but maybe he just feels hugely cheated – out of a wife, a family, a future with the girl who was always meant to be his – forever.

Before he has time to ready himself for another go, Dad is back with the paramedics.

'We need to let these guys do what they need to do, Mark. Will you come downstairs with me please?' Dad leans over me and tenderly kisses my forehead, leaving his lips on my skin just long enough to whisper a goodbye to his *darling girl* before he takes Mark by the arm and leads him towards the door. He needs directing, his brain has shut down. I know how he feels. I feel the ache in my no-longer-beating heart as I watch him disappear from the room. He doesn't look back because he doesn't believe it's happening and I know it will hit him later. His grief is yet to come.

As the two of them descend the stairs together, arms gripping each other's shoulders for support, moving down towards the sound of my mum's soft sobs, the body bag is zipping up around me. It smells synthetic inside with a hint of disinfectant and I wonder rather alarmingly how many have been in here before me.

My body may be leaving the building but there's still no sign of me following it and I'm no closer to working out why. But I do know I don't want to be a spectator, forced to watch this tragedy and everything it will do to my beautiful family. I realise I'm a coward. I want out now. Much easier that way. For me at least. If I could action anything I'd happily stick around. But what's the point when all you can do is sit and stare? It's just going to be torture.

I spend the night curled up on the sofa, watching them all, searching their faces for any clue of what might be coming next. The answer to why I'm lingering has to be within one of them.

Mum doesn't say a single word other than to decline an offer of tea from Dad every now and again. By the time the sun starts to poke its fingers through her net curtains, she's finished reading my notebook. She closes it, places it silently into her lap and looks across the room at them both.

'She was even *more* special than we thought.' She says the words through the very faintest smile.

I'm already past tense.

Chapter Twenty-Five

Jessie

Anyone would think Mariah Carey was in town. Six Louis Vuitton trunks are lined up side by side on the floor of Jessie's enormous walk-in wardrobe, the kind of luggage any true fashionista would crawl on her hands and knees all the way to Paris for. These ones are ready to be filled with everything she needs for three days of thoroughly over the top wedding celebrations. And one super-luxe honeymoon.

A Jimmy Choo evening clutch, frosted with thousands of Swarovski crystals and just about big enough for a lipstick and credit card is swinging from the index finger of Jessie's left hand. The designer's silver mirrored leather four-inch pumps are wedged under the same arm while the other is cradling her mobile to her ear. She's running through some final pointers with Willow Manor's wedding planner. And it kills her to admit it – so she won't – but this girl is tantalisingly close to meeting expectations.

'The vicar has finally agreed to us removing the orange aisle carpet so our guys will get in there in a few weeks and rip it up.' Her voice is full of spirit, so pleased to be confirming the news they have been waiting weeks to hear.

'About bloody time too.' Jessie might be happy to hear it but it never occurs to her to show it with a thank you.

'Quite, yes. The new cream one you've chosen will be laid the night before the wedding and covered so that it remains spotlessly clean until the Saturday morning. I've also taken care of all the arrangements to re-lay the original one after the big day. What would you like me to do with the cream one then, Ms Jones?'

'Bin it. It's no use to me. What was it in the end? The renovations to the spire or a hefty donation to the retired servicemen fund that swung it?'

'Both, I'm afraid. But I can promise you it's going to look incredible.'

Jessie's not bothering to listen now, she's too busy admiring her Carolina Herrera cherry red palazzo pants, imagining how they might look on her in whatever luxurious location Adam has chosen for their honeymoon.

'The florists will arrive at 10 a.m the day before and we will keep the seven thousand David Austin rose heads cool in the old kitchens below the hotel until the last minute so they will stay super fresh for you. The planting on the front lawn is all on schedule so everything will look perfect for the champagne reception, and the oak trees, as you know, have already been removed.' Her voice is laced with a little embarrassment, possibly recalling their first meeting when Jessie bull-dozed her way across the lawn making all sorts of ludicrous demands that somehow have all been achieved.

'And doesn't it look *so* much better for it?' Jessie isn't going to miss an opportunity to snatch another *thanks to me* moment.

'Well, yes, I think once we re-laid all the surrounding lawns I agree it does, but we'll be answering complaints from the locals for a long time to come. Still, that's my problem. The team from Jo Malone arrive the morning of the wedding and they will get all the atomisers in place to pipe Orange Blossom into the ceremony space for two hours before your guests arrive and then seventy candles will be lit forty-five minutes before you make your entrance. They will then return on Sunday morning to replace them with the Blackberry & Bay candles and diffusers throughout the hotel and grounds ahead of the garden party. The scenting will be the perfect distinction between the two events, I think.' Jessie can practically hear the tick, tick, tick as the planner is working her way through the checklist. Time to add something last minute to it then.

'I've been thinking, it would be such a lovely memento of the day if everyone left with an Orange Blossom candle. Please can you arrange for one to be positioned at each place setting. And not the travel ones, the full-sized ones that burn for forty-five hours.'

'OK, another three hundred candles, one for each guest?' There's no incredulity in the planner's voice any more, she's merely fact checking. Just over five months jumping to the borderline insane orders of this bride-to-be has trained her well.

'Yep.' One word that instantly adds more than £10,000 to the wedding bill.

'Right. I'll call them as soon as we're finished and have them couriered here and stored for you. Peggy Porschen has confirmed she will arrive the afternoon before to begin constructing the ten-tier cake, while you are all at the rehearsal dinner at the Coleridge's estate. That's when we will start chilling the Dom Perignon, exactly as you requested.'

'I want it at seven degrees please. No warmer or it's just not right. Now, who have you assigned to look after Hugo when he gets there on the Saturday morning?'

'I spoke to his studio yesterday and I will be greeting him, doing a final walkthrough of all the areas he wants to shoot in and getting all his photographic equipment safely stored. He mentioned he's bringing more than originally expected for the honeymoon, is that right?'

'Yes. He will be accompanying Adam and I on honeymoon too – I want a beautiful record of every part of this celebration, nothing should be missed. Presumably Adam has told him where we're going because I haven't got a clue. And on that note, this next bit is very important.' Jessie is pulling a selection of Heidi Klein bikinis out of a drawer, examining them all for the most flattering cut.

'Hugo only wants the most attractive members of the congregation sat aisle-side. And so do I. These are the people who will be in the shots he takes of the two of us coming back down the aisle, just married. I have selected the appropriate people and I will email you a file later with their details and a head shot so you can identify them. It is imperative these people make it in to the correct seats. And, I don't care what it takes, but my sister Claire must not be visible *at all*.' All of Helen's hard work, the big talking-to she gave Jessie, the cold hard logic she laid out in the hopes of preventing her from alienating her family for good have all been blown away in the final run-up to the wedding, like petal confetti on a summer breeze.

'I want her sat as far from the aisle as possible and I am personally charging you with this task so please don't let me down.' Jessie is beyond caring how heartless this sounds.

There is only the faintest pause from the planner while she computes what has just been said.

'OK. I will make sure you are entirely happy, Ms Jones, please don't worry about a thing.'

'Are there any changes to the guest list?' *Has Annabel broken her neck horse-riding by any chance?*

'No. There are no dropouts – obviously. A few guests want to upgrade to suites which is all under control and Tilly Hunter-Browne has confirmed her plus-one is Dolly Jackson, so I will tweak the seating plan and run it past you again later. The only thing you haven't confirmed for me, Ms Jones, are the speeches and who will be giving one so we can add that to our itinerary of timings for the day.'

'I'll have to come back to you on that.' Jessie is suddenly sounding much less sure of herself. 'One or two are still up in the air.' Jessie disconnects the call and gets that gnawing feeling in her stomach, the sort that only surfaces when you know deep down, even if you can't admit it to yourself, that you're about to steamroller over someone's feelings.

Her dad's speech. She's been stewing on this for weeks. That moment when he stands from his seat on the top table and the innocent tinkle of knife on glass will make her backside clench, her throat dry, turn her into a bottomless pit of angst. How is he ever going to pull this off? He's not. She knows it. Put bluntly, he lacks the skills. He's not a dinner party kind of man, has never held a table of rambunctious guests enthralled while he regales them with clever, fast-paced anecdotes – and why would he, what does he have to draw on? Hours sweeping the playground at the end of the school day, changing light bulbs, unblocking drains – it's hardly the backdrop to a cracking after-dinner speech. Worse, he'll prattle on about how well she did at school, exceeding all the teacher's expectations – like overachieving would be anything new or interesting to this audience – while Jessie is forced to watch the yawns build around the room.

Jessie knows a bad speech will hang in the air for the rest of the day. People made to feel uncomfortable will stay that way. It will be a major, irreversible vibe kill and she's not going to let it happen – not when there's someone else far more qualified for the job.

Henry.

He's already agreed to say a few words at the rehearsal dinner. Once Dad sees how good he is, it will be easy then. It will pave the way for her to suggest that Henry is a better candidate for the day itself. Who says they must follow tradition? This will all be terribly modern and interesting, people will prefer it. Dad can still walk her down the aisle, still have his proud moment, she's not denying him that. But she will save him from the stress of all that inner rehearsal when he should be enjoying the day, from those last minute trips to the gents' for a mental run-through when he could be celebrating with Mum. Save him from the possibility of getting nervous-smashed. *No one* wants that.

Which just leaves Jessie's speech. In the interests of keeping this wedding *on-message* she has decided to give one, keeping the focus well and truly on the future, not the past. She'll centre the whole thing on the huge generosity of Camilla and Henry – it is only fair seeing as they have paid so much towards the wedding. And how welcoming they've been, opening up their lives to her, embracing her into her *new* family now. She's imagining the bent-out-of-shape look on Annabel's face when she says *that*! It doesn't need to be about the Joneses, they'll be sat on the top table for all to see, she's not hiding them away. Guests will see the aisle walk, the mother-of-the-bride loudly blubbing into a fistful of tissues but the more glossing over of Claire that can be done, the better. There isn't much to say anyway and really she should be focusing the word count on Adam, her wonderful new husband, the man who has changed her life in ways she never thought possible. And here he is.

'Hi, gorgeous, have you got a minute?' Adam steps into the bedroom carrying an excitingly large box in his arms, tied with a giant white bow. A grin is spreading across his beautiful face as he sees Jessie's own features light up. 'I wanted to give you something. Your wedding gift. I know it's a little early but, well, I couldn't wait!'

Jessie's heart swells. Adam is one of those rare people who always get it right. The right moment, the right man, the right words. Always so sure of himself. Before he has chance to say another word, Jessie pulls him down to the floor and they sit opposite each other grinning like two kids on Christmas morning while she rips the package open, filling the room with squeals of delight. Whatever it is, she knows he will have chosen it himself, given it proper thought. He has an army of friends, personal assistants and advisors he could delegate to but he's not that sort of man. He'll have done his own research, made the shopping trip, carefully selected it.

It's the square beauty case, wrapped in the classic monogrammed canvas. The one piece missing from her Vuitton collection – and the piece that says *I'm sitting at the pointy end of the plane.*

'Open it.'

As Jessie lifts the lid she can see a white envelope inside with his handwritten note on the front.

To my Darling Jessie, why is it all the love songs are about you? Come away with me on our trip of a lifetime. Yours forever, Adam x x x

Jessie glances up at him through eyelashes that are working hard to hold back the tears.

'Go on…' He's every bit as excited as she is. It's one of the things Jessie loves most about him. Despite the money and the privilege, he's never lost the little-boy joy that comes from making other people happy.

As Jessie opens the envelope, out tumble their honeymoon tickets and itinerary. Three weeks, the presidential suite, North Island in the Seychelles. Her eyes are darting down through the details: arriving by helicopter to this little pocket of paradise where they'll sleep in a driftwood four poster, shower outside under a canopy of bamboo, with butler service, full-throttle twenty-four hour spa, no menus – just a personal chef who cooks every meal to order, and golf buggies to bomb around this modern day Noah's Ark. Just the two of them – unless you count Hugo – in total and utter bliss. And there is no one on earth she would rather share it all with.

'I can't wait to start this adventure with you.' Adam pulls her in to a bear hug and the two of them collapse together on the floor, rolling around like two playful puppies.

'Neither can I. It's going to be amazing, Adam. I just know it.'

Chapter Twenty-Six

Helen

It's Saturday morning in the height of wedding season and Helen has an appointments book rammed full of brides-to-be – at least she did. Two days ago she cancelled every one of them. Personally called each woman and explained: *I'm desperately sorry. I'm afraid I have a personal issue I must deal with. It's unavoidable.* Not once in all the years she's been running The White Gallery has she ever cancelled a bride. Now she's cancelled eight in one hour of back-to-back calls.

Helen knew this day would come – eventually. And when it did, she would have to face it down. When her heart told her the time was right, she would act. Today is that day. This morning she is setting the breakfast table for one. Her hand hovers briefly – habitually – over the second place mat, then no, she refuses to pick it up. She sits at her small dining table alone, picking at a plate of fresh pear and grapefruit segments. No need to extend the extra wooden leaf. It's just her, as it always is. But the sadness is lifting. Determined Helen is nudging ahead, just, in the charge against loneliness.

A pile of everything she needs for the job she must do today is neatly stacked in the kitchen. Black bin bags. A large cardboard box big enough to store a wedding dress. Smaller boxes to take care of Phillip's last personal items. Cleaning products. And a stiff, self-sealing envelope, just the right size to accommodate the passage Phillip left her, the one she has read every single day since *that day*.

Because no one can stay sad forever. Helen knows she can't mourn her life away, especially when she has so much to be happy about: a beautiful daughter who surprised her with a text late last night saying she's *dropping by* today; a thriving business that allows her to feel useful and talented every second of the working day; and in two weeks' time, her first antenatal appointment with Dolly – the first of six sessions that will take Dolly all the way through her pregnancy and birth planning, with Helen fixed by her side for support. Time is finally wearing through her tears and sorrow and she is re-emerging on the other side. Sort of. Nearly. Transformed from the broken shell of a woman who was left alone after Phillip's death to a much stronger businesswoman, friend and mother whose days are full and challenging, just the way she likes and needs them to be. OK, not *everything* is perfect. There was that horribly awkward date with Roger. But the point is, she did it when she could so easily have backed out. That's progress on a grand scale.

And perhaps that is why now she is doing something else that even a few short months ago she never imagined she could. She stands in front of her beautiful wedding dress, hanging elegantly as it always is from her armoire, taking one last indulgent look, before she will pack it away forever. She moves closer to it so her cheek is touching the soft fabric, burying herself one last time in the memories of that special day – on the precipice of the most joyfully full years of her life. She wraps her arms around the dress then allows them to glide slowly down over the silk, her fingers lifting over the delicate glass beads and across the aged lace. Details from a different era but still every bit as potent as if she were standing in the dress today, gazing into Phillip's eyes and promising to love him so much – love him *too* much.

The dress must disappear from daily sight. Too many memories are pressing up against the present now, dragging her back under in those more frequent moments when she pops up for air. Taking big relieved lungfuls of it, only to be pulled back under into the deep darkness below, weighed down by fifteen metres of taffeta. The dress, exquisite as it is, has become a symbol of everything that's holding Helen back. She considers for a moment stepping into it, pulling the still soft material up around her ageing body. One last spin. One last visit to how it used to be before she closes the portal to the past forever. But she can't do it. She doesn't want to. She wants to stay strong, stick to the plan. Get the job done.

She takes the dress off the hanger, spreads it out on the bed and starts to fold it neatly in on itself, taking care not to catch any of the embellishment on the fabric. Then she tucks Phillip's handkerchief into the bodice. This bit is hard. She wonders briefly about slipping it into her lingerie drawer, hiding it at the back so she won't see it every day but she'll know it's there. She pauses. Lets her fingertips stay attached to it for a few seconds longer before she places everything into the box and reaches for the lid. There is one more thing to add. She takes the passage from her bedside drawer, perches on the edge of the bed and reads it one last time quietly to herself.

Speak to me in the easy way
which you always used.
Put no difference into your tone.
Wear no forced air of solemnity or sorrow.

❧

'Thank you, Phillip.' Helen is looking down at the well-worn words – Phillip's very last gift to her. She thinks of the nights she's pinched it between her fingers like her life depended on it, *most* nights in the beginning. Some evenings she slept with it clutched to her chest, then slipped it into her purse the following morning among the first class stamps and dry cleaning receipts; unable to leave the house without knowing it was there. Not any more.

'Please don't think I love you any less, my darling.' The sobs are building in her now. 'But I need to do this. I pray you can understand why.'

Then she places it into the envelope and seals it quickly before she changes her mind. This is the hardest thing – far harder than packing away Phillip's toothbrush that has sat untouched next to hers all this time. His aftershave, too, or what's left of it. That also accompanied her to bed some nights, dotted on the pillow beside her so when she woke, for a brief moment it was almost like he was there, ready to spring to life and get the kettle on.

She's removing the last traces of Phillip from her home, if not her heart, all boxed up lovingly and destined for the loft. But closing the lid on this lifeline is like saying goodbye to Phillip all over again and she can't help it, as she stands looking down at the envelope she's holding with both hands, a tear splashes on to it, one last part of her joining all the memories of him before she slides the lid closed on all of it.

The one thing she leaves is the framed image of the two of them on her bedside table, but even this needs to move. She carries it into the lounge and places it on a bookshelf, nestled amongst her novels and designer biographies. Less visible, no longer the last thing she will see before she closes her eyes each night, but still there, casting a loving watch over her daily routine.

Then she's cleaning: the entire apartment from top to bottom as if physically scrubbing away the stubborn stain of her sadness. The bed is stripped; she attacks its frame with polish, then she's vacuuming the mattress and banging dust out of the pillows, then shooting bathroom spray all over the en-suite.

Kitchen cupboards are emptied and wiped clean inside before everything is re-ordered and replaced. She fills the oven with toxic smelling foam and leaves it to do its thing while she disinfects the floor and all the work surfaces. Three hours later the place smells like a hospital and is show-home spotless. Fresh cut flowers from the garden are placed in the kitchen and lounge, windows are thrown open and Helen upturns the sticks in her jasmine scented oil diffuser sending a waft of pretty scent floating through the air. Somehow she feels this is a new beginning. A bit like the monstrously thorough clean she gave the family home after the school holidays when the kids went back to school – taking all their mess, smells and clutter with them. It's the ultimate cleanse, spurred on by the deadline of Betsy arriving in ten minutes.

There's an uncomfortable suspicion in Helen about her daughter's visit. They spoke just a couple of days ago, covering all the usual stuff and Helen mostly bugging her about whether Jacob's finally fixed the security light at the front of the house that's been broken for two months. Is Betsy drinking too much, partying too hard, does she *ever* just have a night on the sofa? In between all the nagging there was no mention of Betsy *dropping by.* Betsy's visits are usually planned weeks, if not months, in advance and carefully co-ordinated around work schedules, boutique bookings and her daughter's hectic social life. Then the text came last night announcing she would be arriving less than twenty-four hours later. Something must be wrong. The mum panic button has been activated and a long list of catastrophic scenarios are fighting it out in Helen's head when the doorbell rings. Here she is. A bundle of girly energy, alive with ambition and positivity, as always.

'Mum!'

Helen's worries melt as she sees her daughter's trademark broad smile, her corkscrew blonde curls (always a mystery where they came from) bouncing off her shoulders as she hurls herself into the outstretched arms of her mother.

'Come in, come in, but shoes off, I've been going crazy with the polish this morning. Is Jacob not with you?'

'No, he's writing!' Betsy shouts the words over her shoulder, already shooting up the stairs, into the lounge and hopping on to the sofa, feet curled up under her, totally at home. She misses the controlled intake of breath that Helen is taking, pushing her lips together to hold in any judgement of Jacob that may be in danger of escaping them.

'Something is different, Mum. What is it? What have you changed?' Betsy's eyes are all over the room.

Helen looks up towards the loft hatch. 'Oh, nothing, just a quick clean, that's all.' The last thing she wants to do now is waste their precious moments together raking over the morning's activities.

'So, Jacob.' This conversation needs to happen and better it happens face to face than pieced together over countless text messages that Betsy might then feel she needs to hide from him.

'He's on a deadline.'

'Oh, that's a shame.' She doesn't entirely mean it. It might be nice to see him and give him a mild grilling on his work plans but she is also thrilled to have some unexpected one-on-one time with Betsy so they can finally talk.

'Well, it's good actually, Mum, because, guess what? He's landed a book deal! His first novel is going to be published and the advance he's being paid will mean we can really go nuts with… Actually, come and sit down and I'll tell you all about it.'

'That's wonderful news!' Helen is next to Betsy on the sofa, beaming just as broadly. Finally, he'll be paying his way, her daughter can take her foot off the gas a little.

'So, we were wondering, what's the best way to spend this money? What should we do with it that would be really worthwhile and special and great for everyone?'

Oh no, there's some horrible overly generous charitable donation about to be announced, Helen can feel it coming. Poetry to rehabilitate ex-offenders or to save knackered beach donkeys. *Please, no.*

'Listen, Betsy, I think you should be really careful with this because…'

'We're getting married, Mum! Jacob has proposed and I said yes, *obviously*! Woo-Hoo!'

'Oh my goodness!'

'And when the time comes, Mum, I'd like *you* to walk me down the aisle. Will you do that for me, please?'

Helen can't say a thing. She buries herself in her daughter's arms, squeezing her so tightly, sobbing into those sweet-smelling curls, needing more than ever to feel the warmth of her dewy collagen-loaded skin. And the squeeze is being returned, Betsy appreciating, no doubt, the emotions that are surging through her dear mum right now. Helen's eyes stay clenched while her mind fast-forwards to the day, probably about a year from now, her daughter ready to take that incredible step into the future. She can see the dress she'll be wearing, knows exactly which one she will recommend she tries on first, sees herself steadying

Betsy all the way along the aisle through a sea of smiles to the altar. There will be no father-of-the-bride speech that day but no matter. Helen will be there, determined, strong, overflowing with enough love for both of them.

'I'm so, so proud of you, Betsy.' It's two whole minutes until Helen gathers herself well enough to say the words. 'This is the very best news you could give me, today of all days.'

As she waves Betsy off later that afternoon, Helen is aware of a man climbing out of a black Audi across the road. Something about the way his head is dipped, his shoulders hunched with the collar of his jacket upturned like he doesn't want to be seen tells her something is not quite right. He lacks the carefree or clueless demeanour of a passing tourist. She doesn't recognise him as local either but he's heading her way. Although she has never seen this man before something keeps her rooted to the spot, waiting for him in the doorway of The White Gallery where an hour ago she and Betsy were trying on veils.

As he crosses the road without looking, eyes sharply focused on his destination, he pushes open the gate to her front garden and starts to walk deliberately towards her. Now she can see the upset etched all over his unshaven face. There is a brief moment of fear when she wonders what on earth this man might want with her and then the fuses ignite and connect in her brain. Her mind is thrust back to that answerphone message. The distraught-sounding man that never made sense at the time. He's close enough now for her to see two bloodshot eyes trained intensely on hers, searching for some recognition, some comfort. He opens his mouth to speak but only tears escape him. Helen says what she knows he can't.

'Emily?'

Then his arms are around her, head heavy over her shoulder. She feels the weight of him collapsing into her as he whispers a pain-filled *yes* into her ear.

Chapter Twenty-Seven
Dolly

Dolly's eyes flash open, her brain switches on and she's immediately hit with the sense she has *a lot* to achieve today. She just can't remember what. Dodging more deadlines from The Dick? No, it's Saturday. Another gloriously pointless row with Josh? Nope, he's supposedly out flat-hunting for himself *again*. She attempts to throw herself out of bed before remembering she's anchored by the hard boulder that's pressing down heavily on the front of her. Oh yes. Baby prep! And *lots* of it.

The weeks are flying by and Dolly is steering this express train to motherhood with all the gusto she once reserved for star-jump burpees and squat holds. All her obsessive commitment and relentless focus on herself has found a new place to breed, fanned by the underlying competitive edge that seems to swim passive-aggressively around her antenatal class each week. As she's heaving herself slowly out of bed, hands supporting the boulder, she thinks briefly about the eight other women in her class, all first time mothers-to-be, all convinced they know the best way to deliver and raise a baby – regurgitating chapters of the latest baby tome, just like the colicky babies they are all so keen to avoid having.

She winces remembering that first meeting, when she cluelessly arrived fifteen minutes late because she hadn't bothered to Google-map the address, then was forced to do her little intro to the group without hearing what the others had said. She'd prattled on for ten minutes about her job and her social life, making it all sound as glamorous as possible – neatly skirting the lack of loving partner bit – before the teacher finally said *Yes, but how many weeks are you Dolly? Tell us something about the baby* to muffled sniggers from around the circle. Then she sat there, rigid with panic for another forty minutes as her pathetic lack of anatomical knowledge was glaringly exposed to a room full of vagina know-it-alls.

Bloody womb-obsessives she mutters as she heads for the bathroom. But it's staggering the effect a little communal humiliation is having on Dolly. Once shamed, now fully focused – getting ahead of the others with her birth plan and researching her way to the top of the class, determined to be first to buy and pack her hospital bag. Anyway, before anything more can happen today, she needs to execute her morning routine. She waits until the shower temperature is just right before she steps into it. If it turns her skin pink, it's too hot for the baby, she knows that now. She stands there for a few minutes, letting the water fly off the boulder at right angles, thinking about Josh, wondering if he will ever bugger off and give her the space she needs to grow – in every sense of the word.

He's shown practically no interest in her or the baby since she told him she is definitely keeping it. Another epic row was followed by more awkward living around each other, Josh saying he's looking for somewhere else to live but never actually achieving that. Last night she caught him looking at her. As she slumped on the sofa, absentmindedly rubbing her belly, he looked, asked the odd question about pregnancy timings then drifted back off into his own selfish world. She gave up hope of reconciliation a long time ago. Too many horrible things said. Too many insults that can't be unheard.

Dolly steps out of the shower and reaches for her anti-stretchmark oil. She's getting through litres of the stuff. Its bland nutty smell has permeated every item of her clothing and bedding and probably the curtains and carpets too. She's slapping it all over her body now, sending oily splashes up the bathroom walls and over the cupboard doors. Then she's wafting around the room naked while it seeps into her curves. When she finally feels like less of an oil slick she throws on a robe and heads for the kitchen for some iron-rich porridge with a side of smoked salmon for baby brain development.

The remains of last night's cook-a-thon are still sprawled across the work surface. She snaps the lid shut on the box of homemade sweet potato gnocchi and starts to force it in to the last remaining space in the freezer – next to a range of pasta sauces, cottage pies and veggie bakes she's spent the past week making, decanting and freezing, just as advised at antenatal class. Cook now, then enjoy in those first few weeks after the baby is born when you'll barely have the energy to lift your head from the pillow, let alone tackle something as co-ordinated as cooking dinner. OK, she's well ahead of the game with this job but that's how she likes it. She fleetingly wonders whether she should be portioning them for one or two. *Oh bugger him*, Josh isn't her responsibility any more. There is also now a designated cupboard in the kitchen that houses all baby-related kit. The spiralizer had to go to make room for the bottle warmer but it's a long time since she ate a string of raw courgette pretending to be pasta anyway.

As Dolly starts to spoon the cement-like porridge into her mouth, the pelvic floor exercises can begin. She's sucking herself in tightly while the imaginary elevator travels upwards, pausing at different floors before climbing higher and higher then making it's controlled steady descent. Every single day she does them, never missing it, totally committed to the preservation of whatever might be left of her after labour. Well, that and a desperate hope she won't be one of those mothers who has to carry a spare pair of pants around in her handbag, living in fear of an almighty knicker-wetting sneeze.

There is some slightly terrifying internal perineal massage designed to stop you tearing during labour that was explained at last week's class – causing even Helen's normally immovable eyebrows to shoot skywards. This is also about to be added to Dolly's morning routine. But first she wants to research the inflatable balloon contraption you can buy over the internet that does the job for you, negating the need for your own fingers. She just hopes The Dick isn't chancing past her desk the day she's looking for *that* on Amazon.

Dolly dumps her empty breakfast bowl into the sink – something for Josh to do later – and heads back to the bedroom to dress. Her hipbone skimming skinny jeans and bum-hugging jumpsuits moved out long ago and in their place hang a line of wide-legged jeans topped with six inches of belly-warming elasticated heaven and leggings that go all the way up to her boobs, so it's like pouring herself into a giant sock each morning. Dolly knows she will struggle to give these up after the baby arrives. They've become part of her, a line of defence against the haters, just like the *baby on board* badge she never thought she'd wear. On any other woman it was a crushing bore or an aggressive *stand aside people, incredibly important pregnant lady coming through* brag. But somehow now it's OK, more than OK, a discreet ad for everything that is exciting for Dolly right now.

Shares in Amazon are surely soaring thanks to the never-ending arrival of all manner of baby paraphernalia – a fabulously extravagant use for the no-longer-needed wedding fund. It's Gina Ford's *The Complete Sleep Guide* today, now that she's finished her *Contented Little Baby Book* and transferred all the salient points on to cue cards, ready to be easily and quickly referenced when sleep deprivation has pureed her brain. Inspired by one of her over achieving classmates, Dolly just needs to put the finishing touches to the schedule for the baby's first four weeks. The times she will eat, sleep and play and then she's going to add the horrifyingly few mother and baby groups that don't clash with the routine to the calendar on the wall in the kitchen – a level of organisation previously completely unknown to her – but my God did she enjoy sharing *that* in class. She worked out early on that the most together women in the group are all signed up members of the Gina Ford fan club – which is when she ordered her first book. The rest seem to be subscribing to the *let the baby tell you what it needs* school of thought. They are also, coincidentally, the ones with the least attractive husbands and who show up every week having dodged the make-up bag and hairbrush. Decision made.

So, now for today's big task – buying the pram. She texts Tilly, making sure she is ready for their planned 11.30 a.m. call, still an unholy hour for anyone childless, but especially Tilly who is rarely in bed before 2 a.m. at the weekend.

Where Helen has been the wonderfully measured voice of practical calm, Tilly is keeping Dolly grounded, stopping her sliding too far into the mummy world where she might start honking things like *Keep that vape away from my baby!* and *You do know this is a 30 mph speed zone?* That's why, despite having no working knowledge of a pram whatsoever, she's been chosen to advise Dolly on the most expensive purchase of all – on the thing that will be glued to the front of Dolly for the next two years. And just like the marketing strategist she is, Tilly's done her homework. Dolly's mobile rings twice before the dynamically assertive voice of Tilly fills her ears.

'OK, I've been asking around and this purchase is actually *considerably* more significant than you might think, Dolly.'

'Right.'

'Think of this pushchair as the maternal equivalent of the new Miu Miu Mary Janes. It's your gateway to the best invites from the sort of mummy cliques you'll want to hang out with and a brilliant barbed wire fence to those you don't – assuming you choose the right one of course. But that's where I come in. What's your budget?'

'A thousand pounds – or what would have been my accessories budget for the wedding.' She's trying to make light of it but inside it feels like someone is stamping on her heart. Dolly still can't quite believe she's talking about her wedding as something that is no longer happening, when it once occupied so much of her energy, so many of her determinedly happy thoughts.

'Bloody brilliant! That means we don't even have to look at the Maclarens or the Mamas & Papas. I also think we should avoid the Bugaboo. Yes, I know it has a huge celebrity fan base but it's a little too mass market for you, darling.'

'Er… should we be thinking about safety features? Brakes? Three-point body harnesses? Head cushioning?' Dolly is logging on to her laptop at the breakfast bar so she can call up images of anything Tilly recommends.

'All important, Dolly, but if you want to be Cool Fun Mum and blend, blend, blend then we need to get the aesthetics right first. They all have to pass the same safety tests, don't they? But do they all have a coffee cup holder that can accommodate a Starbucks grande latte? Do they all have handlebars slim enough for your Anya Hindmarch changing bag? And crucially the mobile phone attachment that means you can be hands-free gassing all day long. Because, frankly, what else are you going to be doing? And do they *look* the business?'

'Good point. OK, what's your top choice?' After weeks of solo decision-making, Dolly is ready to roll over and be told what to buy. But the thought of joining a new group of women who need to be impressed and entertained every second she's in their company sounds exhausting. More people to judge and quite possibly reject her – just as soon as they work out what a tragic case she really is. Dumped single mum. Not the best intro is it?

'Well, you could look at the Versace stroller, very nice with its brocade fabric and gold trim. Or the Fendi which obviously screams luxury fashion house. But in my opinion nothing beats the Silver Cross Aston Martin collaboration. It's covered in baby-soft suede, the very same used inside the car's roof and it's sold in very few places which means there won't be ten of you with it at sing-along time.'

'It sounds expensive.' Will she now have to endlessly compete for the crown of star new mum when all she wanted was to be snuggled up on the sofa every night, the baby and her wrapped up safely in Josh's arms?

'It is. But here's the really splendid bit. I happen to have a contact at their PR agency who is going to swing you the fifty percent press dizzy, you just need to pretend you write for *Mother& Baby* or something. Then it's all yours for the absolute bargain price of one thousand, five hundred pounds. Do we have a deal so I can go back to bed?'

'Sod it, yes, deal! Thank you so much Tilly. That's the last big thing I needed to get all sorted.'

'Fantastic. Now before I go how's that… *devoted* boyfriend of yours? Found somewhere else to live yet or not?'

'I wish he had. I'll tell you about it all next weekend. We are still on for Adam's wedding aren't we?'

'Are you actually kidding me? This is going to be the most ridiculously lavish event we've ever been to. The sort of wedding that will make Elton John look tight. Apparently Adam's fiancée Jessie is spending more than our combined annual salaries on the canapés. So, yes! We're very much going.'

'Great! Bye, lovely Tilly.'

Dolly is just about to log off when Josh steps into the room and clocks the open laptop.

'You've chosen the pram?' he seems disappointed. 'I was hoping I might help you do that.'

'Why?' Dolly sounds harsher, more incredulous than she intended. Total disinterest and now suddenly she's supposed to consult him on the choice of pram?

'I just thought it might be something I could help with, that's all.' *Christ, he looks sorry for himself.*

'Nope. It's all sorted thanks. Tilly helped me. Anyway, haven't you got a shoot to plan? New York can't be that far off now?' Six weeks ago Dolly might have been pleased – grateful even – for this approach. Not now.

'New York's off actually.' Josh's eyes hit the floor, suddenly the little boy outside the headmaster's office. 'A change of marketing director and global advertising cuts are top of the agenda for the new one. So, it's on hold at least but more than likely canned altogether. I'm gutted.'

Oh. My. Actual. God. He's seriously looking for comfort and sympathy. Wants all the benefits you might naturally expect from a devoted live-in girlfriend – just doesn't want to return the compliment and give a toss himself.

Well she's not going to do it. Dolly's not going to stand there and pretend she cares less about this shoot when she doesn't. Let him feel the bitter pinch of disappointment for once.

'Well, I'm sure you'll work something out Josh, you always do. I need a nap.'

'I admire you, Dolly.' He's trying to position himself so he's blocking her route to the bedroom. Obviously wanting to chat, several weeks too late.

'What?'

'The way you're handling everything. Having the guts to do this. Not being frightened... like me.' *Finally, some honesty.*

'Who says I'm not frightened? Of course I bloody well am. I'm about to have a baby on my own. It's not exactly how I imagined my life would pan out.'

'Maybe it doesn't have to be that way?' He can't even look her in the eye now, knowing full well how pathetically late this is coming.

But Dolly is too tired for this. Too far beyond false promises and vain hopes to go all the way back to square one now. She looks at him standing there, knowing damn well the only reason he's standing there at all is because New York is off, he's been dumped. Well, not nearly as brutally as he dumped her every time he said he didn't want the baby.

'I think it probably does have to be this way, Josh.' She reaches for her laptop, noticing the new email icon flashing at her.

'Tell me something I can do, anything that might help.'

She's looking at him now. *Really* looking at him. All puppy-dog eyes, big soft lips and a chest that looks as though it's seriously benefitted from more hours in the gym recently – all those hours he didn't want to be at home with her. And it occurs to Dolly. She misses nothing about him. Not even the sex.

'Start thinking of girls' names.' She shoots the words straight over her shoulder, without breaking stride. They're designed to wind him and they clearly do. She leaves him standing there open-mouthed and floundering like a man who's just realised with crushing clarity everything he stands to lose. Dolly slams the bedroom door behind her, conversation very much over.

As she slides under the duvet and opens the laptop there is the name in her inbox that once meant so much to her. The name she spent months and months praying would appear.

Dear Dolly,

You'll remember that we spoke about your wedding some months ago and I of course understand that this is no longer going ahead. However, the editor loved your ideas so much that she would like to adapt them into one of our own styled shoots. It would only be fair of course that we ask you to consult with us on the project. It would mean you sharing your list of expert suppliers and being there on the day to help style and direct the images for which of course we would be delighted to offer you the lead by-line credit across the ten pages that we have planned.

If you could let me know if this is something that appeals to you then we will think about scheduling some shoot dates and arrange for you to come in to Vogue House and work through your ideas with the creative team here.

With very best wishes,

Annabel Coutts

Personal Assistant to the editor of Conde Nast *Brides*.

A grin so broad, so cheesy, so genuine starts to spread itself cross Dolly's face, cementing itself there for some time. She can do this! It doesn't matter that she's pregnant. The morning sickness has passed, everything is pretty much organised and she can bunk work for however long is needed. What's the point of being preggers if you can't make it work to your advantage eh? As long as they move quickly there is still time before the baby arrives.

It's a sobering thought, but landing this job brings all the benefits of having the wedding in the first place without any of the all-encompassing negativity of marrying Josh and, despite all the pain of the past few weeks, Dolly couldn't be happier about it.

Chapter Twenty-Eight

Emily

I'm watching my nearly-husband arrive to collect my wedding dress. Could there possibly be any sadder sight? And he's so angry. I can sense the heat radiating off him as Helen lets him in to the boutique, like all his blood has been replaced with liquid rage. I didn't choose to witness this. My spirit just got dragged along for the ride. One minute I'm watching Glo sat motionless on my bed, pink ted clutched to her chest, the next I'm here, like I've zipped through time and space at a giddying pace. But why? Think Emily, *think*. No one else is going to work this out for me.

My beautiful Mark who was always so eloquent, so at ease, has had every drop of confidence stolen from him – he no longer knows what to say or how to say it. Is that why I'm staying close, following him wherever he goes? But what possible use can I be?

Now I'm listening from somewhere buried deep within a rail of tulle as he tries to spit the words out – Helen's brain piecing the facts together quicker than his mouth can form them. It's a whole twelve minutes of huffing and sweating, sitting down, standing up, pacing and fighting the hot, angry tears that are seething out of him before he finally manages to say the words that are killing him too.

'She's gone. Dead, Helen. Brain aneurism.' He's pointing in the general direction of his own head, trying to find a use for his big awkward arms.

Poor Helen. She's quietly crying too now. The two of them, relative strangers really, are in the middle of the boutique surrounded by a halo of white, holding each other and sobbing away, apparently oblivious to quite how weird this really is. It's the first time I pick up on a deeper sorrow that is buried within Helen – something way down in the fabric of her, cellular almost, where no one can see it. But I can feel it. Mark's grief is reigniting something in her that we never talked about. Why would we, I suppose? I was too busy dragging her into my dress deceit. She's so attuned to what he's feeling, I can sense her absorbing it, all the pain that is coursing through him finding perfect symmetry in her.

I have no idea why Mark wants my wedding dress – in fact, I slightly fear for what he has planned for it. But that's why he's here. He's asking Helen if he can pay whatever is outstanding and take the dress today.

'I just… *need* it, Helen.' He's not making any sense, well not to me at least.

'Of course you do. I understand.' I love that Helen isn't asking him any questions, not forcing him to elaborate, and just letting him explain in his own words, in his own time. She can probably see he'd struggle to recite his address right now.

'Glo, her mum, said she chose something really beautiful.' Of course, he doesn't know about the dress switch. None of them does. This could be tricky for Helen. I see the slightest flare of panic crease the skin around her eyes, sense her pulse rise slightly as the same thought flashes through her.

'Can you show me it please, Helen. I'd like to see it first.' Oh God, why is he doing this to himself, to me?

And then a truly gut-wrenching thought occurs to me that's so wrong I struggle to even visualise it properly. Is he collecting the dress because he wants to bury me in it? And if he does, how on earth will I stop him? I won't. The thought is so tragic, I have to look away from them. It's like the sadness of what I'm being forced to witness has seeped into me and is contaminating every part of me, killing off any last remains of life that are still keeping me here. *Please don't do that, Mark!* I'm screaming the words as loud as I can but they're uselessly muffled, like they're weighed down under a tonne of lace and beading that are destined for some happy bride-to-be. If only I was here and not somewhere very cold, waiting my turn for the pathologist's scalpel.

Mark is talking about the dress I should have walked down the aisle in, its expensive hand-woven fabric brushing past my friends and family as I glide along on Dad's arm. The dress I would have twirled around in all night under the spotlight of a hundred camera phones.

'I'll get it for you now. Just take a seat and I'll be right back.'

He doesn't sit. While Helen's gone, Mark walks slowly around the room. He picks up a pair of beautiful baby-blue suede heels and turns them over in his hand, wondering if I might have chosen them too. I expect him to baulk at the price tag, an incredulous snort, at least, but there's nothing. This Mark isn't registering the cost. He starts to run his hand softly along a line of dresses. I can see him coming and pray I might be able to sense the passing warmth of his fingertips – but there's nothing. It's like I'm not even here. I'm not.

What's Helen up to? I can hear her creaking around on the centuries-old floorboards upstairs. She's left the shop and is poking around in her loft, untying a box and retrieving something precious in a small white envelope, then she's swinging the hatch shut and making her way back down the stairs. Secret mission complete. Whatever it is, I hope Mark's ready for this.

When Helen steps back into the shop I'm so shocked by what I see that I'm surprised they don't hear the comedy loud intake of breath from behind the Vera Wang. Helen is holding the Reem Acra dress, the proper Cinderella number, the one everyone wanted me to wear. The dress that put a beaming smile on Mum and Dad's faces – the kind every daughter hopes she'll see at least once in her lifetime. I imagine briefly I might have seen those smiles again when I brought their first grandchild home from hospital. Not now. They'll never know that boundless joy.

It's the dress I felt was far too expensive for a girl who might never wear it. I got that right at least. But of course, Helen and I are the only ones who know that. And I suppose it hasn't occurred to her that I'm here, watching through a thin veil of tulle, clocking everything. She's *actually* going to let him walk out of here with a dress worth thousands of pounds more than I paid for the decoy dress.

Mark cuts through my shock by stepping straight forward and taking the dress. He drops the hanger to the floor and wraps both hands around the bodice, holding it as if I am in there, blood pumping under the grip of the boning. I wish more than anything that I was.

'Was she the last person to wear it?' His tears are building again now and I drop my gaze to the floor, heart breaking all over again. I concentrate all my efforts on visualising my bedroom in the hope I might appear back there but I don't have that much self-control. Whoever wants me here, witnessing this, is keeping me rooted to the spot.

'Yes, she was.' Helen is pulling a tissue out from her sleeve and dabbing away the drops of mascara that are starting to swim around the corners of her eyes.

'I can smell her perfume on it.' Mark is lifting the dress up to his face, knowing the delicate remains of my favourite fragrance are all he's going to get. There is no hair to run his fingers through, no soft cheek to kiss, I'm not about to bound into the room and launch myself at him, chastising him for seeing the dress before the big day. His hopes and dreams are shattering before his very eyes – and mine.

'It's the funeral soon. Will you come please, Helen? I know Emily would want you there. It's at the same church we would have been… well, you know the one.' He's handing the dress back to Helen who zips it in to a dress carrier with lightning speed. I'm not sure she can bear much more of this either.

'I would be honoured, thank you. There is something else I would like to give you, Mark, if that's OK?' I can sense the pace of her heart pick up as she holds the white envelope out for him to take.

'Oh. What is it?'

'Just a little something I no longer need. Please take it and read it. I will pray it brings you some comfort.'

'Thank you, Helen.'

As soon as Mark gets back out to the car he shuts the door and rips the envelope open, thirsty for something, *anything* that might take away some of his hurt. He gets as far as the first two lines…

Death is nothing at all.
I have only slipped away to the next room.

… before his head collapses backwards on to the head rest, his fists balled, pounding the steering wheel in front of him, before I hear his skin rip and tear, sending tiny splatters of blood on to the leather upholstery.

I want to climb inside him and knit his broken heart back together again with a shower of soft kisses. If only he knew how very close I am.

I know blaspheming in church is a real no-no but *Jesus Christ!* Whose idea was it to put me in a white coffin? I'm guessing Glo's. Still, I'll take that over the wedding dress that is mercifully absent today – almost. Mark couldn't bear to have it in the house after all, so it's tucked under my bed in a big brown box but not before Glo cut a palm-sized heart-shaped piece of fabric from one of the underskirts. She's placed it into the coffin with me, where my beating heart once was. My arms are folded so that my fingertips are just touching it, like it's the most precious thing in the world to me. A nice touch. So is the pretty lace bunting that Mark's sister spent so long trawling online for. It's been draped across the back pews. I suppose someone thought it was a shame to waste it.

This place is packed. There are more people squeezed into the pews today than we'd invited to the wedding. My darling family are all in the front two rows, overlooking my coffin and the beautiful framed image of Mark and me that is propped on an artist's easel next to it. I recognise it immediately. It was taken on our first mini-break together to Paris. Our arms are wrapped around each other on the Pont des Arts bridge, following in the footsteps of a million lovers before us. It feels like a lifetime ago, back in the days when we thought nothing of splashing the cash on lovely boutique hotels – long before I worked out how obscenely expensive personalised favours for ninety guests are.

I gulp back a great heave of emotion as I realise I'm wearing my wedding band. I'm so pleased it's there, as close to being married as I'm ever going to get now. Mark has his on too and this troubles me much more. I hope he's not building a shrine to me in his heart that will never be prised open again. Sally will do it. I know she will. She doesn't take her eyes off him throughout the entire service. Not even during her speech where she reminds everyone what an incredible man he is and how he made the best possible choice when it came to me. Her eyes never leave the top of his head, not even to flick to the handwritten notes in front of her on the pulpit. She's only talking to him. He's only thinking of me and the honeymoon that never got booked. The days we were going to spend wrapped up in each other.

Poor, lovely Mum. I'm not sure she's hearing a word of what's being said today. For the forty-five minutes the service lasts, she thinks of nothing other than my first day at school. How she polished my smart patent shoes that morning, bunched my hair, proudly walked me through the school gates then failed to occupy herself until she could race back there at 3 p.m. to collect me.

Dad listens to everything. Then he stands, Lord knows how, in front of a sea of sad, contorted faces and tells them all how wonderful I am, how every single day since I was born he's felt the rush of love that only an adoring father can, refusing to use the past tense.

Then there's Sarah Blake, impeccably smart in a black crepe suit. She's still carrying the weight of all that guilt, preventing her from making eye contact with my parents, friends for decades and now with such a huge hurdle to overcome. I'm not sure Sarah ever will. Helen leaves the service before the end, unable to cope with it all and I watch as one of Dad's best friends who she's been sharing an order of service with follows her out. He's comforting her, turning her tears to a soft smile while something is thawing inside of her.

Several of the children from nursery are sat cross-legged at the front of the church and when four-year-old Peter gets up to read a poem I force my eyes closed. I sit at the very back, next to a pile of dusty hymn books and try so very hard not to hear him talk about my rosy cheeks and how I make the best jam sandwiches. He'll forget me in a couple of weeks, I know he will, but for now his cherubic face is fighting back the tears, bottom lip shaking out the words he's probably been rehearsing all week while his eyes flick to his mum in the third row for support. The tears are streaming down her face too.

Perhaps it's because I've spent the day absorbing everyone else's emotions but I'm starting to feel weaker and less able to read the pulse of the room than I was a week ago. I'm fading. Perhaps when the first shovel of earth lands on my coffin that will be it. I'll be gone.

Except I'm not. I hang around all day and I'm still here watching Dad stare up at the ceiling as late night turns to early morning. He doesn't let go of Mum's hand for a single second until she stirs around 5 a.m. and cries all over his tartan pyjamas. But they're going to be OK. I can feel that. They have each other and that's all that matters for now.

But there's something more I need to see. Some conclusion that needs to be reached before I can go. I feel sure now that it's Mark's anger, which gets more ferocious with every day that passes. Last night he waited until my parents were both in bed, said he would let himself out and lock up when he was ready to leave. Then I watched as he sat in the darkness of my parents' lounge and scrolled through every picture of me on his mobile phone, his angry face illuminated by the screen. By the time he got as far back as our engagement party he was struggling to breathe through the quiet rage that is eating him up. So he took the phone outside, hurled it at the stone patio then stamped hard on it several times until it was an unrecognisable tangle of wires and metal.

This isn't my Mark and I know now I can't leave until I find him again.

Chapter Twenty-Nine

Jessie

The rehearsal dinner entrées haven't even been served and already Henry is bringing the house down. He is standing at the head of the Coleridges' giant dining table, looking exquisite in his dinner jacket, antique champagne coupe in one hand, the undivided attention of everyone else balanced tantalisingly in the other as he addresses them with his usual boom.

'I've told Adam there are three things a husband must say as often as possible if he wants to have a happy marriage – and I know my darling Camilla will support me wholeheartedly on this.'

Jessie's eyes follow everyone else's across the expanse of fine bone china and cut crystal to where a Chanel-clad Camilla is sitting, her warm, entirely unfazed smile indicating she knows exactly what's coming. No embarrassing revelations about to be exposed here.

'You are right. I am wrong. And I love you.' Henry looks thoroughly pleased with himself as the belly laughs ring out around the room and Jessie can't help but admire the man who, less than twenty-four hours from now, will become her father-in-law. She notices again the easy charm that radiates off Henry, so self-assured and never, it seems, having to work at being the most entertaining person in the room. Exactly the sort of person she wants regaling her guests during the wedding breakfast tomorrow. Not, sadly, her own dad who she can see is already wearing the downcast glaze of a man not really in the room, his thoughts, no doubt, on how he is going to follow this tomorrow. Surely it is kinder to save him from that? Why set him up to fail so horribly, so obviously?

Everything about Henry's demeanour suggests he is feeling the polar opposite of Jessie right now. She's stiff with nerves, like someone has thrust a cold metal spike down the back of her feathered Oscar de la Renta dress, preventing her from moving freely through fear she might injure herself irreparably. She has pretty much zero chance of truly relaxing and enjoying the moment – this penultimate evening when all the excitement should build to an almost unbearable crescendo before the main event can *finally*, after so much planning, begin. And she will be declared Mrs Adam Coleridge. Assuming none of the Joneses do anything tonight to halt it.

Adam is sitting next to Jessie's mum, looking like a mini cut-out of Henry, every bit as handsome but positively glowing in his Tom Ford tux, his hair casual, as if he's just raked his fingers through it, fresh from the shower. His arm is carelessly draped across the back of Margaret's chair and Jessie can't help but notice the sartorial gulf between them: Adam's expertly hand-cut jacket that skims his contours as only a suit made just for you can, versus Margaret's rainbow-bright lace dress that's cutting into her upper arms and riding up her thighs causing her to wriggle self-consciously every three minutes. Margaret's sensible shoes are colour-matched precisely to her bag, shawl, earrings and belt – mass-produced, factory made, priced cheaply to sell quickly.

Why she wouldn't just let Jessie dress her for tonight and the wedding still grates, but there's not much Jessie can do about it now. This is happening and damage limitation is the best she can hope for.

Now everyone is seated, Jessie can hear Adam asking her mother how she's feeling about the big day tomorrow.

'I just hope I don't make too much fuss, Adam. I know Jessie hates that. She's told me I'm not allowed to cry during the ceremony or it might start her off. Now I'm terrified I won't manage it and ruin the moment for her.'

She can see the stress on her mum's face, all the pressure Jessie has put on her to behave well, not even allowing her mum to react in the same way a million mother-of-the-brides have done before her. Feeling a wave of guilt, she opens her mouth to reassure her mum, but is beaten to it by Adam, one step ahead of her again.

'A wedding without tears? I'll consider it a personal insult if I don't see you squeezing out a few from the front row, Margaret!'

She knows he's only being his usual kind self but he's also making Jessie look more heartless. Then Henry makes it worse.

'You can cry all over me if it helps, Margaret!'

As Jessie's eyes glide along the table she can hear her mother ask Adam to *just say the word* when it's time for her to serve the pudding she's made. Despite endless protestations from Jessie, Margaret insisted on making her sherry trifle for everyone this evening. Jessie can only imagine Camilla's irritation at losing control of her own menu planning. She probably intended to serve something light and simple – a meringue made with fresh berries from the estate's kitchen gardens perhaps – not some seventies throwback full of shop-bought sponge fingers that in an hour or so from now will be glued to the back of everybody's teeth.

Jessie quickly dismisses the shot of guilt that's trying to nestle in her chest and lets her eyes carry on up the table, her cheeks warming at just how glaringly obvious it is who is a Coleridge here – and who is not. She is bookended by two of Adam's ushers, Sebastian and Harry, who are both well-schooled in the art of dinner party chitchat, allowing her attention to wander around the room while they try to out-banter each other. Jessie's just grateful someone is enjoying the evening.

Adam's grandmother, Sophia, a neat woman in her late eighties who has the look of someone who knows where all the bodies are buried, has been seated next to Jessie's brother, Jason, who appears to have upended an entire bottle of wet-look gel onto his hair tonight. Already Jessie can see the look of undisguised confusion creeping across her face at whatever it is he's muttering into her ear. She can only watch in horror from across the table as Jason repeatedly drinks from Sophia's wine glass, causing a member of the waiting staff to swoop in undetected each time and replace it. Not one other person at the table has noticed this farce, except Jessie. She tries to signal to Jason his mistake but all she elicits from him is a curt 'What's wrong with you!?' and she has to give up before everyone else does notice.

Then his fingers are all over granny's bread roll and he doesn't bother to wait until everyone has been served before his cutlery is clattering loudly into the fish course. If Jessie can just make it through tonight, maybe everything will be OK. Hopefully there won't be the time or opportunity for this level of scrutiny tomorrow.

'I trust you'll be wheeling out some gorgeous bridesmaids for our entertainment tomorrow, Jessie?' Seb is asking loudly so the entire table turns to hear the response.

'No! I mean, I'm not really having bridesmaids. Well, I am but…' The hesitation is coming from a good place, it really is, but it's also causing hurt frowns from her mum and dad and a nasty scowl from Claire. Jason is too busy swigging back his third glass of Chablis to even register it. The last thing Jessie wants to do is out Claire as the much hoped-for gorgeous bridesmaid, only for her to register the awkward silence while everyone wonders how to verbally sidestep the fact that she doesn't exactly fulfil the brief. Of course it's down to Henry to kill the awkward moment.

'Well, if what Claire here tells me is true then you boys better watch out!' bellows Henry. 'Do you know she holds the record at the Feathered Nest for the quickest yard of ale drunk on New Year's Eve? Her name is actually engraved on a special plaque behind the bar, for goodness sake!'

'Yes. It. Is!' boasts Claire.

And how proud your parents must be of you. Camilla isn't saying it, but it's etched all over her face for Jessie to see.

Claire is the biggest surprise of the night so far, looking about as good as she ever has in one of Helen's silk wrap dresses, one with gently flared sleeves in a beautiful shade of bluebell. She is seated next to Henry, and Adam's best man Lucian, a lanky Old Etonian who looks like he might be prone to bouts of poetry writing. The three of them are cackling away as if Claire has just told the filthiest joke of all time – Christ, maybe she has. No, it's actually worse than that. Far worse.

'Jessie, can it really be true?' Henry is asking across the table. 'What your friends did to you on your eighteenth birthday? Claire is furnishing me with so much detail here, I feel I am finally getting to know the *real* you – and my goodness! I just wouldn't have thought it possible—'

'Yeah it's true!' pipes up Jason before Jessie even has a moment to compose her thoughts. 'You should have seen the state of her.'

The image of herself, semi-clothed and tied to a lamp-post on the estate is burning bright in Jessie's mind, causing the heat to flare up inside her. Parcel tape wound around her so she couldn't move, like some awful stag night prank, her friends forced a carrot into her mouth, wedged a huge cabbage between her legs and dangled a tampon from each ear before the flashbulbs started clicking.

'Well, it was a long time ago, I was just a kid really.' Jessie feels so deflated. Like Julia Roberts in *Pretty Woman* when she gets all dolled up for the races only for someone to point out she's still a prostitute. Another brutal reminder there's no point pretending, she's never going to be able to truly escape what has gone before, is she? There will always be someone from the past, a family anecdote, something ready to tear her down.

Jessie says very little after this. She just watches as her mum slops trifle on to everyone's plates, while the waiting staff stand by, not quite sure what to do with themselves – obviously a first. Still, it doesn't stop Henry declaring it *bloody delicious* and asking for seconds, much to Margaret's utter delight.

Then Claire thinks she's being helpful by attempting to clear the final plates from the table. She's reaching for Henry and Lucian's dishes, trying to scrape them off and stack them in front of her before a member of staff swoops in. Not before Camilla has clocked it though. Does the woman miss anything? Then Dad passes the port the wrong way around the table, causing even greater confusion to an already baffled Sophia who looks like she's way past her bedtime.

By the time they are all filing out of the dining room for a nightcap in the library, Jessie has had enough. She's ready to wrap this up, get back over to Willow Manor and on with the rest of her life. Wake up tomorrow to what will surely be a less embarrassing future. While everyone else is getting a refill of port and collapsing into generously upholstered chairs, trying to take the weight off bellies full of leaden trifle – at least Mum didn't bring the squirty cream with her, her favoured garnish – Jessie sits in a large winged armchair, wondering how best to collar her dad. She needs to explain that Henry will be doing the main speech tomorrow and then get the all clear from Henry, who, no doubt, will be delighted. Someone like him hardly needs time to prepare. But this is going to be tricky. Her dad and Henry are holed up in a corner, Henry showing him some old pictures of how the house used to look before the current Coleridges breathed refined life in to it – that is, spent a fortune on it.

'So, big day tomorrow then, Graham, how's that father-of-the-bride speech coming along?'

Oh God, Henry is pre-empting her chat.

'Well, it's all written, has been for months, actually, Henry,'

Shit, this is not helping. Jessie sits, undetected by the pair of them, panicking now about whether to jump up and reveal herself before her dad can say another word.

'Marvellous! Sadly not an experience I am ever going to enjoy, having only one son, but I will be rooting for you.' Surprisingly, it's all back-slaps, bonding and the clinking of heavy glass tumblers between the two of them,

'That's good to know because I am feeling nervous about it, not that I've told Jessie that, obviously.' OK, too late, she needs to stay hidden. He's lowering his voice conspiratorially now. 'As I'm sure you've worked out, she has quite high expectations and I'm so worried I'm going to let her down.'

'You're her father, I'm not sure that's even possible.'

'In this case, I think it might be. The truth is, Henry, I feel like she's been slipping through my fingers for years, growing up and further away from me, from us. It's like the clock has been ticking for a long

time and it's about to stop tomorrow.' There is a sadness to her dad's
voice, that forces Jessie's mouth open, ready to tell him he's got it all
wrong, making her twist in her seat, so close to stopping him say
anything more...

'We're becoming less and less important in her life. From tomorrow
I wonder if we will factor at all. Every day closer to this wedding has
felt like a day closer to losing her really. More than anything I've just
wanted time to slow down. Is that an awful thing to say?'

Oh Dad.

'Of course not. She's your daughter. I can only imagine how hard
this must be for you.'

*Why is it everything that comes out of Henry's mouth is so instantly
believable, spoken as fact, never opinion?* Jessie wonders.

'I keep asking myself, will Adam want to spend time with us? Will
they ever want to come to us for Christmas when they could be here?
I don't want her old school photos to be all I have of her now that she's
marrying in to your family, Henry. But I know I need to face the fact
that you're the people she has chosen to spend her life with, not the
ones who have been foisted on her.'

This is almost unbearable. Jessie has spent many wistful hours fantasising about how Christmases at Swell Park Estate will be the stuff of her
childhood dreams. Big lavish, magical affairs full of every conceivable
luxury. A giant real fir tree, kissing the ceiling of the drawing room,
filling the room with its fresh pine scent and adorned with hundreds
of co-ordinated Liberty decorations. Nothing like the fake thing her
mum drags out of a broken cardboard box every year to cover in highly
flammable tinsel. She genuinely hasn't given a thought to how her
parents might feel about her never being home for Christmas. She was
more concerned with how *not* to invite them to the Coleridges'. The

fact her dad has second-guessed her so accurately makes her stiffen in the armchair then try to sink silently lower.

'Don't get me wrong, I admire her greatly. She's made me a better father actually. You can't watch someone with that much drive and determination and not want to work harder for them.'

Jessie feels a small swell of pride, laced with a much stronger sense of remorse – like every one of the sacrifices she knows he's made, sacrifices she has been selfishly unappreciative of, are pricking at her conscience.

'If she needed a bigger desk, I worked overtime. When the school-books got more expensive, I started working weekends…'

Jessie is looking across the room now, suddenly distracted by the unexpected sight of Camilla embracing her mother, cocooning her while Claire smiles on. *What the hell?* Suddenly, Jessie's fighting to keep track of what the men are discussing while simultaneously trying to lip-read Camilla. Something about *being there tomorrow, supporting, door always open. One family now.* She needs to get over there but she can't, if she moves Henry and Dad will know she's overheard everything. She'll look deceitful. Besides, now that her dad has unashamedly laid bare her deprived childhood, she's keen to hear Henry's take on it all. Is he going to be put off by the picture her dad is painting?

Graham is leaning back casually against the bookcase, his body turned to Henry, inviting his confidence and advice.

'Well, for a start I think you're underestimating Adam—'

'Sorry Henry, I didn't mean it as a criticism, I just—'

'No, no, I know that. I understand you perfectly. But Adam is solid, dependable and the last person to be impressed by wealth alone. We have worked very hard at that. No one more so than Camilla, actually. She won't mind me telling you this, Graham, but she doesn't come from money at all. I'm afraid I was rather predictable and married my secretary!'

'Oh, right.'

'Yes, and she has been a much-needed grounding force in this family. People often jump to the wrong conclusion about her but she has a kind, sweet heart and is quite simply the least judgemental person I know. The only thing that irritates her is people getting her so wrong.' Henry lifts the solid stopper out of the port decanter and refills the pair of them without asking if Graham needs it.

Never more has Jessie wanted to feel the fuzzy numbing effect of alcohol coarse through her. The drug of choice for the socially awkward. She desperately needs her edges to blur, her mind to file what she's hearing somewhere deep back in her brain where it won't be remembered tomorrow, for Adam to appear at her side and tell her everything will be fine. Can someone just *please* be on her bloody side! And why the hell didn't she grab a drink before she sat down?

Her mind trips back now through all the conversations with Camilla, unravelling everything at high speed. The loaded looks, the sideways glances, the confession that she still needs the Debrett's guide, the silences, all those assumed judgements left hanging in the air but which were never actually said. The way Camilla sat at the bar in Claridge's that night, witnessing her undignified spat with Claire but never saying a word. Christ, probably thinking all along it was Jessie who was to blame.

She feels an icy chill creep up over her, the kind that makes it into your bones and stays there, making you long for the comfort of your duvet. The urge to cry is coming at her thick and fast. She mustn't. But everything that is wrong in the room tonight leads back to her, an incriminating trail to the one person who is responsible for all the hurt and misunderstanding.

The realisation strikes like a vicious slap across the face, her whole body feeling the aftershock. So much has been decided by Jessie herself rather than said by Camilla, she's starting to see that now. What a monumental fucking idiot. Not only for causing herself so much angst but for getting Camilla so wrong – and it must all be so bloody obvious to her too. She even tried to warn Jessie. What was it she said that night over supper? *There is no point pretending to be something you are not.*

Why hadn't she listened? She couldn't have been clearer, could she? The shame is strangling her insides. How could she make both her parents doubt their worth – and why has it taken Henry's intervention to point that out to her? How will she ever undo this mess now? There aren't the words or the hours to rewrite it all. She tunes back in to her dad's protective voice.

'I hope Jessie will enhance your life too, Henry, I hope you will allow her to. Because – she'd kill me for saying it – but she's so painfully shy sometimes and crippled by insecurities, feelings of never quite being good enough. On that front, I'm afraid we are quite similar.'

Christ, she wasn't fooling anyone was she?

While Camilla's elegant laugh mingles through the air with Claire's cackle, Henry takes a huge glug of his port and readies himself to draw a line under every concern her dad has.

'My advice is to make your speech tomorrow, Graham, and enjoy it! And do it with great honesty. People want to hear you speak genuinely and from the heart, nothing else matters.' There. He has said it, therefore it is true.

And it's as if Henry knows someone else is listening in on their supposedly private chat – like he just stopped talking only to her dad.

Finally, Jessie knows what she needs to do and there is still time. Just.

Chapter Thirty

Emily

The scent of fresh rose is overwhelming, intoxicating – even to my dulled senses. It hits me before I even make it to the church archway because the bride – perhaps in a moment of utter madness – has completely covered the stone path in what must be hundreds of thousands of fresh petals. This is no mere scattering. This floral carpet is deep – I can see people sinking into its fragrant bed as I pass a few paces behind Mark. The floral archway itself is so dense, guests are squeezing through it in single file, expectations loftily raised for what awaits inside.

Trees. There are actual real, fully grown silver birch trees, twelve of them, lining the aisle. And they have also had their branches stuffed full of rose heads – creating great petal-filled domes above the congregation. Every pew end is covered in them too. It's like the rose room at Chelsea Flower Show – just with more roses. There is a pristine white carpet laid the entire length of the aisle and I wonder who will be brave enough to put the first outdoor shoe on that.

Ten minutes from now everyone will be reaching for the painkillers to relieve the pounding in their heads (I sympathise) from all this heady perfume. Before it's even started this is easily the most flash wedding I've ever been to – and I'm dead. Not ideal, is it? But I'm here for Mark. Today will be difficult for him. Just a couple of weeks ago he was standing at the front telling a very different audience how his very soul was ripped out of him the day I died.

Everyone told him he shouldn't come today. *It's too early*, Dad said. Why risk it? But Mark has known Henry and Adam for years, organised countless big trips for the Coleridges through his travel business, so he was never going to miss it. I thought he might stay just for the service, slip out unnoticed afterwards leaving everyone else to the boozing and dancing. But now I'm not so sure. Sally is with him.

This can only be a good thing, I know that, I *planned* that. She's sticking close. Looking after him. She kept a respectful distance earlier when he visited my grave, placing a beautiful fresh bunch of flowers there – the exact ones he knows I would have carried on our wedding day. I want to tell him not to waste his money – peonies aren't cheap – but today, in front of Sally, is it wrong that I need to see I'm not forgotten yet?

She's doing a good job of steering the conversation away from me, keeping it focused on what's going on around them. But I'm tense, so clenched and dreading the moment when someone from way back is going to ask where I am. Are you even allowed to talk about death at someone's wedding? How will he phrase it? How do you do that without creating an insurmountable flare of awkwardness? Oh God, here we go…

'Ahh, Mark, on your own today, mate?'

Sally is on it. 'Hi, I'm Sally. Are you the bride or groom's side?'

'Mark! Long time, no see, where's—'

Here she is again… 'Would you mind if I drag Mark away? He's needed at the… you know.'

And her swift interventions seem to be working. His heart doesn't feel quite so heavy today, he's even managing a hint of a smile as he embraces Adam's parents.

'Mark!' Blimey this guy is loud.

'So lovely to see you, Henry. And today of all days. Huge congratulations.' Mark extends his hand to shake but this Henry is pulling him closer, getting into his ear.

'Whatever you need, I am here. You simply ask and it will be done. Come and see me at the house, will you? I'd love to talk.'

Mark only manages a nod, I can see he doesn't trust himself to say a word in case the dam holding back his emotions starts to crumble. But I can also tell he's relieved at the confirmation that he was never just a business associate for Henry. And I'm relieved the words are discreet, undetected by anyone else, all too busy taking their seats now.

Just as the fog seems to be lifting slowly from Mark, this is all getting much harder for me. I see he's still wearing his wedding band and I'm slightly ashamed to say I smile this time at the stamp of ownership. Surely he's still mine for now? All those years together don't get cancelled out in a couple of months. He's not available *just* yet.

Maybe it's being surrounded by so many people that's helping. Or maybe it's the fact that a wedding really is the one place on earth where you can't be a misery guts. Even if your own wedding just got cancelled at tragically short notice, it's still not on. You're still not allowed to cast the shadow of gloom over this happy couple's day. Quite a pressure.

As everyone stands, I see Helen at the entrance of the church. She's crouched low, doing her thing. Wafting, lifting, smoothing the dress – totally in her happy place. Then she moves around in front of the bride and takes both of her hands.

'Do I look OK, Helen?' the bride's asking nervously, just as I imagine I might have done.

'You couldn't possibly look any more beautiful, Jessie. Now, if you do nothing else today *please*, enjoy it! Everyone is here for you, rooting for you. And the man of your dreams is waiting for you at the end of that aisle, so go and get him!'

There are tears in Helen's eyes. Wow! Hundreds of brides, a different wedding dress sold every day and *still* it moves her. I wonder if this wedding has deeper meaning for her somehow. I can't read her as clearly as I could a couple of weeks ago but there's more to the emotion today. Maybe there's a daughter she's thinking about, worrying about? The fact I'm struggling to sense things so easily is what's worrying me. First it was difficult to be still here at all, now the idea of going is slightly terrifying. What am I going *to*?

Thinking about Helen makes my mind flip back to Glo. When I left her this morning she was statue-still on the sofa, something clenched tightly in her fist, while Dad packed some of my clothes into black bin bags upstairs. They had been building up to this job – the charity shop run with your dead daughter's belongings. Treasured things they've kept – my first pair of ballet shoes, every framed newspaper cutting charting my achievements and, of course, that raggedy teddy bear from the day I was born – but they both knew, even if they hadn't been bold enough to say it out loud, that progress has to be made, even in the tiniest steps forward. As Dad gets stronger, he's going to be the one to make that happen.

As the door closed behind him, I watched as Glo slowly unfurled her fingers and I saw for the first time what she'd been clutching. A small, soft pink velvet pouch. I knew immediately what was inside. As the tears started to roll down her tired, pale face she loosened the fine cord tie, turning the pouch upside down and spilling its precious contents into her quivering palm. Every one of my tiny discoloured baby teeth tumbled out and I was broken for her. Oh, Mum. Only someone filled with as much love as her could hold on to them for all these years.

These are odd thoughts to be crashing in on me as everyone is clapping the bride and groom's first kiss. He's holding her face so tenderly, eyes full of tears, looking like he never wants to let her go. And that smile. It's radiating out of her, lighting up her entire face and bathing the room in a warm glow of happiness. Oh, to have enjoyed just one second of that feeling with Mark on our wedding day...

Guests are making the short walk through a marquee tunnel that connects the church to Willow Manor. I glance around one of the fine drawing rooms, taking in what a mega bucks wedding looks like. It doesn't have a lopsided, homemade and un-iced cake, that's for sure.

I've counted and there are no less than eighteen members of staff buzzing around, topping up people's champagne flutes far more times than necessary. What I wouldn't give to feel the effect of some of those fizzy bubbles right now, while the old, still-living me hangs off Mark's arm, just two more guests full of excitement for everything we might enjoy today.

Ornate morsels of food that look like mini edible art installations are weaving their way through the crowd on silver trays balanced by staff in white gloves. The whole place is alive with the can't-quite-believe-our-luck energy of the three hundred or so guests. Every now and again a shriek of delight goes up as someone else discovers the... wait for it... dessert room. Thank God none of this lot know my amateur cake was going to be our only pudding.

And then the moment I've been dreading comes. Mark takes his seat for the wedding breakfast, next to a woman with a beautifully swollen belly. *Dolly Jackson*, the place card reads. *Will he be able to handle this,* I wonder. A pregnant woman and all the inherently happy forward planning that comes with her? And then…

'Are you here with your wife?' she asks, noticing his wedding ring. The briefest of pauses hangs between them while Mark readies himself. Sally, two seats away, can't save him now and I catch the torment on her face as she realises it.

'No. I'm not.' It's all Mark can manage as his hand lifts absent-mindedly to the breast pocket of his suit, like he's checking something is still there. Then I see it myself, the passage that Helen gave him that day in the boutique. He lets his fingers waver there for a moment, con-firming its presence and I hear the air escape his lungs with a whoosh of relief that it is. There must be something in the way his eyes are sliding downwards as he declines to elaborate that warns Dolly not to go any further. I like her so much for not pushing him. Others would have. I also like that she is one of those pregnant women who is eating everything in sight, including Mark's starter – he never did like lobster.

For me the speeches are always the best part of any wedding day and I'm determined not to miss them today but as the hours tick by, I'm fighting against an almost unbearable tiredness creeping up over me. It's taking all of the little energy I have left to stay focused, and even so, I'm missing things now, all the subtle conversational nuances are away over my head. Why is Mark laughing? I can't seem to follow the flow of the chat, and who is this Josh that Dolly is gleefully bad-mouthing to the table?

The groom's speech is charming, clever and delivered with the sort of confidence you hope you'll be capable of mustering in such a moment. But oh, it's the father-of-the bride who brings me, and everyone else in the room, to their knees. He's taking us all on a wonderful journey through the love story of the father-daughter bond and it's opening up my heart all over again, making me long to be that little girl back on my own father's shoulders as we run the length of the beach – my hair flying on the salty sea breeze, his hands gripping my bruised and bony knees. On a day when we knew only happiness.

'She is everything to me, she always will be.' He's standing next to her on the top table, holding her hand while he proudly shares with the entire room all those feelings men of his generation are encouraged to keep to themselves. It's all pure, honest emotion. 'I love her more than I ever thought possible and I will continue to until the day I take my very last breath. When she was a small girl, I used to dream about her, waking in the night to check she was OK. Today I have to accept that's not my job any more. Another man has stolen her heart and I am trying so hard not to let that realisation break mine.'

Everywhere I look, women and plenty of men are dabbing the corners of their eyes with the expensive linen napkins, until finally he finishes to an explosion of applause that revives me wonderfully – his reward is a big teary hug from the bride that gloriously goes on and on.

The best man is a disaster. Someone forgot to tell him he should be delivering heartfelt hilarity with a touch of humiliation. Where's the filth? He's intellectualising the living daylights out of his speech, confusing everyone, but frankly that's good because it gives us all some time to compose ourselves before the bride gets to her feet. She has everyone's attention from the get-go.

'Er… this isn't the speech I was planning to give today.' She's actually shaking, shuffling a stack of cue cards nervously while everyone holds their breath before she gives up, abandoning them altogether. Only then does she find her voice.

'It's amazing how easy it is to lose sight of who you really are when you're planning a wedding. Growing up, my family meant everything to me, but somehow I forgot what's important to them and to me. I've spent more time deciding on what you're eating today than in my own mother's company in the past year. That's wrong, and, today, Mum, I want to say I am so sorry for that and I promise you, from the bottom of my heart, it will change now, right from today.'

My eyes slide along the top table between the two older women – which one is her mum, I wonder? Then it's obvious. Not the one with the exquisitely tailored cashmere suit and what I think might be an actual Philip Treacy hat, but the one bawling in to her napkin, then blowing her nose loudly in it. But who cares? I'd give anything to see my mum ruining some expensive table linen right now.

'I'm only here today because of the endless hours my lovely dad spent working so that I would be top of the class, get the A Levels and that university place. Without any of that I wouldn't have landed the job that meant I met Adam. You've shaped my life in the most meaningful ways possible, Dad, and I love you for that – so much more than I have ever shown you.' I have to admire her nerve. She's making me feel a little ashamed that I was so happy for the men to speak for me on my big day... had I made it that far.

'Sometimes you just have to admit you are wrong. People just need to be loved, appreciated and to know that you care and... and... that's the message I'm going to take into this marriage with me.'

She's choking out that last bit and the effect is being felt all around me. The groom is about to explode with admiration, as is Helen, and there is such deep pleasure on the face of the other older woman on the top table, it suggests this might have been a long time coming. Whatever, the crowd is loving it. Only one girl isn't clapping. A haughty-looking type, who looks like her horse might be parked outside. But judging by the way her eyes are fixed on the groom and the speed with which she is necking the fizz, there is a lot more to that story.

The afternoon disappears into a blur of cake-cutting, bouquet-tossing and a truly hilarious moment when the bridesmaid changes into a shocking orange dress and attempts to teach the groom's mother the art of the slut drop. The two of them loll around the dancefloor together, the Philip Treacy long since discarded, laughing so hard and loudly that the whole room wishes they could join in. Even the bride looks a little envious.

By the time it's midnight I can barely feel a thing any more. I'm going; it won't be much longer. Everything is pixelating, the room waltzing away from me. Am I ready? I feel a futile stab of panic lurch through me – but even that is diluted by all the manic emotion filling the room. Sally is telling Mark their taxi is here and it's time to go. As he walks towards her, she holds out a hand, face smiling protectively towards him. She's as proud of him as I am – he made it, got through it. He takes it and as their fingers lace through each other, I feel the fragile, tentative connection of his flesh on hers, him responding softly to her grip. Almost as soon as it happens, they both let go again, perhaps sensing the eyes that might be on them. But I feel it, the faintest flicker of his heart warming, like the dullest ember in the fire coming to life again. I take one last look at my darling nearly-husband, overwhelmed with one final wave of emotion, all the love I still feel for him draining me completely. There is no anger in his face tonight. The warm, gentle man I fell for all those years ago is slowly returning as I so desperately hoped he would.

As they step out into the darkness of the night, I surrender myself to its inky embrace. And I'm gone.

Author's Note

While the vast majority of the brand names and known personalities in this book are real, the characters I have created are entirely fictitious. The village of Little Bloombury is based on Lower Slaughter in the North Cotswolds, a place I love so much I moved as close to it as I could. It has a beautiful nineteenth-century church which is also where I imagined my characters would marry. The Slaughters Manor House sits just next to the church and is what I based the fictional Willow Manor on. Its beautiful drawing rooms are also where a lot of this book was written, accompanied by a stream of hot tea and toast. Swell Park estate – Camilla and Henry Coleridge's property – is based on the Abbotswood Estate near Lower Swell in the Cotswolds. This magnificent property sits in the grounds behind my home (believed to be the original chauffeur's residence to the main estate) and is where I walk with my children at the weekends. I couldn't imagine anywhere more fitting for Jessie's first proper meeting with her future parents-in-law.

A Letter from Jade

I want to say a huge thank you for choosing to read *The Almost Wife*. If you enjoyed it and want to keep up-to-date with my latest releases, just sign up at the following link. Your email address will never be shared with anyone else and you can unsubscribe at any time.

www.bookouture.com/jade-beer

I have met thousands of engaged women over the years. I've shared champagne with them, helped them in to wedding dresses, advised them on cakes, flowers, underwear and just about everything in between. I've eavesdropped on secret live marriage proposals and seen firsthand what happens when it doesn't go the way you hoped. I've sat front row at more bridal fashion shows than I could possibly count, attended the wedding days of perfect strangers and ok, I admit it, even slipped into the fashion cupboard when everyone had gone home and tried on a few of those incredible gowns myself.

But it's always the women behind the wedding dates that have fascinated me most. Because while weddings can bring all the glamour and excess, there is so much more to any woman than the diamond ring she's wearing. It's about uniting two (sometimes very different) families, meeting – surpassing even – expectations, putting your love, taste, finances and style out there for everyone to judge. And all that while still attempting to be a great friend, daughter, mother and, if all goes well, wife.

Every woman has a different take on it, a different way of coping. But when she's re-telling her engagement story for the tenth time this week, what is she really worrying about, trying to gloss over, concealing from the people she loves most? Does she always really want to be married?

The women I meet and work with are so clever and capable and impressive – but even the ones that appear to have the most fabulous, together lives are usually hiding something they'd rather you didn't know. That's what interests me. And that is ultimately what inspired *The Almost Wife*. I hope you enjoy reading it as much as I loved writing it.

And if you did, please get in touch, let me know what you think, write a review if you like. I would be thrilled to hear from you on Instagram on Twitter or via my website. Everyone knows someone who is planning a wedding and as well as being a bittersweet emotional read, this book is also chock full of inspiration for the big day – so spread the word! And remember, I am always looking for beautiful weddings to feature in *Brides* magazine so tell me all about yours!

Thanks,
Jade Beer

@JadeBRIDES

www.jadebeer.com

@jadebeerbrides

Acknowledgements

To every bride-to-be who ever bought *Brides* magazine or came to say hello at one of our events. Your stories, worries, victories and momentary insanities have made *The Almost Wife* what it is – a bittersweet look at the challenges facing some women whose day-to-day lives don't stop the second a diamond slides down their finger. And to my super-talented team at *Brides*, for whom I have so much pride and respect, and especially my assistant Sophie. The LOLs are always loud and long when you are around.

To all the bridal fashion designers whose dresses I have spent several years fantasising about. Sitting front row at your shows has been one of the great privileges of the day job. To David Bell FRCS (SN) consultant neurosurgeon at King's College Hospital London for clarifying all the medical details that would make Emily's story credible; Stuart Hodges from The Slaughters Manor House for allowing me to creep in early morning before guests were awake and write a chapter or two before breakfast. And to the photographer Hugo Burnand who was gracious enough to let me include him in Jessie's mad rants. Thank you, thank you.

To Anne Hamilton who lavished me with kindness and encouragement when I needed it most and for those endless reminders to 'show don't tell'. Finally, I got it! To the novelist Erin Kelly for pointing out all the shortcomings so brilliantly, every one of your suggestions made the story better. And for never getting snarky about the sheer number of emails that came your way all hours of the day and night. Your confidence in this story was more inspiring than I'm sure you could possibly know.

Thank you also for the brilliance of my agent Alice Saunders who immediately understood the real heart of this book and shouted very loudly about it. And to my lovely editor Kathryn Taussig at Bookouture for saying such wonderful things every step of the way. Both women are the best medicine for self-doubt there can surely be.

People say you have to be highly motivated to write a book. Others, me included I think, might call it selfish. Sacrifices have to be made. So as the contents of the ironing basket skimmed the ceiling of the utility room and the children were whisked away *again* so Mummy could attach herself to the laptop, one man picked up all the slack. There is a running joke in my house that by rights this book should have a joint byline on it, that of Stephen Beer, which would be no less credit than he truly deserves. I spent so many hours hoping a book deal would come simply so I could share the good news with *you*. As I always say sweets, you're lucky to be here!

And finally, to the one couple above all others who have shown me the power and importance of a strong marriage. I wonder if even you knew how good it would be when you said 'I Do' on 8th March 1966, Mum and Dad?